The Belle of Collingwood

The Belle of Collingwood

❖

by
Marjorie Day

Library of Congress Control Number:		2016916641
ISBN:	Hardcover	978-1-5245-4774-5
	Softcover	978-1-5245-4773-8
	eBook	978-1-5245-4772-1

This is a work of fiction. Names, characters, places and incidents either are the product of the author's imagination or are used fictitiously, and any resemblance to any actual persons, living or dead, events, or locales is entirely coincidental.

Scripture quotations marked KJV are from the Holy Bible, King James Version (Authorized Version). First published in 1611. Quoted from the KJV Classic Reference Bible, Copyright © 1983 by The Zondervan Corporation.

Print information available on the last page.

Rev. date: 10/28/2016

To order additional copies of this book, contact:
Xlibris
1-888-795-4274
www.Xlibris.com
Orders@Xlibris.com
749058

My sincere thanks to

The kind people of Collingwood Public Library for their help
My wonderful family and friends for their encouragement
The fine elderly people of Collingwood and vicinity who gave of their time to tell me about the old days

Special thanks to

John Haines, for catching the spirit of the book in his cover artwork

Dedicated to

Rheal

Set me as a seal upon thine heart, as a seal upon thine arm: for love is strong as death; jealousy is cruel as the grave: the coals thereof are coals of fire, which hath a most vehement flame.

—Song of Solomon 8:6

Many waters cannot quench love, neither can the floods drown it: if a man would give all the substance of his house for love, it would utterly be contemned.

—Song of Solomon 8:7

CHAPTER 1

I am the Ghost of Collingwood, and I have a story to tell. I am not the only phantom that dwells in Collingwood by any means, but perhaps one of the oldest.

I was here at the beginning and have seen much and felt much and cared much. All of these emotions have not died. They were too strong. Perhaps you may prefer to think of me as an angel who watches over Collingwood and its well-being. It's not that I am fixed here in time for I have gone on to a new life in another dimension; although as yet I have not chosen to return to Earth. If you will, I feel myself a type of consultant ready upon request to guide and interpret for the inquiring historical mind.

The story which I am about to recount is so vexatious to my soul that I must speak of it. As I said, I am not the only ghost of Collingwood. This and other human stories unfold again and again. But enough! Let me commence.

As you or any scholar of Simcoe County may know, this was a lush and fascinating natural land two hundred years ago. The scraggly growth existing today bears pitiful comparison to the mighty trees that once covered this county. The fish, the wildlife, the natural beauty was so breathtaking, so astounding as to attract many a city-weary European to this area. Hardy Scots, Irish, English, and Germans settled here and erected their log barns and cleared the land on the tails of Indian corn growers. Valiant black slaves, some of whom were already emancipated, came here hoping for a kinder and freer life. Many of those proud people intermingled with the white population. Their indomitable blood is ever present in the area today.

Axmen flourished and were the heroes of the day, cutting down the mighty white and Norway pine and giant beeches; mammoths reaching one hundred and fifty feet into heaven and some measuring seven feet through the middle.

My story begins a little later. Collingwood was formed secondary to Duntroon (also known as Bowmore) as a port to liaise with Toronto. With the railway coming in 1855, it was on its way to greatness—the Chicago of the North. You might think that Collingwood at the end of the twentieth century is prestigious in its own right. True, it is a fashionable resort town but then—well—it was something! The port was clotted with big ships and small: schooners, steamers, barques, fishing skiffs, and clippers. Any time of day or night the harbour was alive, bustling. Sailors and their girls would frequent the Globe Hotel, and there were a few stories to be told about that too!

Around 1865, an engineer by the name of Jacob Winters came down from Toronto on one of the first trains to check out Collingwood as a possible spot for his family. He moved here after obtaining an engineering position on the Northern Railway. He built a lovely brick cottage in town a short walk from the harbour and forthwith sent for his wife, Sarah, and three children with whom he had been in a close correspondence. Sarah, the two girls, and a boy arrived June 10, 1865, pale cheeked but excited. The eldest was Mavis at ten years old; the next Caitlin, seven; and Joey, four. At that time, Sarah was again expecting a child and full of the good news for her husband.

As Jacob handed his wife down the train steps onto the red Collingwood clay, she lifted her brown serge skirt and paused. She stared out toward the harbour with trepidation. The cool green water made her shiver slightly even though the hot early summer sun reflected its rays on the rippled surface. She thought it could never look warm - how much worse it would look in winter. The winters in Toronto were horrifying enough. However, the rest of the scene was so delightful, she was quickly distracted. Coming from Toronto and before that by two years from Manchester, England, she was pleased with the freshness of the air in this new country, the greenness of the surrounding countryside, and the simple but obviously thriving community.

They were an industrious couple, Sarah and Jacob, like most of the pioneers to this area; although a little more educated than most. Their daughter, Mavis, was tall, plain, and doe-eyed and obviously obedient. Caitlin was rather prettier and darker, like her mother. Joey was bright-eyed and full of mischief and energy.

In due course, the family settled into life in Collingwood in their nice little honey-coloured brick house. When the new baby was born, Sarah took childbed fever. She recovered but never regained her full health and was obliged to take to her bed. Jacob was distressed and hated to leave her alone while he did his day trips to Toronto. Mavis only attended the school on Pine Street for two years and then left to look after the household duties. At twelve, she was capable and serious.

Jacob would often come home and see Mavis's pale brown head and lightly freckled face stooped over the scrub board or stirring a steamy pot of broth with the dedication of a much older woman. Much though this warmed his heart with love and gratitude to this selfless daughter, his countenance darkened when he looked upon his failing wife, pale and delicate, every movement an effort.

He would take Sarah in his arms at night and then would be afraid to love her—afraid that if he gave her another child, it would kill her. So he would store up his passion as often as he was able. Otherwise, theirs was a happy life. The new baby, another boy, was named Christian; and they hoped with a name like that he would want to enter the church when he was older. But, of course, that would be up to him. If he was a farmer or railwayman, they would also be content.

Caitlin grew older, and where Mavis was practical and obedient, Caitlin was more of a dreamer. There was a wildness and sweetness in her that made her a fetching child. She would throw herself into her father's arms when he came home, and he would swing her high in the air, her tartan skirts swirling over her childish petticoats like the tail feathers of a partridge. Her fine dark hair would never seem to stay in place and would stray down the little girl's cheeks and into her eyes.

It is with great sadness that I see that this past year, 1997, they have taken up the main railway track leading to the old station.

Men at times can be fools. This advanced form of transportation that took so many years and lives to establish, its efficiency yet to be surpassed, is now being destroyed. In its place are cumbersome and dangerous lorries and miles of costly highway, so much more difficult to maintain than railway tracks. Tracks go as the crow flies, direct, unimpeded; trains are romantic and praiseworthy.

Does humanity really progress? In some ways, it is a kinder world. Mark my words, someday soon, they will see their folly and the tracks will return!

This County has seen many changes—layers of life: Indian growers of sunflowers, squash, beans, tobacco, rising and dying, layer after layer. Stands of white pine and beech, growing up and covering the cleared land only to be cut again by pioneers; only the marshes and bogs changing little but now even they are succumbing to the back hoe and the builder.

Mr. Lawrence Delaine, next door, seemed fond of Caitlin, and she enjoyed his company. The widower was kind, decent, and gently spoken. Jacob was comforted to know the man was there in case the girls had problems when he was out of town. The widow Diddi Dolman, two doors down, helped them out by day but they were alone by night in his absences since his wife, Sarah, had died.

Lawrence Delaine turned to the tub of washing once more. He was a man who preferred to do for himself when he had the time. He had been looking out the window at the girl, Caitlin, again. She caught his look and smiled. Nine or ten she was and a beautiful thing. Maybe not really beautiful but definitely fetching.

Her eyes were grey pools of love, adult eyes in a childish face, but they were also wild and as her slender body jumped and danced in child's play, he enjoyed watching the joy of that play. For some reason he felt a kinship when their eyes met. They fastened and held. He'd glance at her two or three times a day like that and he felt the rapport. Then he didn't feel so lonely for Molly any more. It was if a void had been filled. He wondered if the child sensed something of this too.

Caitlin turned back to her romping as she saw Mr. Delaine let the curtain fall. She remembered feeling utterly wretched after Mama wasn't there any more. Papa was trying to fill up the emptiness with lots of talking, activity, nice things to eat, and day trips. When he had two or three days off, he would take them to the lake edge of town, Sunset Point, and the Pretty River valley for picnics and fishing excursions. Mrs. Diddi Dolman, their widow neighbour, would look in on them while he was away on his trips, which was most of the time. But Mavis was old enough to handle most everything.

The four children all felt especially sad for their father who was trying not to look lonely, but they could see that he was crying inside. Caitlin heard the matrons whispering about her father one day at church—something about a woman. Then Caitlin saw him kiss a lady down at the docks one afternoon last September when the winds were getting cold and whistling in off the lake—a long and lingering kiss—like he was hungry and eating an apple. Somehow, she was grateful to that lady because she must love Papa to let him kiss her like that, and Papa didn't look so sad anymore after that. He got dressed up nice again in his black broadcloth suit and went out some evenings with his gold-tipped walking stick, smelling nice with eau de cologne on his handkerchief, which was tucked neatly in a breast pocket.

Her father's destination was the Globe Hotel. Little Gareth Hayes said something bad about that lady and where she lived at the hotel. Gareth was a naughty and precocious neighbourhood boy. He also had something to say about not buying the cow when the milk was free, but Caitlin knew that Papa liked this lady. She could tell.

Mr. Delaine was always kind to Caitlin, and she used to look forward to waving at him in his window. He never looked at her strangely nor whispered the way the ladies of the town did. Maybe that's why she didn't like women that much.

Mr. Delaine always seemed interested in what Caitlin was doing.

"Come in, little fairy," he'd say and smooth her fine black hair. Her eyes were too close together for beauty, but her smile was radiant.

"Take a biscuit and come look at my pictures."

She would edge to the table, biscuit in hand, and look wide-eyed at the boats he had drawn: skiffs and tugs, sails blowing in the wind, and the Collingwood harbour bustling and jammed with all sizes of seafaring vessels. There was even a picture of a boat caught in a severe storm and being tossed about upon gigantic black waves. They were good pictures, and she was interested in the detail.

To Delaine, her looking at his treasures was a kind of strong pleasure; it gave him a sensation like being caressed when her small fingers traced the masts and sails of his creations. To Caitlin, the pictures were good, but she just really liked standing here next to the man whose kind face she had come to look for more frequently. When their eyes met now, or even through a window, she felt a kind of joy. He was so comforting, fatherly, and she had the sensation of having always known him.

Caitlin visits became more frequent—daily. They may only consist of a smile and hallo and a silent being together for a few moments before she left. She began just walking in and he would just smile and sometimes say nothing. Their eyes would commune and that would be all. She began to have a yearning for him.

Three black hornets landed softly on the wooden door frame. Annie sat on the door stoop and eased her tiredness in the deep warmth and sun of the late summer afternoon. Her chores were done for the time being. The Blue Mountains rose gently to the West. They were a beautiful sight to behold. Now that many fields had been cleared, the low range was visible in its hazy glory. This was her favourite time of day. Or was it the sparkling mornings or the starry nights? Her father, Aaron, used to tease her, saying she was a poet at heart for such was her love of nature.

Annie loved the earth, the land. Those she had sprung from were farmers and she had inherited her father's love and respect for nature. She saw the beauty and often longed for the right words to describe it. Someday, she might indeed try to write those words down in verse. She looked again toward the mountains. Now, in 1872, that the land was cleared around Nottawa; its full beauty and the gentle roll toward the mountains on the horizon could be appreciated. It was said that the Huron Indians believed their spirits walked those mountains and indeed they looked a lovely place to wander in those hazy blue hills and valleys.

The McClory farm was just outside the village of Nottawa, which was, and still is, three or four miles inland of the port town of Collingwood. Annie had seen the boy again today in the village. His face with the fine strong bones in it looked like that of a prince. He always singled her out, went out of his way to speak to her. He lived over yonder, toward the mountains. It was said he was betrothed to a young girl from Toronto, daughter of his father's business partner. For some reason, he stirred something in Annie, something alien yet familiar.

"Annie, start the potatoes, would you, dearie?" her mother, Ruby, called as she came in from the summer kitchen. She was all heated up and perspiring from preserving all afternoon and stopped at the doorway to wipe her reddened face with her apron.

"In a minute, Ma." Annie sighed, wondering what it was like to have a husband, feel his bare body next to her at night. She imagined he might smell like fresh moss or maybe her Pa's shaving soap. She guessed if she were married, she might then lose this restless feeling, this yearning.

"Your Pa is coming home soon from the Station." Her mother, coming into the main room of the house, beamed; her kind and sunburned face cracking in a beatific smile. How she loved her Ma and her Pa. How lucky she was compared to some of the other gals she knew. Her folks were always ready with a kind and approving word.

She's a good lass, thought Ruby as she looked at the fair, pensive girl. "Who did you run into in Nottawa today?" she queried, remembering she had sent Annie uptown this mornin'. Ruby was always eager for talk of the neighbouring women. She sampled one of her freshly made dills; its fragrant, spiced tang was refreshing in the heat then wiped her damp fingers on her apron.

"Oh-h, just Franka Dolman with her mother-in-law Diddi Dolman from Collingwood up at the General Store." She paused, waiting for a reaction as she expected her mother would want to hear Diddi's news from Collingwood, which the latter was always very free with.

When her mother hesitated momentarily, not wanting to seem overly eager for gossip, Annie forgot herself and changed the subject, having had some heavy thoughts on her own mind. So in a different sort of voice she asked, "Ma . . . what's it like to be a married woman?"

Ruby was diverted with the girlish question and guffawed good-naturedly. "Why do you ask that, honey?"

Annie blushed evenly, strands of light fluffy hair falling forward as she eyed the painted floorboards. "I think I'm ready for it."

"You have your eye on a fella?" queried an amused Ruby.

"Oh, not really, Ma," softly replied the young woman bashfully.

Her mother smiled to herself, remembering her own youth back in the north of Ireland. "Who is it, now?"

"George Freenan," the young girl now spoke so softly, her voice was almost a whisper.

"That lad has a fiancée, I understand," said Ruby, briskly waving a pesky cluster fly away from her face.

"Yes, but he . . . looks at me, Ma!" retorted Annie with a telltale break in her young voice.

"He's not one of those philanderers, I hope." Ruby paused, looking with mild concern at her beloved daughter but then her expression changed. "Well, I guess he's only human." She smiled indulgently and her eyes twinkled as she added, "You are becoming somewhat of a beauty, my girl."

Annie was too young to be discouraged by another woman on the scene or, perhaps, her later spirit and individuality was just beginning to blossom. Bolstered at this last flattering remark, words came rushing out of her, "She's a city girl, I hear. Probably high fallutin' and spoiled," and was then interrupted when in walked her Pa, Aaron McClory, blue eyes almost turquoise against a sunburnt face.

Crinkling at the corners, her father's eyes winked as he kissed his wife. "Who's spoiled?" His mouth worked into a grin. "Not you, my girl," he said with mock surprise then turned to the merry-eyed Ruby, his good-natured face holding the eagerness of good news. "Well, looks like I'll have paid work for a while yet, Mother. Shipments of furniture—bureaux, bedsteads, lamps, and fancy dishes are coming into Collingwood from Montreal on the train."

His wife nodded in approval, looking pleased that their modest farm income would be thus supplemented, though it meant an inordinate amount of work for Aaron along with the farm work at this time of the year. The pay was good for unloading and transhipping freight from the train to the steamers. Some of it remained of course to stock the mercantiles in Collingwood. Fortunately, he had their boys and a hired man to help with the farm work.

"That wild-eyed girl, Jacob Winter's daughter, was down at the docks again," said Aaron. "Her Papa will have to keep an eye on that lass." He shook his head. "She's growing up and those lads are a bad bunch. Looking her up and down like a piece of goods. Is she a bit simple in the head do you think? She shouldn't be hanging around there."

"No," Ruby firmly commented. "Diddi Dolman, the widow woman who helps them out now and then, says young Caitlin is a bit of a dreamer, not like the older sister, but a very bright girl. Comes of losing her mother."

Annie put the big tureen with tiny blue flowers on the table carefully. Right from Ireland it was and Ma wouldn't take kindly to her dropping it, as it had belonged to Grandmamma. She listened silently but intently to her parents' conversation. Aaron dried his swarthy face on a rough towel and sat down with them at table for the evening meal. Everyone in Nottawa knew who Jacob Winters was for he was the chief engineer of the train. Nottawa was only a few miles from Collingwood and the big lake.

Annie was still pensive when she laid her head on her pillow that night. George Freenan's handsome face still flashed behind her eyes but as she relaxed and sleep came closer, she saw Jacob's wild-eyed youngest daughter who was only a few years younger than herself. She had seen Caitlin a number of times when she had gone into Collingwood with her father. Annie had seen the girl standing at the docks, the wind blowing in her dark hair; the waves rolling in and dashing against the little dinghies. The image must have triggered something in her for when she slept she dreamed a strange dream.

The dream seemed from another place, another time. A coach pulled up and a bewigged footman in full livery costume handed a girl out into the fragrant night air. The girl's hair fell soft and translucent to the top of her shoulders. It was unusual hair. Extremely soft, extremely light and fluffy, giving her an aura of great delicacy and vulnerability coupled with the fine framework of a slender body.

The coachman held her hand high as he assisted her up some steps while she held folds of a deep olive-green velvet gown, which fell from a tiny waistline. The moonlight fell eerily on the pale fluffiness of the young woman's hair and the silvery wig of the footman as she ascended stone steps to a great and awesome grey stone mansion.

Huge double doors opened to an enormous, ancient hall dimly lit with candle sconces. At the far right, a group of men were gathered in a circle around a peer whom they were mocking. In their preoccupation with the roast, and with drinking and scurrility, they seemed not to notice the advent of the frail, ethereal girl.

The girl was excited, happy, because she was to see her lover. A very large winding staircase was immediately in front of her as she crossed the vast hall. A man, obviously the lord of the manor, quickly descended the stairs ignoring all else and came eagerly toward her, apparently expecting her. He was of medium-tall height and darkish with good facial bone structure.

To the girl, this meeting was everything, joyousness. That he wanted her was sufficient. As he led her up to his chamber, deep in the bowels of the house, this was all that she lived for. It was not known what the encounter meant to the lord. The dream was from the perspective of the girl. That he wanted her on a regular basis seemed established. That theirs was a passionate tryst quite evident.

It would be obvious to any onlooker that this was a clandestine relationship—that the girl must be from a lower class and, though lovely, not of a genteel background. The green velvet dress was suitable for the meeting. She had been "fetched" by him from some modest house and groomed for his purposes. This was her only life and purpose, and she accepted it with gratitude. Where she came from was a mystery. But no one questioned the ways of such men as he. And it was understood that a man like that must have his diversions.

This was Annie's complex and subtle dream, and she came alive in the dream in the girl's emotions, and when she looked on the face of her lover, it was George's face.

There is no such thing as a secret in this Universe. I, as the Ghost, know all, feel all, and have access to all records in time.

Silas Conroy threw his shovel down in disgust and reached for his filthy hat. He'd had enough for today. There were more fence posts to dig, but it was too hot. He was tired of pulling boulders from the field and trying to grow anything other than a few potatoes on this godforsaken piece of land on the side of the mountain. It was only good for livestock.

He looked at his potato patch sown haphazardly about stumps that should have been burnt out two years ago had he been a more ambitious man. Most of his fences were still of brush and should have at least been replaced by stump some time ago.

A few sheep hovered nearby pulling at greens. He was discouraged, but Silas was a man who discouraged easily. The yard was strewn with debris and old bits of tools he'd picked up here and there. His outbuildings were thrown up carelessly because he didn't have a lot of patience or perseverance. The neighbours had been helpful at first, so he had a good barn. But he didn't always tend to his livestock and his barns and pens needed a good cleaning out.

Silas had a wife and one daughter. His mate had been unable to produce a viable male child. They lacked for even the basics at times, living on only potatoes and vinegar with drippings sometimes in deep winter. The trip to the mountain village of Singhampton was arduous at that time of the year, and you needed cash money or bartering goods to get your wants.

Emaline came out the door carrying a wooden bucket with slops from the night before. It was already two in the afternoon, and she was just now getting about her work day. Her hair straggled down the sides of a pinched face from an ill-arranged bun. Her mouth was set in a grim line. The sallow face had been pretty once but a hard life and loss of unborn children had taken its toll. There had been a boy child lost in infancy as well. These things had contributed to making her sadly idle and disinclined.

A daughter, Winnie, was their only living offspring. She was a big help and took naturally to the cookstove. Silas meant often to praise her but never did. He had never received praise as a boy and didn't know how to give it. She was tidy about herself and did her best to keep the house respectably clean.

Winnie was a practical girl. Now sixteen years of age, she was smart with the kind of natural animal wit that is usable in life. Not the kind of girl was this who daydreams impossible dreams. Her life had not allowed the luxury of idealism. Work and want was what she had known.

If her mother was too lazy to make bread, they didn't have it; so from a youngster, she realized the relationship of work and comfort. She was also canny enough to know there was no future for her living with her parents. Like as not, she would end up wasting her youthful energies helping them scrape out a meagre life and nursing them in old age (a fate of many spinsters) or marrying a local boy and staying in the same area expending her young life on bringing up a pile of children and growing old on this mountain.

Not that it wasn't a pretty place. Outside her father's poor farm, there were more ambitious establishments with good houses and well-tended gardens, fields, and livestock. She just didn't feel cut out for the life of a farmer's wife.

Not that Winnie minded hard work or domestic duties. On the contrary, she was good at it and took pride in it. And she meant to use her skills to get ahead in life. She knew her looks were passable too. Hadn't Jimbo Laney wolf-whistled at her t'other night at the dance hall in Rob Roy? When she came in with her new dress, everyone had looked at her. They didn't know she had bought that dress in a jumble sale at the church in Singhampton and made it over.

Yes, she was a deft hand with a needle too. Pa had let her have a bit of the butter and egg money for herself last week. He might have his failings, but she knew he appreciated her help around, wanted her to stay at home to help Ma and him.

The other girls at the dance looked at her a bit odd-like because it wasn't considered friendly to dress up too much at the local dances. "Come as you are" was the style. No frills or fripperies. They thought she was trying to get above herself and so she didn't always seem to fit in. For some reason, Winnie didn't really care what they thought. She knew they tittered about her background, knowing some of their hand-me-downs as children had gone her way in charity. She had her sights set far enough above that such pettiness didn't touch her. The boys seemed friendly enough. In fact, Winnie had danced almost every dance, much to the chagrin of a few girls who seemed destined to be wallflowers.

"Winnie, would you dance with me?" called Jack Pallensey. "You are the best dancer here," he remarked appreciatively over the strains of the fiddler who was ripping out a lively reel.

"I like to dance, Jack," she answered as she allowed him to take her arm. "That's why I'm good at it. A person is good at what they enjoy doing."

"Well! That makes perfect sense to me, Winnie. I guess that's why I'm so good at mucking out the ole pig barn." At which they both broke up laughing.

He looked at her seriously after they had stopped laughing and said, "You really are the belle of the ball tonight, Winnie, with that dress and the way you dance."

"Why, thank you, Jack. That's a very nice compliment to give a lady."

"And you are a lady," he said quickly with a soft look in his eyes, "a really fine lady. I mean it."

Winnie was a little taken aback. She hadn't known until that moment that Jack was sweet on her. A little embarrassed, she nodded her thanks for the dance and moved gracefully away from her childhood friend casting her sandy lashes downward as she had read that modest young women were wont to do. Jack was a fine lad, and she liked him genuinely. She felt comfortable in his company, but Winnie didn't want to encourage any young man's court right now. She had other plans.

Noticing a neighbourhood girl slipping out early, she decided to make for home with her on the buckboard. "Nancy, could I get a lift with you?"

"Why sure, Winnie, but isn't this early for you to leave the dance? You usually stay until the end."

"I'm a little tired tonight. We were out hoeing the potatoes all afternoon, and I've got a stitch in my side," she fibbed.

"Oh, that's too bad, especially with your new dress 'n all," Nancy sniffed.

Winnie didn't miss this little barb. So Nancy thought she was getting above herself too. She sighed and felt a bit lonely. Why couldn't she be happy and just fit in? They were a nice bunch of lads and lasses. She just wanted something different.

"Gee up, Maisy, gee up, girl!" called Nancy, and the buckboard lurched forward into the night. Nancy relaxed her hold on the reins. It was pitch-black outside although the night was clear. Their eyes would soon adjust to the darkness and the horse would find its way home.

The cheerful light from the dance hall grew smaller as they rattled off down the road and the gay sound of reels, jigs, and quadrilles followed them until it was slowly replaced by the music of crickets under the enormous blue black sky dotted with myriads of stars and a bright new moon. The smell of white clover and sweet grass wafted from the edges of fields.

"What a lovely night it is," said Nancy dreamily.

"Yes, it's a fine clear night. It will be a good day for working tomorrow."

"Oh, don't mention work. Haven't you got a romantic heart? Doesn't that sky make you think of love?"

"No, it doesn't, Nancy, but it makes me wonder what else is out there that those stars look down on, other than farm fields and bush. What other exciting things they witness."

"Oh, my, such fancy thoughts. What's so wrong with farm fields and trees? I think they're lovely. And moreover, where there's farms, there's farm boys." She giggled. "And what's wrong with that?"

"Plenty. Because I don't want to marry a farm boy! I don't want to live on a farm all my life."

"Oh . . .," Nancy uttered, obviously taken aback.

Boy, there I've done it again. Made someone think I'm above myself and not meaning to, thought Winnie.

"Nancy," she said gently this time, "there's nothing wrong with farms and farm boys. They're fine things . . . for the right girl. I just feel . . . restless, I guess."

"That's all right, Winnie. Each to his own."

Nancy looked at the other girl and wondered what a girl could possibly need other than a well-ordered life on a prosperous mountain farm and a strong, loving man to hold at night. She wished someone as nice as Jack would be interested in her. Nancy tried to understand her friend's feelings.

"I know you have it tough at home sometimes, Winnie. Your Pa has just had some bad luck. Don't paint all farmers with the same brush."

"It's not just that, Nanc. I'd probably be the same no matter what. I just don't think I want to be a farmer's wife."

Nancy nodded silently and flicked the reins to encourage the little mare who was nervous travelling at night. She was wondering why the girl beside her who was not overly handsome held an appeal for the local young lads. There was a certain something about her. They continued on in companionable silence for the rest of the three mile ride home except for when Nancy giggled and burst into singing a cheeky little ditty. Winnie joined in laughingly as she recognized it.

Have you ever been down to an Irishman's shanty
Where water is scarce and whiskey is plenty
A three-legged stool and a table to match
And a hole in the floor for the turkey to scratch!'

Jack had stood at the open doorway of the dance hall and watched the girls drive the buckboard away into the night. He had known Winnie since he was six years old, and they had started school together in the little brick schoolhouse the local settlers built. He didn't see her much since they both finished their on and off again schooling at the seventh grade level. It wasn't considered necessary for farm lads and lassies to go further. They were needed at home to help and didn't always attend regularly. It was often his job to load the box stove in the school and Winnie sat near it. He recalled her twitching uncomfortably in her damp woolen stockings on snowy days, looking up at him and smiling friendly-like.

Jack's parents were unknown to him. He was an orphan who was sent over from England at three years of age and was taken in by a family here on the mountain for whom he worked hard from a child. He had always liked Winnie. Her family was poor and struggling, and she was sometimes inadequately dressed as a child. The neighbourhood ladies had collected hand-me-downs through the church and had given them

to her mother, Mrs. Conroy, who apparently was not so very robust and
didn't have a liking for sewing or knitting.

He knew what it was like to be different. The boy would have liked to
ask to court her, but at sixteen, he was just a hired hand at Lavery's farm
and had nothing to offer a wife. He also knew that Winnie would make
something out of her life. She was not like the two who had produced
her. She was made of more energetic stuff.

𝕭ook 𝕺f 𝕮aitlin

Chapter 2

Caitlin loved to go down to the lake and watch the boats in the cool green water. She loved seeing the steamers come. She even liked the barges. There was one in port today with a deckload of lath. The steamers *Frances Smith* and *Silver Spray* were also in harbour.

Caitlin had been at the dock all afternoon watching them unload furniture and other items. She liked to watch the men working. The atmosphere was different than watching women quilt or bake together. The men were easier with one another, more silent except for some funning around. One would crack a joke and another would gently deride him. A camaraderie—that was it. The difference. The difference was also in their movements. She liked to watch the brown, muscled arms passing packages from one set to the other and their sweaty brows and the way they squinted and looked at her with interest.

It was sunny and the waves were rolling in from the great expanse of gray-green water. It was good being outside and the wind from the bay blowing her fine black hair back from her face. White and grey gulls were screeching their primeval song.

"You're Jacob Winter's girl, are you not?" a black-bearded glowering man called to her.

"Yes, sir," Caitlin said guardedly with her head held proudly erect.

"Your father know you're here?"

"He knows I come down to watch the boats."

The door to the gate slammed and the clerk came down to go over the cargo list and get signatures. Caitlin turned around and went to leave just as Bill Pratz brushed by her accidentally on purpose. Bill was one of the men who had come up from Vermont to work on the wharves.

"Beg pardon, Ma'am, but haven't I had the pleasure of meetin' you afore?" Bill had been ogling the young pubescent beauty for a while to the chagrin of his swarthy boss. He unabashedly assessed her long, lithe form and innocent yet wild grey eyes that reflected the colour of the lake.

The girl did not answer but turned about. His lecherous leer followed; his tall, tanned frame swaying as he watched her disappear.

Caitlin sensed his insensitivity and sexual interest and the abhorrent combination repelled her. Her heart was beating fast. He had brushed her breast on purpose—a forward and ungentlemanly gesture, yet it had excited her somewhat—that raw contact.

She wondered what it was like to be touched by a man in a loving way. She had heard the matrons whisper at afternoon teas and titter, but it stopped short of her hearing too much—just a word here and there about their husbands' amorous ways. But she got the impression that the husbands were all different because each lady reacted a little differently to the topic. Some blushed, like Evie Carlson; some frowned in disapproval; some laughed and some, like Minnie Blake, blanched and looked frightened. Caitlin was so curious about life. She had disturbing dreams and some were erotic.

Caitlin's sister, Mavis, had grown prettier in the last year or two. Her light brows and lashes had deepened into a darker brown and her figure had developed in a womanly way. The long heavy silk of her hair could be seen bent over basins and cookstove. She was a loyal girl and would make some man a fine and serious helpmate. Her face showed virtue galore but little tolerance of frivolity and her father, Jacob, sighed as he realized she had grown a bit dull for a young lass. He felt responsible by allowing her to take on too much after his wife, Sarah, died.

Young Joey, he had no concerns about. He was a normal enough lad, blonde and bonny. Christian, now four, was enamoured of trains and wanted to be a railway man like his Papa. Strong and robust, it seemed all his mother's life and spirit had been sapped producing such an energetic and unspiritual boy. Not that he was not a good boy, just carefree and thoughtless as healthy lads will be.

Caitlin, on the other hand, he feared for. She was too open, too loving and vulnerable. Too spiritual. Some thought her to be wild and fey. She spent much time in the fields of wildflowers on the vacant lots out back in her own company, just walking. He knew her to be truly spiritual and pure in spirit—almost otherworldly. She could go far if there was anywhere in this county to go for a woman. She had gifts, the nature of which, he wasn't quite sure. But such sensitives were sometimes melancholics in later life and he feared for her on this account.

Caitlin was too giving of her trust and he must protect her. Perhaps an early marriage would settle such a girl and bring her to Earth. But he couldn't stand the thought of some insensitive lout smothering all that life and beauty with his narrow vision of life. Jacob could barely admit it to himself but this child, so unlike himself, was his passionate favourite.

At twelve, Caitlin was still a child in body but a woman in her mind. She knew she was encased in a child's body but that she was in love with her middle-aged neighbour.

Mr. Delaine was a plain man by some standards and entering into middle age, but she could only see the beauty of his soul. Then one day something happened.

It started when Mr. Delaine had asked her to shell peas for him one sultry afternoon last summer as he sat on his back doorstep. She came and sat beside him and said she would help. She felt his thigh next to hers; then after a time, his hand slipped up under her skirt slowly, stealthily while the man yet looked straight ahead. Caitlin felt all tingly but slight revulsion at the same time. She jumped up and all the peas fell over the ground.

Mr. Delaine then cleared his throat and said, "Oh dear, I'm sorry, honey. Don't go," and looking as if he were in a trance, pulled her hand toward him. "You won't tell anyone, will you, honey? I didn't mean to embarrass you."

He smiled and she noticed his forehead looked damp and he looked very warm. She looked at the fortyish widower and remembered she had always liked him. He had been kind and was a good neighbour, her Papa had said.

"I just get so lonely, honey," he said softly. His hand was pressing her toward him, and she felt something round and firm on his lap. Her hand didn't seem to want to leave its place. Somehow mesmerized, she stared into Mr. Delaine's eyes and inadvertently rubbed the spot with her hand, not realizing what she was doing. It felt bigger, expanding.

Now she had the urge to run but felt quite inexplicably fascinated with this new discovery. When he saw that her hand was staying, he closed his eyes and sighed. She continued to massage gently, quite enthralled. The buttons of his pants were straining, and he moved his other hand gently over hers to release one or two.

After unaccountable moments, Caitlin stood back flushed and dazed. Then Delaine took her hands and kissed them.

"Forgive me, Caitlin. But I couldn't help it. You must stay away from me. I'm a dirty old man." His voice was deep and softly resonant now, and he was laughing nervously.

She knew she should be enraged, insulted at what had happened, but she felt only strangely happy. Saying nothing, Caitlin turned and left, looking back at him once on the doorstep.

When she was gone from the back garden, the man leaned over and put his head in his hands in despair. From that time on, Lawrence Delaine avoided Caitlin and looked pained whenever their paths should cross.

Mr. Delaine didn't encourage Caitlin's visits like he used to. It wasn't considered proper for him to have a nubile girl in the house alone. Ever since that episode in the garden a few months ago, he had avoided her. But she couldn't stop thinking about their last encounter. The thought of him filled her memory. His pleasure of those moments had been so obvious; it caused a new emotion to be born in her . . . desire.

"Mr. Delaine, may I come in?" she called softly at his door one evening when months had gone by and it was spring again.

"Caitlin, honey, you mustn't come here anymore," he said gently as he opened the door and saw a more beautiful Caitlin standing there in a warm woolen spring cloak. "It isn't proper."

His eyes registered pain and sadness on her mind. Her desire mounted as she looked at his beloved face. Deep in her small womb, she felt confusing pressures and needs. "Please, just for a moment."

He hesitated after looking at her long and pleadingly then let the door swing back, and she walked past him into the house.

Diddi Dolman looked out her hand-knit lace curtains and saw that young girl go into Lawrence Delaine's side door again, for the third time this week. Diddi was a busybody of the highest degree. She didn't think herself interfering. She was paid to look out for those girls of big Jake's.

What did Delaine think he was doing letting a teenaged girl into his house and him a bachelor. Folks'd start talking, and he was too nice for that. Diddi meant well. She was a high-moraled woman and wouldn't seriously have dreamed anything was going on if she hadn't noticed young Caitlin looking at the older man with cow eyes one day and him looking uncomfortable when he looked up and saw Diddi was watching.

The girl was way beyond playing hide-and-seek and paper dolls. And Diddi couldn't endure the idea of the sweet thoughts she must be provoking in the widower. She'd have to say something to Jacob. The girl's reputation was at stake. Caitlin was fifteen now and at a tender, impressionable age. If Diddi had known the whole truth, she would have certainly flown into a rage.

Diddi closed her window and went out onto the step. She smoothed her apron and patted the sides of her hair noting the strays that had slipped down onto her beefy jowls and carefully tucked them in. She then proceeded picking her way across the flag stones that led from her front porch to Jacob's house, two doors down on the right. Mr. Delaine's house was situated in between the two places.

So intent she was on her errand, she forgot to admire her clump of twelfth of July lilies that were now in full bloom, it being a few days past that date. Their orange glory was lost to her as she passed under a chestnut tree, rehearsing her speech for Jacob. She didn't like to rat on anyone, but something just had to be said.

Jacob was home on a two-week furlough. He took this every year on the anniversary of Sarah's death. It was nearing dusk and a lamp had been lit in his parlour, glowing through the bay window of the charming honey and red bricked bungalow on Maple Street. She could see him silhouetted, passing back and forth in front of the lamp with pipe in mouth and hiked up suspendered pants. He was sorting some papers, no doubt from the railway.

She stepped gingerly onto the wooden verandah and, with some trepidation, tapped at the front door. Newspaper in hand, Jacob answered, looking surprised at the late call.

"A fine evening, Jacob."

"Diddi, what brings you visiting so late in the evening? It's always a pleasure, of course." The sweet aromatic pipe smoke wafted out into the still evening air. Jacob stood poised and smiling easily, good-naturedly sucking on his pipe.

"I daresay the girls are at home this evening?"

"Why of course, did you wish to speak with them?"

"No!" Diddi said abruptly and nervously. "I mean, I just want to speak with you alone if that is possible."

"Why, of course, of course, Diddi." He waved her in with a look of puzzlement. "Come into the parlour. The girls are getting ready for bed." He seated her on the sofa.

"That's fine. It's you I want to see," Diddi proclaimed snappishly due to her nervousness.

The crickets sounded outside in the midsummer evening and fresh lake-scented air filtered in the open window. A small fire burned in the parlour fireplace to take the damp of the evening away.

"What is it, Diddi?" Jacob countered, sensing her discomfort.

"It's young Caitlin. I just thought I should give you my observations, Jacob." Her voice had a bossy singsong quality to it as she straightened her dark serge skirt and smoothed her apron once more. She paused for a long moment.

"Yes, go on, Diddi." Jacob was beginning to feel impatient.

"Young Caitlin has been seen going into Lawrence Delaine's house quite often, and at her age, it's not fitting," she blurted out, glad to have said it.

Jacob's eyes widened with surprise and a slight feeling of annoyance. "She's always been fond of Mr. Delaine and he of her. Why, he's almost like an uncle."

Diddi looked rattled. "But he's not her kin, and I've seen how she looks at him."

Jacob's face darkened noticeably and he said evenly, "How does she look at him?" His emotions shifted precariously.

"With big cow eyes!" Diddi's face reddened with effort. "She's taken with him and I think he with her too," she said with a decided whine in her voice now.

At this last remark, Jacob's manner had completely changed. His relaxed manner of a few moments before dissipated. His body went rigid and he looked almost fierce. "I find that hard to believe, Diddi. Mr. Delaine is a respectable man. Is there anything else that would lead you to believe all is not as it should be between them?"

Diddi hesitated slightly somewhat deflated. "No, nothing—just a feeling I have," she said weakly.

"Well, thank you, Diddi." Jacob helped her up with some control. A changed man in the last ten minutes, his former carefreeness of nature had slipped away and a gnawing dread slowly replaced it. Seeing only Jacob's reserve, Diddi had no idea how her words had destroyed his peace.

"I will have a word with Caitlin about this, but I'm sure there is nothing to worry about. I do appreciate your loyalty," he said carefully. "Please say nothing about this to any of the other neighbourhood ladies. A girl's reputation is a delicate thing."

"Indeed it is! I would not breathe a word of this. It shall not pass my lips," Diddi exclaimed righteously. And with that exhortation, she went about absenting herself with great haste beginning to sense the devastation of the millstone she had just dropped.

Jacob held on to the doorjamb as if for strength when she was finally gone. He was aghast. What was Diddi trying to tell him? Mr. Delaine of all people and his own innocent little girl. His mind raced back over the events of the last year or so.

He was always so very busy. Home and off again on trips. Caitlin had always been a dreamer but had she become dreamier of late? Could she have a childish infatuation with their lonely bachelor neighbour, or was there something more sordid going on? Why had Lawrence not found a new wife? Molly had been gone six years now, a year before Sarah. He himself knew two or three ladies who would have been pleased to receive Delaine's suit.

Blast him! He had felt a kinship with the man, partly owing to their shared grief in losing a beloved wife. He went to the room of his daughters, which they had shared all along and saw the girls were in their nightdresses, fine lawn garments he had ordered from Toronto. Mavis's heavy hair was in plaits while Caitlin's, not being overly long, and of a lighter texture, hung free. She smiled receptively at him, her face one of openness and innocence and it wrenched at his heart.

He observed his youngest daughter was growing up, her small breasts showing charmingly through the fine nightdress but her eyes were still the remarkable part of her. They seemed to know more than her age allowed for all the artlessness of her expression.

"Papa, did you come to say good night?"

"Yes, darlings. Mavis, did you speak to Master Kliber about the pianoforte lessons today?"

"Yes, Papa, I am to begin next week." The tawny-haired girl looked pleased as she recounted this.

"Very well, tell me how much he charges and I shall leave the correct amount for you before I depart on my next excursion. Caitlin, might I have a word in private, my dear? In the parlour?"

"Yes, Papa," Caitlin jumped up and grabbed a shawl from the top of the cedar chest. Her dark hair tumbled over the shawl like some young gypsy girl.

When they were both seated on the davenport, Jacob began.

"Caitlin, love"—he coughed—"you are getting quite the grown up young lady of late. You are fifteen years old. I'm sorry that your dear mother is not here to give you advice on the ways and behaviours of young ladies, so I must be the one to advise you in these delicate matters to some extent."

He looked at her to appraise her reactions then continued: "If we were still living in England, you would be having your coming out in the next two years and, due to your family's status, would have the opportunity to be presented at Court. However, here in this primitive but exciting country, things will be a little different for you but acceptably refined I should hope and to your liking." Jacob was feeling more and more uncomfortable and found his words rushing out too quickly so urgent was his wish to get to the bottom of this situation.

Caitlin's eyes were open wide and smiling and had a questioning look in them. He rarely asked her to speak with him alone like this. She nodded in acknowledgment of his words. He coughed again, and she noticed his discomfiture.

"What is wrong, Father?"

He looked at her painfully directly and said, "Something that I hope is worrying me on no account, Caitlin. I'll come to the point. It has come to my attention that you have been seen going in and out of our neighbour's house quite frequently."

She drew in her breath and the expression in her eyes became closed and sealed off. He saw the change and a new fear stabbed at his heart. He continued, "You must know that it is improper for a young lady to visit a gentleman at his home unescorted."

"But I have always visited Mr. Delaine."

"True, true, my dear, but—*ahem*—you are at an age now that childish behaviours must be set aside. Men may start to take an interest in you in a, say, 'romantic' way. I have been meaning to have a little chat with you anyway as I have heard that you are fond of visiting the docks while the boatmen are unloading or the railmen are taking down their cargoes. I must tell you this is a most unsuitable pastime for a young lady of any station but especially since you are my daughter and considered to be of a better class, it is simply not acceptable."

Jacob's voice was changing with his mood, hardening, growing deeper and more ominous. "I have let you run free like a gypsy until now, partly because you have no mother and I did not like to discipline you overmuch. But this will have to stop. Is this clear, young lady?"

"Yes, Papa."

"So you promise me you won't go down to the docks without your sister?"

"Yes, I promise."

"And you won't visit Mr. Delaine in his home on your own?"

There was a long pause. "I don't know if I can stop that, Papa."

"What do you mean!" he said with great consternation.

"I-I . . . care for him, Father. I want to be with him."

Jacob's face turned scarlet and he gasped in disbelief.

"What on earth are you saying? Tell me, child, and I want no lies!" His voice was frightening to the young girl now. She had never seen him like this and it startled her.

"Has Mr. Delaine ever made any advances to you or touched your person in a disrespectful way?" He paused an agonizing moment in his interrogation.

"Tell me, Caitlin!"

The child was paralysed by her father's reaction and could not answer. She was afraid of the look on his face. She could not open her mouth to utter a single word.

"Tell me, Caitlin!" He actually yelled the words this time, not conscious he was waking the household. It brought her sister pounding in her naked feet to the parlour door. There was a long and ominous silence pregnant with foreboding while the father and daughter stared at one another, and finally he said in a voice filled with pitiful, desperate sorrow and resignation.

"You don't have to say anything. Your silence speaks for itself. There is something unnatural going on." And with the sheerest hatred in his next utterance, he said, "That man will pay for this."

"No, no, nothing is going on, Papa." Caitlin's voice was a wail. Imploringly, she offered with desperation half-truths, frantic now.

"He's a nice man. I like him. Please don't be angry with him. He's done nothing." She sobbed and threw herself into her father's arms as she was wont to do as a much younger well-loved child.

Cruelly, he pushed her away at arm's length and looked at her mistrustingly for the first time in her life. That look hurt her more than anything. He spoke coldly now. "Go to your room. We'll speak of this in the morning."

"But, Father—," she begged.

"To your room, I say. I don't want the whole house disturbed."

Mavis looked at her father dumbfoundedly from the doorway with her mouth hanging open in dismay, but he ignored her completely. She turned around on her bare heels and followed a shaken Caitlin to the bedroom they shared. Muffled crying could be heard from the room after the door closed.

The night crept in closer. The sapphire blue sky had turned to raven black. The pretty fluted lamp still burned in the bay window of the pretty brick house on Maple Street nigh on three o'clock a.m. If any indigent or stray person had happened by on the street (or anyone who had been into his cups) he would have wondered why the oil lamp was left on all night until he saw the silhouetted form hunched over, head in hands, grieving . . . grieving like another man who had sat in his back garden tormented by thoughts of the same young girl.

CHAPTER 3

The beauteous sun rose on a perfect summer day alive with bird song and sweet sunlight pouring in windows—sights and sounds of happiness. But the beauty and sanctity of a perfect summer morning only made Caitlin's sorrow seem much greater, her situation the more grave. It was the contrast with her grieving mood, her sense of loss, and the premonition that something terrible was about to happen.

She was confused, ill, and frightened of this new father who had shown himself to her. Usually good natured, easygoing, and affectionate, the man she had seen last night was a stranger to her and the thought of this different father, who bore no resemblance to the former one, increased her depression. This new man was dark-faced, suspicious, and had a cruel expression—not her beloved Papa at all. She was terrified of what he might do to Mr. Delaine. Might he kill him? She had not slept other than for fitful, feverish minutes last night. Her dreams were profuse and frightening. Delaine's face came to her once, beseeching, sad and warning. What would come of it?

In the kitchen, she could eat no breakfast. Her stomach heaved when she smelled the good oatmeal porridge and bacon. Mavis had risen early as usual to prepare porridge in the round black iron pot on the wood stove. Caitlin could only bring herself to drink a ladle of cold water from the pail on the sideboard.

Mavis, with her great diplomacy, had not pressed her sister for answers to their father's strange mood and her tears but had patted her and taken her in her arms last night where she sobbed uncontrollably. Again, this morning, the girl had only kind looks for her younger sister.

"Papa says you're to stay in today, Caitlin." Mavis' eyelids flickered sympathetically as she made the pronouncement.

Caitlin was seized with panic. Suddenly, she needed to go out into the fresh morning air, to talk to Mr. Delaine, to warn him, to lose herself in her field of daisies out back of the house. But she said nothing of this to Mavis, only looked furtively about.

"Where is Papa?"

"He's gone down to the Station to telegraph Toronto about some railway meetings he is obliged to attend. He was away early but will be back by noonday." Looking at Caitlin concernedly, Mavis continued, "You must be here, Caitlin, when he returns."

"Caitlin," she then whispered, "what is this all about . . . what have you done to upset Father so?"

Caitlin looked at her dear Mavis and tears filled her eyes. She tried but could not get a word to come out.

"Never mind. You can tell me when you're ready."

How wise Mavis was, how kind! No one could have a better sister. Caitlin's eyes bespoke her thanks, and she turned to leave the room after scraping her untouched porridge bowl and dipping it in the dish pan. Christian and Joey were just entering the room rubbing the sleep from their eyes, still clothed in their nightgowns and looking like little blonde angels. This normally fond, endearing sight and the joy of their cherubic innocence was lost on Caitlin today. The boys looked at her in surprise as she brushed by them without her customary fond jesting, teasing, and tousling of their lovely heads.

The distraught woman-child went straight to her room and slipped off her nightdress. She poured warm water from a pretty porcelain jug into its matching basin and proceeded with her ablutions. After washing thoroughly with the fragrant soap, she dried herself off with a soft towel and slipped on a summer tunic of pale peach muslin over a fresh petticoat. She then used a quick flick of a silver backed brush on her fine, unruly tresses and tied them back with a matching peach ribbon. She brushed her teeth with soot and salt.

Heart beating fast in her breast, she looked at herself in the silvered looking glass above the washstand and saw for the first time, not a girl, but a woman. Caitlin looked again. The fleeting notion was gone. She again appeared to be the young slip of a girl, the mere child that she was. Then, out the door she passed surreptitiously then down the hallway and hesitated to peek through the tinted door glass. She then lifted the latch and with as much silence as possible closed the door behind her.

She sped across the lawn and around the back to Mr. Delaine's house with an apprehensive look toward Diddi's window. Diddi, she had figured out, was the source of her father's information. The lace curtains on Diddi's window were undisturbed. She did not appear to be home.

Diddi was at the market this morning. It was her shopping day. The busybody had already done her work, her havoc, as such persons are apt to wreck.

Lawrence Delaine had seen the young girl speeding across the lawn and the desirable vision in peach she created and the lonely widower opened the door with a questioning smile on his face. They had been chaste since that first episode three years ago on his back doorstep, but she had still come to see him after his initial reluctance on the issue.

For a while, she had been child and he the beloved friend again, receiver of admiring glances and the kind, beneficent listener and they had shared comfortable, fulfilling silences together. Just together, not touching; in the same room apart but totally, mutually aware. She, examining an ornament or artifact he had collected; he smiling at her youth and exuberance. Innocent visits, but the feeling was strong. It crowded the room and, lately, was building into a tangible presence; so much so that he felt it as a pressure on his forehead and temples—almost like a humming in his ears.

As she had grown this year, away from the child's body and into a lovely young woman, he watched this change with wonderment. Today he let her in the door and, instantly, from her pale, haggard face, Lawrence knew something was amiss.

"What is it, Caitlin?" He shut the door and let her walk by him and into the darkened parlour, which was almost devoid of windows and most privately shaded by bushes in the only two corner windows, away from prying eyes.

Caitlin turned and looked at him, standing only a couple of feet away from the puzzled man. Her lip quivered with suppressed tears. Then her trembling body threw itself at him without restraint. It was the first time they had touched since that other time and the feeling that had been building burst within him and he returned her embrace.

All else was blotted out as they stood in their own space and time. For the first time, their lips met and opened into each other. For the first time, the two met physically and spiritually not as man and child but as man and woman. And their passion for one another that had been held in check all this time was released in a flood of joy. He kissed and kissed her receptive lips, and they lingered on in a mutual state of oblivion.

He pressed her to him and his manhood pressed into her womanhood beneath the soft muslin dress. Then, raising the soft fabric, he discovered her young nakedness and virgin softness. Leading her gently to the couch, he undid his pants and then his mouth first and penis later caressed the petals of her inner rose, moist and fragrant with desire.

He did not penetrate her virginity but allowed the tip of his male part to play on the softness of her outer flesh until desire overcame him. The gentle prodding and rubbing without the pain of first entry caused an almost comatose state of pleasure in her. The sensation of his seed spilling onto her pubic area pushed her over the edge and a wonderful sensation proceeded throbbing from her loins. In those moments, Caitlin lost all her fears in a perfect state of bliss.

Jacob got his business done with haste at the Station. It was a grim business he needed to attend to back at home and his stony look at those unfortunate enough to encounter him that morning reflected the morose change in character that had overtaken him. *The dirty pervert,* he thought. Never again would he think trustingly of a neighbour or acquaintance or be unquestioningly positive of a man's character. He knew from the girl's face, something had happened. He would keep her under lock and key if necessary.

Bill Pratz fancied himself a lady's man and had his self-opinion confirmed at least weekly by one or another town girl. He boasted of his prowess at the Globe Hotel regularly and often got into fisticuffs when one of the men recognized the name of an intended or a girl next door among Bill's conquests.

Not all was truthfulness from Bill's lips. He hadn't been lucky with all those young ladies mentioned but even if he had a fancy for one and a limited conversation, mostly on his part, they might carelessly be added to his list of wenches. He was therefore known as a local Lothario and man about town.

And he had fancied Caitlin Winters and her name slipped out one night after he had four fingers of the fine local whiskey. Eyebrows raised all around for this was not just any wench he had mentioned but the grey-eyed daughter of Jacob Winters, a well-respected train engineer, a man of substance.

Arnold Fotheringill was there that night. He worked under Jacob and was more a right-hand man to the latter than anything else. Arnold was a respectable man, quiet and discerning. He wiped the foam from his mouth with the back of his hand and put his mug of beer down on the counter. He looked with a good measure of distaste at Bill's handsome, leering face and, with nobody noticing, as all were deep into their cups, he left the hotel.

Bill's idea of lovemaking was simple and crude. A willing or not-so-willing girl would be surprised by her skirts quickly raised, knickers lowered unceremoniously, and Bill's sizeable, erect organ pushed into her and pumped rhythmically like the churning of butter until he ejaculated a large amount of semen into his love victim. After a couple of grunts, Bill's male part would slip out and be shaken then the girl would watch either relieved or disappointed as he wiped his penis on his small clothes and tucked it back into his trousers.

If the girl had been a good sport, she'd be rewarded with a grin and a slap on the buttocks or a not-too-gentle pinch of a nipple. If it had been a struggle, she would be ignored and left in a heap. Such was the insensitivity and moral stature of Bill. Women were present in the world to be used for cooking or pleasure—simply that.

Strangely, Bill did not want too often for female company, at first, that is. It may have been his large, raw, blonde handsomeness and dimpled cheek or his wide, irreverent grin that sent pulses racing in some lasses. Whatever it was, it didn't work for him as well as time wore on. Those girls he had molested against their will were unwilling to report him to authorities due to the morays of the times but word somehow filtered out to the townsfolk, men and women who knew that a respectable girl should not be caught talking to Bill Pratz under any circumstances if she valued her reputation.

Jacob Winters, caught up with his occupation as train engineer, and the rigours of being both father and mother to his family, sadly missed out on the gossip about Bill. Bill was a hardworking feller, and unfortunately, this was the only information he ever heard about the lad.

Jacob accused his lass, Caitlin, of being common when he heard from Diddi that she had been seen once again returning from Lawrence

Delaine's house. Diddi had returned from shopping at half past eleven o'clock in the late morning as Caitlin left the arms of her lover.

The furious father slapped Caitlin's face and seeing her mouth soft with recent kisses called her a whore. Delaine had left his home purposefully heading for the Winters' residence shortly after Caitlin left his arms and was in time to hear the commotion. He walked in uninvited as he heard Jacob's raised voice.

"Jacob, I need to speak with you."

"You filthy cad! Get out before I kill you."

"It's not what you think. I love Caitlin."

"You disgust me, you child molester."

"She's not a child. She's a woman now, and I want her for my wife."

"Never, in a month of Sundays! Get out!" Jacob swung for Delaine and the latter grabbed his wrist.

"I'll have the constable on to you if you ever set foot in here again." Jacob pulled himself from the iron grip and shook his fist at the man he once had a regard for.

His adversary stood his ground and said evenly, "I can't let you hurt Caitlin, Jake. She's done nothing wrong." Lawrence spoke quietly wishing to God he had spoken to Winters earlier about Caitlin.

"She won't be beaten. I don't hold with violence, but you'll never have access to her. I'll see to that." Jacob's face was so red and he looked so bilious, the other man was afraid he would have a heart seizure.

"Why, why did you do this to me, Lawrence?" Jacob was losing strength and heart at this point and anger was momentarily forgotten.

"Jacob, forgive me, but I fell in love with her, have been for a long time. Please let me take care of her. I'll be a good husband."

"Get out!" Her father's ferocity and hatred returned with a lightning vengeance. Jacob pushed Lawrence out the door and slammed it in his face.

The despised man walked sadly back home. He didn't blame Jacob one iota. He would have felt the same in his place. What was wrong with him? Was he sick? Was he a pervert? But she was a woman now. But yes, he had wanted her even as a child. He had loved her at nine or ten years of age. But he hadn't touched her until she was twelve. What did that make him?

"Jacob, many men marry young women these days in Collingwood, I have heard. It's the fashion. Maybe, not so much fashion, but being a pioneering community, a lot of single men came out without wives and have waited for children to grow up so that they can take them to wife."

"Yes, but Lawrence Delaine had a wife, Mimi."

"You said she died, Jacob, and now he needs to take another."

"Why my Caitlin? A child. There are women in their twenties and thirties that would gladly have him."

Mimi spoke gently now and looked into Jacob's eyes stroking his hand. "He didn't want them, my love. He wants her."

"But how can a man love a child? It is just crude impulses."

"Delaine is not a crude man from what I hear, and there are girls in town who have married at twelve."

"Well, he won't have my daughter. I'll see to that if I have to put him behind bars."

Mimi turned sadly and looked out the hotel window at the cold grey lake; Lake Manitoulin, some still called it. She loved Jacob but feared for this younger daughter of his whom she had never met. It was true that women had a difficult time in this world, always at the mercy of the men in their lives.

Jacob Winters fell into the depths of a black despair in which he remained for some time. Caitlin was shut in her room supposedly until she could accept the rules of the household and see reason. Her meals were to be eaten there as well. He would deal with her again in two or three days.

When he found this arrangement was upsetting Mavis, Jacob arranged for Caitlin to occupy the attic room, normally kept for out-of-town guests. It was stuffy and hot in the summer, freezing in winter, but it should only be for a short while. She wasn't fit to be in the same company with Mavis. The latter's morals and purity had to be protected from this wanton younger sister.

He must have time to think what to do about this situation. Public humiliation of Lawrence Delaine was out of the question because of the scandal it would cause. Poor dear Sarah. He was penitent and silently begged his dead wife's forgiveness for his failure in bringing up the girl properly. But as time went on, he wondered if Caitlin was just a bad seed; if she was as people had said in the past, "different."

Oh, Sarah! How happy she had been in life, how contented. She had tried to adjust to every new situation for his sake. Perhaps they should never have left Europe with its refinements and strict moral codes.

This strange and crude country did things to people. The old conventions and rules did not always count here. In some ways that was good. Yes, he remembered, there was the negative to be sure back in Manchester. The pretty streets with fine houses were a front for the dank alleyways and dark passages of poverty where horrible things went on, where poverty fostered terrible events and brought out the worst in people.

But Toronto, Sarah had loved. The unhealthy industrial town air of Manchester left behind, she enjoyed the amenities of a small city with the freshness of a clean new country. She loved the social life and shopping.

She also loved her garden, which a gardener and servants kept beautiful. He remembered the large square Victorian garden made up of quadrangles divided by grassy footpaths. Perennials of all descriptions and colours flourished there: hollyhock, daisies, peonies, cone flowers, snap dragons, and climbing sweet peas disguised lowly vegetables grown in the middle of each quadrangle. It was considered vulgar to have the eatables showing. And in the very centre of the square was a formal round garden.

And the house they had there! A twenty-room small mansion with typical Victorian decor. He remembered the modern wallpaper with the fashionably heavy patterned look incorporating olive greens, mustardy yellows, maroons, muddy blues, dusty rose pinks. A richly panelled library boasted a turkey-red carpet on the floor and the filagree wooden room dividers atop the doorways on the second floor were oriental in design and manufacture.

Sarah admired the creamy yellows against white in the finely plastered ceilings with central medallions. The house was warm and cosy with its rich mixture of colours: the orange, maroons, purples, and the strange and unusual patterns and designs. He remembered with fondness his billiard room where he would retire with other gentlemen after a fine meal. They would smoke and play for hours scoring with wooden beads on a string hung conveniently above the pool table using the cue.

Such luxury they lived in there, such privacy! He could still see Sarah enjoying tea in the sunroom; the only really bright and airy room in the luxurious home replete with tapestries and frescoes. She enjoyed its simplicity and airiness at that time of the day and could see the garden from there. Sarah was truly a jewel and he had been lucky to have her for a wife.

Her morals had been scrupulous.

CHAPTER 4

Stay me with flagons, comfort me with apples for I am sick of love.
—Song of Solomon 2:5

Mimi knew that Jacob put his late wife, Sarah, on a pedestal. Had she lived, Mimi wondered, if she may have fallen off it. After all, was there really such a difference between women like Sarah and women like herself? She knew from experience how one incident can change the course of one's life for better or worse—an accident of birth, an inadvertent remark, a careless piece of gossip. They were all in the same when it came to cause and effect.

All this talk about the depravity of his younger daughter disturbed Mimi. She shrugged and turned back from the window and the sight that usually charmed her, but made her feel cold and lonely inside today. Grey waves continued to roll in unrelenting under a cloud-covered, dreary sky. They had no conscience, they had no sense of revenge, right nor wrong. They only followed the laws of nature. So unlike human beings.

Jacob had watched Mimi as she stood facing the window with her back to him. He could see that she seemed to be in deep contemplation, disturbed over the conversation they had just had, but he was too upset to discuss it further. It really did not concern her at all. Right now, he was looking at her hair, which hung loose down her back. It was extremely long and luxuriant. With the pins and combs out of it, it came cascading down in rich chestnut waves full of lights. He loved her hair and would wrap himself in it when they lay together.

As Mimi turned away from the window and looked at him, Jacob didn't want to ask her what she was pondering, what was troubling her. He was too full of his own agonizing convictions about his daughter. He walked up to the sad and beautiful woman silently and took her into his arms, drowning his sorrow in the sublime luxury of her.

Caitlin continued to languish in the attic room for Jacob didn't come to see her after three days, nor even after a week. When asked by Mavis if Caitlin could come out now, he said the time to think would do her good. She was to stay there for now. He seemed to have put his daughter right out of his mind and be ignoring her young existence, which wasn't exactly true but the truth was that he just did not feel up to dealing with the painful situation at present.

Mavis, his eldest daughter, was dismayed and expressed her concerns to her father that Caitlin wasn't eating more than a bird would, and it was unhealthy to be shut in that hot attic without fresh air and sunshine. He relented and said she could be allowed out for a stroll in the back garden twice per day but must return directly to the attic room. He did not want her at the dining table for meals. Her misdemeanour had been too grave. It was all for the girl's own good.

Had Jacob Winters seen the state that his youngest daughter was in as had Mavis, he surely would not have been as severe. But being in the frame of mind that he was at the time, the man blocked thoughts of her out as they were too painful and so to see Caitlin was too distressing to him. He could not bear to look at her at present. Jacob, too, although well educated in a mechanical and techno-scientific line, had little knowledge of medical science, psychology or the frailty of the human body, especially that of a young girl in love who had been through a cruel shock. In all fairness to the fellow, he was not at heart a cruel man but circumstances made him cruel out of his ignorance.

He assured a worried Mavis he would definitely deal with Caitlin face-to-face upon his return from Toronto and his meetings there. He needed some time to think and reckoned she would be amenable to suggestion and have learned her lesson by then. He was also secretly battling with a puzzling feeling of vengefulness toward his "wayward" daughter. He did not try to analyse it as he was not an analytical man in regard to feelings. But it consumed him and threatened to grow bigger—this feeling of betrayal by his daughter. The fact that she had taken his precious fatherly love and cast it aside. She had been his favourite; he could admit it now.

He felt used and betrayed. Her deceit and affection for this other man his own age and old enough to be her father hurt deeply. But instead of feeling hurt now, he felt angry, bitter. The desire to punish was strong. But he was not a violent man..........

"Please, drink the broth, Caitlin. I know it's hot, but it's all you can get down."

Caitlin's eyes seemed larger in her pale face. She shook her head.

"You must eat something. You were sick again today. Have a drink of water then."

Caitlin obediently sipped water from the mug on her tray then looked dully around her. She didn't feel hungry though her stomach was gnawing. It was so stuffy up here with the small window the only ventilation. She'd been here for six days. It cooled a bit at night, thank heaven. Her bed linens were damp with perspiration. There was no point getting dressed for she wasn't allowed out of the room.

Oh, she could have easily slipped out. Mavis would not have stopped her if Papa was not at home. But she was feeling so despondent she didn't even try. Mavis was waiting on her bringing food, emptying her commode and wash water, and trying to cheer her. On one of these ministering visits, Caitlin finally told her sister some of what had passed to lead to this tragic present situation.

"Papa will relent. Don't worry, Cait," the older girl said. "You can slip out any time you want into the back garden when he's out." But Caitlin would not go until finally, having her father's permission that her sister could go out a little, Mavis dragged the sick girl bodily coughing and sobbing down the stairs and through to the kitchen, which led to the back garden.

It was only when the strong light coming through the kitchen window hit Caitlin did Mavis see the drastic change in the girl. After six days in the attic room, she looked emaciated. Her eyes were sunken in her face and her normally round cheeks were hollows. She was stooped like an old woman and could barely walk. She looked shockingly thin and fragile in her nightdress and, though it was warm, shivered uncontrollably. Caitlin's knees appeared about to abandon her to the floorboards. Her teeth chattered like popinjays.

With the greatest concern, Mavis ran to their bedchamber to get Caitlin's warm shawl and bundled her gently through the door to the garden. It was six o'clock in the afternoon and the sun was gentler but still very warm. It was pitiful to see the girl's eyes light up as she looked up at the shimmering summer sky and smelled the fresh, soft air, going from tree to bush touching branches and leaves lovingly. She seemed to regain her look of youthfulness and vigour for a few moments and then she turned and smiled weakly at Mavis. Mavis's heart wrenched.

"Papa is gone for three days to Toronto. I'm going to call Dr. Rostrum. I had no idea you were this ill. Papa will have to let you return to our room. You won't spend another night in that attic!"

"Oh, Mavis!" Caitlin burst into tears and cleaved to Mavis who was again alarmed at how the flesh had fallen off her sister's young frame in so short a time as they embraced.

"Do you care so very much for Mr. Delaine that you would pine away to nothing?"

Caitlin could only nod and swallow to this through tear-brimmed eyes. Mavis pulled a linen handkerchief from her apron and Caitlin wiped her running nose and tear-stained cheeks. They hugged again.

"Caitlin. I don't know everything that happened and I can't say I would approve, but you are my sister and that will always be the same. You always were a little different, but Papa always loved you best. I know. I think you reminded him of Mama."

"Don't say that. I don't want to be his favourite. And I'm not Mama. I'm my own self. I think I must be very different from her. When Mama looked at a flower, she thought of how she could match it to her wallpaper or how it would appear on the bodice of a certain colour gown. When I see a flower, I see it wild and growing in a field, nodding in the breeze, made into a daisy crown for a child. We're different, Mother and I. Papa can't expect me to be like her. You're more like her than I."

"More dull you mean," said Mavis, looking mildly offended with a half-smile on her creamy face.

"No, not dull. . . . . . . just more practical and suited to a life with a man like Papa. I don't know what's in store for me." She frowned and her face suddenly took on a fleeting expression of old age and wisdom. "I love Mr. Delaine. I always have and that's all I know."

"But he's so much older. I would not have dreamed this would happen. Could you not forget him? It may only be a passing fancy."

To this Caitlin did not respond. She just stared at the climbing rose bush about the arbour, which was getting blurry and swimming before her eyes in a profusion of colour. She was feeling weaker again. The fresh air had helped though. The cobwebs were clearing from her mind. But it was not enough to compensate for the shock of finding Love suddenly and being wrenched from its arms.

Dr. Benjamin Rostrum shook his head and muttered as he stomped from the bedchamber with no little noise.

"Where's Jacob! This will never do. Never do! That girl is to have hot milk with a teaspoon of brandy immediately and every four hours during the day, the heat allowing. If it's too warm, give her buttermilk instead. On the verge of pneumonia, verge of pneumonia I say, and in the summer—the worst time." Mavis nodded, taking it in as best she could, trying to memorize his muttered instructions.

"Diddi! Where the devil is that woman!"

At which, Diddi hurried into the room with a defensive look on her face. She bristled.

"What's the matter? What's all the ruckus!"

"The matter is we've got a very sick girl on our hands and she'll need to be looked after properly. Are you up to the responsibility?"

"Of course, I am." Diddi blustered. "What do I have to do?"

"Sponge her face and upper torso with vinegar and water hourly. Give her broth and lots of water, food if she'll take it. We have to get her fever down, and it won't be easy in this heat. Why wasn't I called before now! And what's all this about being locked in the attic room? Jacob will have a piece of my mind when he comes home."

"It was a matter of discipline, I understand," Diddi said officiously, puffing herself up so she appeared almost an average height and quite imposing with her stern demeanour.

"Discipline my foot. Downright stupid I'd say."

Diddi's florid face swelled with indignation. "I'm sure Jacob had his reasons. He didn't mean her physical hurt."

Dr. Rostrum reached over and almost touched noses with Diddi, his eyes bulging.

"I don't know what the lass did to deserve this, but she would have been far better off if he had whupped her hide like the simpler folk do."

He knew Diddi's reputation as a talebearer and wondered if she had had any part in this travesty of parental discipline. Wouldn't be surprised if she had judging from the guilty look on her face. The old busybody.

With that, Diddi flounced out of the room, her bright pink frock far too youthful with its fresh colour and abundant frills. The doctor noted her ample middle-aged waistline. He wondered if she had her eye on Jacob as a potential spouse. If she did, he was sure this interloper was barking up the wrong tree. He had seen that delectable piece Jacob kept at the Globe Hotel. Virtuousness in a woman could be highly overrated, especially when the woman was one such as Diddi Dolman.

When Jacob returned, he listened to Dr. Rostrum's reproaches with a hard and sullen expression. Instead of showing normal fatherly remorse and concern, he boldly requested the doctor to make an examination of Caitlin to verify her virginity. The good doctor's reaction was one of shock and anger.

"Bad seed? Come on now, man. No, I'll not do such an examination. Don't compare Caitlin to Sarah. She's not like Sarah. But a bad seed? She's no different from any other woman. Would you rather her be one of those that spend their time on an invalid couch to avoid their husband's embraces and run down their health so much they die?"

"Are you saying my Sarah was like that?"

"I'm not saying it. Except I couldn't find anything medically wrong with her for a long time. She had recovered from the childbed fever. Only you would know."

"She was a fine woman," Jacob said stubbornly.

"That she was, Jacob. I don't mean to hurt you. I just want you to accept your daughter for what she is. She is not a duplicate or replacement for Sarah. She may resemble her a bit but that's where it ends. Caitlin is a totally different person. If she's not a saint, it shouldn't matter. Perhaps she's a warm-blooded woman. I know you have experience of that. It isn't so bad."

Jacob looked at the old doctor sharply. "It's a small town. I'm a man."

"Of course you are and Caitlin is a woman."

"Caitlin is my daughter—it's different."

"This woman you have, she's someone's daughter too."

Jacob sighed. He genuinely cared for Mimi. The doctor had him there. "Maybe I have been too hard on Caitlin. I'll try to be more understanding, Doc."

Doc Rostrum patted him so hard on the back he almost bowled him over. "I'm glad to hear that, Jacob. There's a good man." He pulled out his watch, which dangled from a metal chain, and said, "Must be running. She's over the crisis now. Be good to her."

Two months passed and Caitlin's life had returned to normal in many ways to all appearances. She regained her health and was looking rosy-cheeked and pretty again. Her appetite had returned. She and Mavis shared their old room, and she was in the dining room for meals again. Mavis was coming along well with her lessons on the pianoforte and the parlour resounded with sweet strains of chamber music on many evenings to the gratification of her father.

Jacob seemed in an amnesia-like state in regard to Caitlin's behaviours of a few months before. He could almost believe it never happened except when their eyes met. There was a difference in their relationship—a subtle guardedness and a disturbing lack of spontaneity. But other than that, to all outward appearances, their relationship seemed the normal affectionate one between a father and daughter.

"Caitlin, how are your studies going?"

"Very well, Father." She never called him Papa now, but if he noticed this or was hurt by it, he never let on. "Mr. Wormsey says I will be able to take my entrance exams soon for the Collegiate."

"Fine, my dear. You know our family believes in a good education for its sons and daughters. Enlightenment is important for the world and it comes through education."

"Yes, Father." Her eyelids flickered momentarily at this remark.

Jacob sighed as he looked at his lovely youngest daughter. He wished they could recapture their former closeness but, alas, innocence was lost and deep down he still had a slight gnawing mistrust of this, his own flesh and blood. It was a sad feeling and he abhorred it. But perhaps this growing apart happened frequently in families as children grew up.

Mimi had begged him to be lenient with Caitlin and he had tried to be understanding of something he was loathe to understand. Lawrence Delaine had fortunately had another assignment which took the surveyor out west to southern Manitoba to examine and give his opinion for the Hudson Bay Company on the suitability of lands for agriculture out there. He had heard this from the newsworthy Diddi for he had not again spoken to the man. Delaine had been gone these past three months. Otherwise it would have been an unbearable situation having him at such close range. The frame house belonging to the widower was boarded up and looked rather pathetic. But Jacob had no sympathy for him. He despised the man now. But with time passing and Caitlin getting on with her life, he may begin to feel indifference toward him.

Mavis spoke up suddenly, "Papa, might I attend the barn dance on the Tenth Line at the Raker's? They have a shindig once a year at this time. Caitlin could accompany me." She looked at her father hopefully. "It would do her good," she said as an afterthought.

Jacob looked quickly at each girl and down at his pipe, which he was in the process of lighting. The girls looked at each other.

"Yes, that sounds fine, fine. Lots of nice young men there, I suppose?" he uttered, thinking of the promise of new social interest for his younger daughter in her own age group.

"Yes, Papa." Mavis blushed.

And so Caitlin and Mavis came to attend the barn dances in the vicinity, and it became a common sight to see the sisters come in arm in arm, the one pretty and dark, the other fair and comely. They were much sought after as dance partners because as well as being pleasing in appearance and known good catches, they were light on their feet and good conversationalists. The Winters girls were considered the catches of the town.

One day in late November, when the frost had taken a firm hold on the ground and its silvery glory promised less work for the young locals and a fine start for the whirl of winter social events that year, all frivolity came to an end in the Winters household.

Jacob came into the house after spending some time in the old Globe Hotel in the company of Arnold Fotheringill. Unlike Jacob's usual moderate self, he was obviously somewhat worse for being in his cups. His expression was grim and he went into the girls' bedchamber. They were happily engaged in mutual hair brushing, a ritual done before retiring and laughing about some silly thing that had happened that day.

"I want to talk to you, you little slut." Jacob's slurred but menacing speech cut the relaxed normality of the scene with brutal clarity. He then proceeded to grab Caitlin by the hair and haul her off the vanity stool. "Into the parlour, girl." He pushed her through the door.

Mavis, gasping in horror, cried, "Papa, what's this about?"

"Never mind. You stay here," he ordered, slamming the door.

"Oh, not again," said Mavis under her breath and started to sob softly.

Caitlin was pushed systematically into the parlour and onto the sofa. She couldn't believe this was happening. It was so unreal.

"Now, you tell me. What have you to do with Bill Pratz? I heard from Fotheringill today that your name came up as a woman of his, that you've fornicated with him."

"No, no! I don't know what you're talking about. I don't even like him."

"So you know him. He apparently named you as his girl."

"He lied!" she cried. She looked shocked but controlled.

"I don't believe you, little trollop. Hanging around the docks when I'm away. You lied to me before and you are lying to me now. You're no good, Caitlin. I tried to give you the benefit of the doubt and this is how you repay me. If your poor mother could see this, she'd be brokenhearted."

"I tell you, it's just lies! That man has a bad reputation. Ask anyone. He's lying!"

"I've never heard ought about Bill Pratz except that he's a hard worker and to think my own daughter would throw herself at a man like that." Jacob staggered a little and caught himself by the arm of the couch. His hot breath stank of liquor, and he looked ugly to Caitlin for the first time in her life.

"I'm not listening to this." She put her hands over her ears, which remark and gesture only further infuriated the drunken man.

"You had better listen to me, young lady. You've had your chance to live in a decent home. You've had advantages that other girls in Collingwood haven't. But all that's at an end. You made your bed and you have to sleep on it. Sleep on it, that's what you'll have to do from now on. Go back to your room now." He spoke now coolly though his bloodshot eyes and waving balance showed what his emotion had driven him to.

The next day Caitlin was called into the parlour at three o'clock in the afternoon from her room where she had been ordered to stay all morning. Bill Pratz stood there, cap in hand, and with a silly grin on his face. A mystified Bill had been summoned there at two o'clock and had been given an offer he could not refuse.

"I don't want to hear any details of what happened between you and my daughter, Caitlin, nor any excuse."

Bill braced himself for a beating as it suddenly dawned on him that his big mouth had got him into big trouble. But, mystifyingly, he was standing there unmolested and here was big cheese, Jacob Winters, not only offering him his pretty daughter to wife but a dowry as well. All he had to do was nod and say, "Yes, sir. Yes, sir." Jacob didn't look at him straight in the eye nor look too friendly, but he didn't slug him nor threaten with the police constable. Bill couldn't believe his ears and then the grim father figure called the girl in and she looked flabbergasted and screamed, "No!" Jacob slapped her across the face and she said no more. Bill wasn't asking any questions. He was going to keep his mouth shut if he knew what was good for him.

Yes, he'd take her on. It was all forming in his mind. Why not? It was time he wed anyway, and he had fancied her. Life was funny. Yes, he'd take her on. He was tired of looking for fresh women and wasn't as lucky lately. He was tired of fending for himself in his shanty for vittles. A wife would go good now. Steady sex anytime he wanted. Wouldn't have to say please and thank you neither. A woman of his own.

And so, Caitlin Isobel Winters was married to William Henry Pratz on December 13, 1873, in the Town of Collingwood. The church minister from the Trinity Church down the street had refused to solemnize the marriage when he was summoned to Jacob's parlour within the week and saw the pitiful spectacle of the sobbing girl, so Jacob arranged for the thing to be done the next day at the home of the Justice of the Peace. The only two others present were Jacob, her father, and a neighbour, Diddi. Mavis had refused to attend.

"Jumpin' Jehosefat! Why on earth would Jacob marry that pretty little thing to that son of a—" Charlie spat into the cuspidor on the floor and ran his sleeve up under his nose. He angrily bit off a piece from a plug of tobacco. The geezer was really upset. He hated Bill with a vengeance. "What's the world comin' to?" After Bill had got little Julie, a neighbour's young lass, in the family way, he had no use for Bill. The girl was sent to Toronto to have the bairn, which was put in an orphanage. The men sitting in the smoky Old Globe barroom the day news of Bill's weddin' broke all grunted in agreement with Charlie. None of them had much use for Bill with his whorin' ways and braggadocio. They shook their heads with pity for the young bride.

Caitlin poured the bucket of water into the wooden wash tub and added a kettle of steaming water to it. She dumped in a bowl of soap shavings and set the tin scrub board in, putting her clothing in first. Later she would do the bed linen and then Bill's heavily soiled clothes at the last. The hard work of washing took her mind from the unhappiness of her life and so it was welcomed. Also, it was done when he was away working so she had the luxury of some time to herself.

Her wedding had been dreary and her wedding night a nightmare. Nothing had prepared her for the assault of body and spirit she had suffered at his hands on that night. Thinking her not a virgin due to her father's rush to have her wed to a virtual stranger, he was insensitive even for himself. It being middle of December, after the brief ceremony they were given a good dinner of ale, chicken, potatoes, and carrots followed by apple cobbler at the North American Hotel on Hurontario Street.

They had gone there with her father and Diddi straight from the Justice of the Peace. Travelling was of course out of the question. After the nearly silent meal, the wedded couple retired to a room for the night. Afterward they would return to his new lodgings at Mrs. Buttle's boarding establishment until spring when Bill would build a small house for his bride on Rodney Street. The building lot was a wedding gift from Jacob. An effort to be genial was made by all except for Caitlin during the wedding supper. She was still in a state of shock so was silent but ate the good food offered because already, her instinct for survival in this marriage had taken hold.

Caitlin had refused new clothing for the wedding and wore her Sunday dress of grey poplin instead. It reflected her solemn mood. If Jacob had regrets of his drunken decision to wed her to Bill Pratz, he never showed nor admitted it. His pride gave him no other choice but to follow through on his word without hesitation and grimly, mercilessly, he did this. He did assist the couple with his wedding present of land and he paid for the two-day honeymoon stay at the North American. He also provided Caitlin with an amount of money sufficient to purchase any practical household items or clothing she might require for her new role as wife to a worker in the shipyard.

Bill had been given a generous sum of three hundred dollars as a dowry. It was expected that he would use this money to erect an adequate structure to house himself and his bride. Other than that, Jacob assured Bill there would be no interference from his quarter. His wife was his own affair. He cautioned Caitlin to spend her purse thriftily as she would now be reliant on the beneficence of her husband, a man of modest means.

Caitlin did not want to even accept the money but something in the back of her mind told her to; that it might help somehow in the future. The only thing she purchased with it was a practical pair of shoes at the shoe store beside the hotel. After ordering these, she kept the rest of the money out of sight for some possible future need. The boarding house, intended for railway men, was warm and cosy as winter surrounded them. In partial return for keep, Caitlin also helped the landlady, Mrs. Buttle, with cooking and chores. Bill did bush work in the winter as no boats came in, and he still had some work unloading on the rails and keeping the snow off the tracks.

She was almost sorry when spring came and she would have to live alone with Bill in their own home. Intercourse was not so painful now, and she bore his attentions as best she could. On their wedding night he had said, "All right, wife, you can take that finery off now, you're with your husband." He smiled his most charming grin and pulled her to him.

"Give us a kiss." Bill smirked and crushed her face to his.

Caitlin tried to push him away, resentment seething, but he growled, "You'll have to watch yourself, my girl. I have my rights now, and I won't be thwarted," his smile fading.

"I know you're no innocent little flower. Fiddling around with an old man were you. That fat old Diddi let it slip, so she did, to my landlady. You'll not be fooling me then with your virginal airs." With which he promptly pulled up her skirts and pushed her back onto the four poster bed.

"I'll give you a taste of what a young, strong man can do for you. What goes in will come out." Caitlin tried to stifle her cries in the hotel and fought him off with silent blows. It was useless. He was strong as a bull. Soon she had the sensation of being ripped apart. When it was over, he looked at her apologetically as he climbed off.

"Why didn't you tell me he hadn't broken you in? Speak to me, lass. Why don't you speak to me?"

For the first time, Caitlin, who was still in a stupor since she knew she would have to marry Bill, seemed to wake up and said, "I'm your wife by law and not by choice. Things past are my affair."

Bill looked at her and blinked. At least she had talked. That was something. He wasn't going to be living with a mute, and Lord, she was lovely.

"Fair enough, lass, fair enough. But don't be too hoity-toity with me for I won't bear it. I'm your husband now, mind."

After some moments, Caitlin got up slowly and drew the curtain round the washstand. She removed her crumpled Sunday frock and her twisted petticoats. There was soap and warm water in the ewer all ready for her, and she was grateful for the comfort of the soft towels. With tears rolling down her cheeks and sniffling quietly, she washed him off her and put on her lawn nightgown out of the velvet travel valise. She took down her hair and walked slowly and painfully to the bed.

Mercifully, Bill by this time was snoring on his side of the bed. His clothes were in a heap on the floor. She crept into her side of the bed and was appalled at how little room she had to sleep. She tried not to wake him, but she needn't have worried for Bill slept soundly. Like an animal, Bill was satiated and not bothered overmuch by the subtleties of human nature. As long as he ate well, had sexual urges fulfilled, and was sufficiently warm, he was untroubled with insomnia or twinges of conscience. He was a man driven by his basic instincts.

Caitlin from then on tolerated Bill's sexual attentions and even a few times enjoyed them, in spite of herself, being naturally a warm-blooded girl. This confused her as they were given without romance or even tender caresses. She was a young woman, and it was natural for her to have some physical responses. But it was purely physical, and when it was over, she was unhappier than ever. His sexual demands were strong. Hardly a night would go by that he wouldn't take her. He would drink often and would then be verbally abusive and take her like a whore. Then there was his jealous nature, which was growing more evident. He had to know her every move. She felt stifled, imprisoned.

She didn't think of Mr. Delaine very often. It seemed so long ago, another happier world full of sunshine, smiles, and quiet conversations. He was away and may never return. She put him out of her mind out of sheer self-preservation. When spring came and she got out for walks, she walked down Maple Street past his house. Someone else was living there now. Her heart sank.

But what Caitlin didn't realize was that he had just rented it to some newcomers for the winter as accommodation was so scarce and he would be back this summer.

"Caitlin, come in my dear sister," Mavis called from the front yard of her old home next door but one to Lawrence Delaine's. She had espied Caitlin while stepping out to shake a braid mat.

The lilacs were blooming and a yellow canary flew up over the hedge. It was late May and all of nature held the promise of easier, happier times. *What will become of me?* Caitlin was at that very moment thinking. My life is over before it's begun. Just turned sixteen and already my life is a ruin.

She shook herself out of her gloomy reverie in response to the voice that called.

"How are you, Mavis?" Caitlin made an attempt to be cheerful as she stepped onto the porch of her former home. "You look lovely." And so she did. At nineteen, Mavis was a looker—a rosy and stalwart girl. Some man would want her for his wife soon.

"Thank you, Cait. Come inside and I'll make you a cup of tea. We'll talk? It's all right. Papa is out of town on a run."

Caitlin felt odd as she crossed the threshold of her old home. It seemed like years rather than a few months since she had lived here. She touched the wallpaper, the curtains, and was reminded of her dead mother who had chosen the fabrics and colours so carefully. She smelled the familiar smells that are peculiar to different places. This home smelled of lavender and wood smoke mingled with the rich aromatic pipe tobacco her father smoked and lingering scents of this morning's oatmeal. Good, clean smells. She felt suddenly emotional.

"How are you, Cait? I'm sorry we haven't had you these past months for supper. Papa has been dispirited and feels you would be better left to your own devices as he calls it."

"That's all right, Mavis. I appreciated your visit and the embroidered tea towels you sent around." Mavis had dropped around earlier to the boarding rooms and found her in a dismal state.

Mavis suddenly felt guilty at her own happiness. She had semi-forgotten her married sister lately after the initial shock of it all. She had lately fallen in love with a farm boy by the name of Samuel Wuthers. He had sought her out after noting her absence at the local socials. He had asked her father for her hand in marriage after one lovely afternoon together in April when he had finally found her at a box social. She had meant to get over to see Caitlin again but had been so immersed in her own happiness and what with seeing to the two boys and all.

They embraced and Mavis put on the kettle to boil. She took down two china cups and saucers, two bread and butter plates, and a butter knife.

"You are looking a little better since I last saw you, Caitlin. Are things better between you and Bill?"

"I'm making do, Mavis. I guess you could say that." She looked uncomfortable. "Let's talk about you. You look so pretty and happy. What is your news?"

"Oh, Caitlin! I do have news." Mavis's eyes glowed with her happiness. "Father has agreed to let me marry Sam Wuthers. Do you remember him? I'm so happy. We'll be married this fall."

Caitlin stood up and embraced her sister again. "Engaged to be married! I'm so happy for you," she said sincerely. "I remember him. He was a nice young man. You deserve happiness."

Suddenly Mavis looked tragic. "You deserve happiness too, Caitlin. How can I be happy when you are so sad?" Tears came to her eyes.

"Don't, please don't, Mavis. It isn't so bad, really. I'm managing. Think of your own happiness. Forget about me. It's just the way of life."

"But it is so unfair."

"Yes, but it was partly my own fault and stupidity."

"No, Caitlin, Father was cruel . . . heartless."

"Please don't talk about it. I want to be happy for you."

A look of intrigue came over Mavis's face. "He's coming back, Caitlin. Mr. Delaine. I heard it from Diddi, that old bat. I can't stand the sight of her anymore. He's finished his work in Manitoba and will be back soon."

"But his house. It's let to someone?"

"They're building a new brick house on Birch Street and will be soon gone."

Caitlin's face looked bright for the first time in months but that look faded as quickly as it had come upon her. "What good will that do me, Mavis? I'm married."

"I don't know, Caitlin, but I think he will try to help you. He was always so fond of you."

"What can he do?" Caitlin looked sorrowfully at her sister. "I'm bound to this man for life."

"You could run away together."

"You're dreaming, Mavis. You've read too many novels."

Mavis looked at her suddenly. "But you were the dreamer, Caitlin, and I was the practical one."

"I'm afraid my dreams have all died, Mavis. I'm a different person now, in touch with cold, hard life," the younger woman replied dully, looking drab and forlorn, her shoulders drooped sadly in a plain brown frock. Mavis took out a level scoop of tea from the caddy and poured scalding water over it into the pot. Her back was turned so her sister couldn't see her grieving face.

CHAPTER 5

My beloved spake, and said unto me, Rise up my love, my fair one
and come away for, lo, the winter is past, the rain is over and gone;
The flowers appear on the earth; the time of the singing of birds is
come, and the voice of the turtle is heard in our land.
—Song of Solomon 2:10–12

December of 1874 came and the inevitable happened to Caitlin. She found out she was carrying Bill's child. This is how she discovered the fact.

After not wanting breakfast one Monday morning, she proceeded to do the weekly laundry. After the arduous task was finished, she threw the items over the rope line to dry. They would probably freeze but would dry out some. Later she would bring them in and finish the drying in front of the fire. Caitlin scooped out a pail of wash water and proceeded to scrub the floor with it on her hands and knees. Suddenly, her head swam and she felt ill. She felt hot. Managing to get up and put the bucket and scrub brush outside the storm door, she came back in and lay down on the bed. After an hour, she felt better but her body felt strange, like it didn't belong to her.

She had noticed recently a feeling of delicacy and light-headedness, she remembered. The monitoring of her monthly flow had slipped her mind. Lately she had been busy with adjusting to the new house and growing within herself the semblance of a new philosophy of existence and a new selfhood.

This psychological change was also inevitable, a metamorphosis from suffering into acceptance and reconciliation with her inner self. For Caitlin was, by nature, as all truly spiritual people are, a person of great inner strength and fortitude. How she came by these qualities is unknowable. But it is a fact that many persons who outwardly appear fragile, dreamy, even flighty and unequipped for this world astound that very world with their display of strength and fortitude at times of crisis. Some others, contrarily, hale and hearty individuals of practical natures sometimes sicken and die in early life or cringe fearfully when real tragedy crosses their path. And so it was with Caitlin, the former scenario.

Shortly after the physical symptoms came upon her, she recognized her condition for what it was and from that point on knew no more disabling fear of her husband. She was from that point on above his abuses and coped reasonably well with her lot. She even lost some of her disgust and hate for him. This came at a crucial time for Caitlin whose health had been failing. She now improved in strength and stamina as she carried this child for there were no longer the severe inner turmoils within her.

The winter months turned into spring, and by early summer, Caitlin was finding it harder and harder to do her chores being heavy with child in her eighth month. She didn't go out much as it was not considered quite the thing for a gravid woman to parade herself about in public. At least Bill had left her alone these last couple of months. She hadn't seen her father since the day she was married, and though he had wronged her, the young woman missed him now, her good memories blotting out the other.

Caitlin wiped the sweat from her brow. She had been preserving all morning and had done down a goodly number in jars of green beans. The door rattled and in came Mavis with a pie in her hands.

"Caitlin, what are you doing working in this heat! Shame on you."

"Well, it had to be done. Bill would be angry if I let those beans go to waste."

"I was out picking wild strawberries in the commons yesterday. Sit down now and we'll have a piece of this pie."

Caitlin lowered herself gratefully onto a kitchen chair and Mavis set about putting the kettle on. She always tried to come when Bill was away. In spite of his absence, she spoke furtively. "Have you seen Mr. Delaine, Cait? He's been back some months."

"No." Caitlin's face changed to the expression of a wounded deer, helpless and vulnerable and resigned to her fate. "Have you spoken with him?"

"I have and he's asked after you. He heard you were married." Mavis looked directly into her younger sister's eyes and her voice changed. "He's confided in me, Cait. He said he should have never left—wouldn't have if he thought Father would do such a crazy thing."

"What use is it to speak of it." sighed Caitlin who, in spite of her spurt of energy this morning, felt suddenly tuckered out.

They had tea and pie, and Caitlin felt better until she tried to get up. A searing pain almost doubled her up. Mavis took charge and made her lie down. "Do you think it's time?"

Caitlin nodded, her face screwed up in pain. Beads of perspiration stood out on her forehead. "Go get Mrs. Coxswain next door. She'll know what to do."

Mavis ran next door for the older Mrs. Coxswain who had acted as midwife for a number of local deliveries. The elderly woman was over in a shot, running across the yard with her skirts lifted up high and a long, grey braid swinging across her back.

Three hours later, Caitlin gave birth to a baby boy. She smiled at Mavis, her fine black hair plastered against her head but she looked really beautiful and surprisingly strong.

"She looks like the Madonna herself holding that baby—a born mother." old Mrs. Coxswain chortled. "Must have been the pie what brought it on. Fruit pie'll do it every time. Gets the gases goin'." The old biddy knew the girl had a hard life with her bloke but so did many others. Life with a man wasn't always a bed o' roses. But the young 'uns, well, they kind of made up for it.

Mavis, on the other hand, looked at the fine-looking boy and turned her face and wept. God forgive her, she had wished it stillborn. So many of the first ones were and after what Caitlin had gone through . . . But no, here was this sturdy baby boy, the image of him to tie her sister forever to that devil incarnate. With a dead child, she may have left him, but now? Caitlin looked at her sister's tears and seemed to read her mind.

"Don't cry, Mavis. It's all right."

She is the strong one now, thought Mavis, and she turned to fetch another basin of warm water for cleaning up. She tried to think happy thoughts. She thought of her soon-to-be marriage to Samuel.

Bill was proud of his son and bragged about him at the saloons like he once bragged about his women. He kept quiet about the latter these days. Oh, he had taken down a lass or two when his wife was big with child. *What was a man expected to do?* he asked the world silently. The lass, his wife, was a cold fish at best. Oh, but the wee lad was a chip off the old block, anyone could see. He had a fine son and a good woman, for all her haughty ways. It was cause for celebration. Bill went on a bender and closed down the saloons at night. He staggered home thusly for three nights in a row and didn't show up for work. It's a good thing the economy of Collingwood was buzzing at that time and they needed men; otherwise Bill would have been out a job, new son or no.

Caitlin had to manage as best she could with a new baby and a drunkard on her hands. It did no good to chastise him. She had learned silent toleration. Eventually, he returned to work sober and she breathed a sigh of relief. But she had to beat off his advances for two months. After she figured she was healed up, she stoically gave in. Things went on much the same as they had except for the baby boy.

Bill had insisted the child be named William after him, and much though Caitlin disliked the idea, she went along with it. She reconciled herself by the sure knowledge that though the babe resembled his namesake, that his nature was innately different. Often when a child resembles one parent, he carries the personality of the other. This was her fervent hope.

Caitlin's life had some happiness in it again. The child became her joy. She loved to bathe and tend to him. And he would love his bath and gurgle happily, splashing wildly. She now laughed again and smiled once more. The young mother would lift her child's chubby body out of the wash pan and kiss his little bottom as she dried him. He was such a sweet little boy. In a way, he had saved her life. He made her forget the continuing unhappiness of her married life.

Bill treated her more civilly now with grudging respect but was often inebriated and Caitlin suspected he saw other women. Once this was confirmed when, in broad daylight, she went downtown to buy some necessaries. She had left young Willie with old Mrs. Coxswain next door. He was getting too heavy to lug around the town, and she didn't have a baby carriage. She walked past a saloon and out burst Bill at that moment, his arm around a woman. He was obviously drunk. He paused for a second surprised and then said, weaving sideways and leaning on the woman with one of his ear to ear grins, "I'd like you to meet my Jessie."

The woman's attractive but hard face expressed a raised eyebrow and a mixture of what could have been the beginnings of pity but ended up as a look of smug mirth and disdain. Caitlin felt like a nickel and hurriedly walked away with her bundles, humiliated and strangely hurt. Yes, it was a sad marriage indeed and only Caitlin's inner fortitude and the joy of her new son to whom she could express her love kept her sane.

Anyone passing Caitlin's window in those days would have witnessed a touching scene. A young, slim matron with hair upswept in a bun playing with her firstborn. It was very like a cameo of the Madonna and her boy with a similarly rustic backdrop. And thus like uncountable women have done since time forgotten, Caitlin did her best to forget any unpleasantness in her life and concentrate on the compensations that God had given her. And time went by and months turned into years.

The years had gone by for Caitlin, and there had been nothing significant to mark them for her except the growth of her boy. It had been six years now since she had been wedded to Bill. They had not had another child. Caitlin had thanked God in his mercy for this.

Her father had virtually disowned her and so she never saw him. Mavis was happily married and the mother of two healthy children. She lived with her husband on a fine farm on the Tenth Line quite a piece from town. Thus, she saw her sister infrequently now as well. If Bill had been a better sort of man, there would have been get-togethers to look forward to where the children would play together and the husbands would help one another. She and her sister could trade recipes and household tips. But with Bill the way he was, they had no real friends, and Mavis could not bear to be around him.

Lawrence Delaine lived in town still, but Caitlin rarely laid eyes on him. In the good weather he was away a lot on his survey assignments and the winter kept people indoors a lot except for the monied or carefree who partook of the winter social scene. Delaine followed bachelorly pursuits and she matronly ones and their paths seldom crossed. When they did, they were unable to have the privacy for a conversation and so only exchanged glances and a few words. The boy was always with her too. Delaine would ask her how she was and then look down at the boy who was the image of Bill but shy and introverted by nature.

"If there's anything I can do for you, at any time . . .," he said once or twice and her eyes fought back tears when he said it. "Just ask, Caitlin. Just ask."

Mimi was beside herself. Jacob was ill. She knew he was. He had been overworking since Caitlin's marriage; she guessed to smother his guilty conscience which he would not, of course, admit to. He was so damnably proud! That man. She loved him with a passion she had never felt for another man and a tenderness too. She had the desire to mother him, care for him. But he wouldn't have that.

She was lonely, so lonely sitting here in this hotel room day after day. It had been twelve years now that Mimi had lived in Collingwood, and most of that time, she had known and been supported by Jacob. But she knew, though he wouldn't discuss it, that the reason he didn't marry her, though he was free to do so legally, was that she was not the lady his former wife was. He was status conscious and would not consider making a woman of her dubious background his wife.

This hurt her beyond all imagination. Now she knew he was ill and he didn't send for her. Mimi had tried to go to his house but that neighbour woman, that Diddi he had talked about, wouldn't let her past the door. She put her head in her hands. It was so humiliating. If she had been another type, she would have forced her way by. But that was part of her problem, had been all her life. She let others lord it over her. She was too soft. She knelt down on the floor and reached under the bed, her long, beautiful hair falling like a cloak about her shoulders. She drew out the valise from its spot. It was dusty and smelled of mould and mildew. *Mould and mildew,* she thought, *the substance of my life.* She had been here before. Another town, another man. Not just another man this time, but it ended like all the rest.

That scarlet woman had her nerve walking up to the door, bold as brass to see Mister Jacob. There was no way, if it was up to Diddi, that piece was getting by her into the house.

Diddi was getting very concerned about Jacob. His breathing was getting rougher and every time she asked him if she should get the doctor in again, he shook his head.

"You're in charge," he said. So she was taking him at his word. The first thing she did with this new authority was to turn the tart away at the door. No point in worrying him about that so she wouldn't mention it. The next thing she needed to do was contact his eldest daughter, Mavis. Mavis knew he had a bad cold but was not aware of the serious turn his illness had taken. Diddi dispatched one of the neighbour lads old enough to be reliable to ride his pony down to the Tenth Line and inform Mavis she was needed in the sickroom posthaste. She was just about to send for Doc Rostrum too when he walked in the door.

"How's my patient? I meant to come back a couple days ago but got tied up with a scarlet fever case."

"Poorly, Doc, poorly I fear. I was just going to send for you though he wouldn't have it." Diddi was actually quite relieved to see the man.

"My God, Jacob!" The old doctor dropped his bag on the floor in alarm when he saw Jacob's grey complexion. "Why didn't you send for me sooner!"

"No point, Doc, no point." He had difficulty getting the words out. Jacob knew he was done for. Something had gone out of him these last couple of years. He didn't have the strength nor will to fight lung fever as it needed to be fought. He was tired, so very tired. The doctor lifted him up in his arms to the sitting position.

"Shall I go and get your daughter, Caitlin, for you? Would you like to see her?"

"Naw" was the response. At the sound of her name, however, an amazing change came over Jacob. His eyes opened wide, colour flooded into his face, and he brushed away the doctor's hold on him. The doctor speedily arranged his pillows as it was evident the ailing man wanted to sit back as uprightly as possible and talk.

The sick man's voice now far from the weak tremulous thing it was a minute ago, burgeoned into a deep, strong, and resonant sound.

"She wouldn't want to see me. Leave it. I haven't spoken to her these six years. Only seen her in the distance, the pitiful thing she's become, dressed in rags and dragging a child, my grandchild along the street like any common household drudge with her urchin."

"And you've never tried to contact her?"

"No, and I've never met the boy." Jacob looked bright-eyed and bird-like at the old doctor, his now skinny neck straining with the weight of his head. "You think I'm hard and cruel, don't you?"

"I'm not the one to judge any man."

"Yes, I was hard on her. But the way I saw it she made her bed and I saw to it she lay on it. She didn't know what side her bread was buttered on. But lately, I've been thinking I made some mistakes."

Then he suddenly sat up in fury. "But, by God, she could have had it different, if she'd toed the line. I would have given her anything." Tears brimmed up in his bleary, red-rimmed eyes as he croaked his words out. "With her fine upbringing, her looks and charm, she could have been the belle of Collingwood!" With that exhortation finished, he sank back exhausted onto his pillows and closed his eyes.

Doc Rostrum shook his head. *Yes,* he thought. *Things could have been very different for Caitlin.* He had seen her too and knew her sad state of affairs. It was sad that the passions of human nature lead men to make such foolish mistakes. It seemed Jacob was just now beginning to realize the folly of his behaviour.

When the prone man did not open his eyes again after a few seconds, the doctor waited to see his chest rise in a great gulp of air. The action did not come. He reached over to feel for a pulse on his neck. There was none. Jacob was dead.

Bill had changed over the years. Any kindness that was in him at the start had seemed to disintegrate. With the regular over-consumption of whiskey, he had become gross and derelict. His looks had deteriorated as well as his pride in his cleanliness and appearance. Instead of the swaggering, handsome dude with fetching smile, he had become a weaving, unshaven, bulgy-eyed specimen whose hallmark was dull-minded cruelty and resentment.

One night, Bill came home in a particularly foul mood. He had had a disagreement with a fellow worker. He complained about everything in the house: her cooking, her manner, the boy, her coldness toward him. He went to raise his hand to her and the small boy came swinging to her defence. Infuriated, Bill landed the boy a box in the ear that sent him flying.

Caitlin went berserk. It was one thing to hit her, but she would not countenance him abusing the child. She flew at him with hatred, her nails clawing at his face. Her physical strength could not hope to be a match for his. He dared not hurt her too badly for he sensed that he was not liked in this close-knit community and that it would not tolerate him if he seriously injured his wife. But Caitlin's face was bruised and sore where he hit her.

Her concern was not for her appearance but the blow he had dealt her son. She knew a blow like that could cause deafness in a child. She must do something. They could not go on like this. She had suffered six years of hell and had stuck it because of her little son. Had she not had him so soon, Caitlin would have had the strength to leave Bill after two or three years. She knew now she would have. But what was she to do with the little child. She could not go to Lawrence with Willie. He might have been charged with abduction. She knew he would have helped her anyway, but she could not risk ruining his life. One life ruined was enough.

But now Bill was beginning to take out his moods on the boy now that he was older. And they weren't at all alike. The difference in character would be more apparent as time went on and the friction would grow greater between them. Little Willie would either be reduced to a speechless, frightened child, or if he stood up to his father, a routinely abused one.

The next day, she didn't want to but had to go to the market because they were very short on provisions. She tried to tilt her hat so that the bruising would be hidden, and because of the blustering October day, she was able to hide the welts on her neck with the aide of scarves where he had grabbed her in fury. She put a warm woolen cap on little Willy, kissing his sad little face.

Hurrying along Hurontario Street, hoping not to be greeted by anyone, she almost ran right into Lawrence Delaine.

"Why, Caitlin!" He had her by the shoulders and was peering into her face, or what he could see of it with hat brim and scarves in the way. The young boy of four stood silently and looked up at the neat-looking man whom he had seen before stop to speak to his mother.

"Your face, Caitlin. It's bruised." His gloved hand touched the young woman's cheek lightly. Fleeting looks of hate and anger passed over his countenance before dissipating from the pleasant face that was not accustomed to harbouring such emotions. In their place was an inexplicable expression.

"It's nothing, really. I'm all right," Caitlin said, trying to hide her face deeper in the voluminous scarves. She was acutely embarrassed.

"Caitlin, the time has come. I must talk with you . . . Now!" He looked very serious indeed.

Caitlin looked apprehensively up and down the street and said almost in a whisper, "You know I can't. If Bill found out—"

"Never mind him." He took her cold little hand and looked meaningfully at the boy. The boy slipped his hand into the stranger's almost automatically and was rewarded by a kind smile.

"There's a laddie," the man, who appeared to Willie to be quite tall, said to him gently. Then Mr. Delaine walked so fast that his mother and he almost had to run to keep up.

"No one will bother us in here." He ducked into a saloon and said, "Barnaby, could you find us a warm corner?"

Barnaby, a smiling barkeep with sideburns, long white apron and broad smiling face, didn't blink an eyelash. He was used to surprises. The proprietor directed them promptly to a table at the back of the room in a corner behind one of the stoves. It was warm and cosy indeed. He brought them some hot cider and some cocoa for the child after a spell. After a few gestures from Delaine, he brought a platter of sweet rolls fragrant with cinnamon and studded with raisins. The astute man had recognized Bill Pratz's poor little wife right away. Caitlin was shaking and her hands wrapped round the warm mug. Little Willie sat still and his eyes roved around the room, which he thought was beautiful, and then rested on this man who looked at his mother fondly.

"I remember when you were just a little lass, Caitlin. I loved you even then."

"Lawrence, you mustn't . . ."

Willie looked up at his mother.

"It's got beyond the point now of being cautious, Caitlin. Never mind the boy. He has to hear this too. It concerns him. I should have taken you away years ago. But I didn't. God forgive me, I didn't. There were so many obstacles. And then you had a child, his child. The man's no better than an animal to do that to you, Caity. Does he hit the boy too?"

Caitlin broke down and sobbed at this. Her head was down and she was nodding. He handed her a handkerchief. The boy looked at him with big eyes. Eyes that he could see were used to seeing his mother cry like this because he looked at her like a dumb animal, dumb and helpless.

Anger grew in him again. Caitlin blew her nose and then spoke with a husky voice.

"You can't do anything to help us. I will have to deal with this myself. Perhaps my sister and her husband can help us. We cannot involve you. You could go to prison."

Delaine laughed. "You needn't worry. It won't come to that. We'll go away—to another town, another vicinity. You will be my wife and son. No one will ever know."

Caitlin dabbed her eyes and looked up at him. The thought of being with him was so joyous she couldn't think of it. He smiled when he saw her expression. "I've been waiting for this moment for years. Now we must make our plans. I have a proposal. Come away with me right now. This very instant. Do not return home. I can have the gig ready and loaded in two hours. A friend can arrange the rental of my house. I was going away in two weeks anyway. You will be gone before Bill comes home from work."

Caitlin felt elated and panicky at the same time. "No, I couldn't! It's too soon. I must think."

He looked at her intently. At least she had not said "no." His heart was full of song. He waited and then she finally spoke again looking him full and strong in the eye.

"When he has gone to work tomorrow, I will pack a small bag, perhaps two." Then she hesitated, not sure what would come next and losing her nerve. Catching her mood, he took over, the ideas flowing into his feverish mind.

"Is there anyone you can trust, a neighbour who is in sympathy with you?"

"Yes, the Coxswains next door. They despise Bill and will keep a secret."

"Good. Take your bags next door then. I know the Coxswains. I will have them picked up by my friend. We must not be seen together in town tomorrow. He will figure it out soon enough. But a delay in his knowledge will give us a good head start, and we will be beyond his reach before he knows it."

A great calm had come over Caitlin. "I will pack our bags as soon as he is gone in the morning. I can be ready by nine o'clock." Delaine looked apprehensively at the boy who stared at him absorbing every word. Caitlin caught the look and said sadly, "Don't worry about Willie. He never talks to Bill unless he is spoken to. He will not confide anything to him. He fears his father."

Lawrence's eyes turned to her again and there was pain in them. "I blame myself that this has carried on so long. I should have moved earlier."

Caitlin said softly, "It wasn't time. I wasn't ready." Her voice held conviction. "I am now."

There was a look of relief on Lawrence Delaine's face. He went on, "After you drop off your bags at the Coxswains, you should leave your house for the market with the boy as if to shop. Then with only one loaf, walk back of the market onto Ontario Street. Follow that street until you reach the first farm on your left. They are friends of mine, the Landrys. Go in and Mrs. Landry will make you welcome. She has heard of you and your plight. Tell her I sent you."

"I know the farmhouse. I will be there."

Delaine reached over and tousled the lad's fair hair. The boy smiled at him shyly. He was quiet, too quiet for a small boy. The man's heart went out to him with his mouth streaked with cocoa and his unfortunate resemblance to his father.

Caitlin was reeling when she left the saloon by the back door. She could not chance running into any of Bill's cronies from the shipyard with Mr. Delaine. A wonderful sense of freedom was upon her and the dull, cool October day seemed the most beautiful day she had ever experienced with the pungent smell of wood smoke lingering in the air. God had surely come to her rescue. She stooped and gathered the little blonde boy in her arms and kissed him.

"We're going to be all right, darling. We're going to be very happy. The nice man is going to help us. But you must keep a secret and say nothing to your father about the nice man."

The small boy looked up at her with his fat cheeks and nodded soberly, pursing his lips. Caitlin smiled at him. Then she whisked him away up the street. She would only buy the brisket of beef for tonight's supper. But no, she mustn't make Bill suspicious. She'd buy some provisions for a few days.

Caitlin thought the morning would never come. Blessedly, Bill fell asleep early in a stupor and left her alone the night. As she bathed the boy and tucked him in bed in his little cot, these thoughts ran through her head. "This is the last time I will tuck my boy into this bed. This is the last time I will look on Bill in a drunken sleep. This is the last time I will spend an evening in this house, look at the moon through this window, hang my dress up on this peg, crawl into bed beside this man, and dread the coming of another day in emotional and physical bondage."

CHAPTER 6

Caitlin got up at the usual time although she hadn't slept all night. Over and over in her mind she reviewed Lawrence's instructions. Then she pictured it all happening. She feared something would go wrong. Then she went over in her mind what she would need to put in her bags.

Although she didn't sleep, she was not tired as she would normally be. The excitement of the plan endowed her with energy. She got up and hastily dressed, partly because of the chill in the room. Lighting the kitchen stove, she went about her usual routine after the morning fire was going. She scooped an extra spoon of precious tea into the pot. What did it matter now? She needed to get Bill going. She hoped he would not be sick from last night's drinking and thereby late leaving for work or worse still, not go at all.

She started the porridge with shaky hands, and while it was bubbling, took a large handkerchief and spread it out on the table. She cut two thick shives from a homemade loaf and then two large slices of cheese which she placed on the cloth and then tied it up in a knot.

"Your porridge is ready, Bill," she said, clearing her throat and brushing crumbs from her apron all the while casting an anxious glance toward the bed. There was no response. After ten long minutes, he was still abed.

"Bill. You're going to be late again." This time she got an irritable grunt.

"What of it."

Little Willie meanwhile rustled in his bed at the sound of his father's voice and sat up rubbing his eyes.

"Mama, Mama. I had a dream. It was a nice dream. It was about—"

Caitlin hurried over to the little boy, looking back uneasily at Bill who was now pulling on trousers over his long underwear. She hugged the child. "Yes, darling. Now get up and Mama will wash your face and you can have a drink."

Bill looked at the boy with disdain. That one got all the attention around here. It was always darling this, darling that, but did he ever hear an endearment or word of love himself? Muttering, he plunked himself down at the table and waited for Caitlin to pour some steaming tea in his mug before he wolfed down the porridge. His head was aching this morning but not so much that he didn't notice Caitlin's nervous behaviour and shaking hand as she poured out the brew. His hand came up and grabbed her wrist.

"What's afoot?"

She trembled all over and almost spilled the scalding tea on him. Her heart pounded as if it would burst from her breast. Surely he couldn't have guessed.

"No . . . Nothing, Bill. Not a thing. I'm just feeling a little feverish this morning. Have the chills I guess."

"That'll serve you right for gallivanting all around town. A woman's place is at the hearth."

A wave of relief flowed over her like a warm tide. She felt it right down to her feet. He didn't know after all. She was safe, but she still shook from head to toe with fear.

Caitlin had a loaf under one arm, and her right hand held Willie's as she walked briskly to the back of the marketplace. Now, only now, did she feel she might really make it to that farmhouse as planned, really get away from Bill. She had been so nervous. Only briefly had her eyes scanned the room of her oppression before she closed the door to the house where her womanhood had been degraded these years by the brutish man.

Cold wind bit into the faces of the two figures, one tall, one tiny, as they headed east on Ontario Street. This street was quite built up now with some small frame houses, a little church and also some fine new brick homes. There were quite a few people milling about. Caitlin hoped against hope no one would stop her to chitchat.

Just as she was thinking this very thought, Mrs. Mabel Quirty called out to her. Panic overtook her. That lady was wife to one of Bill's mates at the shipyard. Caitlin looked up, clenched her teeth, and smiled and waved gaily but kept on going, walking so fast, Willy had to run to keep up to her.

Her heart was thudding in her ears and she did not look back until she left the town houses behind and farmland stretched out in front of her. No one was behind her or likely to notice where she went now. As she topped a little hill and looked ahead, a cream-coloured stucco farmhouse stood in the distance to her left. That must be the Landrys'.

Thankfully, she continued in that direction. As she finally reached the door stoop, shivering and concerned for poor Willy who was very tired, the door opened. A long faced, kind-looking woman in her forties stood there. She must have seen her coming from the distance.

"Mrs. Landry?" Caitlin looked at her apprehensively. "I'm Caitlin, a friend of Mr. Lawrence Delaine."

"Oh, my . . ." Mrs. Landry was momentarily at a loss for words when she saw the woman and child on her doorstep but quickly recovered her wit. "Well . . . Come in, by all means, dear." She stood to the side and gestured. The woman looked puzzled as she led Caitlin to a kitchen which appeared in apple-pie order and bade her sit down at the table. The kitchen was cozy with a large wood cookstove filling the room with warm fingers of heat. Caitlin sat down with relief and pulled Willie onto her lap preparing to make an explanation.

"Mr. Delaine asked me to come here today, you see. He . . . he said he will be along shortly to collect us."

Mrs. Landry's eyes got big. She looked at the woman before her and then at the small blonde boy and then nodded her head in partial understanding. She remembered well their friend, Lawrence, making mention of a certain young woman.

"We'll be going away, you see," Caitlin continued, hoping she didn't need to explain further.

Mrs. Landry paused for a long moment and then spoke, "Well now, that's good, isn't it?"

The woman looked compassionately at the beautiful young woman with a startling streak of white in the front of her hair. The lass looked nervous and upset and no wonder after what Lawrence said she'd gone through. She had the kind of beauty that made possessors of it live a hard life. Mrs. Landry thanked God now for her own plainness and peaceful life.

"You just sit there, dear, and make yourself at home." The woman got up and took Willie's hand. "Come over and sit on this stool. It's just your size an' I'll give you a biscuit." She then went to the hob and put the kettle on. A hot drink is what this girl needed now. She looked right chilled through.

"You're very kind, Mrs. Landry. Thank you." Caitlin said when a hot cup of tea in a nice china cup and saucer was put in front of her. "It's a pretty cup and saucer."

"It's only suitin'. I can see you're a lady from a refined background. I'm glad to be of help to Lawrence. He's been a good friend to Ned an' me."

They passed an hour in which Caitlin told the good woman her story but there were some anxious moments before they heard horses and a wagon pull closer to the house. Caitlin stood up abruptly and wrung her hands. Mrs. Landry lifted the window curtain and hissed, "It's him." Caitlin was so happy that she went to the woman and they hugged as if they'd been friends for years.

"Now my life truly begins," Caitlin said to her. Then in the door came the man of her life, his face alight and glowing, his eyes pools of deep love as he had once seen hers to be as she romped in his garden only a child.

This moment was one of those rare and precious ones that is remembered forever when all else is forgotten. It is remembered over pain, disappointment and tragedy. Gazing into her eyes as he held her in his arms he said simply, "We must leave right away."

"Not until you've had a cuppa." Mrs. Landry said, "An' while you're drinkin' your tea, I'll put some eatables in a basket for your journey. Land sake, I shoulda thought of that afore!"

While Caitlin gazed worshipfully into her lover's eyes, he drank his tea and Mrs. Landry chuckled to herself. Slicing cold beef, cheese, and the loaf that Caitlin had brought, she thought, *I've never seen a pair so enthralled with one another, I swear!* Topping the basket with several juicy fall apples, she handed it to them on the trap. When they had thanked her profusely for her kindness and were off, her brow furled with a worried expression. If that Bill was as mean as they said he was, he'd not take his pretty wife's flight sittin' down. She knew the type. He'd be after her to the ends o' the earth if he thought himself cuckolded. God speed 'em she prayed and, shivering suddenly, went gratefully back into her cosy, warm house out of the cold, fall breeze where things were always safe and familiar.

"The Landrys are United Empire Loyalists, and I helped them obtain that farm a few years back. Have been friends ever since. They're good people."

"I liked her. Where will we go now?"

"As far away as we can get before sunset. The horses will only be good for a few hours and will have to be rested from time to time and of course fed and watered. Then we will have to find accommodation for ourselves and livery for the night."

"And where might that be?"

"Don't worry, I have some ideas." He patted her knee. Her heart beat joyfully now as they drove east along the road that followed the shore of the Bay.

They travelled along that road of many winding curves, the road that, if one kept following it, led to lands occupied only by lumberjacks, Indians and a few settlers. This area would one day be known as Wasaga Beach. But instead Lawrence turned south at a fork toward the new town of Stayner through which ran a good road to Barrie.

Delaine had decided to head toward Barrie, which was the nearest large centre where they could lose themselves. Once there they would not be very noticeable, just any couple with a small boy travelling light. There they would stay for a while and then head on to the port town of Midland. He could safely leave Caitlin and Willie in Midland while he did his survey work in Manitoba for a few weeks. But that was all in the future. His immediate worry was to put some distance between themselves and Collingwood and get some adequate lodgings for tonight.

There were a number of inns along the way to Barrie, but they were a fair distance and an obvious place to look for missing persons on an escape route. He did not want to leave any clues along the way of their whereabouts. A beautiful young woman with a white streak in her black hair and a blonde child escorted by a middle-aged man was an easy description to remember. For this reason he would avoid train travel.

It was almost impossible that Bill could put two and two together and catch up with them on this first day of flight, but Lawrence Delaine was taking no chances. They could have been seen. If word got to Bill while he was at work, well, there's no telling what he might do or whom he might enlist to help him.

As it was, Bill worked on, none the wiser until the normal end of his work day. For some reason his wife flashed into his mind several times today. He kept seeing her white face as she ran over to the child, hugging him and saying, "Yes, darling. Now get up and Mama will wash your face and give you a drink."

He never remembered his own mama ever being that loving and tender to him. All he remembered of her was that she was a small, watery-eyed, cowering woman who shrank from her harsh husband but waited on the man eager to please him, much out of fear it seemed. As a result, he grew up tough without the softness a woman's love can put into a boy and with a disdain for women.

He'd felt a growing resentment to Caitlin lately, and also to the boy. They seemed wrapped up in their own little world. His initial pride in the boy as a carbon copy of himself was now fading. The novelty had worn off, especially when Willie wasn't the brash and hearty little fellow he had promised to be at first. The tyke had become a mama's boy and didn't like his father's rough games and manly ways. Bill was going to put an end to this small revolution going on in his own home.

Caitlin was going to learn to cowtow to him, be a good wife—show a little respect. After all, didn't he support her and the little brat? He was going to set down some ground rules tonight. By Jove. And the first one was about all this gallivanting around town she did. He'd put an end to it. Once a week was enough to go uptown for provisions. He did not want any of the town bachelors getting ideas. Women were scarce enough a commodity, especially when they looked like Caitlin.

Bye, but it was a nasty day. October 17 and already foreboding of winter. Big, wet, cold snowflakes started falling out of a slate, grey sky as Bill walked home. He pulled his blanket coat tight over his vest. Even the woolen scarf Caitlin had knit him didn't keep out the bite of the wind. He was glad the house was only a short walk from the Yard. He'd soon be in his warm kitchen with Caitlin's good cooking wafting up his nostrils and the sight of her pretty head bent over a pot.

His initial reaction when he neared his home was surprise when he saw no smoke curling up from the chimney of the little frame house. The second was dismay as he opened the door and felt the cold kitchen and saw the dark emptiness of the room. A feeling of cold desolation was there in the room, and it crept up on him. The third stage of his emotions was that of anger at the nerve of her not being home at this hour, which was nigh on six o'clock and getting toward dusk. How dare she make him wait for his supper 'til seven or eight of the clock. A man could expect better from his wife when he'd worked all day.

Inside the room, Bill looked around for some explanation in the form of a sign or note. Nothing. It was neat and tidy and no preparation was in evidence for an evening meal. He turned around and picked up the curtain, half expecting her to be coming up the walk and rehearsing the tongue-lashing he'd give her. But no, there was no one coming up the rough stone walk to his house.

His anger turned now to swift fury, and he plunked himself in a kitchen chair and stared at the cold stove with malevolence. An hour later, he still sat there and a cold and dreadful thought came creeping over him. Maybe she wasn't coming home this night . . . nor maybe any other. Maybe she'd up and left him. His mind flashed back onto the events of this morning. Bill recalled her extreme nervousness, her hurry to shush up the child when he started to speak. It all could add up to that terrible conclusion.

His fury was changing into that terrible combination of hurt and hate that drives certain men to desperate deeds. If she'd run off with a man, it would justify all of his fears over these wretched years. She was his, belonged to him, and the idea that another man might take her away, might even be loved by the woman who had never loved him, made him insane with jealousy. He picked up a china cup and saucer and flung them against the wall. The crash cemented the purpose in him and he made for the door.

The younger Mrs. Coxswain opened her door looking frightened but tight-lipped. When she saw Bill's black face, she thought, *Oh boy, we're in for it.*

"No, Bill, I haven't a clue where she is. Saw her heading for the market this mornin' and haven't seen her since."

The stricken man snapped, "What time?"

"I dunno, maybe tenish."

Bill turned around on his heel and marched down her path toward Hurontario Street. He'd get to the bottom of this. A picture was forming in his mind. Her and that Delaine fellow. He's the only man he'd known her to have anything to do with and that one was still alone. Bill needed a drink an' a bite. He headed into Barnaby's, the nearest saloon. The evening was cold but he hardly felt it anymore.

Barnaby served him, thinking the man looked more like a corpse than a living being this night and set a meat pie with some peas before him when he muttered something about some vittles with his grog.

"You're looking rough tonight, Bill."

Bill glowered. "Got woman problems."

Barnaby's brow flinched. "Oh?" This was said with an innocent air for he was used to commiserating with the problems of men.

Just then Phoebus Quirty came in. "Bill! What are you doing in here so early, you old sot."

He turned around to see Phoebus, his mate at the Yard and one of the only men he got on with. The scrawny, wizened man liked his off-colour jokes. Now the latter looked at his buddy's face and said, "What's up? You look like a sick hen."

"Shut your fly-trap."

Phoebus carried on chattering unabashedly. "My Mabel said she saw your missus the day but she was in an awful hurry. Mabel called out to 'er but the lass just waved and kept on walkin'. A might put out was Mabel. As I was tellin' you afore, she thinks Caitlin gives herself airs. Won't rub shoulders with the other Yard wives. But then, I think she's a little jealous," he said good-humouredly. "Your Caitlin sure is a bonnie one."

Bill had gone stiff. "You say Mabel said she was in a hurry. Goin' where?"

"Aye, she said the little 'un was runnin' along of her to keep up."

"Never mind that. Did she say what direction she was takin'?"

"Oh, aye. She was back o' the market and headin' out along Ontario Street."

"Ontario Street!" Bill exclaimed more to himself than anyone else. "Why would she be goin' up there?!"

Phoebus eyed him curiously. "What's eatin' you, Bill? You look awful. What if the lass went for a little walk?"

"She hasn't come home."

Phoebus' eyes got big and his expression changed from one of friendly derision to one of surprise and pity instantly.

"Oh, aye . . . aye. What do you suppose has happened?"

Bill's face looked blacker than Hades. "She's run off. That's whot. I know it."

"By hersel'?"

"No, with a man." Bill's face now looked murderous.

"What man!" Quirty looked stupefied 'cause when would that little lass get the chance to have it on with a man when she was so well placed under Bill's thumb? He watched her as a cat does a mouse.

"I'm not sure, but I feel certain it's with a man . . ."

Why he had forgotten it, he didn't know but now Phoebus Quirty remembered just then one of the other lads at the Yard saying he'd seen Bill's wife in the saloon with Mr. Delaine, the surveyor. He'd thought the lad was cookin' up a story to annoy Bill with 'cause they loved to get Bill's goat and they knew his wife was a sore spot. But as far as he knew, the story had never reached Bill's ears. Now he knew why. It was likely true.

Quirty looked away suddenly with an unmistakable guilty look. Bill, in the heightened awareness of his frenzied mood, caught the subtlety of the look. "What is it? By Jesus, tell me!" Bill's voice verged on hysteria.

The older man shook his head and proceeded with uneasiness. "I don't know if this has anythin' to do with it, Bill, but I heard she was in here a couple days ago with Mr. Delaine, the surveyor. Would ha' told ya, lad, but I thought it were just a joke at the time."

CHAPTER 7

By ten o'clock that night Bill had recruited the help of two or three Yard men, which included assurances that they would come along of him to forcibly bring Caitlin home, if necessary. Although these men didn't have a high regard for Bill, they were men who believed in the inexorable right of the man to his wife and offspring and the undeniable sanctity of it all.

He had also contacted the local constabulary and insisted that that personage find the man who "kidnapped" his wife and child and charge him with this heinous offence. The constable was loathe to move on such an accusation made of a respectable citizen by one whose morals were in question, but by the next day was put in a position of having to do so by the visitation of a lobby of zealous and virtuous matrons who were appalled at such a depraved crime happening in their community. That poor, innocent child being abducted and his mother, a young woman of questionable reputation and even if she herself had gone of her own free will, was she then a fit mother to run off with a lover and deprive a father of his child? It was not to be stood. But the possibility was that they were both kidnapped and justice must be served in either case.

Sheriff McMahon, tired and irritable at being disturbed from his bed last night by Bill and having to deal with these irrepressible women today, reluctantly gave his assurances to the ladies that he would look into the situation. As if he didn't have enough to do for his five hundred per year in this frontier town where saloons abounded, dealing with drunk and disorderly conduct alone. And this Bill was one of the worst offenders. He'd picked that one up off the street and driven him home more than once lest the ice and snow form a coffin for him by morning. Perhaps he should have left him to his fate.

He could read people. Lord knows he'd learned about people in his job and that Bill was a bad 'un. The sheriff felt compassion for the pretty little wife he'd seen in town who did her best to hold her head high, but he had to be objective. If a crime had been committed, it was his job to set things straight according to the law and not his own convictions. The matter would be accorded due action. If the child had been removed from its father unlawfully, it would have to be returned with the mother. If Bill chose to press charges, one or more of the adult parties could be in for a jail term depending on the circumstances.

The aging constable sat down and penned the necessary forms to get the ball rolling. Bill had information that they may have headed east from town. That would make sense as the nearest large centre where they would have some degree of anonymity would be Barrie. They may also be headed south. He would follow up both possibilities. It was unlikely they would have headed west. It was mostly wilderness, farms, and small villages that way with the populace having close connections with the people of Collingwood. At any rate the road ended a few miles outside town in that direction and dwindled into an Indian path surrounded by dense woods.

He straightened his suspenders and lit one of the fine cigars he had got at the new cigar store in town. The little luxury made him feel better about his day and eased his irritable mood. Ah, Collingwood was a fine town. He had to remember that and most of the folks of the best sort and his job often rewarding. He just had to remember not to get emotionally involved with people and their outcomes. Then he'd enjoy life more and things would be easier.

Sheriff McMahon looked at his pocket watch. It was eleven o'clock. He had better ride over to Stayner and alert the constabulary there of the situation. It was an unpleasant task, but he would have to notify appropriate people in Barrie and Toronto of the missing persons by telegraph. He was afraid that two-legged donkey would take matters into his own hands. If he didn't do something to find the people, a further tragedy may ensue. He would talk to a few people today and do some detective work as well. His deputy could fill in for him. He would go for a couple days if necessary and try to catch up to them himself.

Bill came into the sheriff's office just then dishevelled and somewhat the worse for drink. Bill had obviously not been near the Shipyard yet today. The constable took a deep breath and tried to push a feeling of distaste for the fellow aside.

"All under control, my good fellow. Your claim is being looked into. You can go home and wait. I will be in touch."

"How come you've not done nothin' yet? Strike while the iron's hot. They'll be miles away by now. If you're not moving on it, I'll do it myself. I've got friends who know what they're about. Won't tolerate a wife walking out on her husband and taking his boy."

"I thought you said she was kidnapped."

Bill, weaving badly, hiked up his pants and threw his chest out. "Whatever it is, I want 'em back. They belong to me." He poked his finger at his own chest. "I have rights."

The fastidious constable looked at the man before him who appeared decrepit and slovenly both in appearance and morals and said gravely, "You had better see, my man, that you don't take the law into your own hands. If you should do so, believe me, I shall be just as ready to throw the book at you as at them. Now go home and get some sleep. You have a job at the Shipyard, I understand. They'll be wanting to see you back at work soon I should imagine."

"The Shipyard be damned!" spat Bill.

The man was really getting the officer's dander up now. He came near to grabbing him by the scruff of the neck and throwing him out on his ear. Looking very grim now, he said with great restraint, "Out with you now. I have business to attend to."

The constable's face was beet red when he shut the door on the man. Sometimes he wished he was a civilian so that he could wring a neck when he felt compelled to do so and he hadn't felt like wringing a neck for a long time as he felt like wringing that bugger's.

Caitlin, Lawrence, and little Willie had stopped in Stayner, a new town grown up by Nottawasaga Station, for a few minutes. As they drove into town, on the left hand side of the main street they saw a grocery and dry goods store, then an inn, a grist mill, the town livery stable, and after that a harness shop.

"It is tempting to leave the horses and wagon at the livery stable and take the passenger train from Nottawasaga station to Toronto, but I know it's already gone for the day and it would be foolish to wait until the morrow," said Lawrence.

"He could follow us, get the police on us when the train stopped. There's the telegraph," Caitlin spoke evenly and tried to hide the alarm in her voice.

Lawrence looked at her solemnly. "He could do that, to be sure. It will be rough going, but the road is the safest route until we get far enough away from Collingwood."

Caitlin looked to her right and noticed they were passing a confectionery shop, then a general store, and millinery shop. A hotel was next on the south side of the main street and there were several hitching posts in front of it. Lawrence stopped here and got down to tie up the horses to the first post which was just beyond the general store.

"I'll be a few minutes. I'm going into the store for a couple things. You and Willie just sit tight." Caitlin nodded. Lawrence left them in the conveyance and got out to purchase a couple of wool blankets and a kerosene lamp. He wasn't sure what was ahead of them, and it wouldn't hurt to have some emergency items. He had only thrown three blankets in the trap before he left. At that time he had been fairly confident they would be able to get adequate lodgings along the way but now was feeling less so. If worse came to worse, they could sleep under the wagon. It was two o'clock already, and they should cover some distance before stopping for the night.

Caitlin stayed in the wagon and tended to Willie who had been good as gold. She asked him if he was thirsty and felt his forehead, brushing strands of fine blonde hair away from his high forehead. It was a typical mother's gesture and she found to her relief that his brow was cool and dry. Then her attention turned apprehensively to two men who lingered outside the hotel, smoking pipes and chatting. Had it been summer, they would have stayed longer and eyed the pretty young woman and child in the wagon and wondered aloud to each other who she was. But the temperature was dropping and the winds were picking up and the dark grey snow-clouds in the sky bade them be on their way to home and hearth for it was too late in the season for farm work and these men were of an age where they could take life a little slower.

Lawrence Delaine strode over to the general store and thought to himself that he liked this town. Women with shopping baskets were walking up and down the street and men in overalls and bright neckerchiefs were coming into town on buckboards with produce for sale or trade. Two old farmers were chatting affably in front of the hotel. The stores were well stocked and the attendants friendly. A smiling young woman rose up to wait on him with curiosity bright in her eyes as he entered the store.

"You're not from around here, sir?" she said later as she took her time totalling his purchases.

He hesitated and then said slowly, carefully.

"Not unless you consider Collingwood far away."

She looked at him with increasing interest as she laughed.

"Well, we're obliged at getting yer custom today, Mr. . . . . .?"

The cautious man answered her quickly without revealing his name.

"Your prices are more agreeable than those in Collingwood this day. We are visiting an acquaintance in the area and thought we'd take advantage of our trip to make some purchases," Lawrence lied, hoping to distract her.

The woman nodded. She would have liked to ask who the acquaintance was for she was a very inquisitive person but noted the uncommunicative look in her customer's eyes and in his voice; so stifled the barrage of questions that cropped up in her mind. Like "Why didn't the woman come in and make the household selections?" Oh, yes, she had peered out the window and seen a beautiful woman sitting up high on the smart conveyance. But she also saw the look her father, the proprietor, gave herself and so left off any prying questions but not her speculations.

Life was rather dull in the shop day after day waiting on customers, mostly unromantic looking housewives and manure-covered farmers. When she did get someone interesting in the shop, why shouldn't she try to find out something about them? There was more to life than what happened in this little farming town. This man certainly looked interesting and mysterious; plain-looking except for arresting eyes and gentlemanly attire, but cutting a rather romantic figure. *Clothes make the man*, she thought looking at him boldly with a certain admiration.

When the quiet spoken man left the store with his purchases, the shop girl sighed and returned to her work-day routine. Lawrence got back into his seat and said, "I likely shouldn't have stopped here, but we needed some things for the journey."

"Where will we go now?" Caitlin looked at him with glowing trust in her eyes.

The widower hoped he would deserve the confident look she gave him. "I thought we would—" But as he started to explain his idea, great huge snowflakes started to fall all about them.

"Look, Mamma, it's snowing!" Willie cried with glee. He had been very quiet until now, and Caitlin was overjoyed to hear him speak with such enthusiasm. The child turned shyly to the older man.

"Are we going to travel in a blizzard, Mister?" He was enjoying this adventure. Lawrence was tucking an old buffalo robe about their knees as he went to answer the young boy with a smile. Just then he saw the store lady standing at the door looking at them all. He got the horses going without further hesitation.

"We'd better be off," he said as they left the boundaries of the little town of Stayner behind. "Blizzard or no blizzard."

The young shop girl turned and went back into the store. She couldn't resist one last look at the family in the gig. But it intrigued her that the boy called the man "Mister." He wasn't the boy's father then. Well, the man had seemed older than the woman for sure.

Finally the snow came down hard enough that Lawrence sought refuge for the night a short ways later. It was coming dusk. By this time a thin, white blanket lay on the ground. They had stopped for a drink of water at a creek and eaten some food from the basket.

"I know a farmer about a quarter mile in from the road. He will take us in for the night I'm sure." Lawrence turned down what looked like a cow path and travelled for a long way into the bush. He came out into a clearing where lay quite a decent-sized farm, which boasted a small two-storey log house and a larger one of planks under construction. There was also a nice barn.

The Thurstons were surprised to see Delaine whom they had not seen for a few years, but they were very welcoming. It seemed they had several new children since his last visit with them and were virtually bursting out of their four-room house.

"We need lodgings for the night. It's a matter of extreme urgency." Lawrence's face showed his state of mind, and as he went on to give further explanation, Mr. Thurston interjected.

"No need to explain, my good friend. Our home is yours." The man looked at Caitlin and the small boy and some of the truth was plain to see.

"This is Caitlin and her son, Willie," continued Delaine, knowing it was necessary to impart some of their situation. "I have to take them away from an unhappy and dangerous domestic arrangement." He started to feel uncomfortable as his emotions caused a loss of words to express their plight.

The Thurstons looked at one another and at Delaine's pleading face. It was plainly apparent that the surveyor was in love with the beautiful young woman and wanted her for himself. There was no reason to disbelieve his claim of domestic discord for ill-treatment of wives and children was, sadly, not a new or uncommon story. And there was an air about the woman and child that told of long-suffering. Mrs. Thurston's face crumpled with pity and her heart went out to the young woman who was not much more than a girl.

"We're a might crowded in here, but we'll find a nice spot for you," she said. "There's a turn-up bed and a trundle bed upstairs where the children sleep that you can use for tonight or the barn can be made quite cosy and you are welcome to its shelter." She looked at Lawrence's worried face with concern.

Her husband caught her thoughts and said to their guests, "Be assured that your visit will be held in strictest confidence."

No more was said of the circumstances of their unseemly arrival and Mrs. Thurston went about the happy task of comforting Caitlin and Willie and putting the kettle on to boil for tea. The kindly woman drew a curtain in the kitchen back and bade Caitlin refresh herself from her journey. Caitlin gratefully accepted her offer and was pleased to see a nice washstand with jug, basin, and fingertip towels.

It was an unexpected pleasure for the Thurstons to have this company. They delighted in telling Lawrence and Caitlin about their happy, busy life on the rich, sandy-loam farm while Willie played shyly with their children in the corner of the kitchen. The meticulous couple were at the stage now where they were building a new house and had already built a nice, medium-sized barn, which housed well-cared for animals. While the couple was very hospitable, the two opted to sleep in the barn rather than inconvenience the household.

Caitlin was glad Lawrence had purchased the extra blankets for they were quite cosy that night in the barn on mounds of soft hay, which they covered with the old buffalo robes. The barn had several cows and two horses apart from their own and the warmth from the animals' bodies, combined with the well-built walls of the structure, which were two-ply thick, kept the barn warm on the frosty night.

When Willie fell asleep with a peaceful look on his face, Caitlin said, "Now he's released from the shadow of his father's moods."

The two lovers enjoyed the privacy of the place.

"How do you know the Thurstons? They seem very fond of you," asked Caitlin as she settled down on the mattress of hay and rested her weary head.

"Through my survey work, like the Landrys. I've come to know many of the settlers and helped them by recommending suitable properties. It's a small thing for me, but they are often pitiably grateful as they like a tip on a good piece of land when they're new to the area. I'm a bit of a consultant for the township in my free time. I never knew I would be so pitiably grateful in return for what they have done for me this day." He eased himself down beside Caitlin and turned to face her. His hand reached out automatically in a long familiar gesture to stroke her fine dark hair as he had done when she was but a wistful child.

Words were unimportant now and totally unnecessary. They lay and, though it was dark, gazed into each other's faces silently and then slept exhausted but happy in each other's arms. Tonight, the joy of this closeness after so long a separation was enough to fulfill the longing of their hearts. Had it been a prince's bed with fine linen and bed hangings of crimson velvet trimmed with gold fringe, Caitlin could not have been happier than she was in that humble barn.

In the morning, Mrs. Thurston felt so badly they had had to sleep in the barn, she ushered Caitlin into the house where she bade her wash and make her toilette while she cooked them all a fine breakfast of eggs, pork, and potatoes followed by some good strong tea. The lady proudly set her own preserved fruit on the table. Although their present house was small, the Thurstons were now prosperous farmers and their table was more than adequate. Mrs. Thurston was excited by the new house that would be finished before Christmas.

"Come and stay with us again when the house is finished. But take care now on the road for travelling won't be easy in this weather. The ground is soft and muddy under the first snow in spite of the new gravel."

Lawrence knew that it would be treacherous as travelling in the spring but leave they must and make their way to Barrie. Fortunately, the gravel which had been laid on much of the road would help immensely.

The first new day of Caitlin's freedom was bright and sunny. The little storm of the evening before had blown over leaving only a few inches of fresh snow. It was still crisp as they started out. They could not get away before midmorning from the kindly people. The weather had turned very cold and the snow had frozen solid. It looked like their journey would be aided by a more solid ground, but it was still with some trepidation that they returned to the main road and prayed that God would speed them on their journey.

Bill heeded the Constable's advice and went home to rest for an hour or two. The house was cold and dank without a woman there to keep the fires burning. He cleared up the cup and saucer he had broken the day before with the corn broom and lit a fire in the wood stove. Once it was going well, he lay down on the bed he had shared with his young wife. Why had he let old Jacob rope him into this marriage? He could have had a less uppity tart for a wife. Although she rarely spoke back to him and avoided rows, he always knew Caitlin looked on him as a lower type.

Bill had thought shortly after his marriage that he should not have married Caitlin. Perhaps instead he should have gone over to Owen Sound to work. There was good whoring in that town, and he would have been better off marrying a strumpet anyway. It was said they made good wives—knew how to tend to a man's needs. Nevertheless, his possessiveness had continued to deepen throughout this marriage until he was obsessive about his wife.

What would Jacob Winters say if he knew what she'd done now! But then he had been dead for almost a year now and even before that he had snubbed them both since the marriage. Not a penny had she received from his will. Her sister, Mavis, got all his money and the two lads to finish rearing. Bill decided that when he woke up from his nap, he would call on that sheriff again. If his wife and young 'un weren't returned tonight, he'd do something about it. By Jove he would!

Sheriff McMahon was in Stayner by one o'clock and his inquiries had borne fruit. A couple matching their description had been through town late yesterday and had actually stopped to buy some things. An observant young woman even saw what direction they took as they left town—toward Barrie. He was sure it was them for the young woman described them to a tee, even the boy.

There had been an early snowstorm here last night so he figured they may have found a place to stay, a refuge, not far from town for the night for t'would have been hard to follow the road. The constable was in luck for the storm had stopped by early morning, making tracks still visible in the snow. That Delaine was a smart one all right. An educated man. He had assisted one of the original surveyors to this area, a government surveyor, as a young man and had, after learning his craft, spread out to other parts of the province and beyond when this area was settled up. He knew quite a few around here and wouldn't want for those that would be glad to give him lodgings.

There was one thing that might help in the search. Delaine's conveyance was a fine one with extra wide wheels that would make recognizable tracks different from the local farm wagons. If the weather remained this cold as it promised to, he could be tracked thus.

The sheriff sighed. He'd done his part. He'd hand the matter over to the local constable here and get home to his wife who'd have a good meal ready for him. His heart just wasn't in this case. He almost wished that lot would get away; although he didn't know what Lawrence Delaine was thinking, absconding with a young married woman half his age and her son when he owned property in Collingwood. However did he think he would get away with it?

The veteran law enforcer scratched his chin. It was a desperate measure, a crime of passion; if it could really be classed as a crime.

There he was again, questioning the law. It was decided, he'd hand it over to old Sloan. He would be more objective about the whole thing. Anyway, the man had little to do in this sleepy town and had the time to deal with it. From his calculations, Sloan could catch up with them on a fast, fresh horse in a few hours come morning. It was clear and cold now and promised to be a good day tomorrow.

McMahon was tired and irritable when he saw the lights of Collingwood approach. His steed was also tired, and he felt resentful toward that whiskey-soaked sot for running him all over hell's half-acre. All he needed was to see Bill's now ugly face greet him as the veteran constable came to his door at seven o' clock p.m., cold, hungry, and extremely short on patience.

"Well?" Bill stood there arms akimbo, tenacious with stubbornness emanating from his very being.

"My patience is running very thin, my man, very thin. I've been out the day looking for your family and the man who allegedly abducted them. I have located their whereabouts as of late yesterday afternoon when they passed through Stayner. My associate will be on their track first thing tomorrow morning."

"Tomorrow morning! By gad! They'll be out of reach by then. Time is slipping by. I want justice done. I've been wronged!" Bill looked at him fiercely.

The peace officer thought: liquor has addled what brains he had. "Justice, whatever it is in this case, will be done. That I assure you. Now get out of my sight. And I warn you once more. Keep yourself to yourself. The police will take care of this matter."

Bill stood there hopping from one foot to the other, continuing to rant. "I pay me taxes. It's the likes o' me whot hires the likes o' you. You coulda' nabbed 'em yesterday if you was on the ball. Now, like as not, it's too bloody late. As I told you, I got friends who'll help me. I'll get that 'un back and the young 'un. And that blackguard whot took 'em will have to answer to me!" He poked his finger repeatedly at his own breast.

Sheriff McMahon wagged his finger at Bill and said, "I have half a mind to throw you in the lock-up right now. And I will if you're not out of me sight in one second. And mind your actions, man, from here on out."

Bill spun around and stomped off. He went straight to visit the men who promised to help him if he needed to go it alone.

"Bill, don't ya remember there's a launchin' the morrow?" whined Phoebus Quirty looking at Bill dubiously from his bloodshot eyes.

"We'd go with you, you know we would, but the boss said every man jack is to be at the launchin' to help-like the morrow. Them that doesn't turn up is fired . . . gonzo. And that includes you, Bill. He said so. He sent us with a message for you. I was about to come over t'visit you now when in poked yer head."

"He said that, did he?" Bill looked thoughtful. He knew his boss's dislike for him was thinly veiled and though he felt like saying "Piss on it," without his wife and son and his job, he'd likely have to move on from this community 'cause he knew he'd have it tough getting more work. Bill had a little brain. It had shrunk from lack of love in his early life and lack of compassion. The latter attribute had never developed in him as a result.

"We'll come with you day after next if the police haven't found her then. It's a promise," Phoebus said, breaking into Bill's thoughts.

With that, Bill went home with some confidence Caitlin would be returned to him before long, one way or another, and had a fairly good night's sleep for the first time in two nights. He might just let the police handle it. It sounded like they were on to her, slow but sure.

He'd go to the Yard tomorrow, help with the launchin', keep his job, and when that pretty little stuff was brought home, he'd give her the livin' dickens. Did he have plans for her! Like a "loving" husband he'd "forgive" her and not press charges. Then when he got that bit of goods home, he'd hurt her where it wouldn't show. As for that bastard, Delaine, he'd see him sent up for life if he didn't kill him first with his own bare hands.

Call it poetic justice if you like, but the events of the next day were such that some would say Fate or some otherworldly intervention played a part. But then, real life is stranger than fiction say the wise ones.

It was a side launch like all the launchings in Collingwood that day, and Bill was stone sober for a change. He had to put on a good face for the boss. At one time his young, muscular, and tanned, blonde looks and easy if obnoxious smile imbued his employers with confidence in his ability to do the job. Nowadays, with his less impressive appearance, which showed signs of early dereliction and the seediness of a street bum, it was an effort to stand straight and look cocky. Even he knew his penchant for whiskey was showing in his face and figure.

So, today, he compensated by pushing his still hard but stringy muscles to their limit as he toiled along of the other men with hammer on wedge in an attempt to tilt the boat so she would be able to slide down the greased wood into the water. The knocking of wood on wood resounded in the air as they attempted to free the boat from its moorings.

Crowds of large numbers had gathered to watch the late season launching of the paddle steamer SS *Mary Dawn*. All one hundred and seventy-five feet of her was up on stocks on the west side of the railway wharf. Even with the chill day, the townsfolk were all out; the ladies donning their best finery. It was a chance to meet and mingle and witness a proud event for the Town. For many it was their first viewing of a launching and mothers held up their children hoping they would record this grand event in their memories.

As the last wedge was hammered in under the keel in the progressive effort to release the *Mary Dawn*, the foreman yelled, "Cut the ropes. Now let go the chains."

A murmur went through the crowd who strained against the railing to get a better view.

But as the boat slipped down the butter boards, something went very wrong. "Blast it. The stern's going first," yelled the launcher. "Out of the way and run fer yer lives!" he called to the men. They didn't need to be told twice and scattered like toy soldiers as timbers went flying, well aware of the dangers if they delayed. Side launchings were also notoriously unpredictable.

But Bill had caught the eye of a particularly comely lass who was in the front row of spectators and, despite the colossal hazard, had paused to touch his forelock to her in between heavy blows to a wedge. His face broke into a reminiscence of one of his former lasciviously charming smiles as he caught her blushing glance on his rippling muscles, and momentarily, he looked as he had ten years ago, crudely handsome and dashing. It was only for a short moment, however, for an enormous roar drowned out all else, even the foreman's angry bawl.

"I said get out of the way, blast you!"

But it was too late. A split second earlier Bill could have wrenched it free, but while he tugged on his pant leg that caught on a nail, a horrified public looked on as the ship side launched with Bill in its road. As the ship's hull hit the water with great force, a mountainous wave was propelled skyward amidst voluminous spray. The blushing young lady's face turned from coquetry to shock and disbelief and she shrieked.

It all happened so fast, mothers didn't have time to hide the faces of their children in their skirts and they were forced to witness the terrible scene. As the stern hit the water, the bow angled back and the great boat rose up and hit Bill in the head, partially decapitating him in midair. His body disappeared in the wake in the next second. The feckless young girl left off her screaming and fainted straight out.

For those who witnessed it, it was said that it must have been a quick death, quite instantaneous, though terrible to watch. Sheriff McMahon was there himself but didn't realize it was Bill until the foreman did a head count to be sure, an hour later.

Old Sloane had started out early and was sure he was on to the tracks of the escapees. They had likely stopped in at the Thurston farm for the night. Sheriff McMahon had apprised him of the larger wheel prints Delaine's conveyance might make. He saw some likely tracks lead in and out of the Thurston property. But another night had passed in the meantime and he could not be sure. He went into the prosperous little farm and inquired of its mistress if she had of late some visitors. The lady seemed too quick to deny the recent presence of a couple and child in her home.

"Why, those are my husband's tracks," said Mrs. Thurston when he questioned the wide tracks in the lane. She proceeded to blush and Sloan detected something amiss in her manner right away. He decided to call her bluff.

"I must warn you, you could be an accessory to a crime if you don't tell the truth. Harbouring a kidnapper—"

"Kidnapper!" The missus was up at arms. "She was no more—"

"There. I have you."

Mrs. Thurston looked rattled and miserable. "But he's such a good man and the girl seemed willing enough. Happier than larks, they were and the young 'un too."

Sloan coughed, somewhat embarrassed. "I see, I see. Well, the situation may not be all that it seems. But in your best interest and the best interest of your friend, you had better tell me where they're heading and what route they plan to take."

After a lengthy pause in which her expression became one of defeat and worry she let it all out.

"Barrie . . . to Barrie they went on the main road. But please"—and she touched his arm pleadingly—"go easy on him. He's no criminal by my measure."

Touched by her genuine regard for the man, Sloan felt compelled to reassure her. "I'll heed your words of commendation, ma'am, but I've a duty to perform." He tipped his hat to her and left speedily not wanting to waste any more precious time.

Caitlin, Lawrence, and Willie had made good time on the road to Barrie after leaving the Thurstons until one of their horses went lame in the late afternoon and they were forced against their better judgment to stay at a roadside inn while they waited for the delivery of a fresh steed the next morning. They were still far from Barrie. In spite of this risk, they were safely on the road the next morning at a good hour and things looked like they would be all right.

The constable from Stayner was in luck when he stopped by a roadside inn and it seemed three individuals fitting the description of the escapees had resided there the night before awaiting a fresh horse. Not wanting to linger too long, although a mug of ale would have been refreshing, he carried on his way after learning two rooms had been let to a middle-aged man travelling with his niece and a small child.

A weary Sloan caught up to them two hours later and hollered, "Halt in the name of the Law!" as he drew his revolver and pointed it in their direction but aimed the same high above their heads. It just so happened at that very moment his horse, tired from this long journey which he was not used to, chose to slip on a bit of melting ice and as he struggled to regain his footing, inadvertently threw old Sloan onto the road. His gun fell some distance away.

Caitlin and Lawrence had by this time stopped and turned around with fear written on their faces. Disaster had struck. They were found. This almost comic fall of the officer made them realize they might still escape. Lawrence commenced to start up the horses again, but Caitlin put her arm on his elbow.

"Wait, we can't just leave him here. I think he may have broken something." She pointed to the officer who had not attempted to get up but was curled on his side holding one leg.

Lawrence looked at Caitlin searchingly and she at him for a long few seconds. Saying nothing, he got down from the trap and walked back toward the officer.

"Are you hurt, sir?" he enquired politely as he knelt down, ignoring the gun a short distance away.

Sloan grimaced. "My leg. I think it's broken."

"Here, let me." Lawrence palpated the limb gently.

Two hours later, Sloan's broken leg was set, and he was wrapped in a blanket sipping a hot mug of coffee laced with brandy made over a quickly arranged open fire at the roadside. Some evergreen branches and boughs that Willie had collected covered with more blankets made comfortable seats on the ground. They all ate some sandwiches that Mrs. Thurston had prepared. Lawrence remained calm throughout all of this. He turned once to Caitlin and said. "I'm sorry, my dear. I'm afraid I've failed you again." Sloan watched as the young girl touched his face gently and said with quiet emotion, "You have never failed me, my darling."

My Lord, thought Sloan. *If these were criminals, I'm in the wrong business.* Then Lawrence proceeded to tell Constable Sloan the story of how they came to be on the wrong side of the Law.

A few hours later, after night had fallen, Sloan arrived back at his residence; and when his wife saw him being brought in by what looked like those that he was after, she said, "Lordy, Lordy." She looked again at him and said, "Shall I go for the doctor?"

"Never mind, wife. It's been set good. Just get the back room ready for our guests."

"Guests?" she blinked, dumbfounded.

He looked at her irritably. "Yes, guests. Now do what I say. It's been a long day." Then he turned to Lawrence and said, "Don't worry, either of you. Stay here the night, and I'll send word to Sheriff McMahon in Collingwood tomorrow that I'm incapacitated, but I've got some confidential information for him about the case."

The next day, McMahon received Sloan's message and responded immediately with the following.

"Bill Pratz was killed yesterday at the launching of the *Mary Dawn*. Hold investigation of kidnapping. There may have been some misunderstanding of this. Change of instruction. When you are able, find wife and notify of husband's death. Assess situation and use your good judgment in resolving this case."

After the launching, the water was dredged, and Bill's body was found and the Shipyard supplied the finest coffin box that could be had at short notice. He was buried the next day at the cemetery just outside the town limits. It was the strangest funeral the town had ever witnessed for although there was a great attendance, most of the men from the Yard, there was no family, in particular, no wife and every eye was dry except for Phoebus Quirty who sobbed profusely and blew his nose repeatedly. Indeed, Phoebus was the only mourner there who truly mourned. The other men from the Yard stood there and respectfully removed their caps but shifted uncomfortably from one foot to the next, hoping it would be over quickly.

The Town was agog with the irony of it all. The man's wife disappears and then he dies within two days of her disappearance. There were even rumours of the supernatural and witchcraft, but these died down in the days ahead for no one had been on intimate terms with the family and so townsfolk generally went on with their own lives, each one having its own worries and concerns. Death was not a rare thing then, even among the young. This was not the first death at the Shipyard either.

The news of Bill's death left Caitlin and Lawrence staring at each other in disbelief at first and then each watched the other as the heartache of years fell away from their faces and understanding dawned on them. They were finally free. Old Sloan watched them and smiled to himself in quiet satisfaction. This was the kind of case he liked—one with a happy ending. Didn't have too many of those. So the devil got his. And a devil he sounded from what she had told him. He'd use his "good judgment" all right—they were as free and innocent as birds as far as he was concerned. If it's one thing you learn from this business, it is how to be a judge of character and there was no guile in these two. And when she gently told the boy about his father, he saw the boy turn to his mama with a smile on his chubby face and say, "So we don't have to go home again, Mama?" No boy reacted like that over a father who was good to him.

"If I was you, I wouldn't go back there. Not yet. People bein' what they are, well, they might not take kindly—" Sloan blushed as he looked at the pretty woman with the kind smile on her face and then went on. "If I was you, I'd take a nice trip down to Muddy York for a few weeks, let things cool down 'n all. Folks forget quick enough. You won't be quite so noticeable when you go back."

"Excellent advice, Sloan, excellent advice. Thank you." Lawrence patted the good-hearted police constable on the back. "You've been very good to us. Actually, we were very fortunate that you found us that day. Funny how things work out, isn't it?"

"Aye, the Lord works in mysterious ways, to be sure, laddy."

The next day, Caitlin, Lawrence, and Willie took off south for Muddy York or Toronto as it was now known waving at the ruddy-faced Sloan and his good wife who saw them off from the door of their comfortable home. Lawrence wired his employers, and they agreed to postpone his surveying assignment in Manitoba until spring. He could afford to take a little time off.

As they drove off, he was thinking. It wasn't the best time of year for a trip to Toronto. But if it got bad, they could always change to a sleigh. What was he thinking about! Even these little challenges seemed a joyous thing. It was just dawning on him that he was about to begin the happiest time of his life. He looked at Caitlin who had been strangely silent. As he looked into her eyes, he saw that she was so silent because she could hardly take in all this joy.

Book Of Annie

CHAPTER 8

Annie dreamed of her future. She looked forward to the day when she would be a bride. She imagined her wedding day and perhaps a honeymoon at the popular Eugenia Falls, which was a two-day trip by wagon. If a girl was lucky, she would take this trip with her groom up the winding mountain road and through scenic farmlands where they would stay at an elegant and romantic red brick Inn replete with charming verandahs close by the falls.

But for now, Annie had her mind on a certain fellow who she was hoping to impress at the box social at the Sunday school picnic. Like many of the socials, this one had the women preparing a box lunch. The lunch would be auctioned off to the menfolk. It was to be this afternoon, and Annie had her preparations nearly ready.

She had the box filled with two pieces of cake and two roasted chicken legs. The outside of the box had been decorated with great care as it would hopefully be the most splendiferous one there. Like the other women, she decorated her box with bits of wallpaper, coloured tissue, ribbons, or bows—anything that was pretty and handy - a scrap of lace here and there.

The boxes would go on a table, and when time came for lunch, an auctioneer would take charge and the men would bid on them. They would try to notice the boxes as the ladies came in and, if they were sweet on a girl, would try to bid on hers. The man would eat with the girl who made up the box lunch he bought. Annie finished off her box with a big green ribbon bow on top and stood back the better to admire it.

George Freenan attended the same church as Annie on the side road that ran toward the mountain. Sure enough, when the time finally came, George bid on Annie's box lunch, and they sat together under the chestnut tree in the shade and ate silently. George was not shy with young girls, and Annie was not the first girl he had shared a box lunch with.

But for some reason, they spoke not a word to one another. He'd been to many box socials, although they were mostly in the fall and winter. They were gay get-togethers in the cold months. A fiddler would get up and a caller then anyone who could thump on a piano. Together, they would recount the same old lively reels, jigs, and quadrilles and whether a bean social or a pie social, a helluva good time would be had by all from nine to ninety.

Yet, right now, George sat there in the hot, dry quietness of summer on that lawn next to Annie while the tree crickets sang and said nothing.

George was known to be a lad interested in the young ladies. He'd rolled in the hay with a few as well as shared their lunches. But he had become aware of this wheat-haired girl for a little while. Of a sudden, a little lassie with abundant freckles left off her games and came over to Annie.

"Annie, would you play ring-around-the-rosie with us?"

Annie smiled and got up, dusting cake crumbs off her skirt.

"Sure, Bonnie. I need to get up an' stretch anyhow."

She looked shyly at George and said half apologetically. "I like the little 'uns."

"Go ahead, I'll watch. Thanks for the lunch, Miss Annie."

Annie's eyes lingered on him momentarily and then she swung around and ran to join the children who were not much younger than herself. They were already hand in hand in a circle. Annie was barefoot and her long, soft hair hung free over her dull blue jumper. The little girl, Bonnie, turned her head around and smiled back at him sweetly through crooked teeth with a wisp of strawberry blonde hair falling over her sunburnt freckles.

The day was sunny and parched and filled with the opulent magic of summer. Dry weeds crackled and rustled crisply as Annie made her way to the children. George drained a glass of lemonade and leaned on his elbow on some soft grass in the luxury of a full stomach on an easy no-work day. The excitement of the children at play touched him, and he recalled his own carefree childhood with loving parents not so long ago.

Many of these children would have hard and bitter lives as they grew older, he knew. Many were barefoot and some in ragged clothes. But for today, they laughed and jostled one another in the dry, crackling July grass and ran the livelong day heedless of what their future might bring and the stronger for not knowing.

"Come and join us!" shouted Annie. Her cheeks were flushed as she danced and played with the children. George sat up now, smiling affably. Annie broke into a song that was familiar to all.

"Lazy Mary, won't you get up, won't you get up, won't you get up. Lazy Mary, won't you get up, so early in the morning."

The children yelped with glee and joined in. Annie broke free of the children and, revelling in the happiness of the day, danced in the high soft grass of the churchyard around and around, the sun and the heat rejoicing with her and she sang all the while.

"No, Mother, I won't get up, I won't get up, I won't get up."

As she danced, George got up and stood smilingly transfixed by Annie's dancing that was free and uninhibited as that of a wood nymph. The children chirped and joined hands in a fairy circle and went round and round and, periodically, flopped exhaustedly on the ground in a harmony of giggles.

The local women looked on indulgently at the young ones at play and, occasionally, an old geezer clapped in time to the song. The afternoon droned on in happy heat as the harvesters sang out their hearts; it droned on in pleasant pastime.

As George stood there watching the girl, heat in him outside of the heat of the afternoon began to build. Then, in his secret parts, grew an urgency, a prompting so great, he almost walked out and grabbed her to him in front of the respectable matrons. Of a sudden, he longed to crush Annie to him, bruise her lips and loins against his feverish ones.

But as stealthily as the feeling had come upon him, it began to leave as the young girl stopped her dancing and along with the other picnickers started to tidy up the area and his desire was lost in the chitter chatter of the afternoon.

Soon after, Annie left to go home with a neighbour.

George handed his overcoat to Tim Flannagan and rolled up his sleeves to pitch in at the barn-raising bee. He liked physical work and being in the open air in the back settlement. Two men were carrying a hand-hewn beam in his direction. Most of the frame was now complete, and they were about to fill in. First, they had helped the farmer choose the location, taking into consideration the prevailing winds and drainage. The barn would face south to catch the sun. It would be huge, of course, compared to the house and would be built in the style of those in Pennsylvania. A dirt ramp was constructed to the second floor after the first floor, which would house the livestock and the stonework was complete. The wagon could then bring the grain directly into the second floor.

"Are ye goin' ta ventilate the top with pigeon holes? Them is mighty good eatin' fer the family," said an elderly farmer.

"Aye, John," said the owner. "And will ya be able ta come back and help me with the shinglin'? We'll be doin' it in the full o' the moon fer a warm barn. My missus'll put on a good feed fer ya."

"Don't worry" confirmed John. "The whole lot of us'll be there ta help. We'll put cedar so they'll draw together when the weather gets damp."

George helped the men brace the roof with great struts and then stood back and admired their work. The old farmer looked up at him pleased. "Thanks for helpin', George. You always were a good lad. Will ya come back later and help me with the paintin'? I can make the paint meself with red oxide of iron and skim milk. Just need a bit o' lime with it, and we'll be all set ta paint a nice red barn."

"I sure will, Mike. You can count on me."

George's father, James Freenan, was there at the raising too. He was a businessman, a merchant, and of Irish parentage from the south part of the island. He expected George to follow in his footsteps and go into business, his mercantile business. James was community-minded and didn't like to miss a bee. He was well over sixty years of age and still stalwart. James looked over at his son with affection. Why George was his favourite, he didn't rightly know, but he had warmed to the lad from the start. Perhaps it was the boy's vulnerability.

He wasn't a farmer like the other two boys or as hardheaded. But he was likeable though far from perfect. James detected a slight weakness in him. He didn't like killing things and so did not take to hunting. But it was plain that the boy was the one with a head for business. He liked to come to the store. As a boy, he had always had a chatty way, which amused the lady patrons, and he had never seemed bored or restless.

George was deep in his own thoughts this day. He figured a little physical work would distract him from thinking about women for a while anyway. At twenty-one, he was feeling the needs of a man. Amanda Trolley in Toronto was a pretty girl and his intended; his father's choice really but quite delectable, blonde and coy as a kitten.

She was daughter to Gregory Trolley, import and export entrepreneur. He and Father had put their heads together four years ago and come up with a nice little trade in the furniture, textile, and dry goods business supplying Nottawasaga and Collingwood folk with the nicer amenities of life. The trade was appreciated in the "Forest Town" of Collingwood. It was a town that had some regard for an enterprising man.

Yes, Amanda was pretty and sophisticated. She laughed at his country ways and manners; though at times, this made him feel gauche and too much the rosy-cheeked farm boy. He wondered if their soon-to-be union was a good idea after all. But he knew his father wanted him to settle down and be a respectable member of society and raise a family.

His father wasn't a passionate man. Or no, perhaps he was. He was just passionate about different things—his business, his role in the community. George's father and mother were good to one another. Theirs was a peaceful household. Harmonious.

The lad felt the need for a woman, strongly and surely. He wondered if his father, James, had ever felt like that before marrying. If the latter had when he was young, he had never let on to this, his favourite son. George felt that if he did not marry soon, he would be obsessed with his needs to distraction and could never concentrate on building the kind of life he wanted and would therefore gravely disappoint his father.

He had seen that little McClory girl again today. She lived outside the village of Nottawa and her father worked on and off at the dock when freight came in to be transhipped. He was a man of all work as well as a farmer. They were a modest but respectable family.

The girl held an attraction for him. He was not sure why, but she affected him. He wanted to look at her, even touch her. *Odd*, he thought, but being young, George didn't dwell on the thought too long. He put it down to his youthful urges and fancy. Amanda would more than suffice as wife and love mate. Why, any man would be lucky to have a girl like her. And she was determined to have him—he knew. He saw that determination on her face almost the first time they met. It amused George. He recognized the steeliness in her small face. Amanda knew what she wanted and would have it.

A brown-skinned lad, not more than eleven, passed him some hand cut nails and he forgot his previous thoughts, lost in the pleasure of hard work in good company on a sunny, blue-skied day. He looked around and saw the same happiness on the faces of the other men.

It was good to work as a team, as one body, and to forget any differences one had during last night's drinking bout. It was good to be alive in the Dominion of Canada in Collingwood. He would soon be a businessman, have a wife and family like his father before him and his father before him; to grow with this young community, perhaps to be looked up to. Was all this enough? He thought so. What more could there be?

Now Amanda really was not typical of girls of her time in Toronto, in all fairness to those others. She did not mean to be unkind but simply had a selfish streak, which was unknowingly encouraged by an indulgent father.

Being an only child, which was somewhat of an oddity in those times of large families, she had unwittingly been treated like a china doll lest they lose this one and only treasure. Fortunately, Amanda was not prone to hypochondria and was, although petite in stature, a very sturdy and feisty girl, not prone to vapours or other ailments and complaints either. She was self-willed and spoiled, however, and had little regard for the feelings and welfare of others.

George and Amanda were married amidst much pomp and pageantry in Toronto in the year 1874, a few weeks before Christmas. Amanda and her doting father insisted on a city wedding so that he could see his "little gel" enjoy the fineries she was brought up to expect on her wedding day. George's initial suggestion that they marry in Collingwood was met with aghast looks. Needless to say, he did not mention it again. Obviously, he realized, she would want to have her friends around her at the wedding, and they all resided in Toronto, and after all, it was the bride's family who planned the wedding.

So he went along with everything naively expecting that Amanda would adjust to life in Nottawasaga township with a minimum of difficulty. Were not most of the women in Collingwood emigrees from Europe and other parts of Upper Canada? They made out quite well in their adjustments to settlers' lives for the most part and thus did he expect that Amanda, citified though she was, would also adjust. After all, she was born in Canada.

Amanda's father had purchased for his daughter Mrs. Isabella Mayson Beeton's new *Book of Household Management*, which she politely accepted with some forced enthusiasm but tired of after the first two tedious chapters. Novels were so much more interesting and intriguing. However, the section which spoke of handling domestic servants she read and stored this knowledge for possible future reference.

The wedding was opulent beyond description. Bowers of flowers, red and white, adorned the church. There was also holly in abundance and great wreaths of evergreen. Bouquets of red roses decorated each pew and candles and candelabras were lit in profusion giving the whole procession a most glorious air.

Like other Victorian brides of society, Amanda would later preserve her bouquet by drying it and placing it under a glass dome. She had had great decisions to make in regard to her wedding flowers. Should she carry a nosegay of snowdrops like Queen Victoria had done, or should it be a tussy-mussy of bold red roses surrounded by lily of the valley?

The wedding repast would include roasted quail, a fish dish, roast fowl and lamb, game pies, salads followed by cheese, tarts, and bonbons. The music was baroque in nature from a dignified black-clad orchestra situated at the entrance of the impressive church. Their white linen gleamed in the candlelight and their rich wooded instruments complemented the polished banisters of carved oak behind which they sat.

The lofty ceilings of the cathedral could only be termed magnificent and the guests gasped in awe as they beheld the exquisitely decorated church. Amanda was like a vision from a fairy tale as she walked down the aisle, gleaming in trailing white on the arm of her father to the moving religious hymn, Excelsius Deo, sung by a choir soloist.

The reception was held at her father, Mr. Trolley's, military club which was most unusual. These affairs were usually held at the family home whether it be humble or rich. A gigantic yule log was burning on the impressive hearth and most of the church decorations were brought to adorn the military hall.

The meal was begun with a sweet Madeira wine or dry sherry, depending on preference. This was followed by cold cucumber soup. After dinner, the wedding party was served with port and brandy along with large trays bearing apples, walnuts, and aged cheeses. They toasted with champagne and claret punch. The ladies sipped the creamy luxury of fruity frappes, taking care to protect their lavish silk and lace-covered taffeta gowns from spills.

"Dearest, you look bewitching," crooned George to his bride after they had welcomed their guests at the wedding table. (George could be quite smooth, which was part of his charm.) He was mesmerized by this radiant creature in satin lace and netting. Amanda positively glittered with sequins and pearls.

"Why thank you, George. You look ravishing, too."

"Oh, my dearest, I cannot wait to hold you in my arms!" he exclaimed.

Amanda smiled smugly and offered up her lips to him. The guests roared in appreciation.

"Here, here!" Her father raised his arm jovially in a toast.

"To the lovebirds." Turning to his new son-in-law, he announced, "By Jove, I've given you my only daughter, George, because I've come to know you for a gentleman and a man of ambition. You're the son of my best friend and partner. Therefore, no better match could be made."

Mr. Trolley then turned to the wedding guests and raised his glass. "Are they not a handsome couple? He so dark and she so fair? What a bonnie bunch of grandchildren we'll have, eh, Margaret?"

To this there was much cheering and clapping from the party as the old gent turned to his wife, Margaret, who nodded shyly in agreement, her round, moon face a wee bit flushed with wine.

"Treat her like gold, my boy, because that's what she's used to. Ha, ha!"

With that, Gregory Trolley sat down and adjusted his waistcoat over his handsome paunch, grey moustachios twitching from a speech well spoken. They stood out with distinction against the man's round, florid cheeks. He was indeed well-pleased with the match and not a little relieved that his little vixen was settled with a practical, down-to-earth young country gentleman. He hoped she would learn some of the young man's practical ways for her mother had not been very successful in gaining the girl's interest in matters concerning the running of a household.

James Freenan, as father of the groom, then delivered his speech, and with the dinner finished and dessert and liqueurs being consumed, the dancing commenced in the large hall.

"How about a country dance?" cried a gentleman in the crowd. With that, the orchestra, which was made up of a cello, violin, flute, mandolin, and pianoforte, left off their sedate waltz.

"A Christmas song for a Christmas wedding!" demanded a lady guest.

"Something gay," called another. "We wish to celebrate."

"I know just the thing," answered the chief musician. "It is a Christmas song, yet it is gay." With that, he struck up the chords of a lively jig tune. It was an old and familiar Christmas song and the people clapped in recognition and delight.

"What is the name of that song?" inquired George of his bride.

"Why, that is 'A Christmas Day in the Morning,'" declared Amanda.

George was sipping on his wine cordial and found himself suddenly immobile as he listened to the gay melody. He'd heard that tune before! It was so familiar. But where? The young and old alike hooted with glee and cut joyous figures as they hopped and danced across the floor to the song. But for George, an unreality seemed to slip over him, a sadness blotting all else out in a soft fog until all there was left was the music which was evoking strange emotions in him.

> *I saw three ships come sailing in on Christmas Day,*
> *on Christmas Day.*
> *I saw three ships come sailing in on Christmas Day,*
> *in the morning!*
> *And what was in those ships all three on Christmas Day,*
> *on Christmas Day*
> *And what was in those ships all three on Christmas Day*
> *in the morning?*
> *Our saviour Christ and his lady on Christmas Day,*
> *on Christmas Day*
> *Our saviour Christ and his lady on Christmas Day*
> *in the morning.*
> *Pray wither sail those ships all three on Christmas Day*
> *on Christmas Day.*

George shook his head to try to clear the haze. But the music rose and filled his brain with its sweet nostalgic strains until he was transported in a soft, dull cloud back to a hot summer day at the churchyard on the side road where he had bid on Annie's box lunch two summers ago. He saw her laughing face and her downy hair swirling about her as she danced and twirled, twirled, and danced, singing,

> *Lazy Mary won't you get up, won't you get up,*
> *won't you get up.*
> *Lazy Mary won't you get up, so early in the morning.*
> *No, Mother, I won't get up. I won't get up. I won't get up. No Mother.....*

It was the same melody but different words, and it transported him back in time. George saw again Annie's soft, light hair sparkling in the hot sun and her simple, country frock held up as she swished and whirled about in bare feet. He tasted the tart lemonade and felt his hot desire for her. A panic of deep loss and desolation swept over him suddenly.

His trance was broken when Amanda put her hand on his arm and instead of the lemonade he tasted the cloying sweet richness of the cordial in his hand. He was back at the wedding table. Everything looked dark and cool. Amanda's hard, brilliant beauty enhanced by the sparkle of white and diamond bright in the light of the many-candled chandelier came through to his now dulled senses that he attributed partly to the indulgence in too much claret. A strange bleakness came over him but was gone in a few seconds as the hard brilliance of the reception hall and cacophony of voices made him forget that simpler time.

George finally had his bride to himself as they left the hall to cheers and whistles and handfuls of rice. They stepped into the cool, late fall night where a hansom cab awaited them with a fine Percheron on the cobbled street. A driver stood by the horse and deftly stepped forward to assist Amanda into the plush leather seat. George swung up on the other side, and they were off to a charming hotel on Yonge Street for the night.

George had suggested a wedding trip was too much expense for Mr. Trolley. But the man had pooh-poohed his objections and insisted they take at least a fortnight excursion and sojourn before going to Collingwood. Thus a compromise was reached. Instead of taking the train straight home, they would have the hire of the hansom cab and driver who would leave them in Aurora where his family lived. They would go on from there on their own, wending their way home gradually and staying at pre-planned country inns and charming villages. They would meander slowly home, starting north on Yonge Street. It had been an extremely mild and dry fall with no snow so they were able to do this. George was handed a substantial purse and travel itinerary as they departed. A wedding present of a new travelling carriage awaited them in an Aurora livery.

"I will be up to see you in a fortnight with your mother, my dear child. I have business to tend to with James, and we want to see you settled in. We will bring with us your trunks and other things." The elderly man's eyes rimmed with tears owing to the emotion of the moment and the amount of champagne he had consumed. "Don't forget your old father now." He patted his daughter on the cheek.

"Never, Papa." Amanda flung her arms around the old man's neck and kissed him. "George will take good care of me. Don't you worry," she said, looking coquettishly at her new husband. "Daddy will never forgive you if you don't," she gushed plaintively as George smiled sheepishly.

Their room in the hotel was lavish in the Victorian style. Rich scarlet velvet curtains hung from the windows with matching bed hangings. Brocade adorned the walls and there was soft, thick carpet underfoot. A fire burned in the grate of a dainty, marble fireplace.

The room was small but exquisite, and George's bride was breathtaking against this dramatic and romantic backdrop in her expensive white gown with dewdrops of pearls on lace. If George had known the cost of the gown, he would have been astounded. It was worth two years' salary of an average working man in the Town of Collingwood.

Amanda wrapped her arms around her husband possessively. "At last, you're all mine. You belong to me." She kissed her young swain long and hard. He wasn't sure what to do now, feeling suddenly shy. He had had other women, but this was his wife now.

"Would you unbutton my dress?" she requested, seeing his hesitancy. Amanda turned around, and he fumbled clumsily with the many tiny buttons. She drew down the dress from her shoulders and he breathed in.

George had looked forward to this moment for a long while. His wife stood in her satin camisole and petticoat. Her skin was like white marble, and she was small but well-formed. The priceless white gown slipped to the scarlet carpet and she stepped out of it. He was a little surprised at his bride's lack of modesty. But she was such a pleasing sight he forgot about all else. Unfastening her stays, he then lifted her small body and half threw her onto the bed. She laughed tantalizingly and pretended to be offended. Then they both laughed. With the stress of the formal marriage ceremony and dinner behind, he could enjoy his wife now.

George released his ascot, loosened the stiff collar, and undid two buttons on his baggy silk shirt. His now open shirt revealed an extremely thick rug of fur on his chest. He discarded his pants quickly and stood with long, open shirt by the bed. The groom's small clothes shifted amusingly with his growing member.

"What a sight you are!" Amanda giggled. "Just like a furry Papa bear." With a mild sense of shock, he watched her small, white hand dart out and grab his male organ none too gently.

"You must promise me now you'll take good care of me, George." Her voice was a whine.

"But of course I will take good care of you, my darling!" Recovering somewhat, George spoke earnestly. "You're my wife now. We will have a good life."

Seemingly appeased at this, Amanda lay back and her hand dropped to her side, losing interest in its former hold. The young groom was not sure what to do now so he climbed over top of his wife whose eyes were now closed. He kissed her young lips, which seemed passive now and submissive, then drew down the expensive silk, beribboned bloomers and explored his new wife. She barely cried out when he entered her, although the taking of her virginity must have hurt. *She is a tough, little thing*, he thought.

When it was over, she rolled over and put her arms around his neck, and smilingly said, "Good night, my darling."

"Are you all right, Amanda?" he said apprehensively. "I'm sorry that I hurt you."

"I'm fine, George." She pecked him on the cheek and snuggled into his neck. Presently, he could hear the heavy breathing, which accompanied sleep coming from her.

George lay there and looked at the flocked wallpaper and at the ornate French clock on the mantle. Light from the oil street lamps filtered in the window. He smelled the strange but not unpleasant, pungent odour of potpourri and plaster and the collective odours of the room and the city.

He could hear carriages and other horse-drawn conveyances going up and down Yonge Street, even at this late hour. How different the city was. He was tired. It had been a long day. *So this is marriage*, he thought. He felt sleepy, satiated, comfortable, cosy, and well fed and ever so little bit disappointed.

CHAPTER 9

Annie and her younger brothers, Frank and Eddie, would often make the trudge in good weather to Scotch Corners. The road was still treacherous being dotted with quagmire and at best it was muddy. It was a spooky walk, and there were rumours that an Indian massacre had occurred just to the west of Nottawa about a hundred or so years ago at a Jesuit Mission called Etharita.

The old-timers had heard about this from Indians who had passed this information down by word of mouth over the generations. Once, Annie thought she heard drums as they passed a copse of trees which appeared particularly ghostly. But Eddie at twelve was more sensible than her and had laughed her fears away.

The purpose of going to Scotch Corners was multiple. First and foremost, they still got their mail from this point as her family had been among the early settlers who had come before Collingwood was of any significance and was only known as Hens and Chickens Harbour. In 1830, Collingwood was no more than a cedar swamp. Scotch Corners, or Bowmore as it was also known, was the important place in the vicinity. They had some relations who lived at the Corners whom they visited, and there were some good stores there, one of which was run by James Freenan and his son, George. Mr. Freenan had two establishments, one being in Glen Huron which was the main store.

Annie had heard the news of George Freenan's wedding with great disappointment.

"Annie, that young lad you know has tied the knot, I'm afraid, to the socialite from Toronto." Ruby McClory eyed her daughter sympathetically. "I guess he wasn't for you, my dear."

"What boy is that?" her father queried.

"Young George Freenan, Aaron. Annie knew him slightly from shopping at Duntroon."

"Ah, yes." He looked at his daughter searchingly. "A fine young man but a lad for the ladies, I have heard."

Annie's eyes flickered up. She sighed and felt a little puzzled at her feeling of loss. She had hardly known George yet had sensed his interest. Perhaps, as her pa said, he was just a gent for the ladies. Annie was eighteen now and a good age to have her eye open for a likely husband.

"There's a social at Raker's barn this week, Annie. Why don't you go on over? It will do you good to kick up your heels. They say there's a shortage of girls since that poor Winters girl got married. They say her sister, Mavis, was devastated and doesn't attend social functions anymore. Young Caitlin was married off to that Bill Pratz fellow," Ruby said disapprovingly. "You know the one, Aaron."

"Why on earth did Jacob Winters let her marry that wharf rat!" he snarled.

"They say he forced her," spoke Ruby.

"Why in the blazes would he force her to marry that scum!"

"It's all a mystery to me. For the life of me, I don't know. But there seems to be some hush-hush reason."

"Was the girl in the family way?"

"Apparently not. They've been married six months now and she's thin as a rake."

"Well, I'll be damned! That's the first I've heard of it, Ruby. How you women are the first to get this kind of gossip I'll never know. Must be something about the feminine mystique."

"Feminine mystique, my hat! It's compliments of Diddi Dolman, the most newsworthy busybody in the Town of Collingwood. She told her daughter-in-law Franka Dolman here in Nottawa who told Ema Richards, who told—"

"Enough, enough!" Aaron laughed and put his hands over his ears. "How about some supper, woman?" Their mood was light-hearted and jovial once more as they teased one another, secretly relieved that their daughter was not the victim of such a fate.

But Annie did not laugh. Life didn't always turn out the way you wanted, and she felt sorry for Caitlin and for herself too. Why was it her generation seemed to be having problems? Look at her mother and father. They were loving and happy after twenty years of marriage and three children. She envied them and wondered if she would ever have that.

She was eighteen already and no one other than George, now a married man, interested her. And she had to forget him, fast. She couldn't moon over someone who belonged to another woman. She picked herself up sadly and started to set the table.

Aaron and Ruby looked at their daughter and then at each other. They had been hoping to lighten her up a bit. A flicker of worry passed Ruby's brow for her daughter then she hid it quickly as Annie turned around.

"There will be other boys, dear."

"Will there, Ma?" Annie's eyes surprisingly held tears.

"Of course, dear, of course."

Aaron bit his lip. He didn't like to see his little girl upset. Damn it! He couldn't protect her forever, and it could be a cruel world out there. He was still puzzled about the news of Jacob Winter's daughter, Caitlin, being married off to that revolting Bill Pratz.

How could a father do that to his daughter? And him a big wheel 'n all. Supposed to be a high-class bloke. Aaron scratched his head and shook it. The man should have protected the young girl. That's what parents were for. Not let her hang around the wharves down at the lake. Nothing good could have come out of it—a young, pretty girl like that alone and unchaperoned.

On Tuesday, Annie, with Frank and Eddie, made another trip up to Scotch corners and this would be the time she ran into George Freenan. His new bride of six months was milling around him in the store looking at fabrics and dressed like she was going to a soiree. Annie's mouth dropped open, and she couldn't help but stare for a moment at all the ruching on the city girl's skirts.

George and Annie had really never got to know one another very well other than partaking in the church picnic on the side road and a few snatches of conversation when she came to shop—"How do you do" and "the weather is fine today" kind of stuff. Even that day at the church social they had scarcely spoken.

But there had been a rapport. And ever since then he would touch her arm intimately whenever she came into the store and ask her if he might help her in a very attentive way. Perhaps, Annie was now thinking, he's like this with every woman. She felt annoyed at this idea and so decided to snub him today.

George was stocking the shelves with oddments when he happened to look around and saw Annie McClory walk into the store. He felt a slight shock go through his body.

"Why, Miss McClory, what a pleasure to see you today."

Annie took a deep breath and spoke, conscious of his new wedded state. "Mr. Freenan, I hear congratulations are in order." She had been rehearsing this line for when she might see him again.

His face worked gracefully through two or three emotions and then he replied, "Why, thank you."

"How very nice for you." Her lips pursed primly. Their eyes held for a moment.

"Oh, darling," Amanda came singing along, "I must have a costume made from this fabric. Isn't it just too charming?"

"Charming indeed, my dear." George looked docile and slightly henpecked as he looked obediently at the tartan yard goods.

Amanda stopped and looked Annie up and down unabashedly and the country girl turned away embarrassed. Annie pretended to study some velvet ribbon on rolls. She was suddenly conscious of her simple frock and straw hat. What a bumpkin she must look compared to this blonde fashion plate!

"How charming and quaint the fashions are in this village, George. Do you think I would suit gingham, dear?" Amanda spoke condescendingly as she held a bolt of yellow gingham under her chin and once again drew George's eyes away from the demure-looking farm girl.

"Of course, Amanda, you would suit anything." George was at that minute wishing Amanda would serve the customers like most storekeepers' wives, but he could not seem to interest her in this or dusting shelves today.

"Ah well, George, would you get the stock boy to drive me home. I'm getting bored."

"Right away, my dear."

George hated to admit it, but he was glad his wife was going home to the family residence so he could get on with his work. He had been away for some weeks from the business at the time of his wedding. But even now, though six months had gone by since the nuptials, he still had some catching up to do.

Their wedding trip had not gone as smoothly as he had hoped. Amanda had complained about the bumpy ride along the rutted roads and the cold, and once they had got themselves lost, and she was rather cross with him. Getting stuck in the mud at Newmarket did not improve her mood either. Perhaps they had had a little too much of each other's company all at once. She had been quite accommodating, however, in the bedroom. He had no complaints there and, as a matter of fact, was getting quite addicted to having her around.

He showed his bride to the farm wagon after excusing himself to Miss Annie McClory. He kissed Amanda good-bye and she tied her bonnet ribbons and smiled fetchingly.

"I'll have a nice country supper for you when you get home, my love."

"Marvelous, Amy. You are becoming quite a cook."

"Maude is a good teacher," she said with a graciousness that was encouraging.

He smiled up at her, happy she was fitting in and attempting to learn farm cookery. He had had some reservations at first but felt confident today that she would make him a good wife and he would be able to make her happy, given time. Perhaps, with a little patience, he could interest her in helping out at the store.

She trotted off toward the family home, waving back at him. And that was another thing he would like her to learn. She really must learn to handle a horse and wagon on her own. He squinted after her in the midday sun then turned with a sigh back to the store. Perhaps he was being far too demanding. It was a big adjustment for a city girl, but there was lots of time. He remembered suddenly the little McClory girl was there.

He found Annie fondling some expensive, satin poplin with stripes; the kind of stuff city girls wear in tea gowns.

"It's lovely, isn't it?" he said finding himself inadvertently observing the fluffiness of her hair.

"Oh yes, but much too expensive for me. I really prefer the cotton prints in any case. They're more comfortable and suit me better."

"I wouldn't say that." He looked at her and suddenly pictured her looking very different. "I can imagine you in velvet for some reason."

"Oh, really, how odd!" She coloured in spite of herself at the personal remark.

"Velvet, dark green like lilac leaves." He then laughed. "Well, it just popped into my head, Miss McClory. But yes, it's soft and rich, and green is my favourite colour. One never tires of it as it is all around us in nature."

"That is very poetic. You must be a very thoughtful man."

"I try to be. It is nice to see you again, Miss McClory." He felt suddenly embarrassed, but he could not resist touching her on the shoulder to emphasize the sincerity of his remark.

Annie shivered at his touch and heard a little clatter at her elbow. "Oh, look! I've knocked over that spool of white lace." She stooped down to search on the floor as it rolled out of sight behind some bins and barrels.

George knelt down beside her to look also. He didn't know how it happened but all of a sudden he was kissing her. The spool forgotten, Annie found herself wrapped in George's arms and not sure who had made the first move. Time was standing still as it is apt to do in these situations.

Her brothers were you-whoing for her outside as they approached the store. By this time they were restless and ready to go start home. With a start, Annie regained her sensibilities and pushed George away. She glanced around. They were still alone in the store, thank goodness.

Annie adjusted her teetering straw hat and felt suddenly angry as her father's words came back to her, "He's a lad for the ladies."

"Why did you do that?" she said in a quietly reproving tone. "You are a married man." There were tears in her throat now. "It's not fair!"

"I'm sorry, Annie. May I call you Annie? I don't know what came over me. I can't explain it."

"It's all right. Never mind. But I have to go."

He helped her up, retrieving the offending spool of white lace at the same time. "You will come back to the store again, won't you? I do apologize."

"Yes, yes of course," Annie said hastily while straightening her garments. She headed toward the door without further hesitation.

Frank and Eddie met their floundering sister just outside. They had been at the other store to collect the mail. They slouched on the long bench on the porch just outside the Freenan Mercantile, kicking their breeched legs up and down and trying to whistle. When they saw her, they started playing storekeeper.

"It's my cheery pleasure to serve you, madam," said Eddie to his brother, Frank. Frank left off sucking his peppermint stick long enough to snigger.

"Ready, Sis?" asked Eddie, the oldest, and he jumped up off the bench.

"Yes, ready." Annie's breast was heaving and she looked out of breath. Two pink spots sat on her cheeks.

George had followed Annie to the door and overheard the boys. He said to Eddie, "Would you like to be a storekeeper some day?"

"No, sir," answered Eddie.

George smiled. "What then, a miller, a clockmaker, a fisherman, a cooper?"

"What's a cooper?"

"He makes barrels, boy."

"Naw," said Eddie. "I'm gonna run off to sea an' be a sailor."

"I see."

Annie laughed in spite of herself.

"I'm gonna be a farmer," piped up young Frank.

"I'm glad to hear that," said George, leaning on the doorframe.

"Come along, boys," urged Annie, shaking her head. "Now don't lose that mail!"

"Good-bye, Miss McClory," George called from behind standing at the doorway of the store.

"Good-bye, Mr. Freenan." Annie turned and met his earnest gaze. "And . . . thank you." There was forgiveness in her look and something else . . .

Eddie looked at his sister quizzically and then shrugged his shoulders. *Girls!* he thought. He shifted his concentration to the sucker he had purchased at the confectionery counter of the other store. He was at the stage where he was all cowlicks and brown-freckled nose. George could not help but smile at the sight of him.

He watched Annie's slim figure walk northward with her two young brothers and he shook his head. What in the devil had come over him? He didn't even want to know. This would never do. He must be especially careful that this kind of thing didn't happen again.

But in his heart he admitted that there was something about that particular girl that affected him. Avoidance was the only solution, he decided.

Aaron McClory wasn't a teetotaller, but he wasn't a hard drinking man either, lucky for his wife and family. There were many women who waited with bated breath on pay days to receive their husbands' pay packets and were sorely disappointed at the pittance that was left when they finally arrived home. There were five saloons (or watering holes) in Nottawa; one being a proper hotel and many more in Collingwood. It was like running the gauntlet. There were also many large families and mouths to feed that depended on a man's pay in those days.

Ruby was a good woman and Aaron knew it. He was damned lucky to have her and made no bones about it. They had fifty acres in a good location, not a big spread but plenty of room for a nice garden, barn, grain, and hay for a few animals. They kept two cows, four horses, and some pigs and chickens.

There was a new grist mill in Nottawa so they could have their grain ground into flour, bran, and shorts there instead of going the distance to the Old Village, which was now called Collingwood. That made life all the more convenient. There was also, built in recent years, a fairly good general store in Nottawa where the locals could trade their farm goods for new tools, groceries, and material for clothing. Aaron's farm was west of the main road and about a mile down the side road.

"Oh, so you're home, love." Ruby was looking spent but cheerful after her typically long day.

"One of these days, I'm going to dress you up like a queen, Ruby." Aaron spun her around in his arms.

"Aha! What's that I smell on your breath? Not some of our fine local whiskey."

"So you do, but just enough to make me feel amorous." He kissed her on the neck.

"Oh, your whiskers are tickling me!" She laughed but gave little resistance. Still after all these years, his touch sent shivers down her spine. And he knew her neck was a trigger point for passionate feelings and used it mercilessly.

"What's for supper, Annie?" asked Aaron, letting go of his wife as the girl came into the room.

"Oh, the usual, beef stew," she replied dully wiping the back of her hand across her forehead.

Aaron picked up her mood quickly. "Why so glum, honey?"

"Oh, nothing, Pa."

"Still upset over that Freenan lad? Forget him, girl. He's gone and married," he said bluntly.

"Oh . . ." Her eyes squeezed tight with tears and her nose turned pink. Annie turned around and ran from the room weeping.

"What the—"

"She went to Duntroon today," Ruby said by way of explanation.

Eddy's head wobbled up and down expressively.

"That explains it," said Aaron. "She must have seen that fine piece of his. She was floating around the store when I was there last week as useless as tits on a boar. Wouldn't know how to use a weigh scale or condescend to wait on a lady for dress goods. Well, he'll never know what he could have had. Our Annie is a fine girl and would make any man a good wife."

"Now, Aaron. That's hardly fair. His young wife is city bred and hasn't had time to adjust to country ways. It must be very difficult for the poor thing. Give her time. They don't live up over the store like most store folks do so she can't be expected to take to it as quickly."

Upstairs in her loft bedroom, Annie was still reeling from the day's events. She was feeling so many conflicting emotions: sadness, anger, hope, hopelessness, sorrow, passion, desire. And all because she'd been kissed by a married man! But she knew it was no use torturing herself like this. The sad and happy part of it was that now she knew that she loved George Freenan and always would.

Chapter 10

George's father had taken a spell and he was worried about him. James complained of chest pain and dizziness, and the older man was so weak that he had to be helped to his easy chair one night after supper. Once there they had an awful job to get him to rest for he was quite agitated. But this passed after two or three hours much to everyone's relief and he was able to go to bed feeling quite all right. In spite of exhortations from the family, James could not be persuaded to agree to a visit from the local doctor.

George and Amanda had been living with his parents since their marriage.

"There's plenty of room," his father had said. "I like my family around me. There is lots of time to build a place of your own and lots of trees to do it with. They're not going to run out. Right now, I need your help with the business so concentrate on that and keeping that pretty little wife of yours happy." He was awfully fond of Amanda, her being the daughter of his best friend, and she could wrap him around her little finger.

James was a kind and easygoing man, getting more so as he aged. He had been an energetic man in his time. If he had any fault, it was that he cared too much what other people thought or about hurting the feelings of others. But this very attribute had led to his business success as it made him diplomatic and accommodating in his dealings with the settlers.

George was fond of his parents. They had given him a good upbringing and a heritage to be proud of. His mother, Ida, was known to be a lovely person, a devoted homemaker, mother, and wife. She was also thrifty and sensible. She had treated all her children kindly, and when

George was a boy, he knew his cuts and bruises would be ministered to and he would receive a kiss and a hug for good measure.

Mrs. Freenan did not know what to think about her new daughter-in-law, but she did not share James's enthusiasm for the young lady. Of course she would never admit this, but there was something about the girl she couldn't quite take to. She had tried to love Amanda for her son's sake, even went out of her way to be nice to her and helpful.

Ida hoped that she was not one of those mothers who was jealous of her daughter-in-law but thought not as she, too, had been joyous about the news of his forthcoming marriage and eager to meet the girl. James had seen Amanda growing up for he had the opportunity on a number of occasions to visit Toronto on business. Ida considered her husband's business partner to be a cherished friend and his daughter, she had felt, she could hold dear to her heart. At their first meeting, she had embraced the girl and was ready to accept her wholeheartedly. Amanda was pretty enough with her pert nose and blonde ringlets.

The young girl's face was framed by hair parted in the middle and drawn firmly back until clusters of ringlets cascaded over the ears relicving the initial severity of the coiffure. It was the current fashion in society. The look was fetching, especially with Amanda's light shade of blonde hair which was unusual in adulthood. But the coiffure was not the only thing that caught Ida's interest that day but evidence of a stubborn set to the small face. In time Ida found that her new daughter-in-law had a temper, which the young matron found hard-pressed to keep under control at times.

The Freenan household was a large one. In their roomy two-storey log house, which was large enough to be a small inn, seven people already resided.

Those were Buck, Harry, and little Sophie, their youngest daughter; Martha, the live-in cook and housekeeper; Grandpa Freenan who was ninety; herself and James; and now there were the newlyweds. Her first two daughters, Elizabeth and Elva, had been married for a few years now.

She had been fortunate in only having the six children and was, thank God, past the childbearing years now.

It was a full house again with the nine of them. Apparently, Amanda was used to a much smaller household in Toronto.

Mrs. Freenan was disturbed one day when she saw Amanda turn on old Grandpa Freenan when he tried to spit in the cuspidor but caught the bottom of her gown instead. The frail old man was deeply embarrassed and said, "I'm sorry, lass," and bent to stoop and wipe off her hem with his wrinkled handkerchief.

Amanda pulled herself away from his reach as if he were a leper and said scathingly, "You're disgusting. Don't touch me." Her face was full of loathing, and she left the room in a fury. The poor old man was devastated.

"Never mind, papa-in-law," soothed Ida, heartsick for the piteous old man. "She's just out of sorts today. She doesn't mean it."

Another time, she heard Amanda snap at old Martha and then speak to her in a condescending tone like she was a servant. Martha was considered anything but a servant and more a part of the family. The woman had come to live with them after she was widowed a few months, five years ago. She had been a dear friend and neighbour who had lived close by for years, and Mrs. Freenan had begged her to come live with them and help her with the household duties and rearing of the children. She was paid a good wage and worth every penny of it.

Ida wondered about Amanda and her son but supposed he must be besotted with her, young and fetching that she was, and like a lot of men, fooled by her wily ways. She sized Amanda up as a manipulator with her coquettish manners, but the girl could exude such warmth and charm when she wanted to!

Well, she was George's choice or maybe more James's choice. This time she wasn't in agreement with James. The girl was not all she would wish for in a daughter-in-law, but after all, she had been so fortunate in her own family and life, she shouldn't ask for perfection in the girl. Mrs. Freenan senior was, if anything, fair.

Amanda had lived in a fine three-storey crafted stone house in Toronto on beautiful Jarvis Street. The log house on the Tenth Line was very different from what she was accustomed to. She found it difficult in these rustic environs to adjust to what were for her close quarters. She was not used to all of this family around either. At home, there were just her mother and father, her old grandmamma and the household staff. The staff consisted of two live-in kitchen maids, a housekeeper, parlour maid, and the gardener who doubled as butler and carriage man. The staff generally stayed out of sight in the large home unless they were needed.

The young bride found it difficult in this rough countryside without any fashionable entertainments. She was indignant at some of the people she met who she considered uncouth and while there were many saloons; there were no salons. She had cried violently after she unwrapped her father's recent parcel yesterday. He had sent her a handkerchief cap with a paradise feather and a Regency-style turban. Where on earth would she wear such items in this wilderness full of bull frogs and serpents?

One could scarcely set one's foot outside of the door in comfort. The new Prunella gaiters Papa had sent her last month were covered with mud, quite spoiled now in fact after that Martha creature had out and out refused to clean them for her. The woman had even had the effrontery to suggest she clean them herself!

Amanda would have been further infuriated had she heard Martha's comments to Ida. The former stomped into Ida's room, took her apron off, and threw it on the bed. Ida looked up in surprise at her friend and employee. Martha's dear old face was white with rage.

"That yellow-haired hussy ordered me to clean her Prunella gaiters and boots. Would you believe it?" Ida put her hand over her mouth to suppress a laugh. It wasn't funny but Martha looked so comical and Amanda's behaviour was so outrageous, it warranted a good laugh, even if only to lighten the burden of her own worries about the girl.

"Am I supposed to polish her boots as well? If I am, it will be my last day here."

"Martha, my dear friend, of course not!" Ida was alarmed now. What would she ever do without her Martha, her friend and confidante? "I'll have a word with her, Martha. You're not to do anything of the sort. Amanda was out of line. Please don't let it upset you."

By the time George's brothers came into the house, the two women were laughing together as Ida described to Martha how funny she had looked in anger. But the event stuck in Ida's mind and she was beginning to be deeply worried about her household. Even the two who came in from the field looked quizzically at them, and she sensed they felt the new tension in the household.

The brothers, Buck and Harry, had just washed up outside as they had come in from the fields. They were farmers on the acreage James had been granted by the Crown. Since it was a large acreage—two hundred and fifty acres—he planned to split it off and give each boy one hundred upon his marriage. George would carry on the business because he was so oriented. If he liked, he could build a house on the remaining acreage or live in this house.

The girls had married good men with their own land. Ida's husband saw to it that they both had comfortable homes. Although her children had not made any comment to her on the subject, she noticed a slight discomfort in them around Amanda. *My, my*, she thought, *what is this all to come to. Please God, protect my family's happiness and bring peace and serenity to this house. Amen.*

James Freenan had another spell, and George was very worried now. The patriarch had come out in a cold sweat and staggered to his easy chair one afternoon. He complained of a pressure in his chest, and it was apparent he had some difficulty breathing. This time Ida had insisted he go straight to bed and she sent Buck through the cold, darkening November day for old Doc Rostrum in Collingwood.

"You have a malaise of the heart, my dear man," said the white-haired practitioner as he finished up his examination of the patient who was comfortable now after responding well to a dose of laudanum.

"And no more stresses of business for you I'm afraid. I insist on complete bed rest for a fortnight. After that, you may get up twice daily and walk in the house and there about, but you are not to undertake work of any sort for six months. You need rest. And your room must be aired well every day, even though it's coming winter."

"But I can't possibly obey you, Doctor. I have most important business commitments to attend to in Toronto and must be there before Christmas."

"Obey me, you must, Mr. Freenan, if you wish to live more than a few weeks," he said severely, his countenance grim. "You have been very lucky this time. Another attack could be forthcoming on the heels of this one. If you do not relieve yourself of all duties of any sort immediately, I assure you, you will not live to see this Christmas."

"Oh." James shrank back stunned. "I had no idea it was so serious, Doc. Well, I suppose I will have to ease up."

"I am sorry to be so blunt. But I will not be responsible for the consequences if you get up from this bed and resume your normal activities."

Ida was standing at the doorway. She was sorely vexed and dabbing her eyes with a linen hanky.

"Don't worry, Doctor. I won't let him out of that bed. I'm not ready for widowhood yet." Ida was very fond of her husband and couldn't imagine life without his big, blustery presence.

"Bravo, Mrs. Freenan. Now cheer up, Freenan. With proper care and following my advice, you'll likely outlive me. I can see that your good wife will see to your every need. I'm leaving some laudanum for the pain."

Doc Rostrum closed up the black medical bag and put on his worn great coat. "Now, I'll be off before the snow flies. These November days are so unpredictable in this godforsaken country. It was a long ride in the old democrat out here and I'd like to be home in front of my hearth before nightfall." It was only six o'clock p.m. by his pocket watch, but these November days were blastedly short; and if he was travelling after dark, there were few other travellers on the road between here and Collingwood tonight to give an assist if his aging conveyance broke down.

Ida thanked him profusely and blew her nose loudly. She gave him the generous sum of two dollars for which he was exceedingly grateful and pleasantly surprised. He was rarely paid in cash up front and often not at all. But people tried to repay him in some way or another down the road.

Often their gratitude was payment enough when they lived in dire circumstances such as some of those newly settled and living out their first year in this area. His wife didn't always agree when he came home empty-handed after a gruelling ten-hour ordeal of delivering a baby or sitting by a fever-victim exhausted. Martha, the cook, handed him a heavy basket as he left the large log house.

Doc Rostrum got into the old democrat and lifted the cloth on the basket. He felt a lump in his throat and a little misty-eyed as he saw the generous gratuity of a roasted chicken, still warm, currant buns, and a jar of Martha's famous bread and butter pickles. The good smells filled his nostrils. His young wife would have her cares eased considerably about their skimpy larder tonight. They had eleven children and the young ones would fall on this feast with gusto when he got home. Unlike other men, his efforts did not directly produce food, and this was sometimes a problem. They had a cow and some chickens like most people in Collingwood and so had milk, butter, and eggs but rarely killed one of their precious birds.

Ida closed the door behind him and went to see George who was in the parlour and had heard the doctor's booming diagnosis.

"Now, Mother, don't worry," he said, putting his arm around her shoulders. "I'll be able to take over. Papa has trained me well. He'll be able to get all the rest he needs. I will make that trip to the city to trade goods. Let's go up and talk to the old codger." He smiled lovingly and kissed her. "I'll take care of both of you. It's my turn." She burst into sorrowful tears on his shoulder.

"Don't Mama," George said softly, caressing her thick salt-and-pepper hair. "He'll be fine. Just wait." But the ache in his heart told him he didn't believe his own words.

Five weeks later, they buried James. He didn't take the doctor's advice. The older gentleman was up in his nightcap and shirt pouring over inventory lists and fretting over order sheets when he thought no one was around. He took his usual half quart of whiskey a day against the advice of the good doctor who had allowed him only two fingers of brandy at night with milk for sleeping. Milk! Pfaff. He hadn't drunk that since he'd been at the breast. Never could abide the stuff.

James enjoyed his last weeks thoroughly, however, getting great satisfaction from fooling his attendants that he was following their ridiculous rules.

He would leap back into bed and close his eyes convincingly looking for all the world like he'd been asleep for hours when an anxious Ida, Martha, or George would peek in. He would hear their footsteps up the creaky steps to his invalid room. Ida had taken to sleeping with Sophie so as not to disturb her husband's precious rest. When they shut the door again, confident he was resting, he would snigger devilishly and tiptoe once again to his writing desk and light the candle.

George was the only one not fooled by this charade. He wondered why he smelled candle smoke once when entering the room. Lingering outside the room and stepping in place to make a little noise like footfalls descending the stairs, he chanced to hear some commotion coming from the room. He had left the door slightly ajar on purpose and presently saw a faint light of the candle lamp fall through the slit in the door.

Peering quietly through, he saw father's night-capped form at the writing table sticking his turkey feather into the ink well. He heard muffled chuckles coming from the older man and knew his game. George smiled to himself and gently closed the crack in the door. How he enjoyed this father and how he would miss his sense of humour and guidance when he was gone.

It was a shock to poor George when that time came so quickly. James had enjoyed those few weeks of invalidism as his pain had subsided and he could enjoy his practical joke of fooling the nurses. He took a flying leap back into bed after being particularly naughty one night; doing some book work and imbibing a good measure of whiskey, which he had got up in the night and swiped from the pantry. After hearing footsteps on their way up the stairs to his room, he leaped into bed with a gleeful smile on his face and his heart seized on him. He landed face down on the pillow and managed to turn his face to the side but that was his last effort. They found him seconds later dead as a door nail.

There was a great wailing in the house for James had been greatly loved. Ida was devastated. And George, more than the other boys, felt the loss severely. He had become very close to his father in these last years, partly because of the business connection. It had helped him understand more about what drove the man who had little time to spend with his children years ago because of the nature of his business. George felt honoured to have had the chance to get to know this naively funny but astute businessman with the childlike penchant for practical jokes.

Even Martha was great in her suffering. Never again would she hear James Freenan's energetic wake-up call in the morning as he got up first to snitch a lardy biscuit from the pantry and rouse any lingering sleepyheads hollering, *"Daylight in the swamps!!"*

CHAPTER 11

She heard it as she lay in her bed—the song of the frogs, the wild green sweetness of it, but how could it be? It was only April, and a layer of snow still lay upon the ground. Ice covered the ponds. But yes, she could hear it—the unbearable sweetness and hope of their song, the surpassing joy of it. Annie's life had carried on dreamily since that day she and George had kissed at the Freenan Mercantile.

After that experience, most other things seemed mundane. Finally winter melted into early spring which soon, in turn, gave way to bounteous summer, but Annie hardly noticed the passing of the seasons. She went through the motions of her daily routine of helping Ruby with the household chores and gardening. She got to be a deft hand at quilting and had loved to spin for it gave her time for quiet contemplation. She would sit in front of the window with her soft hair falling loose about her shoulders and was a serene sight for any chance visitor or passer-by; their farmhouse being close to the road. But as time wore on, she wasn't serene inside anymore nor content in those quiet pastimes.

One early fall afternoon Ruby, who had been observing her daughter with growing concern for some time, finally confronted the distrait girl.

"Annie, you're so restless these days, precious. Your attention is rovin' like a gypsy. What are we going to do with you?"

"I don't know, Ma." The girl smiled a crooked little smile at her mother.

"I don't think there is enough here to interest you, dear. Why don't you apply for a situation helping a farmer's wife? It would be something different for you, and you'd earn a little money of your own."

"Folks around here don't have cash money to pay out, Ma. Besides, you need me here. I couldn't leave you."

"Not all farmers are so hard up for cash. There are some that are growing rich. And you'll be leaving us soon enough when you marry. I might as well get used to the notion now."

"Huh!" Annie looked pained. "I'll likely be an old maid like the Misses Willoughby."

"Not you, Annie. Never you." Ruby's voice held a note of conviction. "Winter is coming again and the dances are soon to start up in full swing. You're nineteen now, and while that is still young to me, there's a number of lassies around here your age that have been married a few years and have two or three children by now."

"Mmm hmm . . ." Annie felt uncomfortable talking about marriage these days. Ruby didn't scold her daughter for mumbling. The woman sensed she had broached a painful subject once again. Sighing, she turned back to the long stockings she was knitting.

Annie was down in the dumps and felt even worse when she heard the news of the death of George's father. She didn't know why it made her feel so sad. She hadn't known the man well, but he had always been so kind and cheery when she had seen him in the store. She wouldn't be the one to hold George and comfort him in his time of grief. His wife would. Annie would have liked to comfort him. She said a little prayer for George and for the soul of his father and ended it with a request that God forgive her for loving a married man.

Ida Freenan missed her husband very much. She missed the warmth of him at night and his bristly old face and in general his kind, dear presence. And to think his old father of ninety-five outlived him. Poor old Ebenezer had deteriorated since his son's death and mostly just sat by the fire. That was five years ago now. Only his little great-granddaughter,

George and Amanda's little girl, Susan, could bring that old sparkle to the ancient man's bleary eyes.

Today, Susan was playing with her fine bisque doll on the hearth rug in the kitchen. Ida didn't scold the child for bringing the expensive doll into the kitchen for the old man enjoyed watching her so. Instead she simply went and got an older rag doll and replaced it quietly. She put the lovely golden-haired doll with the pink organdy dress away in the child's room.

George and Amanda had another child, a boy of eighteen months, now. Her son had added a wing to the house for his wife and growing family even though the salt-box-shaped log house was already a good size. Ida placed the beautiful doll on a shelf in little Susan's room. Her grandfather Trolley had sent it down from Toronto on the train last Christmas. But little Susan was too young to appreciate its value and the value of other things, such as ridiculously costly bed hangings over the small bed, which she would soon grow out of.

The tiny girl preferred to climb into bed with Grandma at night and the elderly woman looked forward to her little grandchild coming into her room as the shadows fell. Ida went to her room earlier these days. She would take the little girl onto her lap on the rocking chair by the window and would sing "The Grandfather's Clock" to the little one who would beg her to sing the same song every night.

The grandfather clock was too big for the shelf
So it stood forty years in the hall.
It was taller by half than the old man himself
Though it weighed not a pennyweight more
It was bought on the morn of the day that he was born
And was always his pleasure and pride
But it stopped short never to go again
When the old man died.
Tick tock, tick tock, tick tock . . .

The little girl refused to sleep in her own bed most nights and Grandma looked forward to the comfort of having her little

granddaughter with her as well. The elderly woman liked the feel of the
little child's warm body close to hers.

Sometimes before she dozed off, Ida would hear voices raised in
argument coming from the new wing of the house. Then she would
sing another song for Susan to drown out the voices. When the little girl
was fast asleep, she would lie awake and wonder if this would ever be
a happy home again like it was when she and her husband brought up
their children. Buck and Harry were gone now. Each had built his own
home on his inherited acreage. Only Sophie, Great-Grandad, Martha,
George, and his family still lived here with her.

The atmosphere of the house had changed since her husband had
died. No, since Amanda had come here. But she was grateful to have
George with her still. What would she do without him and her new
grandchildren whom she adored? She could see her husband, James, in
young Charlie. Ida guessed she was likely just getting old and she didn't
want to interfere with her son's life, so decided it was best to mind her
own business.

George had been very busy since his father died. His mother used
to help out in the store two or three days a week, but she couldn't bear
to go there since James died and she was getting on so that it was too
much for her. Without her wonderful help as well as his father's, it was
extra demanding. Time went quickly. He had had to hire staff to run
the second store for there was only himself and his sister, Sophie, now
to serve in the Duntroon store.

The stores, seeing to ordering for them, selling, accounts, and
building an addition to the house for his wife had taken up most of his
time. He hadn't felt the latter necessary but had done it to humour his
wife who, he found, was susceptible to moods and demands. She felt that
they needed more space and privacy and he gave in to her pleading.

There were fifty acres left with the house, but he didn't have time to tend them so he let out thirty acres to a man who supplied them with wheat, oats, and hay to meet their needs as payment of the rent. They only kept a few farm animals. The rest of the land was more than adequate for that and their vegetable garden.

Becoming a new father took much of his time also for he adored his children and wanted to give them more attention than he had received from his own busy father. Lately, he had developed a hearty respect for his father's inadequacies in this area. George was so busy now, he didn't have time to realize he was growing more and more unhappy in his personal relationship with Amanda. Her often petulant manner he had excused because of new motherhood and the stresses and strains thereof.

Amanda had become a passably good cook and was fussy about her children's cleanliness as in her own toilette. She seemed to be moderately helpful around the house to the other women but more efficient at delegating work than doing it herself.

This would not have bothered him if she had taken an interest in his business affairs for he would have welcomed her help with the accounts and paperwork. He would have even welcomed her presence in the store. However, any attempt to interest her in business accounts and inventory had met with yawns and looks of boredom.

Amanda helped with preserving but contributed little to the gardening efforts, which work fell mostly on Sophie and his aging mother who should have been able to start to take life a bit easier now. The young wife spent much of her time in winter reading novels of which her father kept her in good supply or doing fine needlework on a frame in the parlour.

She complained that George's line of work kept them from enjoying the winter festivities and entertainments. Amanda scorned the practical but necessary jobs of knitting and abhorred the long wool knit stockings though did not hesitate to don them herself as the temperatures plummeted.

And Amanda had changed toward George in a rather disturbing way. From the submissive bride he had married, Amanda had become a disinterested sexual partner, only occasionally welcoming his advances. She seemed to fall asleep quickly when she went to bed and sleep deeply.

He had supposed it was a temporary situation caused by new motherhood and would pass, but as time went on, Amanda failed to become the responsive wife he had hoped she would be. He finally decided that likely this was the nature of women; that, for them, sexual urges were of secondary importance to other aspects of life, particularly those women of gentle breeding.

He shrugged off this problem as George was wont to do concerning things of an emotional nature. He was upset though that Amanda had been snappish with his mother and sister, Sophie, within his hearing once or twice and when he broached the subject with her, it provoked a quarrel. He also asked her if she could be of more help with the hoeing and planting of the all-important vegetable garden. She had pouted for days after that. He didn't bring up the subject again so as to keep peace in the household.

He knew that Amanda considered herself a gentlewoman and so the latter did not feel it appropriate to have to milk cows and other such lowly tasks. Being city bred, she did not realize that the settler women, even those of gentle breeding, had had to learn equality and tuck in to do numerous humble tasks such as baking bread, milking cows, and churning butter.

All these things a farmer's wife must undertake if her family were to be successful in this new country. Her husband also must undertake many physical tasks that in England and other parts of Europe would be done by labourers.

This country was the great equalizer. Social status was of much lesser importance here. And George was glad it was this way. It was so much more companionable. He had learned these things from his father who knew of the old country and its ways.

CHAPTER 12

Let him kiss me with the kisses of his mouth: for thy love is better than wine.

—Song of Solomon 1:2

Annie found a station with a farmer's wife in late spring of that year. Her mother was secretly relieved and noted the presence of two sons of marriageable age on the prosperous farm. She had been concerned about Annie's future. The girl now worked for Mrs. Starkey on the Sixth Line who had a brood of little ones too young to help on the farm and two adult stepsons from her husband's previous marriage. Widowed at the age of fifty-two, Willard Starkey found a wife three years later. She was servant to some gentlefolk who stayed briefly in the area on their way to Harriston to stay with relations.

Alma Starkey was forty at the time and had given up hopes of marriage long ago in England. She was a comely enough woman who had been prized as a kitchen maid and later held other household positions of increasing responsibility. Her employers reluctantly gave her up, but they were good enough to realize this was her chance to be mistress of her own home. They settled a generous sum on her along with their good wishes.

Willard Starkey found in Alma a competent wife and she had delighted in presenting him with a new baby every year for four years running and was proudly carrying the fifth. Mr. Starkey joked that it was fortunate her child bearing years would come to an end within the next decade.

His eldest son, Manfred, from his first marriage was capable, serious, and at thirty, had worked hard on the thriving farm for enough years that his father bought him fifty acres just adjacent as payment for his years of cheerful labour. Wyatt, the other boy, had apprenticed with a blacksmith and was now doing his smithing right on the home farm but planned to remove his business to Collingwood and pursue other ventures as well such as the carriage and harness making trade.

Their mother had only had the two boys and had become barren after them. At forty-eight, she had developed a malignant growth in her abdomen, which she had thought was a late conception. It was only at a late stage that her massive girth was discovered to house not a child but a tumour. She died at what was thought to be her seventh month of pregnancy. The doctor failed to detect a baby's heartbeat and upon palpating her swollen abdomen made the gruesome diagnosis. She died two weeks later. The doctor was distraught over this case. He could have, if he had been a skilled surgeon, tried to remove that beastly mass that grew like a monster with its black tentacles inside her. But alas, Doctor Rostrum was a mere country doctor and by the time he was called, she was too weak to be transported by train to Toronto.

Annie fit in well with the Starkeys. They were happy, jovial people who treated her well, and Mrs. Starkey liked having another woman around to talk to. She was quite the chatterbox. She told Annie many stories about life in England in one of the big houses, and Annie listened fascinated at the difference in life in that country. She wished she could go there somehow and see it all for herself. Alma told of a life that was not all struggle and work as pioneering times in Collingwood were. They had fine architecture, fancy coaches, elegant soirees, theatre, and balls. The matron neglected to recount the lot of the desperately poor in the fine cities who didn't have the benefit of hope and clean wholesome poverty that the new Canadians had.

One day Annie sat listening to Alma and her imagination drifted magically, envisioning the grandeur that Alma spoke of. A question came to her mind. She wondered if her mistress missed it all very much. But she detected the woman's pride in her home and children and her new sense of freedom. It was a dream come true for her, this new life.

She had enjoyed the old life in the fine mansion, but Annie had sudden insight that all this was an unexpected bonus, showing the bounty of life.

Mr. Starkey came into the house at that moment, a big bear of a man with a broad chest, long hair to his collarless shirt and full whiskers. He kissed his pregnant wife with gusto, and Annie blushed seeing from the look in their eyes that they loved each other. She was glad Mrs. Starkey hadn't just married him for the material advantages and security. She liked Alma.

The Starkey farm had some sugar bush, so they made their own sugar in big cakes. There was even a milk house, and Annie helped milk the cows and set the new milk in pails in the cool building. The cream would rise, and they would skim it off. She and Alma would make wonderful butter, some of which would be sold in Stayner. A lovely little tributary of the Batteaux River ran across the back of the property in those days, and Annie went back with her neck yoke and two wooden pails to fetch the daily water for the house.

She met Manfred on the way back from the river one summer day, and he tipped his hat to her saying, "Ma'am." His eyes softened when he looked at her and with the instinct of a woman she knew that he wanted her. They would meet as she came up with the water because this was the last duty she performed before the evening meal. He would come up at the same time tired from the fields to wash up for supper.

This was the time of the season when the men cut the grain with a cradle and bound it up. They used horse power to cut the grain then they had to bind the sheaves up and cut them with a cradle or reaping hook. In the summer, many days, the men would eat and then go back to the fields until dusk.

Annie would spend one Sunday a month with her parents. She would leave Saturday evening and Manfred drove her to her home, four miles northwest of his farm. Her father, Aaron, would bring her back on Sunday after supper.

She had been with the Starkeys for almost four years now and knew Manfred was getting close to a proposal of marriage. Alma had hinted once or twice that her eldest stepson would make a good husband and the lack of subtlety did not escape Annie. She had been happy here but didn't want to complicate her relationship with the family by refusing their son. It would possibly be the end of her employment with them. She admired Manfred and liked his brother, Wyatt, but did not feel especially drawn to either one of them, although, like their father, they were fine-looking men and undoubtedly good catches.

Her parents really looked forward to her visits now, especially since her brother, Eddie, not quite seventeen years old, had gone off to become a sailor on the lakes. Ruby and Aaron were most upset but he had his heart set on it so they did not try to stop him. There was only the one boy left at home now, young Frank. On her Sunday visits home, Ruby would ply her with questions about the Starkeys.

"What do you think of the elder boy?" her mother would ask her.

"Oh, he's all right, Ma."

"Just all right? He looks like he has an eye for you, honey. Sits up there proud as a peacock beside you when he brings you home in that wagon on Saturday night. All dressed up fine he is."

"He's always headed into town for Saturday night socializing."

"Oh, is he." Her mother looked disappointed in Annie's apparent lack of interest in the upcoming young man.

"He's a very eligible young man, Annie. Don't scorn him. There's a lot worse."

Annie felt slightly offended at this admonition and a bit confused. She was still in touch with her memory of George, although she'd only seen him at a distance or unbeknownst to him in the past few years. She remembered his arms around her that day in the store at Duntroon and the feel of his lips on hers.

"Manfred isn't what I'm looking for," she said quickly.

"What you are looking for, my girl, isn't available to you." Ruby looked at Annie with a look of sharp perception in her eyes. "There's no use mooning over that young Freenan boy. He has a wife and two children now, and you're not getting any younger."

Annie's lip quivered at the bluntness of Ruby's statement.

"Don't lose this chance, dear." Ruby's face and tone were softer now, beseeching. "I want to see you happy with a fine man like your father."

"But you love Father, always have," Annie protested.

Her mother looked down half-ashamed. She knew the girl was right, but she looked at her daughter and thought. What a waste! Her own fears had been confirmed. It was still thoughts of that wretched storekeeper that were keeping her beloved daughter from a wonderful marriage with a fine man.

Manfred proposed to Annie at the end of the summer when he took her home to her parents one Saturday night. He pulled over to the side of the road and removed his hat.

"Annie, I've known you for four years now since my stepmother brought you into the house. I know you to be a good woman. I'm inquiring with deep respect if you'll be my wife."

Annie had dreaded this moment and now it had come upon her. She looked into his hopeful face and said as kindly as she could, "I'm flattered and honoured by your offer of marriage, Manfred, but I wouldn't be fair if I accepted it."

"Why on earth not?" Manfred looked disappointed and agitated.

"Because I'm not in love with you," Annie said simply and reluctantly, looking away.

"I see," said Manfred sullenly. His disappointment hung like a black pall in the air. "Thank you for being so honest." He resumed the horses, and they continued on in silence to her mother's house.

After that things felt slightly different at the Starkey household. Alma was guardedly friendly, the spontaneity seemed to have seeped from their relationship, and although nothing was ever said, Annie noted the difference. Other than that, everything went on as usual. The only other thing different was that she didn't come across Manfred every afternoon when she came back from the river with her load of water.

Mr. and Mrs. Starkey usually did the trips into town themselves to get their grocery and clothing needs from the shops in Stayner. Alma enjoyed the excursions usually done on Saturday, market day, once a month. It being late summer, Mr. Starkey and his sons were busy in the fields from dawn to dusk and Alma had a summer ague that was leaving her feeling miserable for the second week in a row. There were a few provisions needed, and so Annie was sent by herself to Stayner to pick up the necessaries.

"Mind, you get me the oil of cloves, tea, and some mustard, and it would cheer me to have some yard goods for a new dress. Get me some red calico or blue and white print, three yards, and choose some for yourself if you like. I'm giving you your month's wages in advance. Here's a list of the other things I need. Have a good day of it, dear. It will get you away from my cheerless company for a while."

"Are you sure you'll do without me, Mrs. Starkey? You should be resting. You're not strong yet."

"I'll be fine, and I'll manage the supper all right. They'll have to do with simple fare tonight. The mutton soup from last night will have to suit. There's plenty of bread, butter, and cheese and those pies that you baked yesterday."

Annie tied her sun bonnet ribbons and wore a light summer cloak as it was still the cool of early morning. She bade Alma good-bye and went outside. Wyatt had hitched up the democrat for her and the horse was stomping and snorting, eager for an excursion in the fresh dewy morning air. It wasn't long before she turned east on the government road toward Stayner, the road which led from Duntroon (Scotch Corners) east to Stayner and beyond wound its way to distant Barrie. It was essentially a level trip of about three miles from here on to reach Stayner. She passed some cleared farms with stump fences and two or three farm houses which were set back quite a ways from the road. Up ahead, she saw a traveller coming toward her. As the wagon approached, she was stunned to recognize the driver as George Freenan whom she hadn't seen for three years! Her hands trembled as they signalled the horse to stop.

"Whoa, Bella."

George was just returning from an early morning jaunt to Stayner to pick up some stock for the store from the train at Nottawasaga station.

"Why, Miss Annie. Is it truly you? It's been that long since I've seen you."

"Yes, Mr. Freenan." She looked at his face hungrily and noted his changed appearance. He looked older, strained, and more mature. But he looked pleased to see her.

"Have you a moment to stop and share your news with me? It's such a fine morning to meet an old acquaintance."

"Well, I suppose that would be all right," Annie answered. "Just a short break and I must continue on my errand. I'm working for a family on the Sixth Line. I trust you know of the Starkeys."

"But of course." His eyes flickered with recognition. "The industrious Starkeys are well known in these parts. A fortunate place to find employment."

George helped her down from the wagon and looked searchingly at her. She looked tantalizingly the same, fresh and sweet but more real and alive, more vibrant than he had noticed in the past. He reluctantly let go of her hands.

"How are your wife and mother, Mr. Freenan?"

George's eyes flinched almost imperceptibly. "Thank you for
inquiring. They are both well. My wife and I have a daughter and son
now, and my mother is in good health." He hesitated. "Please call me
George, and may I call you Annie?"

"Yes, I suppose that would be all right . . . George." Annie savoured
his name on her lips and became aware that she felt ridiculously happy
to be here in the middle of the road, talking to this man who had been
at the back of her mind for so long.

Then she remembered again his recent loss. "I was sorry to hear of
your father's death. A kind gentleman." He nodded in acknowledgment
saying nothing.

The sun broke out suddenly from the haze of the morning and
bathed them both with its warmth. She shaded her eyes as she looked
up at George. He had children, now, she thought. He was a father.

He spoke now. "You . . . You haven't married then."

She shook her head finding herself unable to respond verbally to
this.

"The Starkey boys. One of them is your intended?"

"Oh, no." She suddenly found her voice. "I'm just employed there . . ."
Her voice trailed off.

Annie took off her bonnet and looked around. She wondered what
anyone would think if they happened by and saw these two standing
there looking at each other foolishly. But no one was coming on this
well-travelled road. It was very quiet with only the calls of birds and the
rustle of grasshoppers and the sound of the light warm wind rustling
leaves in trees. The horses stood very still and occasionally shook their
heads and snorted. The day was one of those perfect ones with a pure
blue sky. It was starting to get hot. The late grain was red and ripe in

the nearby fields. And Annie was alone in the middle of the road with the man she loved.

There was an overgrown orchard that came up to the road on the north side near to where they stood. George reached out and picked a ripe apple and gave it to her.

"An early apple. Try it," he said. "Some refreshment for a weary traveller." He picked one for himself and bit into it.

She stared at the apple for the longest moment and said, "I am weary." A tear suddenly came to her eye, and she felt overcome with emotion. She bit into the apple and chewed its tart juiciness feeling acutely embarrassed. George was staring at her, and she fought with the tears which were stubbornly welling up in her eyes. Her nose felt damp and she fumbled for a handkerchief and dabbed at her nose self-consciously, feeling very uncomfortable. She had the desire to get away from here now, to run.

"It's the grain. It sometimes affects me," she said, wiping her nose delicately. "I must be going. It must be getting on for eleven o'clock." Annie was already mourning, mourning that he would soon be gone as she fingered her pendant watch. There was no hope, no hope.

"Of course, I mustn't keep you," he said quickly, noting her sad countenance. Her look was unbearably melancholic. "I hope we will meet again soon."

Annie nodded, discarding the remains of the apple and turned toward her wagon unable to speak. George went to help her up, but as he put his right hand on her waist and reached for her left elbow, the feel of her impelled him to turn her around and look into the suffering eyes. She was so vulnerable, so irresistible. His actions were automatic after the first touch of her. He gently drew her close and kissed her softly on the mouth. Then he kissed the tears away from her eyelashes. A small cry escaped her throat. He kissed her again and she gently, submissively returned the embrace. They broke apart to look at each other then they fell together, resuming their kisses, passionately now. Annie's response was no longer merely yielding. They stopped once again after a while to smile at each other, smiling amidst their kisses.

At some point in all this bliss which seemed a part of the sunshine and the beauty of the surrounding countryside, George took Annie's hand and led her deep into the orchard. On the road, the two horses stood quietly and nuzzled each other. He laid her on the soft meadow grass, and they melted into each other's arms. It was as if their faces melted together and their bodies were one mass. In intimate relations Annie felt more a part of him than she felt a part of herself. Joy exploded.

When they had rested in each other's arms, they got up and their lips met again in that deep communication which was for both of them so fulfilling.

"Can you come by this way next Tuesday morning?"

"I'll try."

"I'll look for you, Annie."

The two democrat wagons separated and went in opposite directions. If it had been possible to view the scene from above, it would have appeared that as the wagons parted, suddenly Time started to go by once more on its unrelenting way. There were horse-drawn conveyances coming from both directions which would soon converge and pass. It was as if they had been held back in limbo until the couple had finished their tryst, frozen in time.

Chapter 13

Behold, thou art fair, my beloved, yea, pleasant: also our bed is green.
The beams of our house are cedar, and our rafters of fir.
—Song of Solomon 1:15–16

Annie managed to return to the same spot the next Tuesday using an excuse that she wanted return to Stayner. She had seen some nice dress goods on sale for fifteen cents a yard on her last visit and now decided it had been folly not to buy them.

Alma had forgotten to put a couple of items on last Saturday's list anyway so was amenable to Annie making another trip into Stayner to get her some white sheeting and pillow cottons. She looked at Annie quizzically, however, because of this unusual request to make a return trip for such a frivolous reason. It was unlike Annie. But, she thought, perhaps the girl was having a change of heart about her stepson. The change of mind about the new dress could be an indication.

"Do go to town again, Annie, if you like. I could use one or two extra things and Bella enjoys the run, to be sure. I can see you have your heart set on a new frock." She smiled indulgently at Annie whom she was ever fond of despite the girl's previous rejection of Manfred.

"I thought I should save the money," explained Annie, feeling better if her falsehood contained an element of truth. "But I've noticed this dress is getting quite worn at the cuffs and won't bear mending again."

Alma laughed heartily. "I don't want it said I have my household girl going about in rags. Get some plain-coloured cotton for new aprons while you're about it. We might as well get right spruced up."

Annie smiled in amusement at Alma. She forgot her guilt momentarily at her deception of her employer.

"You're so kind to me, missus. I've so enjoyed working for you."

Alma looked slightly taken aback.

"Well, it's not coming to an end, I hope."

"Oh no, of course not." Annie was wrenched back into her new reality. She felt both elated and apprehensive. She had been in what felt like a mystical trance since her meeting with George. Unbelievable happiness had come into her life. It had overridden any feelings of guilt or fear for the future. It was so strong, that it blotted out all else.

And yet, soon after, she felt its antithesis: a terrible longing for him and that feeling of mourning again because she was not with him every moment. Now she could at least look forward to their planned meeting of Tuesday, which was finally approaching. She could see him, kiss him, touch him again. Once in a while a feeling of futility would torture her. She would hear her father's words again: "He's a lad for the ladies." But then she would remember how he kissed her, how he held her, the kind and loving look on his face. She had felt his hunger for her.

Tuesday morning shone bright like a diamond, the dew drops melting away and evaporating into the August sun. Bella was hitched and ready for her, frisky in the morning air. Annie was living her dream. On her way to see him. Would he be there?

"Take yer time, Annie. You worked twice as hard yesterday to make up for today. You didn't have to. We could have done the baking tomorrow." Alma stood there looking at Annie with her hands on her hips. "My, you look chipper. I wish I looked that fresh and pretty first thing in the morning, teeth gleaming like pearls. Oh, to be twenty-four again." Alma tittered and gave the horse a slap on the rump.

Annie laughed. "Don't let the little 'uns get the better of you today." Alma let out a mock groan and made a gesture as if to shoo her away with her apron. Annie rode off down the lane waving her hand above her head. As she turned from the lane, she could see the little ones descending on their good-natured mother. They were tugging on her skirts, and she knew the middle-aged woman would have a busy day. She felt a twinge of remorse for her deception. But she knew Alma was a lucky woman, lucky in love. She had her man with her in a loving family, something she herself craved but might never achieve. It had to be the right man for her. It couldn't be just any man—no matter how perfect he may be.

Annie's heart was thudding with anticipation. She called "Haw" and the horse turned left, starting toward Stayner. She saw nothing on the road ahead of her. Then a wagon came into view. It was painted bright red and as it approached she saw the familiar forms of the Misses Willoughby come into sight. The spinster ladies slowed down to speak to her.

"Why, it's Annie McClory. What are you doing out here unescorted on this lonely road?" called one of them.

Annie drew in her breath with disappointment and said, "It's perfectly safe to travel here alone. I'm doing some errands for the missus who is watching five children."

The spinsters looked at each other and seemed to read each other's thoughts. *Like two black crows in a nest*, Annie thought, *with their black bombazine dresses without the relief of even a scrap of white lace.*

"Well! I don't know what the world is coming to when young women are forced to travel on their own exposed to the dangers of a new and savage country," said the elder.

Annie smiled wryly to herself as she replied, "I thank you both for your concern, but I don't see any Indians on the warpath nearby, although there was some movement back in yonder bush. But it might have just been a bear or a wolf."

The misses' eyes bulged and their necks stretched. One of them let out a beeping sound. They strained their eyes into the distance. "Well, we had better be on our way," croaked the eldest, Matilda.

"Oh, let's, Tilly!" the youngest, Drusilla, exclaimed with a shiver.

Matilda drove off promptly pair in hand with ample use of the cowhide, whipping the poor beasts into a fast trot. The road behind them became a cloud of dust as they made their way with the greatest of speed in their attempt to reach safer territory. Annie couldn't help but laugh and her laughter turned into a bounding joy when she saw another wagon approach in the distance and instinctively knew it was his. She trotted Bella as far as the orchard that marked their last meeting.

George's face finally came into sight, and she sensed his eagerness to see her. He jumped out of the wagon and came to help her down. She was in his arms, and he was kissing her passionately and endlessly. Then he glanced searchingly up and down the road. George paused to tie both horses to a tree this time, and they made their way into the orchard ducking low branches. He pushed her gently against a tree, and he made love to her right there and her joy was complete. They then collapsed onto the meadow grass and he started to talk. He told Annie of his wife and how she could be difficult at times. He poured out his troubles and cares to her. Annie listened and weighed them in her mind and in her heart. Some of it she didn't want to hear as it was too disturbing to imagine him with Amanda. But she listened nevertheless.

Being a Tuesday, rather than Market Day, the road was still quiet when they returned to the horses.

"I can't meet you like this again," Annie said, looking into George's face. "The missus looked at me strangely when I wanted to go back to town so soon."

The young man's face took on a look of worry now. "It's not going to be easy for either of us."

Annie had already been considering the future. "There's an old settler's cabin that's deserted down the road from the Starkeys. It's set back in the bush. There is a path leading to it, and I go there sometimes when I walk. It's so quiet and peaceful there."

"I know the one. Trees have grown up around it now. When do you take your walks?"

"Near the end of the week. I have some free time then in the mornings."

George thought quickly. "I often make trips to Stayner in the morning to pick up small stock at Nottawasaga Station and make some deliveries once a week in good weather. Sometimes I don't require the wagon as saddlebags suffice. I'll meet you at the settler's cabin next Thursday morning if you can come. I'll be on horseback. I should pass the Starkey farm at about half past nine on my way to the cabin." Suddenly, his face was tragic. "I feel so guilty," he said.

"Don't." she shook her head. "Don't." She put her arms around him and pressed close to him. He touched her cheek and said, "I must go and so must you. The cabin next Thursday at midmorning." He helped her into her wagon and turned thoughtfully to his own conveyance.

Annie got home at half past four, in time to help with supper. Alma was tired from a hectic day and was glad to see her servant come up the laneway. Annie went in with the parcels which she left in the kitchen and then went to her room to change into a work dress. She hung up the good dress hurriedly on a peg and donned an apron. She then went down to help her mistress with the meal.

"I haven't started supper. The bairns were hangin' on to me and I could hardly get a thing done. Your dress goods are bonnie, Annie, but why did you buy plain brown stripe?

"It's only for a daily dress, ma'am."

"Oh, aye, 'tis a practical colour right enough, but with those pretty calicos in town, I thought you'd had in mind something more gay, blue and white print, say." It struck the older woman as being a bit odd that Annie was all fired up to go to town for a simple brown stripe dress. But she put it out of her mind. She had more pressing concerns. Little Matty had just come in the door looking like a street urchin, hay in her hair, heavily soiled face and hands and a runny nose. She grabbed the child deftly as a mother cat and soundly wiped her nose with her handkerchief. Setting the squirming three-year-old down, she thought, *Eeh, what an afternoon I've had!*

The next morning was washday. Annie hauled water from the river filling every available container while Alma collected the items for laundering.

"Mr. Starkey and Manfred are going to dig a well out front of the house so as you won't have to haul water anymore from the creek." Alma looked at Annie proudly after this statement. The girl smiled at her fondly but made no comment. Alma thought, *The poor thing is exhausted from carrying all that water every week for laundry. P'raps she'll think highly of Manfred for making her lot easier.*

Cheered by the thought, Alma fairly bounced through the house singing an English ditty and gathered bundles together. Lastly, she stopped at Annie's room. Annie had removed her bed linens and neatly folded them apparently wishing them to be washed. *That Annie is a neat one*, she thought, and *she is particular about her Sunday dress*. She saw it on the peg and took it down to see if it needed a rinse out.

Her eye caught a dark spot on the back of it near the bottom. Her brow knitted as she looked closer at the mark. A grass stain and quite large at that. She found it curious that Annie would have such a stain on her best dress when she had only worn it to church and to go on the democrat to town. She brought the dress down and said, "Shall we give this a rub? There's a mighty grass stain on the back of it."

Annie looked startled. "Oh?" She came right over, looking a little jittery. "Oh, that. I must have done that at the Sunday School picnic."

Alma said nothing but recalled the picnic had been in July, and she distinctly remembered they had laundered this dress since then. With the benefit of Alma's good homemade soap and the wooden scrub board, the stain was duly removed and no more was said about it.

The settler's shanty became George and Annie's refuge. George brought a thick horse blanket on their second visit there and spread it over some hay. That was their bed. It was getting into the middle of September now, the time of the rains. Annie went to the cabin early and lit a fire in the small stone fireplace. By the time that George arrived, the cabin was dry and cosy.

"Ah, some light and warmth. What a welcoming sight." He smiled and ducked to kiss her as she was sitting on the wood floor minding the little fire. She looked serious. "I shouldn't have come. The mistress looked at me like I was queer going for a walk in the rain. I told her that I love to walk in the rain and feel it on my hair."

"And do you?" George sat down beside her and put his arm around her and stroked her hair, which was soft as goose down.

"Yes, I do, but I have to say this dank and musty weather isn't my favourite. I prefer the spring rain." Then she said no more for he didn't allow it. It was always like this. He was hungry for her and, prompted by the short time allowed, wasted little time on preliminaries. When they had loved, he said, "We can't go on like this, you know. Sooner or later we'll be found out." He looked serious, too serious.

Her heart gripped. What was he about to tell her? She knew he was right but true to the nature of women in love, she lived for the sweetness of these moments. "What then?"

"I have a wife and two beautiful children. Amanda is a cold woman. I let myself drift into an alliance with her. Now there is very little I can do about it. There is that obligation to her and especially to my children."

Annie swallowed. "Do you love her?"

"I don't think I have ever been in love."

"Are you in love with me?"

He looked at her and spoke slowly. "I don't know."

Annie was appalled. What was she to him? She hadn't stopped to think that he might only want her for her sexual favours. Theirs was such a passionate relationship. But she hardly knew him. She didn't understand the nature of men.

They met at the cabin one more time after that. It was a beautiful early October day. The sky was perfect blue and the leaves red and gold shimmering in a slight breeze. Alma noticed Annie's restless behaviour that morning.

"I think I'll walk for a while. I need some air. Is it all right?" she said weakly. Her mistress looked up at her as she turned from the oven with a tray of biscuits in her hands. She nodded once, and Annie was taken aback by the look in her eyes. It was at once sad, knowing. She hesitated momentarily and then went quickly out the door after hurriedly donning a wool shawl.

My God, she knows something is going on, she thought. But it was too late to worry about that. Annie was a woman out of control, driven, and she could not turn back now. It was past ten o'clock already. As she reached the point in the road from which the cabin was situated, she heard a horse snort and knew he was there before her. Her feet had wings and her hair floated softly behind her shoulders as she ran through tall weeds to the cabin.

He was at the door waiting for her and silently took her hand, leading her into the humble shack. They cleaved to one another and time stood still. She drowned in his kisses and they were as one flesh. Annie felt like she had burned her bridges behind her and this was her only life. She lived to be with him. She chose his love over her pride, over her love for her family, over her loyalty to her mistress, over her sense of self-preservation.

Later, he confronted her with discomfort in his eyes.

"I don't know how to say this to you. But I don't think I can go on like this. It's unfair to you because I cannot leave my wife, and I could not bear to lose my children." He felt her stiffen and she drew back from him. He continued, "I have seen another man, an acquaintance of mine, who took leave of his wife for a mistress and his was not a happy outcome. I feel so terribly guilty, deceitful to both of you. I don't think I can continue this affair."

Annie stared at him disbelievingly. How could he talk about his needs and disregard her so totally! She was shattered. She had given herself to him, risked her reputation and employment to meet him clandestinely. He was simply letting her go, discarding her. It wasn't that simple. She couldn't just turn off her feelings.

Suddenly, she was angry. "What was I to you? A reprieve from a cold wife? I have needs too. Things are not so easy for me either."

George hung his head. "I'm so sorry. I shouldn't have given you false hope." He looked in agony.

Annie was frantic. *He's weak*, she thought. *He just used me like one of his girls before he was married. I'm just another girl that he'll forget.* She couldn't say any more hurtful things to him, however, she had the misfortune of loving him too much, and she knew that part of what he said was justified.

"Very well. I know you're in a difficult position. It was partly my fault." Her voice sounded devoid of emotion, cold and flat. "This will be our last meeting. I accept that."

"Annie"—he took her by the shoulders—"I hope we can still see each other from time to time . . . be friends." He looked at her with tenderness.

His suggestion was so ludicrous to her in her present state, she felt like screaming, but all she did was to force herself to nod. She felt like pounding his chest and then collapsing in his arms sobbing. But what good would that do? So she simply said, "Take care of yourself and I wish you happiness." She could hear herself saying it and it sounded cold, like someone else talking.

He looked miserable as she walked past him. He tried to embrace her once more, but she could hardly tolerate the touch that would be his last. Heartbroken, she walked through the bushes and tall grasses, then down the road back to the farm oblivious to everything around her.

George waited for a few minutes and made his way back to the highway past the Starkey farm—a forlorn figure on horseback. His anticipated sense of relief was outweighed by other confusing emotions. The largest of these was a puzzling sense of loss and emptiness. He wondered what he had accomplished by hurting this girl. But he knew they couldn't continue on this way. My Lord, what if she were to conceive a child? He felt better now realizing he had done what was necessary to protect her and himself by preventing such a calamity.

Neither George nor Annie noticed Manfred who was coming up over the ridge bringing in some late hay. He saw Annie making her way back to the farm. She looked in a state of mild disarray, and he watched as she stopped under a tree, silhouetted against the western sky, to adjust her skirts and smooth her hair. Then she hurried on a little farther before turning into the lane. At the time he was kneeling down to check one of his horse's hooves for he thought she had a loose shoe. Presently, he heard hoof beats and then saw a gentleman ride by on a sorrel mare.

Curiosity getting the best of him, he walked out to the road, but the lone rider was too engrossed to notice him. The horseman turned at the highway toward Duntroon, and it wasn't until he did that Manfred remembered where he had seen the man and the horse before. Of course! He was the storekeeper at Duntroon, Freenan's son and heir.

He wondered what young Freenan was doing in this vicinity and then suddenly it hit him. Manfred visualized Annie with her mussed appearance. Thoughts flooded him; her strange refusal of his marriage proposal and her unmarried at twenty-four and a servant in his stepmother's house. Another girl would have jumped at the chance to be the future mistress of a successful farm. He left his work and followed the path backward of the man on horseback.

It was easy to follow the fresh hoof prints in the dust. They stopped at a growth of young trees a quarter mile down the road. He hadn't been down here for a long time but recognized the footpath to an old pioneer cabin set back in the bush where he had played as a child. His heart sank as he followed the hoof prints along the path and which led right to the door of the shanty. Growing indignant and angry now, he flung open the door and looked in dismay at the red and blue horse blanket on a makeshift bed on the floor.

Annie stood in the moonlight at the window in her snow-white petticoat. She watched as a shooting star coursed the midnight sky and then fell to earth. She felt numb now. She was tired from her emotions, from fighting tears all day. She felt a type of peace now. The Starkeys had been strangely silent at supper, even the children. She was glad this sad day was over.

But the future stretched out bleakly before her. She thought of the Misses Willoughby and her own probable fate, spinsterhood. She felt suddenly sorry for them. Or perhaps she would marry a man whom she liked but did not love? A better end, or was it? She thought of her parents. She had been born of love. Suddenly her legs crumpled beneath her and she slumped on the floor her head falling forward onto her knees. Her body was wracked with sobs as her silken head shone softly in the moonlit dusk of the room.

Some distance away in his comfortable home, George was looking out at the same moon. He was thinking of the girl with the soft, light hair, the hair he would no longer touch and the face he would miss seeing. He let the curtain drop and looked across at his wife lying with closed eyes in the luxurious bed.

CHAPTER 14

Annie continued her tenure with the Starkeys only two months after that. One day she felt a quickening in her body. With the instincts of a farm girl, she knew with a certainty she was carrying a child. At first the idea infused her with a sudden joy, which was quickly replaced with fear and foreboding for the future.

Annie had kept her secrets about her love and now suffered silently with this new one. The secrets were like a wedge that drove itself between her and Alma. Their formerly close relationship was now stilted, unnatural. One day Alma brought things out into the open when Annie looked again sad and distracted as she had for most of this past month.

"Is there something bothering ye, lass? You can tell me surely." The woman wiped her floury hands on her new cotton apron and turned to this girl of whom she was very fond. Annie said nothing for a moment and then burst into tears. Alma held her and patted her back. "Now, now, it can't be all that bad. Give over and tell me."

"I can't!" Annie spoke between sobs. "I can't tell anyone."

"What you think is a secret may not be as secret as you think," the woman said kindly. "I know there's been something afoot with you. Manfred has some knowledge of it."

"Manfred!" Annie exclaimed. "What would he know of it?" Then she remembered how Manfred had acted strangely this last while. He looked at her now with resentment, even suspicion at times. She thought it related to her refusal of him. He acted coldly toward her lately. Now she understood why. He must have seen something, perhaps George riding in the area and suspected the truth.

"It's a man, isn't it?"

"How did you know?" Annie looked at her.

"Manfred found your meeting place and put two and two together. He saw the young man."

"Oh no!" She covered her eyes; then pulling straight and composing herself, she said. "I'm sorry he had to discover it. I didn't mean to hurt him."

"You did lass, you did," Alma said quietly. "He was right taken with you. Still is, mind."

"I'm to have a child, Alma." Her eyes were pleading. "Does that shock you?"

Alma looked startled. "So you are, lass, so you are . . . and that's what comes of such meetings. I'm surprised but nought shocks me. It's happened to many a lass afore you. But what, tell me, does this lad have that our Manfred doesn't?"

"I don't know. It's something I can't explain. It's been there a long while before I met Manfred. It was always there between us."

"I mind that the fellow is the married storekeeper. Manfred recognized him. Why else would a girl have to meet a lad in secret like. You've got yourself in an awful pickle, my girl. I won't be one to judge you, but others will, you can count on that. What are you going to do?"

"I have no idea what to do. I've only known for a couple of days now." She touched her stomach and fell into weeping again.

"There, there now." Alma handed the distraught girl a handkerchief and patted her hand. "I'll make you a nice cuppa and you can sit for a spell. There's an answer to every problem. Things look brighter after a cup o' tea, I always say." Alma's mind was clicking and turning over.

"I have to tell you, Annie," Alma spoke after they finished their tea. "You didn't strike me as the type to get burnt in the bushes, pardon my expression. Manfred was rip-roaring mad when he discovered that makeshift bed in the cabin." She burst into loud chuckles and slapped her thigh.

That was just what Annie needed. She started to laugh too, and it soon turned into hysterical convulsions, tears streaming down both their cheeks. It was a good thing the men were far out in the field for they would have demanded to know what was so funny had they been within one hundred feet.

Alma knew how to be discreet. She hadn't been a valued member of the staff of a big house in England for nothing. Her husband was kept innocent of Annie's predicament, and she didn't breathe a word of it to any soul other than her eldest stepson. She believed both their happiness might still be retrieved if a union between the two could be arranged, even at this late hour. Such was the altruistic nature of Alma. She knew the lad was still besotted with the servant girl.

Manfred's black eyes enlarged as he listened to his stepmama's confidences the next day and a look of distaste passed his countenance. It was soon replaced by a fervent look of hope. He wanted the girl still but his former opinion of her was altered. Manfred thought about the situation for days.

He watched Annie, studied her, and saw that she was troubled, not her former carefree self. He took a kind of pleasure in taking his time. There was no rush. She was going nowhere. After a time he felt almost glad this had happened. She was more vulnerable now. She would accept him meekly and with trepidation. He felt a sense of power and control over the situation.

By the time Saturday rolled around, Manfred was feeling good again about himself and about Annie. He had been pleasant to her all week, doffing his hat when he met her with her neck yoke coming up from the river. She would look at him quizzically but began to relax and feel happier as her relationship with the Starkeys became more comfortable again. So it was with high spirits on Manfred's part and a grateful attitude on Annie's part that they left for the trip to her parents.

It was Saturday afternoon, the month end day off. She was thinking about how she would tell her mother the news about the child and pulled her cloak tighter about her in the chill November air.

"Look yonder, Annie, a nice patch of Michaelmas daisies still in bloom." He stopped the horses and jumped off the wagon. He came back and handed her a big bunch of the wild purple asters smiling up sheepishly at her.

"Why, thank you, Manfred. So unusual for this late in the year. They're lovely." She blushed, embarrassed by this out-of-character gesture of his. Manfred always seemed to have difficulty expressing his feelings.

A little ill at ease now, she wished the four-mile journey would soon be over. Something in Manfred's manner disturbed her. Presently, he pulled the horses to the side of the road. He turned to her and said, "Annie, I'm goin' to ask you again. You know the question. Will you marry me?"

Annie looked at the handsome man. She had been thinking about him. He was not unattractive. Could she grow to love him? She could be his wife and save herself from disgrace, have George's child and no one be the wiser. But when she looked into his ebony eyes, it wasn't at all like looking into George's blue ones. There was no depth reaching out to her, no communion of souls. Difficult as it was to turn down this expeditious solution, she just could not do it. "I'm truly sorry, Manfred, but I cannot in all fairness accept your offer of marriage."

Manfred's face darkened. "Then what in the devil are you going to do with a bastard child and no husband?"

Annie's head jerked back. "So you know . . . It's something that I will have to deal with. Please take me home." Though she felt uncommonly shaky, her words came out with dignity.

But Manfred was not going to be shaken off so easily. "Tell me first what hold that storekeeper has on you. Why did you choose him over me?"

"I can't tell you why. It's something I can't explain. It's over now, but I can't marry you. I don't love you."

"So you love him, a philanderer. I have no respect for your fancy man. You choose a married man with children over me then."

The look on his face alarmed her and the sweat stood out on his brow. He reached over toward Annie and tried to kiss her. His lips felt like bland wet rubber. Her only sensation was disgust. She pushed him away. "Don't do that."

He laughed a humourless laugh. "You might get to like it." He put his hand on her breast. She slapped him across the face in an instantaneous response. His other hand was already pulling at her skirt. He was a strong man and not in his right mind at the moment, she could see. She screamed shrilly. At this, he let go of her and she made to jump off the buckboard

"Wait, wait," he said, putting up his hands, palms toward her. "I won't touch you again. I promise I'll take you home now."

Annie looked at him carefully and then nodded; her heart in her throat. They drove in silence to her parents' house, and she got down by herself with her bundle. He said nothing else to her and, looking straight ahead, whipped the horses into a gallop down the road.

Manfred went straight into Collingwood and hit the first saloon he came to. He sat for hours over his whiskey at the bar and talked to no man. After a few whiskies, Dan, the barkeep heard the man saying, "Slut, slut," and wondered to whom he was referring. *Drunk talk*, he thought, but it looked like some girl had done him wrong.

Later on, Rose O'Drury laid her white hand on his shoulder and bent her perfumed bosom toward his face. His aching eyes looked up at her pretty painted face and she gave him the old "come hither" look. She led him back of the barroom to a tune of wolf whistles and jeers where her lavish room was. Rose didn't make up to just any feller. She'd had her eye on Manfred these last few weeks.

Manfred pushed the burgundy feathers aside from the deep scarlet gown and kissed her snow-white neck. He was too drunk for preliminaries, but Rose knew the ropes and assisted him. Soon his breeches were off and his troubles were dulled in the voluptuous white softness of Rose. She was all soft kisses, twining limbs, and sweet perfumed hair.

When he awoke the next morning there she was, still beside him. The pillows were stained with her paint and her hair was free and natural, devoid of pins and feathers. She looked like an innocent child lying there.

He thought of Annie and his want of her, his disappointment, his judgment of her. Here he was in bed with the town whore and her looking beautiful like an innocent child. Annie kept talking of love. He realized that Annie symbolized a good wife to him—thrifty, moral, and good in the kitchen. Had he loved her? Perhaps the idea of her. He looked down at this cherubic creature asleep beside him. Dyed red hair and remnants of lip rouge on her face. Rose rolled over and opened her smudged eyes.

"Manny, oh, Manny, you're still here." She kissed him and pulled him to her. Passion overtook him and he kissed the painted lips and played with the masses of bright hair.

"Rose, you were good to me last night. Thank you."

"Come again to see me, will you?" She looked at him with a tear in her eye.

That tear caught at his heart. He got out of bed feeling a little confused. "Time to get some breakfast, Rosie," he said kindly. She watched him as he washed at the stand. He pulled the bell cord and hollered out the door. "Some breakfast and some more hot water please, and thank you!"

CHAPTER 15

Annie was more than a little shaken as she went through the door of her parents' house.

"Darling, you're home!" Joy flickered over Ruby's work-worn face as she put down the bowl she was stirring and hugged her daughter. She held the girl at arm's length and noted her ashen face.

"Are you all right, dear? You look like you just seen a ghost."

"I'll be all right in a minute," Annie said without conviction. She sat down on a kitchen chair, torn between relief to be out of Manfred's clutches and dread of what she was about to tell her mother.

"That young buck was in an awful hurry. You'd think it was a Wild West show the way he raced away." Ruby's eyebrows crinkled. Sensing something was amiss, she said, "Tell me your news, Annie."

Annie started hesitatingly and then came out with the whole story. Ruby's face passed through a number of expressions reflecting her tumultuous emotions—from pity, anger, worry, sorrow to love. She did not interrupt nor say a word, however, until the girl was finished.

When it was all out, Annie looked up at her mother bleary-eyed. "I'm so sorry I brought you this trouble," said Annie sadly, observing her mother who did indeed look tired and worried, but Ruby's expression changed again to one of deep contemplation. She put her arms around the girl and held her. Annie felt such a comforting feeling of relief now that the story was told. They held each other for a long moment. It was very healing to Annie—that embrace of acceptance.

"Oh, my dear, my dear. Why couldn't you have married the nice elder brother and had an easy life. You had to fall in love with that womanizer."

"Please don't say that, Ma. You don't know either of them," and she proceeded to tell Ruby about Manfred's treatment of her on the way home.

Ruby looked angry. "Well, you're certainly not going back to that house! I thought better of that family. You'll stay right here with us. We'll take care of you."

"But what will people say?"

"Never mind what they say. An idea is coming to me. This sort of thing has been handled with grace before."

"I won't give the child up!" Annie cried.

"No, not that. Give me some time, but I think I may be ready to have another baby. I'm not over the hill yet you know," her mother said with a wry smile.

Aaron was not as understanding as his wife. He was really shocked and hurt at the news. It was a week before Ruby could get him to see reason. He was all for hauling George Freenan out on the street and giving him a licking. Annie was terrified at the prospect and after much begging and tearful pleading was able to get his promise he would do no such thing.

Her biggest hurt, however, was the look of disappointment in her father's face that outlived the anger. As time went on though, Aaron not only adjusted to the situation but played his part admirably in the little plot Ruby cooked up.

"It may not fool everyone, Annie," Ruby admonished, "but it will save face and those who gossip are often ignored by the nicer folk who want to believe the best of people." This was said with cautious optimism.

The plan was that Ruby would feign pregnancy. Later, a theatrical approach would have to be made as she made a couple of public appearances with a well-padded tummy. Since gravid women were not often seen in public (it was not something to be displayed), a couple of sightings of a seemly bulge would be sufficient.

The news could be spread in various ways. Only one or two people would be taken into confidence. One would be the midwife, old Mrs. Coxswain. Annie knew that Alma Starkey would not spread news, but she wasn't at all sure of her stepson, Manfred. They decided not to worry about what he might say. Young Frank was still at home but of course he could be trusted.

Their plan was not a totally new idea and had been carried out by others in the past with some success in her mother's memory. And so it was that Aaron mentioned to a number of comrades his wife's "condition" and so it was with God's mercy and old Mrs. Coxswain's help that a healthy baby boy was born to Annie the next spring.

Although there was some rumour circulating around town, it was generally accepted in genteel circles that Ruby had borne a late child and no more was thought of it. Annie had kept to the house and saw no one for the last three months, which was easy enough as they had few visitors. She would go up to her room when someone did drop by. Had it been later on, around harvest time, it would have been almost impossible to hide her. She would have had to "visit relatives out of town."

During those long months of pregnancy through bitter winter storms, Annie thought constantly of George, of her love for him, and secret joy at having their child filled her. She began to long to hold the babe in her arms.

It was also a heartbreaking time for her, with that feeling of mourning, of not being able to see George, not being able to share the truth with him. She prayed to God, thanking him for her dear parents who were kindness itself to help her in this crisis. She knew some other parents would have dealt an unkind hand to a pregnant daughter and that she had been spared this special type of misery.

Under no circumstances must she tell George the truth, Ruby said. It would ruin his life and do her no good. Annie agreed to this. It seemed unhappily logical to her at the time. She had no energy for confrontations anyway. She thought often of remembered kisses and embraces. She built a shrine within herself to the memories of those precious events of love, reliving in every meeting the ecstasy of her lost love. It somehow placated her, filled the emptiness of the long hours to live in this dream world. And she was not without hope, "the hope that springeth eternal in the human breast." Hope that, through some miracle, she and George might someday be reunited.

She felt joy again when old Mrs. Coxswain held her baby out to her. She searched earnestly in the baby's face for a likeness of George and was not disappointed. When the kind old woman had done her duty, Aaron drove her home and gave her a generous sum. The old woman was pitiably grateful, he could see. He knew she could be trusted with the secret. She had seen much and was wise.

"Thank you, old mother," he said. "I'll not forget your help and your promise."

"Your secret is safe with an old woman. But don't judge the young lass too harshly. She has a big price to pay for her moments of pleasure."

Aaron nodded and helped the old crone down. She spoke as though she had memories of her own youthful passions. He looked at the grey frizzled hair done in a simple, thick braid down her back, which was arched by a dowager's hump. Although she appeared quite spry, she must be very old, perhaps in her eighties. And yet he could almost see her as a young girl, see beyond the still-bright sunken eyes and the thickened features. She would have been pretty too, he bet.

Back at the house, Annie was in tears. Ruby had decided to lecture her, seeing the inordinate look of joy on her face when she handled the newborn child. Better she should hurt her now than see the girl hurt tenfold later on.

"You'll have to forget he's yours. From now on, get it in your head that he's my child."

Annie started to weep and Ruby remonstrated, "It's for your own sake, Annie. I'm not trying to be cruel. You must treat him like a brother. Start by thinking of him as one or people will know and your future will be one of no hope of respect from society, no chance of finding a husband. Is that what you want?"

"I don't care about a husband. Since I've seen the babe, I care nothing for society."

Ruby's brow darkened. "It's not only for your sake. He will be an outcast, a bastard if they know. His life will be unhappy."

Annie hadn't thought of that. There was nothing she wouldn't do to prevent her son from suffering. She had loved him at first sight and even before he was born. She agreed to everything Ruby said—for his sake. And so it was, Annie was given the child to suckle, but after two nights he was kept in a cradle in Ruby's room. It was her plan that the child must know her as mother. He would be brought up to think that Annie was his sister. This was the second heartbreak for Annie.

The months went by and the green lush of spring turned into the mellow, golden warmth of summer. The baby was christened in the church in Nottawa and named Henry. He was a cute little gaffer, and Annie stood silently watching the reverend father bless him as her mother stood smiling with him in her arms. Her father looked proud. He had become very fond of the pretty baby.

To look at the couple, Annie thought, you would swear they were the real parents. There was nothing to describe the feeling she had standing there that day. She had forfeited her right to be a wife and mother. She was a shadow person lingering at the fringes of life, which was passing her by. A deep grief engulfed her.

Her mother looked nervously at her. Was her daughter going to spoil things? She looked so miserable. People would notice. A large number of their neighbours attended these functions. It was cause and excuse for great celebration; a break in their toil-worn lives to experience social life, levity, and celebrate new life. Annie's sad face was ruining everything they had planned so hard for.

Annie caught her mother's worried look and suddenly came to. She realized how close she had come to folly. A bright smile formed itself on her face. She came up to her mother and kissed her and then her father. "We'd like you all to come back to the house for a lunch in honour of my new baby brother." The words almost stuck in her craw, but she forced them out. She took the child from her mother's arms and held him up toward the congregation. There was applause.

Ruby and Aaron looked at each other and sighed with relief. The hardest part was over. The child was accepted as theirs, and Annie would fulfill her role as a sister. She would be free to have a respectable life again and perhaps marry in time.

The summer harvest came and went that year with much ado. It was a bountiful one. Ruby was glad she had her daughter with her. They cooked and baked to feed the gangs of men that came to help with the threshing. They felt a new closeness and laughed together at the baby's antics. He was four months old now and looking more like his real father. Annie wondered what he would look like in a few years.

Some of the young men on the threshing gang had eyes for Annie and a couple of them tried to engage her in conversation but were disappointed when she politely answered them but disappeared quickly into the house and showed herself only when she must to help her mother with the serving on the long harvest table out on the lawn

A few of those neighbour's sons were on the lookout for a likely wife as women were in short supply and noted her devotion to helping her mother and baby brother. Had Annie been a little more than just civil to them, they would have planned a return visit to Aaron's house some Sunday afternoon.

Eight years had passed now, and Annie wondered where the time had gone as she waited for the doctor to leave the room where her son lay languishing. Finally, the old medical man came out of the door, looking greatly fatigued and shaking his head, not noticing Annie and heading to the kitchen to tell Ruby there was no hope because it was the diphtheria.

Annie ran into the room to the bedside of the child who thought of her as sister. The child, delirious with fever, and exhausted from convulsions looked at Annie's face and called, "Mamma?" Annie drew the child up into her arms and said what she'd wanted to say all these years. "Yes, baby, Mama is here." The boy looked up at her with glassy eyes.

Ruby stood at the doorway now listening to Annie's words. She looked at the feverish body of the young boy, barely eight, who lay almost immobile on the sweat-soaked bed. Then her heartbroken look turned to Annie. It held disapproval, guilt, and indescribable sorrow. She turned away and left her daughter to the pitiful length of privacy that was left to her with her child.

These past eight years had been dreary years for Annie, and although her parents had not said anything, she knew they were saddened that she had not married in that time. There had been no Sunday afternoon courting visits from young men in their parlour for her manner had been discouraging to any would-be suitor.

She was now thirty-two years old and well into spinsterhood. And the child, her child, lay beside her very ill, a child who had never known who his real mother was. Her heart gave her such pain; she didn't know if she could bear it.

After the boy died, Annie felt like day had turned into night. It was the strangest thing but a dark veil had physically fallen over her eyes making the day dim even when it was sunny. So dark was her depression and so deep her despair that this manifestation occurred. She could not sleep at all, and when it seemed she did, she would hallucinate. She felt as though she were going out of her mind. Eddie came home on leave from the boats when he heard but neither he nor Frank who were both grown up men now could console their sister.

Terribly thin and haggard with lack of sleep, Annie ate little. The neighbours began to whisper. Didn't the girl collapse at the funeral? It happened when the minister read the lines "Dust to dust and ashes to ashes." Perhaps the old rumours were true. It was her child. And she acted so strangely now. She would go by without a greeting, looking wild-eyed and haggard. At the Nottawa General Store, she would forget her order and stand speechless and teary-eyed before she turned and ran out of the store.

Finally, Annie looked so ill that Ruby was beside herself.

"Aaron, something has to be done about Annie. She can't go on like this. She's going to kill herself."

Aaron stared at the wall in front of him. He didn't seem to hear the tears in his wife's voice. The grief of losing young Henry had taken a great toll on him also. He had aged ten years in two months. Ruby put her head down on her arms at the table and sobbed. "I couldn't bear to lose her too."

It seemed with great effort that Aaron drew his dulled eyes from the wall to his stricken wife. He too had been almost immobilized these past weeks. If the neighbours had not come in and done it for him, the crops would still be standing in the fields. He had cared for the animals and done the odd small job around the farm, but his energy was all but sucked from him. The boy had been both son and grandson to him. He knew now that he had loved Henry even more than his own sons.

He spoke then. "We'll send her away for a spell. If she gets away from the farm and us, she'll get away from the memory. Maybe she'll heal then. It's all we can do for her."

Ruby's head came up and a slight glint of hope passed over her face. She thought for a moment and then spoke. "My sister Rachel in Cobourg would take her in. She hasn't seen her for twenty years but took a liking to her as a child. Her little 'uns are all grown. It's a nice town, Cobourg, and right on a lake like Collingwood. She still writes to me regular. I'll write to her today."

CHAPTER 16

Amanda had gone to bed early. George knew she was sulking again. He was beginning to know her very well after twelve years of marriage. He was sorry that she was not happy. He didn't love her or even particularly like her anymore, but he didn't like to see her unhappy. She was his wife after all and the mother of his two dear children, and he felt like a failure.

He should have never taken her away from the society that she loved in Toronto. Why hadn't he been able to see that she wouldn't fit in to a rustic life? But he had been so young, so besotted with her charms. His mother and Amanda had never grown close but had developed a polite relationship which was tolerable only because of their mutual love for the children. But George wondered sometimes how much Amanda loved the children. She would sometimes use them as pawns to manipulate situations and people.

A loud knock suddenly resounded on the front door. George wondered who might be calling this dark December evening. The hour was getting close to nine in the evening according to the grandfather clock in the hall.

"Come in, by all means, come in," he shouted, hoping for some cheery company to ease his blue mood. Perhaps a boyhood chum had come to take a glass of ale with him.

When the door did not open immediately, he strode with some eagerness to it and flung it open. To his surprise a shivering, long-haired, scantily breeched man with a rather wizened face stood there. He wore a city coat of velvet and his footwear was hardly suitable for being out and about on a snowy night. It was a moment or two before George recognized him as one of the staff from his wife's former home.

"May I come in, sir," he squeaked, his teeth chattering from the cold. "It is I, Forbes, Mr. Freenan and I bear sombre news."

George's face fell and he showed the man into the parlour where a cheerful fire was burning. "News? From where? My dear man, you haven't journeyed all the way from Toronto!"

"Yes, sir. Sadly, I bring you news that Mr. Trolley, your father-in-law, is dead."

"Dead! Why I only saw him not two weeks ago and he was brimming with health." George was truly shocked. He was fond of his papa-in-law who, since his father's death, had sought to form even closer ties with him and be a real father figure.

"Alas, he collapsed and died four days ago. It was thought to be a brain seizure. He died within the day."

"But why haven't we known before this . . . a telegraph?"

"Mrs. Trolley thought it would be too distressful for Miss Amanda to be notified thus. She insisted that she be told in person."

"The burial then is over?"

"He was buried two days ago, sir."

George sank into the parlour settee and ran his hand through his hair in despair. "But how ever am I going to tell her? She'll go wild. He doted on her. She was everything to him. She'll be devastated."

"I will tell her for you if you like, sir. She may take it more calmly from me. I knew her from a child," offered Forbes.

Just then Ida showed herself. She'd been listening at the door. "You are her husband, George. You must be the one to tell her. She's a woman, not a child." The thin short man had just now quit his shivering, which had in part been due to apprehension in delivering his message. He looked at the magnificent elderly woman who stood like a statue and thought she looked like one of the fierce angels from the Book of Revelations, most intimidating with her swirls of iron-grey hair.

"You're right, of course, Mother. I must be the one to tell her," acknowledged George but not without some trepidation.

George walked slowly feeling a great fatigue come over him as he approached the door of the room he shared with his wife. Amanda was lying in bed, but he knew she was not asleep. It was a ploy of hers, he had come to recognize over the years, to avoid lovemaking. For some reason he felt bitterly annoyed at it this night and his bitterness gave him the courage he needed. But he was still gentle when he said, "Amanda, I know you're awake. I have some news you must know. Get up."

"What?" She sat up rubbing her eyes and looking exceedingly irritable. "I was asleep. What is it?"

"My dear, I'm so sorry to have to tell you that a messenger has arrived bringing sad news. Your father has passed away." He stopped, waiting for the storm to begin, the wailing, the shrieks. But there was only silence. Feeling even more disturbed and concerned, he went to take her compassionately in his arms. She pushed him away with great force.

"Leave me alone."

"Amanda . . . I . . ." He tried again to touch her, comfort her.

"Don't!" she said, pushing him away once more, this time with fury. "Don't you realize what has happened to me? I've just lost the only person who ever loved me," she blurted out. Then she cupped the sides of her head with her hands and rocked forward and back, forward and back.

George, deeply hurt by her words, turned slowly and left the room where his mother and Martha were standing waiting for him and wringing their hands. He looked at his mother and then Martha and said, "Martha, kindly see to our guest. Bring him refreshment and ready a room for he and his companion. I will have the hired man stable his team. He has brought terrible news. My father-in-law is dead." Martha's eyes got big and the old woman shook her head. She was sorry Mr. Trolley was dead. She'd enjoyed the visits of the blustering kind man over the years. Ah, but weren't they all getting old. She sadly coerced her increasingly arthritic frame to bend to her will and perform the requested tasks.

For the next week, Amanda did not let George near to comfort her and the house was a drear place indeed. She stayed mostly in her room and when she ventured out was uncommunicative. She dined alone.

"George, have you a wife or have you not a wife?" Ida said finally, fed up with sending trays to Amanda's room and seeing her son treated so dismally. "I know the girl has suffered a cruel loss. It's a shock and she was very close with her father. But she has you and the children to see to and she has to buck up."

"I don't know what to do, Mother." George looked at her sadly. "I suppose I have to face the fact that I haven't made Amanda happy in all these years. If I had, she would turn to me for solace."

Ida's face crumpled, and she took her son's head in her hands and then embraced him like he was a boy again. "My dear boy, don't be too hard on yourself. You can't get honey from a vinegar barrel. Lord knows you're not perfect, but you've tried." With tears in her eyes, she said, "Son, I have waited for years for you to come to me and tell me about your unhappiness. It hasn't been between you and Amanda like it was between your father and me. I know. And I know that no two couples are alike. But there's not that love between you, is there? And I'm not talking about the courtin' and sparkin' kind of love. I'm talking about the kind and caring love that comes to be between two people who like and respect each other over time."

George felt strangely comforted in his mother's arms. He guessed it was something that maybe a man never grew out of—the need of the loving arms of a woman.

"I should never have brought her out here, Mama. She was used to better."

"Not better, son, just different. But yes, she was not suited for the kind of life that we consider a good one. She doesn't share our values. I tried to stay out of your affairs. I didn't want to be an interfering old goat. I said to myself, leave them be. But there were times when I had to bite my tongue."

George looked at her guiltily. "Yes, Mama. I know she wasn't always civil to you. That bothered me. But I figured you could stand up for yourself."

Ida cackled. "That I can, boy, that I can. Don't worry about me."

George looked at her gratefully. "I'm glad we had this talk, Mama."

Ida smiled, feeling tears wanting to come to her eyes. "Before I die, I want to see you happy, George. I want to see this house happy again, like it was when your father was alive."

More than anything that happened tonight those words touched and wounded George. If only he could make her wish come true.

Christmas 1886 came and went, and the Freenan household was little changed. They managed to get Amanda to come around a bit a week before Christmas and so were able to cheer the children with stories of Saint Nick and get them to dreaming about sugar plums and toys even though they were getting a bit old for that kind of thing.

It was decided to postpone telling them about their grandfather until a later time. It was too hard on them right now to experience the moods of their mother. Fortunately, Amanda's old nanny parcelled up some things that the children's grandfather had already ordered for them months before anticipating Christmas. Such a doting grandfather, no child had ever had.

The New Year brought some improvement in business for George for which he was grateful because times had been hard these last five years. This, however, was a pittance compared to the lavish inheritance Amanda received according to her father's will. A lawyer had been to see them from Toronto when the weather allowed to speak with the heiress. Of course, he pointed out since Amanda was married, her husband had control of her fortune. George was astounded at the estate left to his wife, whose mother could carry on in her current lifestyle, being a wealthy woman in her own right.

The New Year also brought rumours to George's ears. Being a storekeeper, he was often the recipient of choice bits of gossip which he could not politely refuse to listen to. But his body became rigid when a particular name was attached to this most recent tidbit. Apparently, there was a spinster who was rumoured years ago to have had a child out of wedlock but no one could be really sure because her mother claimed the baby was her own. Now the rumour was going rampant again because the boy child had died and the spinster daughter had gone berserk since the death rather than the supposed mother. The child had died of diphtheria at the age of eight years. The spinster's name was Annie McClory.

George was in a mild state of shock when he heard this. He hadn't really thought about Annie much in all these years. He had pushed her to a part of his mind where she didn't cross his daily conscious thoughts. It was just something that had happened years ago. As working hours drew to a close, his mild state of shock somehow deepened. He became distracted with this rumour.

He thought of the sweet, vulnerable girl he had wanted for a time with passion. He could hardly remember. He was trying now to recall.

Yes, he remembered she was sweet, he remembered her hair, yes, her hair—it was unusual, light and soft and her smile. It was just for him. It was coming slowly back as he allowed it, as he let the door of his memory open.

Oh, it wasn't that he hadn't seen her over the years. Yes, he had caught a glimpse of her from time to time. They had even passed on the street, and with discomfort, he had asked her how she was. She always seemed to be with a small brother. Her mother's youngest, he'd supposed.

Now a niggling thought came to him, one that flashed into his mind as soon as he'd heard the rumour. But no. It couldn't possibly be. She would have told him. Or would she? He had broken off the tryst if he remembered. But it was during such a short interval that they had seen one another. A few weeks, a month or two at the most. They had only lain together a few times, yet enough to conceive a child.

George closed up the shop slowly and methodically. Something was growing inside him. It had been growing all day. It was a strange bright ball of light. There was something he was beginning to realize. He didn't notice the cold sharp air as he left the store and hitched up his horse. What he did notice was that the day was still bright although it was past five o'clock. The days were starting to get longer. It was a strangely beautiful afternoon and his senses felt keen.

He noticed the tart smell of the leather harness mixed with the sweet aroma of burgeoning earth that rose up in the air where the snow had melted or been scraped clean by hooves and sleigh runners. It was a strange preliminary smell that promised that spring would again touch the earth with its soporific wild sweetness.

When he arrived home, George walked straight past everyone without noticing anyone or anything to his bedchamber. Then he proceeded to pace up and down the room until Amanda came in and said, with no little chagrin, "Whatever are you doing, George?" He stopped immediately and looked at her as if seeing her for the first time ever with new eyes. He saw before him a woman not in the first blush of youth but nevertheless still handsome. It was the first time in weeks she had initiated conversation with him, and he could see she was finally coming around.

He put his hand lightly on her shoulder and said, "Sit down, Amanda. Please sit down." She looked up at him questioningly and was about to rebuke him, but must have thought the better of it seeing his agitated state, so obeyed his request.

"Amanda," he started, "you haven't been so very happy here these last years, have you?" He looked into her eyes, directly and kindly.

Amanda felt surprise for if she had come to know anything about her husband in these last difficult years it was that George did not like directness nor confrontation. She had always thought him selfish. He never seemed to elicit her ideas and feelings.

"Well!" she responded. "So you're finally interested in my welfare." She knew this was not entirely fair for in his own way George had tried to be good to her in a rustic way.

"Yes, Amanda. I'm concerned for your happiness. What can I do to make you happy? I know that I have failed to do so in the past."

Suddenly, Amanda's initial curiosity about George's mood turned to deep bitterness, a bitterness that had built up over years of personal misery. The feeling was so acute it nearly overpowered her, so negative and accusing was it that it made her feel faint.

With resentment in her voice so deep it bordered on hatred, and changed her voice to a shrivelled replica of itself, she asked, "What can you do to make me happy?" She laughed a hollow laugh. "You can give me back the years you stole from me. You can give me back the soirees and balls, the cultured friends I would have had, had I not had the misfortune to become your wife." So forceful, so scathing was her response that George was completely taken aback and, for once, though he was a man who could usually respond verbally to a situation, was

completely dumb, standing immobile as she swished by him out of the
room.

The next day, George closed up the store early. It was a Thursday.
There would be a few surprised people expecting to do trade in the store
and not too happy about it either after a special trip out, but it couldn't
be helped. He had been reliable enough all these years and always at
their disposal. This thing that had been preying on his mind was more
important. He had to deal with it.

He harnessed the horse to the sleigh and headed north toward
Nottawa. He had to see her, talk to her. Would she be lucid? He
shuddered to think of the lovely girl he had held in his arms gone insane,
"berserk" as they said. What form had her infirmity taken? Would she
be wild-haired, unwashed, vacant-eyed? He found he didn't care. The
desire to see her again had started yesterday to grow, just a little at first.
Then he had tossed and turned all night after he had let that door in
his heart swing open.

It was half past the hour of four when he pulled into the laneway he
knew to be the family farm of the spinster. Another thought struck him.
She had never married. Why? She had been an alluring and pleasant
girl. There must have been offers. His heart wrenched with the answer
his mind gave him.

He was eager to see her now, more than eager as he jumped out of
the sleigh and tied the reins to a tree. He half expected to see her face
at the window looking out at him, but the curtains remained motionless
as he walked to the door of the neat clapboard farmhouse.

Aaron heard the bells of a sleigh from the barn where he was doing
chores. He was finally able to go about his business again after the death
of the boy. But he was still dismally depressed. For a moment he had a
wild hope that the sleigh was bringing Annie home, but he sighed as he
pitched hay to the animals for he knew this couldn't be true.

Ruby had just received word from Cobourg that their daughter
would not be coming home until spring. Aunt Rachel had some cheering

news, however. She said Annie was starting to come round and partake in some of the social gatherings. She felt that her melancholia was showing signs of lifting.

Aaron stopped his pitching again and leaned on the hayfork. He peered again through the partially open door of the barn and saw a man hovering at the door of the house. In better times, he would have welcomed the interruption and chance to chat with a visitor whether he be friend or stranger.

But he didn't have it in his heart for socializing these days. He had got into the habit since the boy's death of avoiding neighbours and with that hopefully eluding gossip. His wife could deal with whoever it was. When he satisfied himself the man looked well-dressed and therefore safe enough to leave to his wife's capable manner, he turned again to the feeding of the stock. When he looked again at the door of the house, the man had disappeared inside. His sleigh and horse stood tethered. Aaron shrugged his shoulders and carried on with his chores.

The mild winter of that year was followed by an early spring. By the middle of March little rivulets of water were running in the roads in the Town of Collingwood. The buds on the trees were fat and bursting with their secret knowledge of nature's schedule. Many of the birds had not even migrated that year so there were still flocks of wild pigeons to be seen throughout the winter.

Winter in Cobourg had been even milder, being a little more southerly, and Annie had been renewed in spirit by her aunt's kind ministrations and wise advice. Aunt Rachel knew the whole of Annie's history out of necessity. Being a practical and no-nonsense woman with few illusions about life, she had accepted the information in a matter-of-fact way without shock or dismay. Having visited her sister in the backwoods settlement of Nottawa some years ago, she had much sympathy for this niece who had grown up without the benefit of society and its culture.

Notwithstanding, she was not a little impressed that the girl showed some signs of gentility and a pleasant, demure, but capable nature which she attributed to her sister's good upbringing. She was happy to show to Annie the amenities of Cobourg after the young woman was sufficiently recovered from her nervous affliction to go out of doors in public.

A long period of bed rest and convalescent care including a light, but nourishing diet had been necessary to get her on her feet again. The girl's constitution had been severely run down from a refusal to eat. The doctor who had been in to see her on a number of occasions had been informed that she had suffered a traumatic loss of a relative.

"I have seen this condition before in women," he said in front of Annie to her aunt. "It is a hysteria brought on by a great trauma." Then he turned to Annie. "Some women never get over it, but I see from your face that you are a young woman of great inner fortitude. Your eyes and your silence tell me that you have suffered much. But let me tell you this and it may help you. Forgiveness is the great healer. If you can forgive those who have done wrong to you, it will speed your recovery. Guilt is the great Liar who afflicts women such as yourself. Don't believe him else you will be lost. I don't know exactly what your story is and I don't need to know. But I can tell you this, my girl. Guilt is making you ill. If you can forgive yourself, then you can be healed. All my phials of medicines and tonics cannot help you if you cannot do this."

He patted her on the shoulder as she looked up to him with tear-filled eyes. "Ah, I have touched on something I see. Annie McClory, I can tell that you are not the kind of person who would knowingly hurt anyone nor do a wrong that you could avoid. My business has taught me the nature of people over the years. You are a young, healthy woman still. Forget what is in the past that troubles you. You are a woman of value. You have much to offer. In your future lies happiness, perhaps a husband and children, if you allow this to be. This is all I will say today. I know I'm an old windbag."

The physician then closed his black leather bag and got up. "Listen to your aunt. She is a good woman and will do her best to help you. The rest is up to you, my girl."

Book Of Winnie

Chapter 17

"Winnie, your father will be soon wantin' his supper," Emaline whined standing at the door, her hair askew. Winnie was making bath soap outside in a pot suspended over a fire pit.

The weary girl looked up and nodded and stopped her stirring. Winnie poured the hot pork fat mixed with beef tallow, bayberry, and lye into a large pan to cool. The next day when it was hardened, she would cut it into squares. She left the soap to go to the smokehouse where she took down a hen that her Pa had killed about an hour ago and left there for her to pluck.

She took the bird outside and lay it on a stump; then went to the house and brought out a kettle of boiling water to pour over it. It would be easier to pluck now. When she was finished, Winnie came back to the house and slung the chicken onto the wooden bake table.

She then grabbed a wooden bucket and went outside up the rise to the spring and filled the bucket with sparkling water. She wished her mother was more self-reliant. She was feeling more and more hemmed in here. The more she did around the place, the less her mother seemed to want to do. They would never come up in the world and better themselves at this rate.

Back in the house, she proceeded to wash the chicken and clean out the inside. Her mother looked at her questioningly. In answer to that look, Winnie said, "Why don't you just make a boiled dinner tonight, Ma? It'll be easier." Her mother looked blank and then nodded slowly.

"I have to get back to the soap. Might as well make some laundry soap while I have all the setup," Winnie said in way of explanation.

Her mother looked mildly disappointed but went to the cupboard and pulled out some items answering, "Here's the borax and ammonia." She had hoped Winnie would save her the trouble of starting dinner. She felt tired and wanted to lie down on the couch bed in the kitchen. Sleeping was a comfort. It made her forget that her life was not all that it should be.

Winnie had been doing a lot of thinking lately about her future. She had to do something soon. She was becoming more and more frustrated with her life. She felt like a wild horse that was tethered and trying to break free.

The house was becoming increasingly oppressive to her. She even hated the smell of it when she walked in the door. It smelled damp, dank, and unclean to her. With all her efforts put into keeping it decently clean, it was an impossible task without the help of her mother who was slovenly about her own person and barely lifted a finger around the home. There was laundry and scrubbing to do as well as cooking and baking.

Winnie did the best she could, but now that it was spring, the kitchen garden needed to be turned over and planted, an arduous task. Her father could have helped but would only tend to the potato patch, which was planted haphazardly. And she had to keep an eye that the animals were properly fed and watered for he could not always be relied upon to do this.

If she had had any more time, she would have mucked out the pens and barn, but that would have to be her father's responsibility for she had too much on her shoulders already. It bothered her to go into the barn and see the manure deep in the stalls from ancient neglect. It would be an enormous job to get it as clean as it should be.

In the winter she did most of the knitting and mending as her mother wasn't a good hand at it and simply didn't bother about it anymore. Now her mother had begun leaving the preserving for her to do as well and it was all too much. The time had come, and Winnie knew that she had to break away from them or reconcile herself to a lifetime of drudgery.

But how could she do it? Where would she go? Girls had to be careful going out on their own. It just wasn't done. It was a man's world and the only options open to a female were homemaker and wife, teacher, housekeeper, and such like. If you were married to a man of business, you could run his store or manage his affairs. Some women were known to become quite powerful but a young lass without means was prey to the worst of men and might end up in sordid circumstances. She didn't want that. What was she to do!

Collingwood was a pretty town situated in the basin by the Bay and sheltered from weather by these very mountains where Winnie lived. She had only been down there once as a lass of seven when her Pa had taken her in with him to buy some harness. They usually made necessary purchases in Singhampton, a mountain village with good amenities.

The Blue Mountains were a small range but lovely. Except for a few cliffs along the escarpment, the smoky blue hills sloped gently to the basin containing Collingwood and the harbour. If you travelled to the edge of the escarpment most northerly facing Georgian Bay, which she had on a few occasions with her family to visit a family that farmed nearby, you could look out on the most breathtaking view of the bay and also see Collingwood, which was about four miles away at that point.

Winnie thought hard. She was good about the house. She hadn't enough schooling perhaps for teaching but knew enough to teach children their letters. She read well. Perhaps someone in the harbour town would take her in as household help and to assist with the young ones.

Collingwood, so she heard, was getting some fine houses built and was very prosperous. There was work for men in the shipyard, railways, liveries, and smithies. She finished the soap and stood back to admire her work. Tomorrow, there would be a lovely pile of white bars. Yes, she got satisfaction out of a job well done. She would be happy as a domestic with accommodations in a nice clean house with "genteel" people and a small wage.

She even thought of the possibility of becoming an apprentice to learn dressmaking. Something clicked in Winnie's mind. She realized she had finally made the decision to leave home. From that point on her mind was in gear. The practical aspects of the change started to come to her. She began to prepare for her adventure.

But she must be secretive about this until the right moment. They would try to prevent her from leaving otherwise; not so much out of parental love and concern, she felt, for her safety as out of their growing dependency on her.

Winnie's seventeenth birthday had just passed. It was supposed to be the time in a girl's life when she was introduced into "polite society" or so she read in the society column of the newspaper. Her friend Nancy's father was a reading man and let her have old newspapers when he bought them. It was something to do on a lonely winter's night to read them when the wind was howling outside and her parents weren't very good company.

Huh, some polite society she was going to be introduced to stuck up here with her Ma and Pa. Even Ma had her youth and opportunities back in London, England, where she was brought up. She told stories of fine big houses where she had worked as a maid from the age of fourteen, so Winnie knew from her stories about the finer things of life that she was missing.

Her mother, when she was in the mood for reminiscing, described the silver plate, fine linens, carriages, ball gowns, fine food, and handsome gentleman of that world. But Emaline, as a parlour maid, had married her father, a stable boy. Oh, they had been full of dreams and ambitions at one time, she gathered, for a better life in the New World, but the hard life of a pioneer had turned them sour somehow.

Instead of stimulating and challenging them, they had allowed life to defeat them. But Winnie couldn't blame them. "Judge not lest ye be judged," the Good Book said. They had had many hardships and tragedies and who knows if a better man and woman would not have succumbed to discouragement if they had experienced similar trials?

But she could not dwell on this and allow pity to shake her purpose. Out of necessity, she must break away.

As with most things, when a decision is made, Life reaches out and shows the way. And so it was with Winnie. Before long, she heard of a woman in distant Collingwood who was ailing and needed help with her big family. This family lived on the outskirts of Collingwood, about two miles from the dock along Hurontario Street.

It was through Nancy's mother she heard this as Mrs. Lasmithe had a sister in Collingwood. They had gone to visit them at Easter for a treat even though the roads were terrible. They had broken an axle on their wagon and become mired down in mud. Fortunately, Mr. Lasmithe was a cheerful sort and, by Providence, got them fixed up and on their way. Anyway, Nancy's aunt knew of the Lacroixs and had inquired if Nancy might be interested in a position as housekeeper and nursemaid. Nancy declined but said she might know of someone who would be interested.

"Winnie, what do you think?" Nancy said excitedly. "It's your chance to get away." She didn't know why she felt so happy for she didn't want to lose her friend's company.

"Oh, Nancy, it is a good prospect! Aw, but I should wait until the preserves are done and the garden is in."

"That'll be almost fall, Winnie. Don't be foolish! You know what the winters are like hereabouts. Wouldn't you be better off to go now with the good weather ahead of you in case it doesn't work out?" Weather was always an important consideration in any plans country folk made. The dread of being at loose ends, unequipped in the severe local winters was omnipresent.

"Oh, dear me." Winnie's young brow furrowed and she felt overwhelmed all of a sudden. "I don't know if they could manage the summer without me."

But Nancy stood firm, her innate loyalty showing. "And what about the winter, Winnie? They won't manage well no matter what time of the year it is. You know that. My advice to you is to leave and the quicker, the better. They'll have to learn to cope. You told me the more you do around the farm, the more they expect and the less effort your ma makes. Remember?"

"You're right, Nancy." Relieved at the support of her friend, she looked at Nancy fondly. "If I'm going to make a break, I have to do it now, or very soon. I don't want to miss this chance." She hugged Nancy. Suddenly, she felt sure that this was the right decision. With that knowledge came strength.

"Can you get word to them that I will take the position?"

Nancy thought for a moment. "Our Joe is taking a load of wood into town on Friday. He can stop at Mrs. Lacroix's and take her a note. Can you pen a note and I'll put it inside my letter? She can read well, Aunt Renie says. I was to respond by letter if I changed my mind."

"Good then!" Winnie's heart was unexpectedly light. "I have a great mind to write the note now."

"The sooner, the better. By the way, Winnie. She has a funny name. It's pronounced 'Lacroy' but you spell it L-A-C-R-O-I-X. It's Frenchified I think."

"My, that is a strange spelling. Let's go to my room now. I have writing materials there. Ma won't think anything of it for I sometimes go in there to write a letter to my cousin. Let's do it now before I change my mind." But she knew she would not change her mind!

Winnie didn't know how to broach the subject with her parents. Nancy had come over in the buggy with the news this morning that Mrs. Lacroix wanted her to start as soon as she could and if she was able to make it down to Collingwood on her own, she was welcome any time.

Nancy had come in as she was clearing up after lunch. "Winnie, let's go out and take a walk in the sunshine. 'Tis a lovely afternoon."

"Oh, that would be grand, Nancy!" Winnie was glad of the interruption in her day of drudgery.

"I'll help you dry the dishes first."

Emaline walked through to the scullery to see who was talking to her daughter.

"Oh, hallo, Mrs. Conroy. How are you today? I've come to visit Winnie."

"It's Nancy, isn't it? Yes, I'm not so good, very tired. Winnie, have you finished the dishes yet? I was hoping you could do a couple of loaves this afternoon. There's only half a loaf left in the pantry." She smiled charmingly at Nancy. "I don't know what I'd do without my Winnie . . . my health, you know."

"I just want to take a walk in the fields with Nancy, Ma. I'll be back to set the flour rising after a spell. Then I'll make us all a nice cup of tea."

Emaline nodded, relieved she wouldn't have to exert herself this afternoon. The making of bread was such a chore—all that kneading and thumping—and, so often. It was enough to wear a body out. She needed rest, rest. She held her hip, which was stiff from damp and inactivity and walked slowly to the settee where she lay down.

Winnie glanced her way embarrassed. Her mother looked awful and did not appear to have washed herself or combed her hair for a couple of days. Her hair was lank, and she knew it hadn't been washed for weeks. But Winnie refused to argue with her. She was too busy with other things. The least her mother could do was look after herself.

"Is your mother unwell today?" Nancy inquired politely as they left the house.

"No," said Winnie grimly. "I hate to say it, Nancy, but she's lazy. Often, I wonder if she has something wrong inside to make her so lacking in life and energy. But she just sits on the sofa or lays on that daybed and stares into space, like she's in a daze. I think the trouble is in her head."

"She does seem worse than the last time I saw her," Nancy acknowledged. "Winnie," she said fervently, "get away now . . . or you won't be able to. I don't mean to be unkind about her. But I'm afraid if you stay you'll be more and more beholdin' to her and him. Maybe she'll snap out of it if you leave."

"Maybe she will. I think she might. But either way"—Winnie looked directly now at Nancy—"I'm going. It may sound cold, but I've made up my mind."

Nancy looked relieved. "That's good, because I've got word from Mrs. Lacroix. She's happy with what I've told her about you in my letter. She wants you to come as soon as possible. And guess what! She has a pianoforte. And she said if she likes you, she will teach you the pianoforte as part of your wages."

"The pianoforte! Fancy me learning something as high class as that. I'll be a real lady, I will." Winnie's eyes were bright with the news of her acceptance. They both giggled. They passed behind the smokehouse and put their hands on each other's shoulders and jumped up and down with the joy and exuberance of youth.

The next day Winnie baked again and filled the larder with bread for the family. She packed a box with her few bits of clothing and the small amount of money she had saved from times when her father was in a good mood and rewarded her for her hard work with a coin or two from the egg money. She put the box out in the bushes when no one was looking. She had a feeling they would be resistive when she told them of her plans but wasn't in the least prepared for their reaction.

"You're what?" Silas Conroy's eyes bulged wildly. "You've gone behind our backs and planned to leave us? That's the thanks we get for bringing you up and keeping your belly full!"

"I'm sorry, Pa. I didn't mean to sneak around. But I wasn't sure I'd get the position an' so didn't think I would tell you until I knew." It was a slight fib and she bit her lip.

"Who's going to help me with the household things?" Emaline whined. "You're an ungrateful girl."

"There's not that much to do if you stick at it and don't spend all your time on the couch. There are families with a lot more in 'em than ours to do for."

Silas's temper flared up and he got up and slapped Winnie broad across the face.

"Don't speak to your Ma like that ever again," he snarled. Winnie weaved from the blow. She touched her stinging cheek. She'd have a bruised face to take with her to her new job. She was suddenly sick with anger and could hold her tongue no longer.

"I'm not going to stick around here and do most of the work. I'm not like you. I want something better." Her outburst ended in hot tears.

Silas's face turned black with fury. "So you don't think we're good enough, Miss High 'n Mighty."

"We've fed and clothed you all your life. You owe us something," Emaline spat out venomously. She had a look of vindictiveness on her face. Winnie had not seen this side of her before. The slatternly woman seemed to have energized and rose up to the occasion. "You're not going anywhere, Lady Jane, unless we give permission."

"But I've already been accepted, and I don't want to lose this chance."

"The answer is no. You're not going off this property," said Silas. "Your mother needs your help. Now finish clearing up those dishes and get to bed. You have a long day ahead of you tomorrow, my girl, as I'll need your help cleaning out the stables. It's high time they were done, and since you have so much extra energy for dreamin', I might as well put it to good use." He grinned humourlessly showing his bad teeth and chewed on a piece of grass he had brought in from the field in the breast pocket of his overalls.

Smarting and hurt with indignation, Winnie looked at them both clearly for the first time. She saw them now for what they really were— how others saw them; not the victims of fate she had supposed them to be but the authors of their own lives. They didn't really seem to care about her or her future. Her mother left the kitchen, her sallow face flushed dark with anger, her movements surprisingly spry.

New plans formed in Winnie's head. She walked over to the table and started to clean up the mess left from supper, slowly, methodically, her mind ticking, ticking, all the while. Her breath came fast as her heart thudded.

The air was thick and stifling in the house, smelling of anger, unwashed bodies, and stale clothes. She couldn't stand it anymore. It was closing in on her, smothering her. She felt for a moment she would faint but her anger wouldn't let her. Her head felt ready to burst.

After the last dish was put mechanically in its place in the rough cupboard, she took her apron off and poured some hot water into a basin. Her parents had gone up the cramped and creaking stairway to bed and the house was now silent. She carried the basin to her small chamber behind the kitchen and proceeded to have a good wash. She felt sticky from toiling all day and from the heat of her emotions.

She was still thinking, thinking. A new moon was visible through her window. Her room was on the main floor so she could get up first and light the wood stove in the morning winter and summer. Her parents' room was in the small upstairs floor. Presently, she heard her father's snoring and her mother's heavy breathing coming in little strangled gasps intermingling with the snores. Winnie looked out at the new moon again. It was to have been a new life for her. When would she get another chance?

The answer came back to her, maybe never. She looked around her in the dusky room, which was little more than a cubicle. She didn't feel a part of this house anymore. Something in her had already left it. She would shrivel away here if she had to stay.

Instead of reaching for her nightdress, she put her frock back on. She looked around her. There was nothing else here in this dim, tiny room she wanted to take with her except the warm woolen shawl on the bed, which she had knit last winter. She threw it about her shoulders and opened the door, going through to the kitchen.

The house seemed to whisper to her, "Go, go." The old clock ticked softly on the mantle. All of a sudden it chimed and she almost jumped out of her skin. Recovering somewhat, she slipped out the front door of the poorly built frame house and closed it softly behind her. The warm night air hit her with its damp freshness. It was wild and welcoming.

Her heart was still thudding as she went to the bushes where she had left the box. It was a good thing she had prepared for the worst but hadn't thought she'd have to sneak out in the night like this. Winnie lifted the box, which only weighed a few pounds and began to walk down the path that led to Nancy's house. It was about a half mile. She hoped she didn't meet a wolf or bear along the way but didn't worry too much about this as the fate she was escaping was worse than that.

Her hands were getting sore from the binder twine on the box and she was shaking like a leaf when she reached Nancy's lane. Someone was still up as a light was coming from the kitchen. As she trudged toward the house, she heard, "Hey there, who goes?" Nancy's father, Liam, was coming up from the barn with a lantern.

"It's me, Winnie . . ."

"Is all well at home with your folks, Winnie?"

"They're fine but I need some help," she said, her voice breaking suddenly into a quaver.

"Come on in, Winnie." Mr. Lasmithe held the door open lifting the lantern and peering curiously at Winnie and her box. Fancy her trotting through the bush this late at night. Something was surely amiss and he was not surprised after what Nancy told him of that family.

"Come in and we'll make you a good cup of tea."

"A cup of tea?" called Mrs. Lasmithe from her room. "And who's our visitor this night?" She came out, hair wrapped in rags and in her long white night things. Seeing Winnie, she called gaily, "Oh good, another woman. I can come out as I am. Hi, Winnie. It's been a long time since I last saw you. What's up?" But by the look of that welt on the girl's face, she hardly had to ask. At the sound of Winnie's name, Nancy was out like a shot.

"What's happened, Winnie? Tell me! What did they say? What did they do?"

"Whoa, hold yer horses!" Mr. Lasmithe frowned, seeing Winnie's discoloured face. "I can see you two have a secret. Let's be out with it. What's going on?"

With that, Winnie sat down with a sigh on a kitchen chair, fatigued after her hard day's work and night of emotion. Over tea and re-warmed currant scones lovingly served by Mrs. Lasmithe in her curling rags, the story came out. By the time it was all over, it was midnight and they were all yawning.

"Nothing can be done tonight, Winnie. But I'm all for you, after what Nancy has told me and what you've told us tonight. Young people have a right to go their own way. I wouldn't want to keep Nancy or the others here against their will."

Little Andy had crept out into the kitchen unable to sleep and smelling the warm scones. After eating his fill of this unexpected late treat, he curled up in his mother's lap and went to sleep with his thumb in his mouth. The housecat, Whiskers, had also come out to see what all the fuss was about and was treated to a little cream in a saucer from the pitcher on the table.

Mr. Lasmithe got up and stretched. "You can sleep with Nancy tonight, and in the morning, I'll take you into Collingwood. Then I'll go and speak to your father. I'll try to make him see reason. The Lacroixs are a respectable family and you are past fifteen. I don't like to interfere, but since you're Nancy's friend, I'll do this for you. I wanted to go into Collingwood anyway soon. Now off to bed, the lot of you. You too woman. Gee, you look becoming with those rags in your hair." Mrs. Lasmithe rewarded her husband for this last remark with an elflike grin.

CHAPTER 18

When Winnie got to the Lacroix residence, Mrs. Lacroix opened the door eagerly and was relieved to see a pleasant-looking young girl in a gray fustian dress with a face she felt she could like. She so needed help with her brood, and this girl looked like she could fill the bill—a sensible-looking girl who looked capable, friendly, and clean. She was apparently seventeen years of age.

The Lacroix family were from Scotland despite their French name. The Scots and the French had long been allies and intermarriage was not uncommon down through the centuries and the union that had brought the Lacroix name to Scotland was a very old one. This family had been drawn to Collingwood by the blossoming ship-building industry. Mr. Lacroix's father had been foreman at a giant shipyard in Scotland so his son brought with him a wealth of knowledge from his native land.

They had come across the Atlantic on a fast-sailing brig, paying the extra sum to do this rather than endure the weeks of extra sea voyage on the slow moving lumber boats that returned from England with their crowded human cargo. Having a little capital, they were able to purchase land of their choice close to town and erect a pretty frame house in their first year in this area. Mrs. Lacroix was now the mother of four pretty and healthy Canadian children although she herself was not strong since she had contracted the scarlet fever last fall. Fortunately, only herself and her eldest got it and both recovered.

As Winnie was shown through the house, she looked admiringly at the solid staircase. So many people just had the drop-down ones.

"Let me show you your room, my dear, and then you can meet the children."

Winnie took in the freshly applied floral wallpaper as she was led through a sunny parlour and her eyes didn't miss the handsome pianoforte to her left.

"There are three bedchambers upstairs and one down. We will put you in the downstairs one for now although as nursemaid you really should be near the children, but the house isn't large enough to accommodate that."

They stepped into a good-sized room freshly decorated with striped pale pink and rose wallpaper with a trim of full-blown roses trailing with ivy around the top of the walls. The bedstead was carved oak. There looked to be good linen sheets on the bed, which were turned down over an off-white loomed counterpane. There were two windows and from them hung gay chintz curtains with pink and red roses. On the floor by the bed was a cheerful scrappy rug. It was a lovely room all in all. Winnie was almost speechless.

"Do you like it?" Mrs. Lacroix smiled knowingly.

"It's so beautiful!" breathed Winnie. "The most beautiful room I have ever seen." She looked at the pine washstand with a sparkling china ewer and basin.

"We have been fortunate, Winnie. We haven't had to endure a lot of the struggles some people have had coming to this country. We have God and our family back home to thank for that. Not all people have the good start we did," she said kindly. "Not that it was all easy. We've had our challenges and hardships too." Indeed, the ravages of Mrs. Lacroix's recent illness still showed on her wan face.

"It's . . . it's such a lovely home." Winnie couldn't help but compare this ambitious first house with the modest abode from whence she came on the mountain.

"I'm very glad you like it, my dear. Now why don't you refresh yourself from your long journey. I had thought you might arrive this morning. Gertie will bring you some warm water to wash off the dust of the road and you can put your things away." Her eyes fell on the small bundle and then on the girl's face that looked happy but strained and pale.

"Gertrude will also bring you in a cup of tea—real tea mind you, not that concocted stuff—and a slice of bread and butter. Then you can rest for an hour or so. I'd like you to help with supper tonight. Gert will call you at four o'clock to get up. You will meet the children and Mr. Lacroix at supper."

Winnie eased herself down on the comfortable bed after her tray had been taken away by Gertie, who was just a young slip of a girl. She closed her eyes thankfully. Mrs. Lacroix had been so kind. She could have got right to work but the rest was so very welcome. She must have been more tired than she thought for she fell asleep right away and awoke about an hour later. Opening her eyes, she looked at the bright and pretty wallpaper and suddenly remembered where she was. A faint tap on the door was Gertie waking her to help with the meal. She got up refreshed and went to the kitchen. Imagine, having a real kitchen separate from the rest of the house!

Although the house was beautiful, Mrs. Lacroix was really up to her ears in work, Winnie could see, and was not herself accustomed to cooking. She had managed as best she could in the kitchen with some daily help from the young girl of eleven, Gertrude, who was inexperienced herself although quite willing. Winnie did not realize it, but she had overslept the hour by quite a bit. Mrs. Lacroix had not let Gertie awake her for the woman thought the young girl looked like she needed the sleep. Consequently, it was five o'clock when she went to help and the meal was pretty much prepared. Winnie sized up the situation quickly after eating the unappetizing supper that the two had prepared.

At half past nine o'clock, Winnie was in her room for the night and the rest of the house was quiet. She looked at the pretty room by candlelight and could not believe she was here instead of her small dingy room on the mountain. She wondered how Mr. Lasmithe had made out talking to her father. The two would have been in a state when they came down in the morning and there was no fire, no coffee nor porridge made and she was gone.

Winnie sighed. She hadn't wanted it to be like this, but they had given her little choice. But now, she was here in this fine home. And the people liked her. Yes. She could tell they liked her already. And she wasn't going to look back. No, she was going to look ahead to a bright future. Tomorrow she would ask Mrs. Lacroix if she could have some paper and pen a note to her parents explaining that she was sorry she wouldn't be coming home but that she would send them some money from time to time when she was able.

The next day Winnie offered her assistance in the kitchen and was gratified when her efforts were met with much appreciation, especially from Mr. Lacroix.

"What a delicious-looking supper!" he exclaimed when she set the simple meal of beef stew with dumplings in front of him. "Where have they been hiding a talented girl like you?" He tucked his napkin in his collar and took up fork and knife.

"On the mountain, sir." Winnie smiled wryly. She was going to like Mr. Lacroix, she thought.

"Prayers first, dear," Mrs. Lacroix said, smiling.

"What? Oh, yes, of course, my dove." Mr. Lacroix reluctantly took his attention from the feast before him and said a fervent and somewhat speedy grace.

The simple but well-cooked meal was savoured and enjoyed by all. Winnie ate with them and felt a strange sense of happiness and content. She looked about her at the fine linen table cloth on the carved table; at the sparkling dinnerware and fine china that had been lovingly packed and shipped from Scotland. There were even candles on the table in silver candlesticks. All these fine, expensive things and yet they relished her simple stew like it was something marvelous!

She listened to their bright and cheerful conversation on a number of topics and her eyes took in the lace curtains on the window and Mrs. Lacroix's fine dress, which she had put on just to come to dinner. How different this was from home. The children were quiet at the table for this was one thing that Mr. Lacroix demanded although he seemed easygoing with them in other ways.

When dinner was finished, Mrs. Lacroix said, "That was lovely, Winnie. I can see we're going to be very happy with your help in the kitchen. Tomorrow you can begin lessons. Gertie will come in at seven to do the dishes tonight, so you can spend the evening getting acquainted with the children."

The Lacroix household was comprised of Mr. and Mrs. Lacroix and four young children, the daily maid, Gertie, and John Culp who was combination gardener, stable man and odd-jobster. The latter personage was a quiet, unobtrusive Englishman who was used to obedience and totally trustworthy. His quarters were on the main floor behind the kitchen areas.

The upstairs of the house, Winnie soon found, was divided into two main areas, that being the large bedchamber of Mr. and Mrs. Lacroix and separated by a hall, a long room which comprised the children's sleeping quarters. Each child's room was only partially separated by a wall so in the daytime the one open room was converted conveniently to a play and schoolroom area with the help of two benches.

Here, Winnie endeavoured to fulfill the role of school mistress. The children were Ada, six years; Martin, five; Mona, three and a half; and little Lucinda who was only two. The children were too young save the eldest, Ada, to attend school and since it was inconvenient to send just one child, Mrs. Lacroix decided home study would suffice until they were all old enough to attend school together.

She was quite adamant about them receiving an education and herself had tutored the eldest ones, Ada and Martin, when her health and time had allowed. A bit apprehensive about this part of the job,

Winnie soon felt better when she discovered she had a natural teaching ability that belied her mere seven years of schooling.

She was able to impart the rudiments of reading and arithmetic to her pupils in a way that was enjoyable to them. She loved to read them stories and, when a circulating library was established, was able to borrow some good story books as well as Bible stories for their entertainment and learning.

Winnie loved to go into the town of Collingwood with Mrs. Lacroix. Between them, they managed the three children with ease. The youngest was left at home with Gertie. It was such a pleasure to walk the main street in town. The first time she went, Winnie was like a wide-eyed child. There was so much more to see than in Singhampton, which was little more than a village.

A fine main street greeted her with every manner of store. Mrs. Lacroix enjoyed the girl's wonderment and treated her to afternoon tea at the International Hotel, which was on the east side of Hurontario Street near the newspaper office.

"I so enjoy another woman's company," Mrs. Lacroix confided. "It has been such a pleasure having you, Winifred, these last few weeks. Your help with the cooking is a godsend. That roast of beef you cooked on Sunday melted in our mouths. And the children are like little angels now, so attentive to your lessons. It's such a burden off me. You don't know the whole of it." Mrs. Lacroix dabbed at her eyes that filled with sudden tears. "I was never used to such work, I'm afraid. I was not brought up to a life of drudgery such as I have known since I've been in this country."

Winnie was distressed to see her kind employer so distraught and touched her hand.

"Never mind," the woman said, blowing her nose loudly. "I have your help now, and it is such a delightful country. Don't mind me. I'm really very grateful for my life. It has been just . . . just such an adjustment, you see." She hesitated. "But of course you wouldn't know, poor dear. I know you've had great difficulties already in your young life. And you've managed so well."

"You've been so very kind, madam. I'm very happy to be in your employ."

"Well, Winnie"—Mrs. Lacrosse sniffed and smiled, looking quite recovered now—"shall we go now that we've had our tea and look at the other shops? With your help, it isn't a chore to take the children out. They do so enjoy an outing. We'll stop at the confectioner's and then we'll look at dress goods! I think it's high time you had a new dress."

"But, missus, I—"

"Never mind. This will be my treat apart from your wages. We'll look at yard goods at Lindsay's. He always has a good selection. Mind you, Freenan's Mercantile at Duntroon is also a must to see but that's another journey."

By four o'clock, Winnie was satiated with shopping. They'd been to the butcher shop, the shoe shop, and to Mr. Telfer's bakery as well. Among other things she carried her own bag, which contained the makings of a new worsted frock and some hair ribbon. Mrs. Lacroix had also insisted on a new bonnet for Winnie. John was waiting for them at the livery stable. He enjoyed these shopping trips for it was a chance for him to come to town and socialize with the local men in the saloons and buy some whiskey and tobacco to take home.

The next few evenings were spent by the fire stitching the new dress as the evenings were getting cool. October was upon them, and Winnie sighed as she looked at her surroundings. She felt like a part of this family. Mr. Lacroix sat in his fine armchair smoking a pipe. The hour was eight o'clock and the fine Edinborough clock chimed on the mantle. She looked down at the red turkey carpet that gave the parlour such warmth and character. Gertie came into the room with a silver tray bearing Mr. Lacroix's evening glass of port. It was the young maid's last duty of the day, and she would now be on her way.

The children were cosy in bed upstairs after their bedtime story their new nursemaid had read them. Winnie returned to the parlour and sat down in front of the fire once more to take up her sewing. After a few minutes, the penetrating heat of the cheerful blaze had a soporific effect on her and her mind began to wander from her stitching.

She visualized herself walking downtown in her new dress. She imagined gathering its luxuriant folds and going to step from the buggy. A handsome, swarthy gent in a plug hat and soft kid gloves jumped to offer his hand saying graciously, "A lady should not descend on her own. Pray, allow me." He kissed her outstretched hand and—

"Winnie, don't tire your eyes in the firelight! There's plenty of coal-oil in the house. Light the lamp and save your eyes." Her mistress's cheery voice broke through her reverie.

"Yes, ma'am, thank you."

The thought struck Winnie now how ironic it was that she was treated better as a servant in this house than she had been as a daughter in her parent's home.

CHAPTER 19

Christmas brought much festivity to the Lacroix household. Garlands of hemlock and spruce were draped in the parlour and around doors. A fine fat goose was ready for the pot and the snow was early this year, making sleighs and cutters a necessity for travel. There was much hilarity in the household as neighbours dropped by and were offered a glass of Mr. Lacroix's favourite port. Mrs. Lacroix's health had improved dramatically, and she attributed it to the easing of her household burdens.

Winnie had become indispensable to her, and the girl revelled in her new importance. She didn't forget her sense of humour, however, and was always ready with a kind word of encouragement to Gertie who was coming to adore the older girl.

Mrs. Lacroix continually bragged about Winnie's culinary expertise and skills of home management to her lady visitors. As a result, Mrs. Lacroix was envied by every matron of comfortable means in Collingwood who made her acquaintance, and there weren't so very many of these in 1873.

Over the next two years, it got to the point where they were vying as to who could lure Winnie away from the lady's employ to grace her own household. The young girl's now impeccable appearance and manners were duly noted. Mrs. Lacroix had groomed her well and taught her the art of proper service. It was rumoured that Mrs. Lacroix also taught her, with her own hand, the pianoforte. This latter was true in part.

Winnie was hardly expert at the instrument but, during the dark and dreary days of winter for two years running, had been given instruction almost every evening. Mrs. Lacroix's hope was that the girl could play well enough to cheer her and perhaps they could arrange a musicale such as she was used to in her old home across the ocean.

Winnie was a very eager pupil, and Mrs. Lacroix considered, after a time, because of the girl's value, that she would add the music lessons as a sort of rise in her salary. Cash was very hard to come by in those years and goods very expensive.

"You have a very good ear, my dear, and you are picking it up satisfactorily. Oh, how I long to see a concert such as they used to have at home. One day I shall go to Toronto to see one. I do crave for some culture and refined music."

Winnie sat and nodded. She drank in every word of her mistress. She studied the way the lady talked and walked, the way she dressed. Winnie's appearance had changed a great deal already. Her simple homespun dress had been replaced with a dignified black everyday dress. Her hair was sedately coiled at the back of her head. Her carriage was more erect and confident. Her pert nose remained the same as was her readiness to smile.

Winnie had sent home money several times but had never been back to visit. The idea of going back to that place filled her with dread. She felt guilty about it but still had nightmares about being in the shabby house. She knew she may have to go someday but couldn't bear the thought of it just now. Everything in her life was so good. This was her home now, her life.

One day, Gertie came in with a note on the tea tray for her mistress who opened it eagerly and then exclaimed.

"Winnie, I have exciting news! We are invited to a soiree."

"How nice for you, madam," replied Winnie who hardly flickered an eyelid as she expertly poured out the tea.

"I said we, Winnie." She looked up from the invitation with bright eyes. "Mr. Lacroix, myself, and you, my dear."

"Me, madam?" Winnie asked incredulously.

Mrs. Lacroix laughed. "Yes, you indeed. Why, it will be wonderful for you. And I have so longed for some genteel company. A new family have come to town and built a stately home. Mr. Lacroix has been following the construction with great interest. It's on Third Street."

"I heard Mrs. Glover say that street would be full of big homes one day," offered Winnie.

"Right you are, my dear. That is the rumour. I have been so eager to make their acquaintance. Business people of good background from Lower Canada."

"Do you think I should go, madam?"

"Yes I do, Winnie." She looked at the girl searchingly. "Somehow I feel it will be good for you. You are meant for better things I think."

"But what would I wear?" Winnie's voice held self-doubt.

"I should think a new dress would be in order. Something expensive yet understated." She looked again at the invitation and let out a little cry. "But there isn't time!"

"My black taffeta will suffice."

Mrs. Lacroix glanced up from the invitation and her eyes quickly ran over Winnie's young frame. "No, let me think . . . I know! I have just the thing. It is in the trunk. A little tuck here and there and it will be perfect." She rushed to her bedchamber and Winnie stood up half-expectantly. The older woman came back presently with a lovely beige crepe tea gown with glitters here and there about the bodice. A most unusual shade it was for there was a definite hint of salmon in the colour.

Winnie gasped. "I couldn't possibly . . . it's too beautiful."

"Nonsense. It no longer fits me and has been in that trunk for years. It will be perfect with your muted colouring."

"You mean to say mousy colouring," Winnie half-joked, smiling good-naturedly.

"No, Winnie, you could be quite fetching with the right clothes. Oh, let's try it on you. I feel like a young girl again." She giggled.

Winnie tried on the elegant gown, touching the delicate fabric with care and reverence lest it fall apart on her. She didn't have Mrs. Lacroix's statuesque form and the dress sagged disappointingly on her more petite frame.

"Hmmmm . . . Let me see," Mrs. Lacroix commented. Hastily, with unexpected skill, she pinned the shoulder and then the waist and fashioned the extra fabric into a bustle effect at the back. "Come, look, my dear."

Winnie stepped up to the glass and could not believe her eyes. That elegant creature standing before her couldn't be herself. But yes, it was! "How did you do that, Mrs. Lacroix?"

"I never told you, did I? My mother was a milliner, and I helped her as a girl. I was lucky and married a prosperous businessman who has catered to my every wish. Yes, I wasn't always comfortably off, Winnie. I know what poverty is although as a child I never knew want. I only saw the worry it caused my mother."

"You've made it look so elegant." Winnie couldn't stop staring at herself in the mirror.

"It is you who make it elegant, Winnie." Mrs. Lacroix's eyes went enigmatic. "You have something. A way about you. I believe you were meant to wear gowns like this. I don't know why I say this. I shouldn't be saying this to my servant. You could go a long way. It's an intuition I have."

Winnie was deeply touched and looked at her mistress with glistening eyes. "That is the kindest thing anyone has ever said to me."

Mrs. Lacroix looked embarrassed. "Well, enough of this female prattle. Why don't you get out of the gown, and we will pin it properly. There are only two weeks before the soiree and there is much to do!"

The night of the soiree was one of great excitement at the Lacroix home. Mrs. Lacroix had chosen a puce gown, very elegant, from her trunk. "Years out of fashion," she said, "but people don't worry about such things in this country of less shallow values. Fashion is a great waster of funds when it changes every year, disallowing the wearing of perfectly good finery."

"Now the matter of coiffure," Mrs. Lacroix said as she made her own toilette. "For you, a simple chignon will be the most effective way to dress your hair. Your face and form are small and the dress has ornament enough. A chignon will most become you tonight."

Thank goodness the wind had dried the muddy April roads enough to travel, thought Winnie. Fancy having a soiree at such a time of year. She donned her simple but well-cut brown wool cape and was glad tonight for having made this extravagant purchase last year. Mr. Lacroix had begged off going to the soiree due to a feverish cold and congestion on the lungs so he and Gertie stayed with the children. Winnie drove the covered buggy the two miles north to Third Street.

When they arrived, at eight o'clock p.m., a number of other conveyances were either parked or on their way in or out of the circular drive. A couple of stable boys were giving assistance. Lights glowed from all windows and made the large house look very festive and impressive. Winnie had never seen so fine a house. It was made of brick with so many windows she could scarcely count them. There was an impressive balcony on the second floor and the white portico around the massive front door gleamed in the moonlight.

There were two gentlemen standing casually at the front door in swallow tailed coats and tall, silk hats; apparently there to assist ladies down from their buggies and to direct traffic. One man appeared to be a servant, from his manner, a butler perhaps or valet. The other appeared to be the host.

Winnie was handed down from the conveyance to a fine cobbled driveway. Before she knew it, she was whisked inside the small mansion and stood trying not to gape at the luxury that surrounded her. Her hat and cloak were gracefully stripped from her, and she gripped her reticule as a sea of smiling faces seemed to descend upon her. Some of them she knew for they had been visitors to the Lacroix residence but barely recognized them in their finery.

"Mrs. Lacroix and her protégé, Miss Winifred," announced the butler after examining their invitation.

They were escorted to an adjoining drawing room, which was large and boasted a fine black marble fireplace and, wonder of wonders, a chandelier, the like of which Winnie had never seen. Her mother had described such things to her as a child from her experiences in the big houses in England. The chandelier shone like a myriad of stars with its candles illuminating the night.

At the same time, Winnie's eyes fell on an impressive oaken staircase circling gracefully to the second floor. Plush red carpet ran up the length of the stairs from the foyer. The banisters were of carved and scrolled oak and polished until they gleamed with rich brown lights. All this opulence was almost too much for Winnie. She didn't notice that people in the room were looking at her.

"You look lovely, my dear, in that splendid dress." It was Mrs. Glover, their frequent teatime guest, fanning herself rapidly. "That colour and style become you, Winnie."

"That's very kind of you, Mrs. Glover." Winnie blushed. "It is such an honour to be invited here tonight."

All of a sudden, her thoughts were stolen away from the neighbourhood woman as a young man with black hair and a golden skin crossed the room. He was exotically handsome with a sensual mouth. He looked quite confidently dashing, and he spoke easily to a woman in a green silk gown. Something made him turn around so that she saw him face on from across the lofty room. The young man stopped talking and stared back at her for a moment then resumed his conversation.

Party food was spread on the table and a lunch was composed of all sorts of delicacies. Winnie could hardly take her eyes off the dark-haired man, however, but with some self-discipline redirected her attentions after a little while.

"He's Sam Woodrow, a young entrepreneur from Halifax. Quite available but a flirt with the ladies as you can see." Mrs. Lacroix smilingly recounted as she caught Winnie's evident interest.

"Oh, is he? He certainly is good-looking," Winnie responded with slight embarrassment thinking sardonically that at least he wasn't a farmer. He must be a professional man who had had many exciting experiences and been to different places, even cities.

Mrs. Lacroix was flagging down their hostess and excitedly talking to the woman she had only met once before but liked.

"What a lovely get-together! Are you too excited about your new home? Everything is exquisite. I do so envy you. Adelaide Dudsworth, this is Winifred. She has been a great help to me."

"So I have heard." Mrs. Dudsworth looked at Winnie kindly and with interest. "Your skills are the talk of the ladies in town, my dear. Welcome to my home. I do hope you both have met everyone."

"Yes, we're just in the midst of doing that."

The elegantly attired lady of the house smiled easily at the two women and offered graciously, "Let me help you. Oh, there comes Gordon Welch. He owns that enormous new house down the street. Quite a millionaire I think. Made a fortune on the stock market. Old and new money they say. Keeps a large household staff."

She pointed out an aging but distinguished man of a slim, compact build with an air of vitality and prosperity. He had sharp, black eyes and silver-greying hair and sipped a brandy pensively as he studied the people around him in the room. His eyes fell on Winnie, and they lingered there momentarily. There was a bit of a commotion outside and the butler announced a new guest.

"Miss Eulalie Peterson."

All eyes turned to the door as a raven-haired young woman of exquisite beauty and charm entered the hall. From her face, her bosom, her apparel, to her graceful deportment, she was completely captivating. Her dimpled face smiled at those about her and they were one and all enchanted.

"Who is that beautiful girl?" asked Winnie feeling drab and mousy in the shadow of such splendour.

"That is Eulalie Peterson, Winnie. Talk of the town since she arrived here with her uncle. He's brought her up since a wee lass when her parents both died of the fever when they came across on an immigrant ship from Ireland. She has lived with her Uncle, Gordon Welch, in Cornwall and then Chicago when his business concerns took him there," Mrs. Dudsworth was offering this background to Winnie who listened with great interest. "They say she has had a number of suitors since she came to town but refused them all. With her beauty and charm, she could well become the belle of the district."

Certainly, Eulalie's dress was of the latest fashion for anyone who could recognize it. Her hair was coiffed in the little ringlets drawn forward over each ear. The gentlemen all commenced to mill about her, much to the chagrin of the ladies and her lively, interesting conversation could be heard like the tinkling of bells in the background sounds of the soiree. The likes of Eulalie Peterson with her charm and sophistication had never been seen in Collingwood. And this was one of the first "society" parties to be held in the town.

Finally, polite society was taking hold in this wilderness settlement. There would be many more affairs like this as the town grew and prospered. And Third Street with its magnificent giant elms was an appropriate setting for the building of a number of stately homes celebrating the hoped for bottomless prosperity of this frontier town. It would be the jewel in the crown of the community, an area where culture could flower.

Later, when most of the guests had departed, Mrs. Lacroix and Winnie lingered on savouring each precious moment.

"I must try just one more morsel of that gorgeous salmon mousse. How is your fruit cup, dear? What a spread! One wouldn't think one was in the middle of the wilderness, would one?"

Winnie hadn't said too much this evening. "Mrs. Lacroix, I feel so inadequate when I talk to people. Would you teach me the art of interesting conversation?"

Mrs. Lacroix looked at her with that analytical look of hers. "You've been watching Eulalie at her antics. Don't try to be like her, Winnie. Much of what she says is drivel. I got close enough to hear her. What you want to be is less interesting and more ladylike. You're already halfway there. Just be yourself, not an affected featherbrain like her and you'll capture the interest of men."

The much-touted Eulalie had retired with a couple of other guests, namely her uncle, Gordon Welch, and not surprisingly the handsome dark Sam Woodrow, to the upstairs library. Their host, Mr. Dudsworth, approached the two women and bowed deferentially. "Won't you join us upstairs for a nightcap? It's more intimate there now that the crowds have dispersed themselves." He smiled charmingly and offered each of them one of his arms, and they climbed together the elegant staircase.

Winnie couldn't believe she was being escorted by this distinguished older gentleman up a rich staircase lined on one side with ancestral portraits. "My father and mother, and over there is my grandmother, Lady Standleigh." Mr. Dudsworth pointed to a portrait of a very young girl of about seventeen in a crimson velvet gown. At the top of the landing were more pictures, this time of pastoral and hunting scenes. There was also a dainty fireplace and a few occasional chairs and of all things, a large pianoforte.

"What a lovely spot!" Winnie exclaimed admiring the cosy alcove with the cheerful fire.

"Do you play, my dear?"

"Oh, just a little, sir. Mrs. Lacroix has been kind enough—"

"Ah, well, then you must play for us a tune," Mr. Dudsworth insisted.

Winnie sat at the piano and played one of the ballads she had practiced last winter and felt she knew passably well, "Greensleeves." As the last note faded, she heard, "Bravo, Miss Winifred, bravo." It was Sam Woodrow, the handsomely dark young man.

"Yes, that was fine, fine. You have a musical talent I can see," said Mr. Dudsworth. "We should have had you play for our guests earlier. But of course that is presumptuous of me for you are also our guest."

"I . . . I would have been pleased to."

"In that case, we must have you again when we plan a musicale."

"A musical evening, how exciting!" Mrs. Lacroix fairly glowed with anticipation and clasped her hands.

"Do let's go to the library for a sherry." Mr. Dudsworth encouraged.

A glass of sherry was put into Winnie's hand, and she looked at its amber richness in the crystal glass. She had never consumed spirits before although she knew her mother had tippled and there was usually some gin on the cupboard shelf at home. She took a sip of the strong wine and savoured the sweet, nutty flavour. Pleased with it, she downed her drink in short order. She felt warmth all over and was miraculously relaxed. The amber-skinned Mr. Woodrow looked over at her with amusement. She contemplated the fact he had bothered to discover her name. A minute or two later, she wished she hadn't drunk the strong wine so quickly as she was feeling quite giddy.

The lovely Eulalie lounged like a sleek black cat in an overstuffed armchair looking all the world like she was exceedingly pleased with herself. Her uncle came over to Mrs. Lacroix and asked if he might be introduced to Winnie. Apparently, Gordon Welch had had the pleasure of Mrs. Lacroix's acquaintance earlier while Winnie was chatting with someone else.

"I'm charmed to meet you, young lady," he said with a genteel smile. "I hear you are a lady of culinary accomplishment as well as a budding musician."

Winnie coloured as she looked up at the quietly imposing man.

"I'm afraid my cooking is only rudimentary. My mistress is overly kind and has helped me to learn a little on the pianoforte."

"Your candid answer is refreshing. But I'm sure you are modest about your capabilities." His eyes travelled over her neat form in the elegant gown, and he took in the classic simplicity of her coiffure. "Have you met my niece? She is about your age, I believe."

"No, I have not had that pleasure."

With that admission, he took her arm and led her to the chair, which contained Eulalie who now sat up with the bearing of an Egyptian queen.

"My niece, Eulalie. This is Winifred. I'm sorry but I don't know your surname."

"Conroy," responded Winnie as she looked into the limpid eyes of Eulalie and she thought, *This girl has never done a tap of work in her life I'll wager*. And then Winnie felt her confidence come back to her. She was no longer overawed. Her work ethic gave her self-respect. She could hold her head high. She had nothing to be ashamed of, lowborn or not. *Mind you*, Winnie thought, *some are meant to be held up high in life. They're not born to work and struggle.*

"Charmed, I'm sure." Eulalie smiled beatifically and then looked a little bored. "You're Mrs. Lacroix's maid?"

"Eulalie! Mind your manners."

"Not at all, Mr. Welch," retorted Winnie speedily. "She's perfectly correct. I am paid help and consider myself lucky to be in Mrs. Lacroix's employ. She has assisted me a great deal. You see, I'm from a poor family."

"Ah, that charming honesty again." Gordon Welch turned to his niece. "Eulalie, you must learn that there is very little class distinction in Collingwood society. People work shoulder to shoulder with all sorts, from gentle folk to labourers, to farmers. They forget their differences and this is as it should be. I am from a poor background myself, Miss Winifred, but I worked hard, was lucky, and helped by a great many people."

"I'm sorry, Uncle. I didn't mean to insult Miss Winifred. I was just surprised to see a maid at a society affair."

"I believe that Miss Winifred is somewhat more than a maid to Mrs. Lacroix, Eulalie."

"Please. I'm not at all offended. I just feel so happy to be invited to an affair like this and to be able to meet people of society. It's something that I have always dreamed of."

"Ah, we have an ambitious girl here," Eulalie scrutinized Winnie.

"Miss Winifred, would you care to come and look at Mr. Dudsworth's library?" Gordon Welch gave Eulalie a disapproving look and took Winnie's arm leading her to the impressive cherrywood shelving that held a great number of beautifully bound volumes. "You must not pay my niece any attention. I have spoiled her, I fear. But she is a kind girl at heart and suffered an early loss of both parents."

"Please don't apologize. I understand. She's perfectly within her right to question my presence here among these people of high society."

The young Sam Woodrow was standing at the sideline observing the social interaction of Winnie, Eulalie, and Mr. Welch with amusement. He refilled his brandy glass from a nearby decanter on an exquisitely carved small table and then joined Eulalie in casual conversation. Winnie could see them within her vision as she talked to the older man. She was aware of thinking that they must be very well acquainted. Mrs. Lacroix looked disapprovingly at Woodrow from her perch on the sofa and said to herself, "I wouldn't trust that young scallywag. An adventurer if I've ever seen one."

On the other hand, Winnie was finding Mr. Welch quite charming and interesting to talk to. She found herself at ease with the older man. This surprised her. The hour was getting late, and it was about two o'clock a.m. when she and Mrs. Lacroix left the Dudsworth residence.

"Won't Mr. Lacroix be very worried about you?" Winnie said anxiously.

"Oh, no. He'll be fast asleep. These society affairs sometimes go until almost dawn. There are so many dangers in this new country he's forgotten to worry about such things. In Scotland, he wouldn't dream of letting me go unescorted this time of night. It's different here. This is a rural area and people help one another a lot. They depend on one another. And class distinctions are less. The classes mix quite happily here without even thinking of it." She looked at Winnie. "There's something uplifting about that."

CHAPTER 20

Aweek later, a note came to the Lacroix residence addressed to Winnie. Winnie was at that time helping Gertie with the baking of pies. It was a Friday. She wiped her floury hands on her apron and went to her room to read the note. Who could it be from? Not Nancy surely with that expensive stationery. She opened the letter that was sealed with wax and it read:

> *Dear Miss Winifred:*
>
> *I would like the pleasure of your company to take afternoon tea with us on Tuesday, April 17, if it is possible. There is a matter of some importance concerning your future I would like to discuss with you at that time. My niece, Eulalie, will join us for tea. I trust that your employer will allow you to attend. Feel free to show her this note. I send Mrs. Lacroix my kindest regards.*
>
> *I will send a driver to pick you up at two o'clock p.m. If you are unable to attend, you may tell him at the time.*
>
>
>
> *Yours sincerely,*
>
> *Gordon Welch*
>
>

Winnie recalled with pleasure the older gentleman who was so kind to her at the Dudsworth gala. She felt both excited and curious. It sounded like she might be offered a position of some sort. She thought guiltily of Mrs. Lacroix. How bold it was to invite her help directly leaving out the mistress of the house. Mrs. Lacroix would certainly be offended if she showed her the invitation. But it would be almost impossible to keep it a secret with the driver pulling up to fetch her. Winnie made up her mind to show her mistress the invitation after supper when they had put the little ones to bed.

When the time did come that she showed it to Mrs. Lacroix, she had expected her to be somewhat offended but the lady was absolutely livid.

"How dare he approach my servant directly about work! Why, it's obvious that he's planning to steal you away from right under my nose. So that's the way the Americans operate when they come here. If he had approached me directly at least he would have been more honourable."

Winnie was going to say he wasn't American but had only resided in that country for a time, but there was no use in speaking back to her mistress who would have been even angrier. Winnie was very disappointed. She would have to send the driver away when he came next Tuesday.

"Winnie, I hope you weren't intending to accept this invitation." Mrs. Lacroix looked at her with suspicion.

Winnie struggled to choose her words carefully. "I was curious to know what he had in mind."

"I see," said the lady rather coldly. "So you're not so very happy to stay here with us."

The flustered young girl sought to be honest yet diplomatic.

"I . . . I have been very happy here, madam."

Mrs. Lacroix was somewhat mollified but quite aware the girl had skilfully evaded answering the real question.

"Well, we'll speak no more of this just now. I'm really quite fatigued ce soir. Would you fill my ewer with hot water, Winnie? I believe I shall retire early. And please prepare a hot toddy for Mr. Lacroix. His chest is still quite congested."

"Yes, right away, madam." Winnie felt both dismayed and hurt at the woman's accusative tone. It was so unlike her. But the young domestic realized that she had forgotten for a while that she was her mistress's hireling, not a friend and that this was a mistake in itself. The lady was a beneficent mistress but one who demanded loyalty and respect. For all her talk of equality among the classes, she was still conscious of her own position and background.

Mrs. Lacroix came around and the issue seemed forgotten within a couple of days. Winnie decided to forget the invitation and be grateful for her present stability. She had never been so well fed and clothed. She told herself she should be grateful for what she had accomplished. But Winnie was a girl of ambition and questions came to plague her from time to time like "Why miss this exciting opportunity?" and "Haven't I earned my reputation as efficient household help by a lot of hard work?" and "Do I want to remain in this household forever, a servant in someone else's home?"

She tried to push these thoughts aside and get on with her work, but they would pop through at the oddest times—like when she was serving dinner to the family or when she was teaching a lesson in reading to Ada and Martin.

The weekend passed with dismal weather. Everyone seemed to be in the doldrums and Mr. Lacroix's cold appeared worse, which was not surprising with the continual grey, drizzling downpour. The usually cheerful and uplifting home seemed uncharacteristically sad. Winnie felt an odd sensation as if a bubble was building around her and about to burst.

Then it happened. A messenger arrived with a note for Mrs. Lacroix. Her best friend, Agnes in Stayner, was abed and exhausted after the birth of her fifth child. Could she possibly come and stay a day or two with her? Of course, Mrs. Lacroix could not refuse such a request. She left her sick husband and children in the care of her servants. Gertie would live in for the two days instead of working the usual ten hours per day.

Mrs. Lacroix left in the afternoon for the long trip to Stayner. It would take her a good two hours but her friend's husband would meet her half way. The hired man, John Culp, would drive her and return when she reached and met her other driver at the halfway point.

After she was gone, Mr. Lacroix refused to stay in his room, preferring to convalesce in the parlour on the couch in front of the big cheerful fireplace. Winnie and Gertie had to tiptoe about the house and shush the children, which was no easy task. It being a Monday, the arduous task of laundry was tackled and finally completed.

The next day was lighter work. There was only the ironing. Gertie put the sad irons on the stove to heat. Winnie gave a brief morning school lesson to the children from the ABC and spelling book. That finished, she occupied them with colouring materials and cutouts. She came downstairs to see how Mr. Lacroix was faring. He had finished his breakfast. The porridge and tea was gone and so she took that for a good sign.

"Feeling better today, sir?"

"Oh, much, my dear." His cheeks looked rosy and he looked a little sleepy. "Think I'll have a little snooze. I suppose it's bloody inconvenient for you having a big lump like me in your way in the parlour."

"Not at all, sir." She flushed at her fib but smiled to herself at the same time at his curse word. He wouldn't have dared in his wife's presence. She saw him eye his port decanter fondly.

"We will simply dust around you, sir."

"Ha, ha! That's a clever girl. What's for lunch, Winnie?" He always liked his food.

"Gert will make you a cheese soufflé."

"Oh, splendid. She's become quite a little cook since you've been with us. Have to give you some credit. Don't mind me, just carry on." He was already dozing off, so Winnie didn't bother to tell him the cheese soufflé was one of madam's recipes. She had never made anything so fancy at home on the mountain. The girl tenderly pulled the crocheted coverlet up over his shoulders. She had made it for him as a gift last Christmas and he always used it. Winnie had become quite fond of Mr. Lacroix.

She went to the kitchen and said, "I'll take over now, Gertie. Why don't you take a break and go upstairs to mind the little ones?"

"Oh, do you mind"? Gertie loved the younger children and would sit in the rocking chair and just watch them play with their blocks and dollies on the braid rug in their room.

"Run along. I'll finish this ironing and put the things out for lunch. He wants a cheese soufflé. I'll get the cookery book out and measure the ingredients for you."

"That'll be fine, Winnie. Oh, I hope someday I have some little 'uns like those two. They're so bonnie. I just love 'em."

"You'll make a wonderful mother, Gertie, and wife too someday."

The young girl blushed. "Do you really think so, Winnie?"

Winnie smiled. She hoped Gertie would find a nice man and have an easier life than her mother who had ten children other than Gert and a man with a penchant for whiskey. She knew without that young girl's wages, the family would be short of food. But Gertie never complained about her lot. She was always cheerful and willing to work. Winnie thought, *I wish I was as nice as that young girl. I left my parents and them struggling. But I couldn't go down with them. If I were like Gert, I would have stayed there and cheerfully catered to them for years.* This candid look at herself made her pensive.

I know I'm not a bad person, she thought, *but I'm not as good as Gertie. I have wants and dreams that need to be fulfilled and I'm willing to pay the price, whatever it may be.*

The grandfather clock struck eleven as Winnie dusted its rich mahogany cabinet. She continued her domestic chores with rigour. By half past twelve the morning chores were done and the house was in apple-pie order so she and Gertie had their midday meal. Mr. Lacroix had lunched and drifted back to sleep.

My, but he was sleeping a lot, Winnie thought briefly. Gertie was looking a little tired as well so Winnie suggested she have a nap with the children. Unaccustomed to a rest at midday, the grateful girl said, "Oh, Winnie, a little snooze would be heavenly. I usually do that on Sunday when I'm at home."

Winnie sat down to do some needlework and was surprised to find she also dozed off. It must have been the rainy day that made them all so drowsy.

Gertie awoke her at half past one o'clock. "A gentleman is here to escort you to tea!" Gertie looked surprised and questioning. "He's in the kitchen out of the weather."

"Oh . . . oh dear! I had forgotten," Winnie said without offering an explanation. "Will you make him a cup of tea, Gert, and tell him I'll see him shortly."

The girl left the room and Winnie went to get up, her mind racing. She would have to write a note of apology to send back with him. She got to the dressing table in her room, which doubled as a writing desk and started to write with pen and ink. Then she suddenly put the pen down and looked at herself in the glass. Hardly missing a beat, Winnie put the pen and ink away. She took off her work dress and reached for her new blue wool frock and put it on. She combed out her hair and redressed it in a neat chignon at the nape of her neck then grabbed her cape and umbrella. She was going to go to the tea! Mrs. Lacroix need never know.

Winnie went through to the kitchen where the driver, a small older man with a brown cap and the inevitable whiskers, was sipping tea and eating a hot scone. "Good day, sir. I'm sorry to have kept you waiting. Take your time with your tea."

"I'm finished, ma'am. Very kind o' you." He stood up and brushed crumbs from his vest jacket and smiled a bashful smile.

Winnie turned to the gawking young girl beside him and said, "I'm going out for a while. I will be back in two or three hours. Please keep an eye on everything for me. Mr. Lacroix will want his tea at four o'clock and so will the children." The Lacroixs still held to the British late dinner hour for the evening meal most nights. "I'll be back to help you prepare supper."

Gertie looked incredulous, but Winnie gave no further explanation. The older man helped her into a fine buggy with a fringed hood and plush seats. Then they were off.

I can't believe that I did that, thought Winnie who had acted more from reflex than from brains. Winnie felt she had taken a significant step that might change the course of her life. How very true this was she would learn very soon. What a blessing it is to us that we are not able to see into our own future; that a veil of mists is before us. Otherwise, we might never dare to take a step away from the secure well-known path of our lives seeing the frightening events that lay before us. If Winnie had known what would ensue from this impulsive behaviour of hers, she would have cowed in dread and thanked her lucky stars for the modest security now present in her life.

The handsome surrey finally pulled up to the enormous Italianate house on Third Street in Collingwood to which she had been invited. Winnie gazed up at the massive exterior of the red brick mansion with buff-brick quoining, which boasted hip rooves, numerous gables, and ornamental chimneys.

The house, which the driver proudly informed her was named Trelawney, sat on what must have been five town lots and appeared to be two and a half stories high. Virginia creeper already graced its facade giving the house an air of mystery and age although it was recently constructed. To say that Winnie was overawed would be an understatement. When she saw this castle of a house, she knew it was not for her to stay indefinitely at the Lacroix's.

With anticipation of talking to the charming Mr. Welch once more and of hearing the hoped for offer of employment, she descended from the buggy in the rain onto the circular drive with the driver's assistance and entered the fine mansion. A housemaid with a white frilled cap and apron over a dignified black poplin dress answered the door. The maid took her umbrella and cape to dry them out in the warm kitchen.

Winnie thanked her escort, whose name was Edward, and looked around her with an almost proprietorial glance. The other home where the soiree had been held belonging to the Dudsworths could not hold a candle to this remarkable place. It was twice as big at least and the furnishings larger and heavier with ornate carving.

"Tea will be served in the morning room. They're waiting for you, ma'am." The maid opened one of the large double doors leading to the morning room, and there Winnie was surprised to see the young and handsome Mr. Sam Woodrow and Mr. Welch's niece, Eulalie, awaiting her.

"Miss Winifred, what a pleasure to see you again," said Sam Woodrow who arose and looked deep into her eyes before he bent over her hand which he gently kissed. The sensation left her tingling and a spontaneous thought came to her mind. My daydream has come true. She thought of her vision of that night by the fireplace of the gloved gentleman with a tall silk hat handing her out of a conveyance onto the main street—a striking similarity, how odd! She was beginning to feel that the world was her oyster. Things were working out for her in an oh-so-perfect way.

"Have a seat, Miss Winifred." Eulalie lazily gestured to an overstuffed chair covered with heirloom petit point.

"Where, I pray, is Mr. Welch? I am looking forward to seeing him again." Winnie boldly looked about the elegant room for the man she had come to see.

"Oh, I'm afraid he wasn't able to make it." Eulalie smiled and her look seemed one of self-satisfaction. "He was called out of town on business. My uncle left this morning bound for Chicago on the steamer, *Silver Spray*."

"I see." Winnie's voice held disappointment, and she tried hard not to let it show in her face. "When will he be back?"

"It's very hard to tell. He received news by messenger yesterday that caused him to have some concern about his business investments in Chicago. He decided to leave right away to investigate the rumour." Eulalie paused to pour tea from a beautiful silver tea pot and now her facial expression was unreadable. She handed Winnie a cup. There were little cubes of snowy sugar in a bowl and wedges of lemon in a small hand-painted dish.

"Lemon! Wherever did you get such a thing," Winnie exclaimed, quickly struggling to maintain her poise, at the same time trying to gather her thoughts at this new development. She mustn't let her discomfort be too obvious.

"When one has money, one can obtain anything one's heart desires. Actually, they are readily obtainable in Toronto. Uncle simply ordered some up on the train" was the response from Eulalie, which drew a quiet sigh of discouragement from Winnie.

Tea was fairly uneventful as Eulalie talked about the fancy dress balls and masquerades she had attended in Chicago and her trip to Europe three years ago with her Uncle where she had participated in a London season, attended literary salons and really been exposed to fashion and polite society. Apparently, she had been the debutante of the season and had had several marriage proposals, one from the son of a duke. Her braggadocio was becoming tedious to Winnie who hoped to end it by inquiring, "Why did you not marry the duke's son?"

Eulalie looked at her incredulously and said, "And break my dear uncle's heart? I am his only family and he would want me to marry a Canadian or at least have the commitment from my husband that we would live near him in Canada."

The handsome Mr. Woodrow said little but watched Eulalie with amusement and indulgence while interjecting the occasional enigmatic glance at herself. Winnie suddenly had the uncomfortable feeling that there was much more between them than friendship. She looked up at the mantle clock on the hand carved oak fireplace. The hand was at half past four. She had better get back. She didn't like to leave Gert alone with the children and the ailing Mr. Lacroix for too long. She looked at the remnants of the tea—cucumber sandwiches and cake— and remembered she had promised to help Gertie with supper.

"I really had better be going." She made as if to rise. "I didn't realize the hour was so late."

"Yes, of course. I'm sure you have domestic duties to see to. I'm sorry you missed my uncle but he is often forgetful of such things."

Winnie felt slighted at Eulalie's obvious put down and patronizing attitude. She felt a further sense of discouragement. Gordon Welch had obviously not left any instruction with Eulalie to mention a position. Perhaps it wasn't a position at all he referred to in his note. It could have been mere advice he wanted to pass on to her.

"Edward will take you home. Thank you for joining us, Miss Winifred. Your presence was a charming addition to our tea hour." Eulalie rang the bell. "We have so many servants in this house, you would think one of them would appear when you ring."

So, Winnie thought, *they already have all the servants they need.* Feeling not a little deflated after her sanguine expectations, Winnie allowed Edward to help her into the surrey and they were on their way. This time her eyes were not on the silver harness nor the graceful way the Percheron horses moved.

Oh well, she thought, *at least I got to see that fine house.* But she would not have gone against her mistress' wishes if she had known it would turn out like this.

They were almost at the edge of town when the one of the wheels caught in a hole and gave them an awful jolt.

"Lawdy, I hope we ain't broke th' axle," Edward cursed. "'Xcuse my language, ma'am." The wet spring weather had changed the road into a quagmire. When Edward got down on the muddy road, he further exclaimed, "Tarnation! Th' axle's bent and me without a tool to me name along of me."

They sat on the road for half an hour before someone with the right tools came along and was able to help Edward mend the axle. "Well, this should hold out to get you home, miss," Edward said finally with relief.

Winnie looked at her watch with concern. It was nigh on six o'clock in the afternoon. What a day this had been! Poor Gertie would be wondering where she was, and it would be hard to explain her absence to Mr. Lacroix when she was out so late. She never should have gone against Mrs. Lacroix's wishes!

It started to rain harder; it had not stopped all day, and the damp, cold night air gave her a further feeling of misery. Even with the umbrella up under the covered buggy, she was feeling wet and cold. Finally she saw the light of the Lacroix house. It was almost seven o'clock and practically dark.

She felt glad to be near home and looked forward to the warm parlour fire and the smells of supper coming from the cosy kitchen. As they drove up the laneway she noticed there was a strange buggy in front of the house and a man who looked like the local doctor, Doc Rostrum, getting into it. A cold fear struck at Winnie's heart. Something was amiss. She thought of Mr. Lacroix. *Oh my dear Lord!*

Edward dropped her off at the front porch and was in a hurry to get back to the warm kitchen of Trelawney where the servants would be soon gathering to have their companionable supper. Winnie got down herself and hurried up the steps to the door of the house.

She was surprised and flabbergasted when Mrs. Lacroix herself opened the door and coldly took stock of her, saying, "So you have decided to return to us."

"Mrs. Lacroix, you're home early!"

"So I am. You're surprised, I see, after abandoning my home, children, and a sick man for hours."

"I . . . Mr. Lacroix, is he all right?" Winnie could hardly speak, so devastated was she by her reception.

"He's a very sick man. The doctor just left. You can come in and get out of those wet things. I'll want to talk to you later about this."

She stepped aside and Winnie came through the door with her head hung down with shame. Gertie was standing there wringing her hands. She had obviously had a trying afternoon. Winnie went directly to her room and changed her dress. Then she came out to the kitchen. Gertie was there shaken and pots were about to boil over on the stove. Winnie smelled something burning and pulled out a somewhat scorched roast of beef from the oven.

"I'm sorry, Winnie. I didn't mean to get you into trouble." Gertie was almost in tears. "Everything was all right until Mr. Lacroix started coughing and choking. I thought he was going to die. I pounded him on the back and he could breathe better but he was still bad. So I sent John for the doctor."

"You did well, Gertie. I'm the one who should apologize. I should never have left you alone."

The girl had obviously been seized with panic. "I didn't know where you were and the children started to cry when they thought their Papa was very sick. They were frightened, Winnie. Then little Lucinda upset the pan of water I was sponging Mr. Lacroix's forehead with. He got so hot of a sudden. Then Lucy cried louder. I was just trying to mop up the mess when Mrs. Lacroix came in."

Gertie stopped to take a breath and then raced on. "You see, Miz Agnes's neighbour offered to stay with her and so she didn't need Madam any more. Madam says she was worried about Mr. Lacroix so Miz Agnes's man brought her all the way back. When I saw her, I was so relieved I cried."

Winnie was dumfounded. How could a calm orderly house fall into such chaos in such a short time, and how did Fate arrange such an untimely arrival for the mistress of that house? How incriminated she herself was now!

Winnie did her best to retrieve the dinner, and it was almost passable when served at nine o'clock, an hour later than usual. The children had calmed down and were in bed shortly thereafter. Poor Mr. Lacroix was unable to eat anything but drank some clear tea and was resting comfortably.

The master was apparently out of danger, but his cold had come close to pneumonia said Doctor Rostrum. He had been sleeping too much according to the old doc who explained his throat had become congested with phlegm, which caused the choking and coughing. The medical man insisted he be propped up in bed with three pillows and sleep thusly.

"Sheer nonsense," said Mrs. Lacroix. "That doctor has strange ideas. Everyone knows that solid rest is imperative for a cold. But he would have the sick up and walking about."

The doctor also insisted that the sick man's room be aired. Mrs. Lacroix was also disdainful of this suggestion. Fancy, exposing the poor man to the damp, spring night air and chilling him further. Nevertheless, the doctor's instructions were followed to the word. When things had settled down in the house, and Gertie had gone to bed upstairs with the children, Mrs. Lacroix called Winnie into the parlour. The woman stood facing the fire with her hands clasped behind her back.

"Madam, I'm so terribly sorry for everything," uttered Winnie meekly.

"Yes, I'm sure you are, Winnie." She turned around and looked directly at her servant and the look in her eyes made Winnie's heart sink. "But I'm afraid that is not good enough. You deceived me by going behind my back to that tea. You left my children and sick husband with a young girl who couldn't be expected to cope with such responsibility alone."

"About the tea, Mrs. Lacroix—," began the girl but Mrs. Lacroix would not let her finish.

"I don't want to hear about it, Winnie." She pulled a small cloth bag with a drawstring from the pocket in her dress and held it out to Winnie. Her look was cold and unreadable, but Winnie thought she saw pain there. "Here is a month's wages. I want you gone first thing in the morning. John will drive you back to your parents or wherever you wish to go."

"But, madam, please. I don't want to go." Winnie's voice was soft and weak with suppressed tears.

Mrs. Lacroix's face flickered with some unrecognizable emotion. "I'm afraid it's too late for that. I can't possibly keep someone on that I cannot trust."

Winnie's hands came up to her cheeks as if to shield herself from this trouble, and she shook her head in disbelief. Mrs. Lacroix's face was immobile as she walked by the stricken girl. Stopping close to her as she passed, she put the drawstring bag into Winnie's apron pocket. "Take it. You may need it," she said and then, "I'm sorry it had to be like this, Winnie." She then walked briskly out of the room and up the stairs.

Winnie stood for a moment and then slumped down on the red turkey carpet in front of the fire. She felt so cold and shaky. How could this have happened to her? How could everything she'd worked for collapse all in one day. Her life had been going so well!

When the fire began to die down in the hearth she had always found so cheerful, Winnie lit a candle from it and walked slowly to her room. It was the last night she would stay here. She had meant it when she said she didn't want to leave.

CHAPTER 21

At seven o'clock in the morning a pale-looking Gertie came into Winnie's room with some warm water and filled her ewer. Her white frilled cap was askew, and she didn't look like she had slept.

"Oh, Winnie!" Gertie put her arms around Winnie who was sitting at the side of the bed after a restless night of her own. "It's all my fault you have to go. If I could handle things better on my own, Mrs. Lacroix wouldn't have been so angry."

"Nonsense, Gertie. You're becoming a grand little worker." She touched the girl's cheek and said, "You'll manage just as well as me. You're ready to run the household now. Mrs. Lacroix doesn't really need me anymore anyway."

Gertie sniffed. "It isn't right, Winnie. You've been so good to the family."

"I did something wrong, Gert. I went to see someone about another position against the mistress's wishes."

"Oh, Winnie!" The little maid brightened, straightening her cap. "Then you have somewhere nice to go to?"

"No." Winnie smiled gently, trying not to show the young maid her heavy heart. "The gentleman I was to see was away on business. It wasn't for certain."

"Oh." Gertie looked serious again. "Madam told me to tell you that John will be ready and waiting to take you away at eight o'clock. I'm to make you up a breakfast tray." She looked down now, saddened.

"There's no need for any breakfast, Gert, but a cup of cocoa would be very nice."

Happy to be able to do something at least to help her friend, little Gert scampered back to the kitchen to make the cocoa. Winnie sighed and began to gather her things together. It was a sad task indeed. Winnie didn't have a portmanteau so put what she could in the carpet bag she had purchased for shopping expeditions.

After she used the warm water Gertie brought to have a wash, she wrapped the remainder of her things in a tartan shawl. There were tears in her eyes as she noted the difference in her possessions since she had left her parents. Winnie then packed two new dresses besides the one she had on. That was all she could carry along with her other things such as spare under things.

One other dress, a still good, grey flannel day dress she couldn't take. She would take her umbrella. In her reticule, Winnie put the eight dollars in wages. She took a cigar box from the top drawer of the bureau and counted her small savings, wishing now she had not sent so much home to her parents. She had kept so very little for herself. But then everything had seemed so secure. A disaster like this had been so very unexpected.

She was just tucking some spare linen handkerchiefs and warm woolen stockings into the carpet bag when Gertie came in with the cocoa.

"Thank you, Gertie." She held up the grey flannel dress. "I'd like you to have this dress. It will fit you with a little adjustment."

"Oh, thank you, Winnie, but I wish you weren't going." The young girl looked so sad. Winnie put an arm around her shoulder.

"There, there. Is the mistress up?"

"No, Winnie. She's staying in bed until midmorning. I just went in to empty the commode and see how Mr. Lacroix was. He looks brighter today."

"That's good." Winnie felt some relief and a little less guilty now. "Well now, I'll be on my way." She had half-hoped that Mrs. Lacroix would change her mind overnight, but it seemed this was not to be.

She kissed Gertie good-bye and the young girl pressed a hanky to her nose as she waved good-bye to Winnie at the doorway. John was there ready for Winnie and tipped his hat to her, looking a little woebegone.

"Where shall I take you, miss?" he said as he huddled into the collar of his coat.

It was a cool, frosted morning but at least drier and brighter. Winnie had thought but briefly of where to go. Most of her thoughts had been ones of self-condemnation last night as she'd tossed and turned on her bed. But she knew that she certainly wasn't going back to her parents' home on the mountain.

"To Collingwood, John," she said abruptly. "Would you kindly take me to a good decent hotel? Do you know one?"

John looked mildly startled. "Aye, miss, that I do," he said with which he whipped the horse, and they were off in a northerly direction once leaving the laneway.

As they rode silently along the rutted road into Collingwood, Winnie was glad of John's terse and silent nature. She was lost in her own thoughts and feelings and welcomed the silence. She had enough money to stay a couple of days at a hotel. She needed time to think. There she could plan her future. There was only one thing she knew for sure. She was not going back to that mountain to live with her parents. The young woman had had a taste of a different kind of life, and she was bound and determined to pursue it. She wasn't sure her parents would take her back now anyway.

She pulled her wool cloak tighter about her shoulders. The morning sun broke through the clouds and shone brightly. The air smelled fresh and clean. The dwellings of the town were now in view and she could see the lake far away at the end of the main street and a bit of the masts of the boats in port.

The lake looked grey and cold but invigorating. Presently, John came to a halt in front of a hotel.

"You can stay here, or I can take you to a boarding house around the corner. It's respectable and less dear. I know the landlady."

"I think I'd rather stay here for now, John, but would you give me the lady's name who keeps the boarding house?"

"Aye, she's Mrs. Buttle and it's the pink painted house near the railway station."

"Thank you, John. I'll be going now."

"Miss . . . if I can be of further help to ye, send me a note and I'll do my best for ye."

Winnie looked at him with gratitude. "Thank you so much, John. That's comforting."

"I don't know what happened 'atween you and the missus, but I always liked you, Miss Winnie. The place ran a lot smoother since you come."

She said good-bye to John and carried her few possessions into the North American hotel. The clerk looked agog at seeing a young unescorted woman at his desk. Recovering somewhat after her polite but formal request for a room, he spoke, "That'll be $1 per night, miss. How many nights shall I put you down for?

"I'm not sure, but would you put me down for one for now."

He gave Winnie a long key and helped her up the staircase with her bag. Her room was on the second floor overlooking the street. When the door closed behind her, she looked around her with a feeling of relief. The room was actually quite nice.

It looked clean and was decorated with floral wallpaper. There were muslin curtains on the two windows which faced onto Hurontario Street and a dressing table on one wall with a large looking glass. She drew back the counterpane on the bed and felt even better when she saw clean white cambric sheets underneath. She then returned the spread to its original position and took off her hat and gloves. Winnie felt suddenly chilled and exhausted. She noticed a wool blanket on a table and carried it to the bed. After removing her boots, she lay down and pulled the blanket up over her shoulders.

Winnie fell into a deep sleep. She had hardly slept more than an hour or so last night; she had been so upset. The young girl awoke after a couple of hours and felt warm and cosy. It was a moment before she remembered where she was, in the North American Hotel. A woman's voice was calling, "Madam . . . Madam," and then she heard some light taps.

"Are you all right, miss?" Winnie got up and opened the door. A young maid with tousled brown curls and rosy cheeks stood there. "Would Madam like a tray in her room?"

Winnie realized she was hungry. She remembered she had had no breakfast other than the cocoa.

"Yes, that would be fine." She smelled something delicious wafting up the staircase. "What do you have today?"

"You're in luck, lady. The master has cooked a roast of beef."

"So early in the day?"

"It's nigh on one o'clock. Them that's hungry don't pay no mind to the hour."

"That will be just fine then, but not too large a portion."

The little serving maid came back with a well-laden tray. There was a glass of ale and a bowl of rice pudding as well as roast beef, boiled potatoes and cabbage. "Will there be anything else, Miss?"

"Could I possibly have some hot water for washing, please? And could you tell me where the water closet is?"

"We can add the lunch to your bill, ma'am. It is fifty cents and the water is ten cents. We deliver it once a day free—in the morning." She pointed to the end of the hall at the back of the building. "Take the stairs at the end of the hall, and they will take you to the facilities out back."

"That's fine and thank you."

When the wee lass had left, Winnie thought, *If I stay here long, I'll soon be through the little money I have and then what will I do?* She had counted eighteen dollars and seventy-five cents as the sum total of her wealth. That was including the eight dollars that Mrs. Lacroix gave her for one month's salary. Not a great deal of money if it cost her one dollar per night for lodgings and almost that much again for food per day.

The meal was just what Winnie needed after the rest. She ate at a small table in front of one of the windows and watched the goings-on in the street. She listened to the wagons rumbling and squeaking, children's and men's voices, and once in a while she'd hear women's voices raised in greeting. They were cheerful sounds of unloading and bustle. She liked the sounds of the town. *I wouldn't mind living right here on the main street,* she thought. Renewed by the rest, the food, and the friendly manner of the serving girl, she decided she would go for a walk on the street to take the air.

Winnie noted the commode cupboard was well stocked with towels and a china chamber pot for night use. She freshened up with the water the maid had brought and checked her appearance in the glass. The comfort of the room and the rest had done her good. She felt less anxious about her future. She would visit the midden out back of the hotel to relieve herself and then take a constitutional in the fresh spring air. It would clear her head.

When she went through the main room of the hotel to go out, it was almost empty. No one sat at the dining tables, but there were four or five men sitting on stools at the bar. The proprietor stood pouring out grog for one of the men as she passed self-consciously through.

"I trust your lodgings are satisfactory, miss." The man's dark, short hair was parted in the middle and he wore the side burns and handle bar moustache common to men in his trade. He looked immaculate with a white shirt covered by a satin vest, which was embossed with small flowers. His right arm had a band above the elbow.

"Quite satisfactory, thank you, landlord," she said this quickly and reservedly, not inviting further discourse.

"O'Rafferty is the name, ma'am. I'm pleased to make your acquaintance, Miss . . ."

"Miss Conroy. The pleasure is mutual I'm sure."

Winnie put on her most dignified air emulating Mrs. Lacroix. She briskly left the establishment realizing it would be folly to invite familiarity. Above all, she must deport herself with the behaviour, the bearing of a lady. When she left the hotel, the men turned to the proprietor. One of them commented, "A young lady staying on her own, is she?" Eyebrows raised all around.

"Aye, it's unseemly but she checked in this morning," said O'Rafferty who had a lively penchant for local gossip. "She's Mrs. Lacroix's girl, I mind. I've seen her in here with that lady for tea. Something is amiss, therefore, I'd say." His voice was almost a whisper now, denoting a mysterious situation.

Winnie enjoyed her walk in spite of herself. She looked in the shop display windows on those businesses that had them as she headed north on Hurontario Street's east side. She passed the butcher shop, a cigar store, and general store. She took her time. There was no rush. It was an odd feeling walking alone in the town and knowing that no one was waiting for her, expecting her back at a certain time. It was a lonely feeling.

There was something invigorating and exciting, however, in the smell of spring around her. It almost made one feel like taking off for parts unknown. She could smell the wet earth and the green shoots of new growing things. This stimulation brought on by the soft spring day offset the great fears that Winnie had for her future and prevented her from being in a state of deep melancholy.

It started to rain and she put up her umbrella, thankful she had remembered to bring it along. Men passed her, tipping their hats and women nodded smilingly. So far she had not seen anyone she knew well enough to speak to except for some of the shopkeepers from her previous excursions.

Then, as she crossed Hurontario Street to the west side and passed the saloon on the corner and the tailor shop, she saw Mrs. Glover, one of Mrs. Lacroix's, friends sheltering under a shop awning. Not sure if she wanted to run into the lady at this time, she lingered in front of the post office wondering if she should turn around and retrace her steps. But before she could make up her mind, she felt a firm tap on her shoulder.

"That is you, Winnie, is it?"

Her heart sank as she heard the woman's spritely voice.

"Why hello, Mrs. Glover, what a surprise."

"I'm so glad I ran into you, dear," said the officious-looking little woman. "Would you relay a message to your mistress for me? I'd like her to come for tea tomorrow if she can. The ladies are getting together to form a hospital committee."

"I'm afraid I shall be unable to deliver your message. I . . . I'm no longer in Mrs. Lacroix's employ," blurted Winnie as she now met the woman's eyes boldly. The woman would know sooner or later anyway.

Mrs. Glover's eyes got large, and she was obviously thinking hard. "Oh, I see, and have you another position then?"

"No, I don't." Winnie saw the woman's interest perk up, and she allowed her own hopes to blossom. "I'm staying at the North American Hotel at present."

The woman's eyebrows shot up. "Well then, you are looking for a position, I presume?"

"Yes, as a matter of fact I am," Winnie offered, hope beginning to rise fervently in her.

"Hmm . . ." The woman's gloved finger tapped on her lower lip. "Would you care to drop by to my home on Pine Street tomorrow at seven o'clock, Winnie? I would very much like to talk to you."

"Yes, I'd be most pleased to do so." Winnie attempted to show her interest without seeming too overly eager.

"Excellent. I will see you then." Mrs Glover looked like the cat that had swallowed the canary. "I suppose I will have to send a man with a note for Mrs. Lacroix. It is most important we get started on forming a committee. A hospital is so crucial for our town. Don't you agree, my dear?"

"Yes, indeed, Mrs. Glover, quite crucial." Winnie's spirits were beginning to lift. She felt almost elated now. It seemed that her problems may be over quite soon. Mrs. Glover had a lovely home in town. The lady was quite competitive by nature and liked to have more than one servant in attendance on her household. She also entertained a great deal, Winnie understood.

"Tomorrow at seven p.m. then. I'll expect you to be punctual."

"Of course, madam."

And so they parted, both happy. Winnie continued on her walk with increased enjoyment. She returned to the hotel by five o'clock and asked that a light supper be sent to her room. She was not comfortable eating in the dining room among strange people.

Presently a tray with bread and butter, barley soup, and stewed fruit was brought up by the same maid. There was also a mug of tea. Winnie looked at the young girl with interest as she set down the tray on the small table.

"Thank you. What is your name?"

"Sally, miss."

"Do you live here?"

"No'm. I live with me Mam, the widow Granger, in the old village. In the bad weather I sometimes stay here if there's a free room."

Winnie nodded. She wondered how easy it would be for someone like herself to get another job. She had no reference. But then, she would likely get on with Mrs. Glover. The lady knew her work and had thought highly of it. So there was no real reason to worry.

Winnie's sleep that night was relatively untroubled in the comfortable room. The fact that there were only eighteen dollars between her and destitution was pushed out of her mind in this pleasant place. She was still in shock from her unpleasant dismissal, and her body needed the healing quiet and rest provided here. She could not afford to get sick for there was no person to care for her. She must make her own way in this world it seemed.

The sounds of trading and business had long since tapered off as evening fell. She had retired early and had lain in the warm bed listening to the sounds on the street, which changed in nature as the night wore on.

There were gulls calling and doors slamming from time to time. Presently, sounds of fiddle and honky-tonk piano filled the night air with jigs as saloon business increased with the later hour. From time to time she'd hear a man cuss as he walked drunkenly home to his family or to a lonely room or shanty. Here and there a dog barked in the night and another would answer him from afar.

Then it became more and more silent. The wind picked up, and she could hear waves coming in off the bay and the crack of great pine trees banging together in the surrounding forests. This was still a new and fearsome land, mostly wilderness except for the few settled areas such as this thriving but small community. The silence of the night when the reality of the vast wildness around this tiny vestige of civilization descended, made Winnie feel small, alone, and vulnerable. Finally sleep overcame her.

CHAPTER 22

Winnie was awake and wrapped in her warm shawl over her flannel petticoat when Sally brought up warm water for washing in the morning. The day was cold for late April and overcast, and she was glad when she was finally dressed although the room was beginning to warm up nicely from the stove pipe that ran up through the floor. But what would she do today?

Her appointment wasn't until seven o'clock p.m., and she was hoping a position would result from it. Mrs. Glover would be having the ladies including Mrs. Lacroix over this afternoon. She felt a little reticent at the thought but shrugged it off.

She would have to wait until seven o'clock to see the lady. She worriedly took stock of her finances again. She had better pay her bill now because she couldn't afford to stay at a hotel any longer without dwindling her savings.

"I would like to pay my bill," she said at the hotel desk.

"Will you be leaving then, miss?"

"Yes, I no longer require the room."

The young spectacled clerk scratched his head and added up a column of figures. "That will be one dollar and seventy cents please."

Winnie pulled out the required amount and gave it to him. She went back to the room to get her things together, and Sally was just coming out of her room with a slop pail in each hand. She looked tired and wan today but smiled with her usual friendliness.

"You are off then, ma'am."

"Yes, I am. I'm afraid I will have to find some cheaper accommodations until I can find a situation."

"Well, good luck to ye, miss. Perhaps we'll meet again."

"I hope so, Sally, and thank you for your service."

The girl carried on with her morning task of going from room to room, emptying wash water and chamber pots. It was heavy work and involved numerous trips up and down the back steps with pails until she finally had the rooms tidied. Then it was time to help with lunch.

Winnie was glad she would get a better position than Sally and would be relieved when she spoke with Mrs. Glover this evening. She was hoping to be taken on then and there, thereby saving the price of another night at a hotel.

The day began pleasantly enough, except that she had to carry her belongings with her and was quite tired after the first couple of hours. She almost wished she had arranged to stay another day at the hotel but it was so dear. Winnie had walked around the town for an hour before she found a suitable place to have some tea and something to eat.

She felt conspicuous upon entering the victualizing establishment on her own. She carried her carpet bag, umbrella, and bundle tied with the tartan shawl. Her hat was about to fall from her head, and she blushed with embarrassment.

Cold and shivering, for it was a raw day, she sat down with relief at a small table. Several pairs of eyes came to rest on her. She was the only woman there alone.

Pretending to ignore the intrusive glances, she slowly pulled her gloves off her freezing hands. The wind blowing down the main street from the lake was bitter for a spring day. Her boots were covered with the red clay of Hurontario Street, and she looked down at them with consternation. How was she to present herself to Mrs. Glover this evening with muddy boots?

Presently, a woman came over to serve her. She felt better after the hot tea, which was put in front of her and the scones and cheese that followed. It was her first meal of the day. She had paid her bill and was just thinking that she had stretched the time long enough over her small meal rather than take up her burdens again when the jingling bell over the door caused her to look up.

The door of the victualizing house opened and who should come in but young Mr. Sam Woodrow. Her eyes brightened when she saw his handsome, swarthy face. Perhaps he could tell her if Mr. Welch was now home from Chicago or when he was now expected.

She raised her hand in greeting, and he smiled and came over to her table.

"Miss Winifred. What a pleasure!" He removed his hat and looked at her with friendly curiosity. "What are you doing here all by yourself? May I join you?"

"Oh, do, please." Winnie was glad to see a familiar face, someone she could talk to. She was feeling very lonely at this moment.

"I see you are finished and about to leave. Please stay and have another cup of tea with me. Would you like something else?" He sat down and ordered a light repast from the serving woman and more tea for Winnie.

"Mr. Woodrow, I am glad to see you. I've had something unfortunate happen and am no longer with Mrs. Lacroix. Could you tell me if Mr. Welch is back from Chicago?"

Sam looked surprised and thoughtful touching his forefinger to sensual lips. "I was over there this morning to visit Miss Eulalie, and she still didn't know when her uncle would return. He sent a telegraph to say he would be back by next week at the earliest."

Winnie's fleeting look of disappointment caused the young man to continue and he asked, "Pray tell me what passed that caused you to leave your mistress?"

As Winnie told him the story, there were tears in her eyes.

"I say, what unfortunate timing for you. It was harsh to turn you out altogether, I would say, but I'm sure she acted in the passion of the moment so was not responsible for her actions. What are you going to do?"

Winnie composed herself and tried to make her voice sound cheerful. "I think I might be offered another post. I have an appointment this evening with a prospective employer, a Mrs. Glover. Do you know her?"

"Ah, yes. She is somewhat well off. You might have landed on your feet this time."

"I do hope so." Winnie smiled ruefully.

"In the meantime, how are you spending your day?"

"I checked out of a hotel so I have nowhere to go until seven o'clock."

"It's only noon," he said, checking his time piece. "Could I interest you in going for a ride in my buggy to pass the time?"

"Oh, that would be most kind of you." Winnie's eyes brightened. She finished her tea while the suave young man ate his meal, and she looked forward to passing the afternoon with a sheltered ride and genial company.

After Sam had finished his repast, they left the premises amidst inquiring gazes, and after he retrieved his horse and conveyance from the nearby livery, they got into the surrey wagon which was harnessed to a charming roan mare. He turned to her and smiled and she thought it was like the sun rising the way his smile lit the handsome features.

"Well, we're off," he said and looked at her with that friendly, curious smile again before he whipped the horse into a slow trot.

There was such an earthy quality about Sam. Winnie turned self-consciously and looked ahead. She thought she had never seen such a handsome man. His black hair was coupled with an aristocratic aquiline nose and wide mouth. Fine teeth showed white and even when he smiled. His skin was a golden, honey colour, which hinted at some long-forgotten exotic parentage. The smooth face was clean-shaven except for a thin, well-trimmed moustache framing sensual lips. The moustache was unusual and appealing in these times of prevailing bushy facial hair on men.

She tried not to look at him. All of a sudden, she was conscious of her own plainness, her muted colouring, colourless eyelashes, and pale skin with the suggestion of freckles.

"Would you care for a drive in the countryside?"

"I suppose that would be all right if we don't go too far."

So he drove her outside the settled area of town up around the lakeshore roads and southeast over the Pretty River where a fine bridge was constructed by the mill. It was called Shannon's Bridge, he said. Then they passed the farms on the outskirts of the town.

"I'd like you to see my house."

"You have a house?" she asked, quite surprised.

He simply smiled a secretive smile and drove her down a street he called Minnesota where a lot of construction seemed to be going on. It was a lovely street lined with large beautiful trees. He stopped the surrey in front of a log house of great size. The bulk of it was impressive. But it was a shell of a house; not yet completed.

He said, "This will be my first real home in Collingwood when it is finished. I'm putting down roots here, it seems. I've decided to stay here and open a business, be a respectable businessman." Sam grinned a sly grin.

"What kind of business will you open, Mr. Woodrow?"

"I plan to set up a trade in windows and sashes. There will be a great need for such items as the building in town continues. People will no longer be content with rough shanties and log cottages."

"I would adore to see the house inside."

They got out and walked over a plank set in the mud to the opening of the house. The smell of raw timber was rich and fragrant. They now stood in a hall off which was a large room on the left where an impressive fieldstone fireplace had been already set outward from the wall.

"It's lovely," she gasped.

"You haven't seen it all yet." He led her back through the hall and up a stairway to the second floor.

She felt a little odd for she had never been this alone with a man before. It was damp and chilly in the unfinished house, and she shivered in her inadequate cloak as they stood on the spacious landing.

"You're cold," he said and with a graceful suddenness drew her to him. His gesture was so sudden and yet she had sensed something like this might happen. He smoothly encased her in his arms, and his mouth was soft and firm on hers before she could even think.

Winnie felt herself sinking into the warmth and magic of the embrace. His mouth was warm and wet and tasted of fine tobacco. His skin was freshly scented from the shaving parlour. She got hold of herself and attempted to extricate herself from his clasp, her cheeks burning now, the chill of the empty house forgotten.

"Oh, you're a sweet little thing," he said softly. His hands were caressing and overcoming her efforts to push him away.

"Please, stop," she said feeling both heady and frightened. "I want to go."

"Winifred, I can tell you don't want to go." His voice was a whisper now, and he was pressing toward her again with those sensual lips.

She felt his breath on her face and his determination to have his way. She broke free of his grasp and the soporific state that enveloped her. She stumbled across the landing and down the stairs.

Thoughts raced through her mind. She saw the men in the hotel bar looking at her appraisingly, a young woman on her own. She saw Eulalie and Sam laughing at her, with their perfect physical beauty; laughing at her, a naive mountain girl from a low-class background. She saw Mrs. Lacroix's disapproving face. She must get away from this man before he took advantage of her. What damage had he already done to her reputation? She was seen leaving the victualizing house with him. And what more would he have done if she lingered further in his arms?

She ran across the wooden plank to the buggy, slipping in the mud at the edge and getting the bottom of her skirts soiled. She heard him call after her but was now frightened of him. So she grabbed her things from the buggy and hurried down the street, slipping into a copse of cedars out of sight, hoping he would get into the buggy and drive off.

Through a hole in the bushes she saw him stand at the roadside looking perplexed. He walked up and down the road for a hundred yards or so in each direction. Then, shrugging his shoulders, he got back into his conveyance and drove off.

Winnie backed away from the opening in the cedars and looked about her. She was in an empty lot that had been cleared ready for construction. Stumps stood up from the ground all around. The cedars she had hidden behind and a few other trees had been left standing for reasons of future privacy, it was evident.

She looked at her brooch watch. It was still just three o'clock. She gathered her location was only about a twenty-minute walk from Mrs. Glover's Pine Street home for they had come almost full circle around the town. But she would have to wait for the appointed hour. Mrs. Lacroix would be there now, and she didn't want to run into her.

She paled a bit as she wondered if Mrs. Lacroix was talking about her. Surely, Mrs. Glover would comment on seeing her. She must wait until seven o'clock. She did not want to seem desperate for a position.

My, but it was chilly and what a sight she must be with her muddied hem and boots. The sky had cleared a little and some welcoming rays of sunlight filtered through into the place where she stood, bag and bundle at her feet. A large dry log lay in the clearing where some sun streamed through a tall backdrop of trees.

At least it was private here, away from prying eyes. The shaken girl wanted to be alone for a while now. She gratefully took her things over to the log and sat upon it in the blessed rays of sunlight. She felt a little warmed and drew her cloak about her and rubbed her thinly gloved hands together.

She would rest here for a while and think. Winnie felt like crying but could not allow herself. She mustn't ruin her appearance further for the appointment. Winnie's heart still beat fast from the penetrating kisses of Sam Woodrow but her trust in him had been violated, and it was hurtful that he thought so little of her to treat her like a common street wench.

Her emotions were tumultuous, the overriding one was an encroaching fear, fear that she had tried to ignore or overcome to this point. The comfortable hotel room had numbed it, given her a false sense of security. But she was alone, so very alone in the world and she felt it now.

The singing of the birds around her were some comfort for they seemed determined to cheer her up. The sun got quite warm for a while on the log and her chilled body soaked in its mesmerizing warmth. Once, a tiny red squirrel visited and looked up cheekily twitching its tail.

She laughed in spite of herself when it ran up a tree with its tail straight up in the air and scolded her soundly.

After sitting on the log for a long time, she felt the cool air descend on her as the short spring afternoon vanished and early evening encroached. The warming rays of the sun had disappeared behind the tall trees at her back. She got up stiffly from the log and went about the business of brushing off her skirt and cleaned up the muddy boots as best she could with some dead leaves and twigs. She then brushed her hands off and looked at her watch. It was five o'clock.

Winnie decided to walk to get her blood moving and pass some more time that way. She headed out to the road and in the direction of the main street, Hurontario. She felt cold and hungry, but it was just a short time now until her appointment, and Mrs. Glover would likely offer some refreshment.

Finally, after walking up and down two or three streets more than once and evoking a few looks of curiosity, it was time to go to Pine Street. Suddenly energized, Winnie was now eager and anxious to see Mrs. Glover. Her shoulders and arms were tired from carrying the carpet bag and bundle and her feet felt damp and cold in her boots.

She had been with Mrs. Lacroix shopping one day when the latter had chosen to call briefly on Mrs. Glover so Winnie remembered where the house was. When the weary girl finally arrived in front of the painted white house with black trim, it looked inviting in the descending dusk with glowing lights in the windows. A charming oil lamp fixture was attached to the wall outside of the door on a bracket and it had been lit for the evening.

She gingerly knocked at the door. It was exactly seven p.m. She had planned it thus so as not to appear overly eager. There was no immediate answer to the knock. Two or three minutes went by and she knocked again. Then at last Mrs. Glover herself opened the door.

Winnie smiled hopefully at her. But alas! The woman emitted a strange, unfriendly air. She took in the girl's somewhat rumpled appearance down to the soiled footwear. Instead of inviting Winnie into the warmth and cheer of her hallway, Mrs. Glover stayed put at the door and stared at her.

When the woman hesitated, Winnie offered by way of reminder, "Good evening, madam. You asked me to come around at seven o'clock this evening." Winnie's speech was faltering now, her confidence slowly ebbing away.

The stern-faced woman finally broke silence and replied, "Yes, I did, young lady, but I'm afraid circumstances have changed. I have no need for more help at this time," she said bluntly. Her inferred meaning was obvious.

The girl stood there helplessly looking at her. The woman's face looked cold and accusing. Winnie felt shocked and tired. Mrs. Lacroix must have told her of the circumstances of her dismissal then. But, of course, she would have.

Winnie could only nod and say, "Yes, I understand," in a weak and trailing voice before the woman rudely closed the door on her. Winnie stared at the closed door. After a few seconds, she turned around and walked down the steps to the street.

She had waited all day for this, all day. She walked slowly down Pine Street, her bundles feeling like leaden weights now. The reality of her rebuff sank in and she felt fear and worry overwhelm her. The sky opened and it started to rain again. Where would she go now? That was when she realized she must have left her umbrella in Sam Woodrow's gig.

Winnie then thought of the boarding house that John had told her about. But it was late in the day to approach the landlady and a long walk from here in the rain. It was getting quite dark now. Miserable and sick at heart, Winnie made her way back to the main street. She would try to get a room back at the hotel for another night if there was one still free.

She threw her shoulders back and lifted her head high and with as much dignity as she could muster, walked into the hotel past the inevitable loitering men at the bar and to the renewed surprise of the young male clerk she had dealt with previously, asked for a room.

"My plans have changed. Would you be able to accommodate me for another night?" The clerk looked at her wet hair and clothing and said, "You're in luck, miss. The rooms are all gone 'ceptin' the one you was in." Winnie visibly breathed a sigh of relief. He looked at her tired face and the bundles he supposed she had lugged around all day.

"Would you like a tray sent up, miss? There's still some hot vittles in the kitchen."

"That would be most kind," she said gratefully as she looked into the knowing eyes of the plain young man.

"Let me help you with those." He carried her things up for her, and she looked fondly at the floral wallpaper and homely spread as he lit the oil lamp on a wall bracket and a candle on the small table for her.

When he had gone, she sat down on the bed in exhaustion. What a fool she had been to expect that Mrs. Glover would still want her after she learned from Mrs. Lacroix the reason for her dismissal. Loyalty was prized above all things in a servant, and she had been disloyal. As well, to her discredit, she had been irresponsible by abandoning her duties when she was sorely needed. The gravity of her situation was now clear. No one in this town might hire her because of her mistake.

A little knock sounded on the door, and Sally entered bearing a tray. "Oh, miss!" Her face brightened. "I'm glad to see you again. I thought you was gone fer good the day." The girl's familiar face and friendly smile gave comfort to Winnie's heart.

"I'm afraid my plans went awry." She took the tray of steaming lamb stew from the girl and set it on the table. "It's nice to be back. I've had a trying day."

"Ach, you're not the only one, miss, but this is my last duty and I can go home now."

"Would you do me one more favour before you go? I desperately need some hot water to wash."

"Certainly, miss." Sally returned in a flash with some hot water and a small pitcher of cold for drinking.

Winnie was so grateful she slipped her hand into her purse and gave the girl a ten-cent piece. "Here is something for your trouble and kindness." She knew the girl must have had a long day with little reprieve.

"Why thank you, miss." Sally looked at the coin with big eyes and pocketed it reverently. "But it's all in me job to do for you."

"You have been more than helpful. And please call me Winnie. We're about the same age, and I'm just a working girl like yourself."

"Winnie, that's nice and friendly-like. Good night, Winnie, and thank you. I'll let you tackle them eats. You look right tuckered out."

And so she was, tuckered out. She sat down at the little table when Sally left and ate the hot food and drank the mug of ale they sent up. A warm feeling of well-being crept into her, but she was so tired it was an effort to peel off her clothes and have a good wash.

She lastly sponged off the hem of her skirt. She looked at her boots with chagrin and decided to pay Sally to polish them on the morrow. With all this done, she locked the door and blew out the lights.

In the warm clean bed once more she at last found rest. The night sounds of the street were becoming familiar to her now and comforting. What a day she'd had! She'd been kissed by a man and had been refused a job. But it would all sort itself out in the end, she hoped. It was amazing how a friendly word, a hot meal, and a warm bed could make the world seem a kinder place. Winnie closed her eyes and began to slip off to sleep. She saw Mr. Welch's face then Mrs. Glover was rebuking her coldly then she was in Sam Woodrow's polished embrace.

CHAPTER 23

The next day Winnie awoke with an aguish feeling and could hardly get out of bed. *Drat!* she thought. Sickness was something she didn't have need of right now. Her joints were stiff, and she felt like she'd fallen off a horse. And her throat was sore. When Sally came in at ten o'clock, she was still lying abed.

"Miss . . . Winnie, are you ailin'?" Sally enquired with concern when she saw the girl's peaky face.

"I think I'm coming down with an ague. It was that damp chill day yesterday that did it, I fear."

"Well then, let me bring some hot tea and porridge up to you."

"That would be fine," Winnie said drearily. She'd hoped to go to Mrs. Buttle's boarding house on Huron Street today but she couldn't present herself indisposed to the lady. There were great fears of pestilence in boarding houses since the upsurge in typhoid, diphtheria, and ship fever; and she might turn her away thinking she had a serious ailment. She would have to spend another night or two at least here, it seemed, until she was over this fever.

Winnie managed to get dressed and went downstairs after breakfast to pay the room for two more nights then returned to her room and didn't venture out for the rest of the day. It was raining again and did so for most of the day.

Sally was good to her and tended to her needs, so she needn't go outside at all. On the third day, Sally helped her wash her hair and did some hand laundry for her. She was starting to feel better. But after a walk outside, Winnie knew from the heaviness in her chest, she had best stay at the hotel in the warm, comfortable room for a while longer rather than move to an unknown place with new strangers.

It was a full ten days before Winnie was recovered completely from the ague and feeling strong enough to seek work and lodgings again. Her savings were severely dwindled now. The extra services she paid Sally for along with the hotel room and meals resulted in a large bill to pay, fourteen dollars in all. She now only had four dollars and a half left to her name, but it was worth it to have her health back.

She must find a position immediately though! An idea had come to her. She would approach Mrs. Dudsworth who had the soiree last month that had so changed her life. Perhaps she needed help and would give her a chance. Winnie put on her best dress, a fine blue woolen, and dressed her hair in the chignon which complimented her. With freshly washed stockings and shining boots thanks to Sally, she completed her costume.

It was a dry and sunny day and only a ten minute walk to the Dudsworth home. She felt hopeful again with her health back and now that the weather was getting warmer, things looked brighter. She raised her gloved hand and knocked at the door of the fine house remembering her pleasant evening there. A well-groomed maid in black and white answered the door.

"I have come to see your mistress."

The maid looked her up and down quickly and seeing she looked a lady said, "Come inside, madam. May I take your hat and cape?" She led her into the fine library room she remembered from the party. Winnie breathed in wonderingly again as she gazed at the crystal chandelier in the entrance hall. How she would love to live in this house, to work here. Her reverie was broken by a sharp "Ahem." She turned startled to see Mrs. Dudsworth by the door.

"What can I do for you?"

"I . . . I'm Winifred Conroy. I used to work for Mrs. Lacroix. I met you once."

"Yes, I know who you are," Mrs. Dudsworth said coolly though there was a smile of sorts on her face.

Winnie's heart contracted as she took in the aloofness of the woman but she pressed on. "Would you by chance be in need of household help?"

"If I were, Winifred, I should not be able to hire you."

Mrs. Dudsworth spoke plainly but without apparent malice. She pulled a bell cord and her servant girl appeared quickly.

"Yes, madam."

Winnie began to move slowly toward the door, taking her queue that she was about to be escorted out. But instead of issuing that command, Mrs. Dudsworth ordered the girl to bring some tea.

"Won't you please have a seat, Winifred. I think you deserve an explanation."

Winnie was filled with discouragement as she sat down. At least the lady was being gracious in her refusal.

"I suppose you have heard that I left Mrs. Lacroix's household and the circumstances."

"Yes, I heard all about it from Mrs. Lacroix herself. An unfortunate state of affairs. Mrs. Lacroix was most upset. We have become close friends in the last few weeks. She is the first real friend I have made for a long time, and I value that friendship.

"She was upset with you, not so much because of what you did, but because of your special relationship and status in her household. Had you been an ordinary servant, she could have forgiven it, almost expected it. But you two had grown close and she treated you almost as an equal, which for a woman of her background is exceptional. She went out of her way to promote you. So you see, it was doubly wrong in her mind what you did. Doubly disloyal."

Winnie hung her head in silent acknowledgment of the truth of those last words and felt renewed shame. "I'm so very sorry that I hurt her. I was very fond of her."

"Now, now. I know you are sorry. But you mustn't be too hard on yourself."

The door opened and the maid came in with the tea and some little tea cakes.

"We will pour, thank you, Mabel."

The maid looked apprehensively in Winnie's direction for the girl looked visibly upset. She closed the door snug behind her to allow for privacy.

"Dry your eyes, child, and have a cup of tea. Lemon or cream? Sugar?"

"Cream and sugar, please." Winnie sniffed and took the fine china cup offered her with shaking hands. Any other time she would have marvelled at the fine china but now she was only vaguely aware of its hand-painted beauty which strangely intimidated her. All that she was and had been—a simple rural girl from a lowly background was descending upon her.

"Don't be too hard on yourself because I for one understand your ambition." Mrs. Dudsworth looked at Winnie with compassion. "You do seem a girl who should get on in life and one who appreciates the finer things. I cannot hire you, Winifred, because I value my new friendship with Mrs. Lacroix very much and would not do anything to hurt her or cause a rift between us."

Mrs. Dudsworth then changed the subject gracefully and chatted agreeably about a number of irrelevant things after that in her pleasant, ladylike way until Winnie finished her tea of which she had two cups and ate some of the tea cakes. At her mistress's request, Mabel also brought in a small tray of lemon curd, which her mistress insisted Winnie indulge in sampling. After a while Mrs. Dudsworth personally saw Winnie to the door and wished her well.

Winnie was grateful to the woman for her candour and kind treatment. Strangely, she felt a little better although her prospects were still poor indeed. She returned through the pretty spring day to her room to plan her next move.

She sat on the bed and counted her money again. Four dollars left and no job to go to. If she went to the boarding house now, she would have to give a large amount for a week's board, and she would have almost nothing left and no prospects for earning more. So she did nothing.

She spent the rest of the day walking in the sun and thinking of the few alternatives open to her. She could go back to the mountain and perhaps stay with Nancy and her family but that would be accepting charity. They would not turn her away, though. Winnie couldn't bear to live with her ma and pa again. That would be like going backward in time to a place where she hadn't been happy.

She would stay here one more day and then she would contact John, Mrs. Lacroix's man. See if he would drive her to Nancy's place. She would pay him the last of her money. She should contact him now, send a messenger today, but Winnie didn't have the heart to make that final plan—that final admission of the defeat of her dreams. So for tonight she would pretend everything was going well.

She would try to be happy and listen to the sounds of the night street again as if this was her town, as if Collingwood was her real and permanent home. She had come to love the place as she walked the streets and nodded to the shopkeepers.

It was eight o'clock. She had a good supper tonight and was about to retire for the evening in the comfortable room she thought of as her own now. She heard Sally's familiar knock and expected she was bringing her some hot water for the little maid would be wanting to be off home soon.

"Miss Winnie." Sally's face looked unusually bright. "There's a gentleman to see you."

Winnie looked up very surprised. She followed Sally to the landing and saw down below from the back the silver-streaked head of a well-dressed man. The familiar-looking head turned around and looked up the stairwell at her and she saw it was Mr. Gordon Welch!

"It's all right, Sally. You can send him up." Her heart had taken a bit of a jolt. She went back to the room and waited. Presently, Gordon Welch entered the room, hat in hand.

"My dear Miss Winifred." He smiled a most kindly smile.

"Good evening, Mr. Welch. Please take a seat." She pulled the only chair in the room toward him and sat on the side of the bed herself.

"I have just returned from my trip to Chicago, and I received a note from Mrs. Dudsworth (that worthy woman) recounting your recent trials and tribulations. I am so very sorry to be the cause of all of this and apologize tenfold for my absence from the tea I expressly invited you to."

"I understand you had urgent business to attend to," spoke Winnie, struggling to maintain her reserve.

"Yes, I would most definitely have incurred some serious losses of capital had I not returned immediately to Chicago to rectify a certain situation that had developed there regarding my investments." He coughed slightly and looked at her intimately. "Mrs. Dudsworth tells me that not only were you dismissed, but that you have been ill."

"Yes, that is true, but I am quite over it now."

He looked around him at the room. "It is a passably comfortable room but staying here must have caused you some undue expense."

"Yes, I'm afraid it has taken practically all the money I have. I will have to leave tomorrow." Winnie's lip was quivering slightly at this admission.

"And where will you go?"

Winnie looked at him and now she was fighting tears. "I have nowhere to go," she said. "But I'm hoping that some friends on the mountain will let me stay with them until I am able to make some new plans."

"My, my, what a position I have put you in. First of all, I would like to reimburse you for the hotel stay since it is my fault you had to come here." He pulled out a roll of bills from his pocket, peeling off what looked like a large amount. "I trust this will cover everything. Is twenty-five dollars enough?"

Winnie was about to protest weakly when he said, "Put it in your reticule right now please. There is something else. If you have forgiven me a little, I would like to make you a proposal. My niece, Eulalie, has need of a lady's maid. To this point I have been unable to find a suitable local girl. She had one in the last place we lived, but the girl did not want to travel far from her family and so stayed behind. I feel that you have the necessary qualities and training to fill the position. I'm surprised that Eulalie herself did not try to hire you on the spot when you came to tea. I had mentioned it to her and given her leave to do so if she wished."

Winnie was taken aback. "Why no, she didn't mention it. Perhaps she doesn't feel I am a good choice."

"Nonsense. Eulalie has her peculiar ways and that might account for it, but I can see nothing lacking in you."

Winnie coloured as he looked at her with a somewhat admiring glance. He was an older gentleman in his late fifties, perhaps, but still a man, she thought.

"You will accept the position then?"

"I would be most grateful," she said sincerely. She liked this man. She remembered their most pleasant conversation in the library the night of the party.

"That's good then. I will send my man Edward around to the hotel to pick you up at ten o'clock tomorrow morning. Is that satisfactory?"

Winnie's head was swimming. "Most satisfactory, sir."

He smiled and bowed over her hand, a gesture most unusual for a man addressing his newly hired servant. Then he left the room promptly.

Needless to say, there were curious looks from the usual bar patrons as the distinguished gentleman descended the stairs after leaving a young girl's room about whom they had been speculating these past twelve days. One of the men went so far as to follow the man to the door where he stood aghast as the man entered a fine coach pulled by four aristocratic horses.

Winnie looked out the window and saw the greying man get into the elegant carriage led by four horses with plumed headdresses, an impressive sight on the main street of the small town. Serenity enveloped her. A great burden of worry was lifted from her. It was as if she had never suffered.

Not only did she have all her money restored but a job and not in any ordinary household but the largest house in the town of Collingwood! And it seems she had found a new mentor. Mr. Welch had been more than kind . . . more than generous.

CHAPTER 24

Winnie had been lady's maid in the big house now for three months. She was happy except for the fact that she didn't like her mistress. Winnie found her condescending, and there was an edge to the young socialite's voice when she addressed her servant.

Somehow there was a tension between them. Although Eulalie had not been overtly unpleasant, Winnie sensed a discomfiture between them which at times came across as thinly veiled hostility on Eulalie's part. Winnie supposed she was one of those women who preferred the company of men than to confide in women.

This alienation from her mistress provoked a feeling of loneliness in her. Although it was not profound, it was deepened further by correspondence from Nancy who was to marry Jack Pallensey, her former classmate and friend. While happy for Nancy, whom she perceived had long loved Jack, Winnie felt an inexplicable sense of loss.

Winnie had a splendid room, far nicer than the one at Mrs. Lacroix's. It had a large armoire, an impressive painted iron bedstead with a canopy, a large window looking out over the street for she was on the second floor, and its own fireplace.

The walls were painted cream and brown, and there were yellow velvet draperies on the windows, matching bed hangings and a gold damask counterpane on the large feather bed. It was a tastefully decorated room with good furniture. There was even soft fawn-coloured carpet underfoot throughout the room.

Winnie was astonished with the luxury of her quarters. This had been a proper guest room, and she knew that Eulalie had been incensed when her uncle insisted Winnie have the Yellow Room.

"She is only a maid for heaven's sake. One of the rooms in the attic would suffice. And as for dining with us at the supper hour, why can she not have a tray in her room like most upper servants or perhaps she would enjoy the company of her peers in the kitchen?"

"Come, come now, Eulalie. You should enjoy the companionship of another woman at mealtimes. I'm sure you are bored by my company at times. And as for the Yellow Room, why should your maid, who has a special status in the household, reside in the attics when we have five guest rooms in this capacious house? There are, after all, only the two of us in this house apart from the servants."

"Very well. Have it your way, Uncle." She kissed him fondly on the cheek, her own face dimpling charmingly. "I just didn't want her getting notions above herself and thinking she was as good as us."

Her uncle gave her a dubious look but said nothing. Winnie slipped quietly away from the outside of the carved oak, panelled library doors where she had been waiting to speak with her mistress but had inadvertently caught the gist of the conversation. So it hadn't been her imagination. Eulalie did resent her presence. Eavesdroppers never hear good of themselves.

But what could she herself do about it? Nothing she could think of except perhaps hope eventually for a different position in the house. Perhaps that of housekeeper. That was really more to her liking anyway. They didn't have a live-in housekeeper other than an elderly woman who came in and saw to the running of the kitchen along with Cook and supervised the young parlour maids.

Gordon Welch himself saw to the household accounts when he had the time, but it was rather a hit or miss affair and Eulalie did not show an interest in taking on the responsibility. So it was when a large ball was planned that Winnie saw her opportunity to offer her services in this department.

She was bored with the limited duties of her position anyway and was already offering to help occasionally in the kitchen. The kitchen staff had been surprised but rather pleased at her help, and Eulalie had not seemed in the least interested so she had gone ahead and made it a regular occurrence.

Winnie enjoyed the company of the other staff who were a down-to-earth and homely lot. Cook Ainsley was a plump and jovial personage and of course lived in along with the two kitchen undermaids in the attics.

"Mr. Welch will be wantin' his afternoon sherry." She directed a pointed glance at one of the undermaids, Tessie.

"Let me take it to him, Cook. I wanted to have a word with him anyway," Winnie interjected.

"Thanks, love. You're a good help to us here. I'm glad you're not one of those lady's maids whot gets above herself. You don't mind dippin' your hands in a little flour."

Winnie smiled to herself. "I enjoy all your company down here. It sometimes gets a little lonely up there." At least Cook didn't think she was trying to get above herself. She took the drink on a small silver salver into Mr. Welch's study where he would be at this time of day.

"Ah, Winnie. My sherry." He sat amidst a disarray of papers on his desk and looked relieved at the interruption. "These household accounts that Cook has given me—what tedium when I am not in touch with the household happenings! How am I to know if the butchery bills are what they should be? I do wish Eulalie would take some time away from her preening and card parties to take an interest in the household accounts."

"I would be more than glad to give you a hand, sir. I have experience from Mrs. Lacroix's, and really, I haven't enough to keep me busy."

He looked at her with interest in his sharp, dark eyes. "I notice you've been helping out in the kitchen and seem to have developed a rapport with the staff. I'm afraid Eulalie is a little standoffish with them. That does not go down so well with village people who like to get to know their masters and mistresses. She's used to city living, you see. It's all she's ever known until now. It's difficult for her here without the theatres, shopping, and high society life of the city."

"She has never had a mother to turn to for womanly advice and company so I can understand that it must be hard for her to relate to women," Winnie proffered.

"Your observation is most astute and understanding. I wish she could open up a little more to you. She would find a loyal friend in you, I perceive."

"I would be honoured to be considered her friend, Mr. Welch. I understand, sir. I truly do. I know what it was like for me up on the mountain. I longed to come to the town to see the lights at night, to visit the shops and see the bustle on the street. It must be difficult indeed for her when she is used to a city. May I be of some assistance to you both in helping with arrangements for the forthcoming ball?"

Mr. Welch's brow relaxed, and he leaned back in his leather chair. "That would be wonderful, my dear, if you could put your mind to it along with Eulalie. I'm sure she would appreciate your help."

Winnie looked at her master, suddenly shy. He had called her "my dear" in his rich, soothing voice as if she were his own daughter. There was something very comforting about him. He was so overwhelmingly refined. He never raised his voice nor showed negative emotion. He was a true gentleman, immaculate from his white collar to his polished shoes. His movements were measured and graceful, his smile kind and the look from his deep brown eyes could be soft as well as discerning. She wondered if he had ever had a wife. No one had spoken of it.

So it was that Winnie helped Eulalie with the planning of the ball, which was to be a harvest ball. There were many things to tend to: food, decoration, guest lists, invitations, and entertainment; not to mention theme, and a new gown for Eulalie to match that theme. Should they have a masquerade ball? So many decisions and so little time. Winnie was pleased for this opportunity to perhaps gain a better rapport with her mistress through the medium of preparations, and Eulalie did seem to open up and be friendlier with her in her excitement about the upcoming event.

Sam Woodrow was a frequent visitor to the household to see Eulalie. Winnie had found this very disconcerting at first. His surprise at seeing her ensconced in the household was evident, but he had greeted her with his customary smooth charm.

"How very pleasant to see you again, Miss Winifred." He did not allude in any way to their last meeting.

Eulalie had seen the looks that passed between them. Winnie said nothing but inclined her head. What could she say even if Eulalie hadn't been there? Her pulse quickened at the sight of this particular young man, but each time he happened by, Winnie carefully avoided him or discreetly excused herself when caught in his company.

"I do believe the little country wildflower is trying to avoid you, Sam. What did you do to her? She's obviously infatuated with you."

Sam grinned at her and said, "You're so beautiful when you're jealous, Eulalie. As you say, she's only a simple country girl. So what have you to worry about?" His look was enigmatic.

Emaline grabbed the envelope from Nancy's young brother's hand with a grunt and didn't wait for him to take his leave before she shut the door in his face. The boy didn't expect to be asked in to the rundown house because he knew Emaline and Silas still bore a grudge against his family for spiriting their daughter, Winnie, away.

Emaline ripped open the sealed letter and let the written pages fall carelessly onto the bake table, which had not seen a mixing bowl more often than it had to since her daughter had left cold three years ago. The slatternly woman's chief interest was in the paper money enclosed, and her eyes brightened like hard black coals as she counted out the bills.

"Huh!" she uttered in half-disgust. She brushed back a greasy bang of hair and sat down on a grimy kitchen chair. Her Winnie had gone to work for that rich old fart six months ago, and she expected more than this paltry amount coming from her daughter's earnings at the big house.

The truth was that, although Winnie was making more money, she sent her mother a lower percentage of her earnings now. Security was an ever-present worry for Winnie for she had had a scare when she had been let go by Mrs. Lacroix. As well, Eulalie's indifferent and sometimes hostile attitude toward her did not make her feel overly secure of her present position.

Winnie was also vaguely aware of her mother's growing avarice from little comments she read in Nancy's letters and especially her mother's occasional simpering notes complaining of her hard lot. Still, though Winnie sent a smaller percentage, it was a still generous sum which was given from the heart and not out of necessity.

Emaline lethargically picked up the discarded tissue paper and began to read her daughter's laconic letter. It's polite brevity revealed little or nothing of the girl's life or state of emotions. Emaline felt a twinge of remorse and then an enormous flood of self-pity swamped her. She shakily pulled out the small soiled drawer in the table and drew out a flat glass bottle containing a clear liquid. She pulled out the cork and with teary eyes, threw her head back and took a long thought-killing swig of the gin.

CHAPTER 25

The night of the ball was fast approaching. Eulalie was enduring fittings for a new gown. Winnie was busy with food orders. Many delicacies such as seafood, fancy cheeses, and candied fruit would be sent up from Toronto. Even musicians were to be specially brought in on the train. Winnie learned a lot from Eulalie about how to decorate for a ball. Potted palms, ferns, and other plants were brought in from the greenhouse to decorate the conservatory. Since it was still summer, the garden would supply roses and chrysanthemums.

Eulalie seemed elated and much friendlier as the night of the ball drew nearer.

"You will need a new dress, Winnie. You will be assisting me in my job as hostess."

"Yes, miss."

"We will have fun choosing something nice for you. It will be my gift to you for all your help to me with the ball."

The guest list included everyone in and close to Collingwood of social importance, many of the local businessmen, the more prosperous farmers and their wives, and some unmarried sons and daughters. Guest lists were borrowed from an acquaintance or two. Finally a list of considerable size, which included eighteen couples and numerous singles, was compiled and the invitations were ordered from the printers.

Winnie chose a simple but elegant gown to be made for her, devoid of ruffles and of a soft aquamarine colour. She had no jewellery save some jet and silver earrings, but it was not her place to be ostentatious for she was only a lady's maid. She decided to twine a matching light blue velvet ribbon in her hair in a Grecian style to enhance the simplicity of her dress and distract from the absence of jewels. A soft fawn-coloured fringed shawl of lightest wool that she had purchased from the mercantile out of her salary completed her look.

The night of the ball Winnie helped Eulalie dress her hair in an elaborate mass of ringlets. The glossy, raven hair was crowned with a Spanish comb. The young socialite looked delicious in a light strawberry taffeta gown with a daring neckline and voluminous skirts housing numerous petticoats.

Eulalie's eyes sparkled like the diamonds at her throat. She was in her element. She lived for parties and balls. She was like a dying man breathing in the elixir of life as she made her preparations. Her cheeks glowed, and her lips went blood red. Winnie thought she had never seen such a beautiful creature but thought that Eulalie had forgotten in choosing the colour of her gown the harvest theme of the ball.

Tonight charm and vitality oozed from Eulalie's very pores. Her nature was simultaneously magnanimous and fascinating. Coquetry was an art to her. Every man with a drop of red blood would halt at the sight of this woman as she entered a room. Even the musicians foundered at the sight of her. Eulalie was Desire manifest from her black silky eyes and ivory skin to the curve of her neck and breast and her small waist. And she loved every minute of the attention. She drank in their admiration as an actress on the stage finds ecstasy in an adoring audience.

Perhaps she was meant for the stage, Winnie thought as she watched her mistress in action surrounded by spurned suitors hoping for another chance, a crumb of attention; unmarried sons of prosperous farmers and, alas, husbands of wives who stood like wallflowers as their men made fools out of themselves over this coquet.

Winnie thought, *Oh, my, those women will never forgive her if they are neglected this evening. How does she ever expect to make friends in this town if she flaunts herself like this!* So she sped to the ladies in question and with as much grace and charm as she could muster, persuaded them to tour the house and find the eatables. The women were grateful to be saved from their humiliation by the sedate assistant hostess and with a backward glance at their truant husbands gladly followed her.

Winnie was extremely busy thus all evening between diplomatically heading off Eulalie's brazenness and greeting new guests as they arrived while her mistress was dancing numberless dances. Mr. Welch was a charming host and looked like he'd stepped from a band box. At twelve o'clock, most people partook of the lavish buffet meal while the musicians took turns with their breaks. The music floated outside where many people wandered through the gardens on account of the fine weather.

Winnie had planned to retire after the lunch, befitting her position as a lady's maid. She was about to do so when Mr. Welch approached her.

"I haven't seen you dance this evening, Winnie." He had adopted the habit of calling her this informal name.

"Oh, I'm not sure it would be fitting. Besides, no one has asked me."

"Nonsense, I wouldn't have you here and not enjoy yourself. Do you like to dance?"

Winnie's face brightened. "Oh, I adore to dance, sir. I used to dance up a storm on the mountain, and I've been enjoying the music tonight ever so much."

"Well, then, would you do me the honour of partnering me for this next dance?"

Winnie—used only to dancing jigs, reels, and quadrilles—was delighted as he swept her across the floor in a Viennese waltz. Although she didn't know the high-class dances, she had been watching Eulalie and was able to follow Mr. Welch admirably.

"You dance very well, Winnie. I want to thank you for what you have done to help prepare for this event and especially what you have done this evening."

Winnie's eyebrows shot up.

"Yes, Winnie. I've seen everything that you have done tonight to counteract my niece's frivolous behaviour. Delightful and alluring though she is, Eulalie often forgets that her hostess duties also include the ladies."

Winnie felt a little embarrassed. "She is especially beautiful tonight."

He looked at Winnie with a strange light in his eyes now. "Yes, she is beautiful but you . . . you are something very unique, my dear." He eyed her pale aquamarine dress and the matching velvet ribbon in her hair. She blushed at his glance. It was strange being held in the arms of her master. She felt mixed sensations of a confusing nature. Then the waltz ended and he was leading her to the edge of the room.

"I would like you to meet a business contact and friend of mine. A charming couple." He led her toward a handsome couple who stood at the sidelines. She had seen them earlier and had noted though a striking pair, they did not look very happy. The woman was blonde and pretty but had a petulant expression on her face. The man was good-looking with a friendly open face showing good teeth when he smiled at her.

"Winifred, my dear, I would like you to meet Mr. and Mrs. George Freenan. He has the mercantile at Bowmore. I'm sorry. It's called Duntroon now, isn't it?"

"Duntroon and also known as Scotch Corners. I'm pleased to make your acquaintance, Miss Winifred." He looked at his host questioningly. "What a charming hostess you have, Gordon. But your taste is always impeccable." He looked kindly at Winnie.

Winnie, embarrassed at this error, said, "But I'm really not the hostess. Miss Eulalie—"

"But of course. You are her assistant and what a big help you have been to her this evening." The diplomatic young man smiled warmly, showing his fine white teeth and turned to Mr. Welch. "You must employ her more often in this role, Gordon."

"I intend to, George. And Mrs. Freenan, may I tell you that you look surpassingly pretty this evening."

Amanda Freenan brightened. "Why, thank you, Mr. Welch, I'm sure." Thick, golden eyelashes fluttered on her ivory cheeks. She reminded him a little of his niece.

Amanda had been delighted to get this coveted invitation but since their arrival had been strangely unhappy in the beauty of this house and she felt resentment toward her husband, George. All she could do was think of how much grander this was than their own rustic home. She had also been watching Eulalie all evening and remembered when men had swarmed around her too in Toronto like bees around honey. But what was she now? A haus frau married to a marginally successful small-town merchant.

As Mr. Welch took Winnie away into the conservatory, he said, "Poor George. Alas, business has not been going that well for him since the recession. He is working harder than ever but has had to mortgage one of his stores. And his wife, I suspect, though lovely, is not one of those women content with a good man and a moderate lifestyle. Used to better things with a rich father."

"Oh, how unfortunate," Winnie said with sincerity. "He seems like such a nice man."

"None better in my opinion. A little soft though I think. Let people buy on credit when times were bad. I always try to include them in these affairs. I like George, and it means a lot to his wife to get out into society."

"I can understand that." Winnie looked at the fair woman compassionately.

Of a sudden, a familiar face appeared by her side.

"Hallo, Miss Winifred. How enchanting you appear this evening. May I have the pleasure of a dance?"

Mr. Welch looked at Sam Woodrow with an unreadable glance and then at Winnie. "Go ahead, my dear. You're only young once. Don't let an old man like me monopolize you. Just watch Sam. He's a knave and a scoundrel."

Sam Woodrow laughed and whisked her away to the dance floor. "This is the first time I've had a chance to apologize to you." He looked deep into her grey-green eyes, and Winnie thought she saw a look of sincerity steal across his features. "I got out of line that day in my house. I worried about you, running away from me like that. I felt a real heel."

"You were a heel. What you did was despicable." She felt her face grow warm and her body quiver and shake. Was it her remembered helplessness or the current closeness of his body and his overpowering masculinity?

"I'm sorry, Winifred, but there is something about you. You're different from the women I usually meet. You're not a coquette but neither are you a naive innocent nor a fool. If you fell in love with me, I would be very honoured because I know you are a woman of worth, of strength."

Surprised and overwhelmed, Winnie found herself melting with his words, his charm and mystery, his maleness.

"I must retire now," she said in struggling self-defense. "I accept your apology. But I am very tired."

"Please, just walk in the garden with me awhile. I want to get some air."

"No, I'm afraid that is not possible." Though relaxing in his presence, Winnie wasn't going to put herself in a compromising position again. She had learned her lesson with this man.

"You must, Winifred. I have something important to say to you."

She looked into his amber eyes, which were framed by impelling black eyebrows and answered with some caution. "Very well. But just for a few moments." They walked through the garden and the sky was deepest indigo. The night was soft and wrapped itself around them. The air was sweet as the wine being served from the butler's tray. Perhaps she had had too much of that. It was like a dream walking in the garden of the beautiful home with this most handsome of men. His scent wafted to her in the soft air and he turned and lit a thin cigar smiling innocently at her.

"I can't seem to get you out of my mind. I was going to try to find you, but I thought you had taken a job with the lady you mentioned. Eulalie told me of your long stay at the hotel later. Had I known you were there still, I would have tried to help you."

"That's all in the past. I have a good position now."

He took her by the hand and looked into her eyes. "I'm sorry that I was ungentlemanly, but as I said you . . . you . . . affect me."

They stood, lips not far apart, and Winnie found herself in a quandary. All that surpassing masculinity, the very aura of him. It was that awe in her again. That awe of a man like him.

They were standing thus when she heard Eulalie's voice calling.

"Sam . . . Sam."

The state of her thoughts and feelings was broken. Oh my God. What was she doing outside alone with Eulalie's beau!

She looked guiltily up toward the verandah. Fortunately, the cedar hedges were hiding them. But they could see the skirts of her rosy dress in the moonlight turn and go back into the house.

The two fugitives looked at one another, and without a word, Sam put out his cheroot in the grass and took Winnie's arm to lead her back to the house. His face looked serious, subdued. As they entered the room, Eulalie turned from speaking to a guest across the room and looked at them both momentarily then turned again to the guest.

Winnie then excused herself and went up to her room.

CHAPTER 26

All in all, the harvest ball was a great success. But if Winnie had hoped to become closer to her mistress, she was sorely disappointed. Eulalie was back to her distant, cynical behaviour again, and Winnie was puzzled anew. She decided that their personalities simply clashed and so was glad when Mr. Welch gave her more and more of the housekeeping responsibilities.

"Winnie, I would like to show you the accounts," Gordon Welch said out of the blue to her one day when she had been called into his study on another matter. "Do you still wish to take on more responsibility?"

Winnie looked at this face that was becoming familiar and dear to her. His eyes held a vulnerable look but also what she perceived to be a hidden excitement.

"I would consider it an honour to help you with the accounts, sir."

So they worked side by side on the accounts all afternoon until his desk was orderly with neat stacks of paper.

"Now with your help this afternoon, this mess finally is in some semblance of order. If you can carry on from now on, it will be a great burden lifted from me. I find that my business affairs have been demanding more and more of my time lately."

"Don't worry about the ledger, sir. I will do my best to keep things in order and will report to you regularly on the status." Winnie was grateful for the background in running a household she had gained at Mrs. Lacroix's. "I'm so glad to be able to be of assistance to you."

"Are you Winnie?" His voice was soft like velvet as he looked at her searchingly.

"But of course, sir," Winnie said quietly and felt compelled to turn and leave the room quickly away from his penetrating gaze.

Christmas at Trelawny was like a dream for Winnie. The house was decorated with fir boughs, and Mr. Welch had a large balsam spruce tree erected in the hall. It was ornamented with silver and glass balls and sparkling garlands of coloured beads. He explained that the royal consort, Albert, had brought this tradition of decorating a conifer tree from Germany. Winnie went shopping with Cook to the market and admired the festive displays of meat, which were decorated with evergreens. There was beef, mutton, and all other meats that were fat and eye-pleasing.

Another ball was given at Trelawny on the day before Christmas Eve. The food was mountainous and the guests gay. It was a very happy time for all. Eulalie was in the company of Sam Woodrow and looked happier than Winnie had seen her. Winnie tried not to think of Sam and the attraction he held for her.

Mr. Welch called Winnie into his study on the afternoon of Christmas Eve. "Winnie, I would like to thank you again for your help with the arrangements for the Christmas Ball. Last night was a great success. I had a number of compliments on my hostess. Eulalie did not even attempt the role, I noticed."

Winnie's smile turned to a look of perplexity and she looked down. "I didn't mean to get above myself, sir."

Gordon Welch smiled a slow smile and hesitated a moment before he spoke. "You will always get above yourself, Winnie. But that's all right. It's the way you're made. And I'm glad for the way you are."

"But your niece, sir. This is all seeming to make her dislike me the more."

"She doesn't dislike you, Winnie." He coughed and looked up at her. "Eulalie is merely jealous of you."

"Jealous! But why!"

"Because she is in love with Sam Woodrow. But you must know that, Winifred. It is patently obvious."

Winnie searched her fevered brain for words. "Of course I knew there was a close friendship between them. But I thought . . . I thought . . ."

"You thought they were just dallying with one another. Well, that may be on his part but not on hers. She has been miserable thinking that he may have an interest in you."

Suddenly, everything was clear to Winnie. Eulalie's strange unfriendly behaviour was so explicable in this context.

"I . . . I don't know what to say, sir."

"I won't pry into your feelings, Winnie. Although you are my servant, I don't consider myself privy to your innermost thoughts." He looked somewhat discomfited and slightly fatigued now. "What I will say is that you have become a valuable asset to this household. Your handling of the accounts and household affairs has been most commendable. Your skills as a hostess are becoming superb. You have a way of making people feel welcome and a natural charm and dignity."

"Thank you, sir. It is something I enjoy. I have been very happy here." Her eyes were shiny now with tears. "I don't know what would have become of me—"

"Now, now." He got up and took her hand. "You would have been fine . . . But I am glad that you grace my house now."

She didn't know if it was her gratitude that made her feel so emotional but she had the warmest sensation at the touch of his hand. She left his presence with a new knowledge; not just the reason for Eulalie's coolness but the sure knowledge that her position in this household was not dependent on Eulalie. As she walked slowly and thoughtfully to her room, a young parlour maid ran up the stairs after her.

"Miss Winnie, Miss Winnie, Mr. Woodrow is here in the front parlour."

"Miss Eulalie is in her boudoir," Winnie responded automatically.

"But Miss Winnie. He's wantin' a word with yerself."

Winnie stopped in her tracks and turned around. She went down to the parlour where Sam was standing hat in hand, his feet planted far apart.

"Would you kindly shut the door behind you, Winifred?"

"Why yes, Mr. Woodrow," she replied with some surprise at his tone.

"And stop calling me mister if you please." Sam was looking wild in the eyes and not his usual suave and composed self.

"Very well . . . Sam." Winnie found herself looking around uncomfortably as if for some mode of escape. She looked at the clock hoping he would realize he was keeping her from some duty.

"You are still avoiding me," burst out Sam. "Every attempt I have made to approach you in the last months you have made some excuse to leave my presence."

"I have good reason to avoid you."

"So! You still blame me for what I did that day. Let me tell you something. What I did that day was because I am irresistibly drawn to you. I told you there was something about you." He walked toward her. She refused to back away, be intimidated by him. She obstinately held her place. He put his arms around her and kissed her fiercely. She struggled as fiercely and then relaxed and fought no more.

When they broke apart, he told her, "I love you, Winnie. I want you to marry me and come to live with me at my new home. It is now finished and ready for you. You will never be a servant again." Winnie's surprise was overwhelming. Confusion flooded her. She was speechless. He put his fingers to her lips.

"Don't say anything now. I am going and will be back tomorrow for your answer."

He kissed her forehead gently, and without saying a word, she watched the handsome man smile at her and turn toward the door. The handsome and dashing man of her dreams. When he left, she smoothed her hair and left the room. It was approaching the dinner hour. Mesmerized by the day's events, she retired to her room and lay down upon the bed.

At supper, she was silent throughout the meal. Mr. Welch and Eulalie looked at her curiously. Eulalie seemed unusually agitated. "I hear you had a gentleman caller today." Her voice quavered and cracked when she could hold it no longer.

Winnie looked at the condemning eyes of the beautiful Eulalie and saw in them, recognizable now, fear. Without commenting on Eulalie's inflammatory statement, she got up, returning her napkin to its place and said quietly, "Please excuse me." Eulalie looked at her with hurt anger in her eyes. Mr. Welch had a strange look on his face she could not fathom.

Once out of sight of the dining room, Winnie almost ran to her room and threw herself once again on the bed. "What am I to do? Whatever am I to do?" she asked herself.

The shadows of the day had long since fallen. It was Christmas Eve. She was making everyone in this household unhappy tonight when they had been so good to her. Yes, even Eulalie. She had been good to her even though she feared losing the man she loved.

After some time, she got up and went to the pretty writing desk. She looked out the window above it, which was placed the same way as the window had been in that hotel room not so many months ago, so that there was a view of the street.

The snow had started to fall prettily. The yellow velvet curtains felt soft and warm in Winnie's hand as she drew them all the way back from the pane. It was a beautiful Christmas Eve with ice blue snow on the ground and she could hear sleigh bells as neighbours visited one another to share good will and cheer on this holy night.

She drew out a piece of writing paper and began to pen a note. It was late, around ten o'clock p.m. The house was strangely silent. The kitchen undermaid, Bessie, tapped on her door and brought in some hot water.

"It's an odd Christmas Eve, Miss Winifred. Peaceful-like. Both Miss Eulalie and the master have retired early."

"Thank you, Bessie. Are you going home to your family for Christmas?"

"Yes, ma'am. The goose is all cooked downstairs in the kitchen to be served cold tomorrow. The plum puddin' is in the larder. Only half the servants will be here the morrow. It was kind of the master to let us off on Christmas Day. Another would have made us wait until Boxing Day."

"Well, you have a lovely time with your family. I'll be thinking of you sitting at your Christmas feast."

"Thank ye, ma'am." Bessie always addressed her as a lady. "And a grand feast it will be! What with Mr. Welch's generosity 'n all. He's given us all a nice Christmas box."

When Bessie left to wend her way home to her family on Rodney Street, Winnie stripped down and had a wash. Then she took down her hair at the dressing table and brushed out its soft, brown length so it covered her shoulders. Still naked, she stood up and looked at her pale body in the glass. Then she donned a floor-length wool wrap and picked up a candle in its holder and the freshly penned note.

She opened the door to her room and closed it softly behind her. Eulalie's room was almost opposite her own. She tapped softly and then slipped the note under the door. Winnie paused for a moment but heard no movement in the room.

At the end of the long hall was Mr. Welch's bedchamber. She walked past two guest rooms and an upper floor sitting room. When she reached the door of her master's room, she stood for a moment and looked at it. Then she put her hand on the doorknob and without knocking opened the door and went in, closing it behind her.

The room was lit only by the light of the fireplace. She looked at the large bed but the covers were intact and it was empty. As her eyes adjusted to the dim light, she put her candle down on a table and walked further into the large L-shaped room. She had never been in this room before. Two wing chairs were placed in front of the fireplace, angled toward it on each side. The bed was on a platform to the far right. She could now make out Mr. Welch's silhouette in one of the chairs and his hand holding a glass of brandy.

She walked into the range of his vision, and he looked up at her. His collar was open and his tie undone and hanging. It was the first time she had seen him in an informal pose. He spoke softly and evenly. "What have you come to tell me, Winnie. Are you leaving me?"

Winnie said nothing. She stood in front of the fire looking at this man. This man of fifty-seven years who was greying and distinguished and very kind. And then she knew of a surety that she had made the right decision. Still saying nothing, she opened the robe and let it fall at her feet. He sat there with the glass of brandy in his hand and stared at her.

"Why are you giving this gift to me, Winnie?"

"Because it's Christmas. And because I love you."

He looked at her long in the eyes then he put his glass down and stood up. He took her hand and led her to the large bed.

Eulalie was in hot and bitter tears when she heard a tap on the door. She chose to ignore the tap rather than let one of the servants see her in this state. It wasn't until an hour later she noticed the note at the bottom of the door. She picked it up with curiosity and turned up her oil lamp. It read.

> Dearest Eulalie:
>
> I'm sorry if I have caused you any undue concern in regard to Mr. Woodrow. I have no interest of a romantic nature in that gentleman. I hope that you and he will soon marry and have a happy and prosperous future together as it is obvious that you are devoted to one another. And I hope that you and I may become good friends.
>
> With deepest sincerity,
> Winnie

CHAPTER 27

As the train pulled into the terminal at Collingwood on a fine spring morning in May 1887, two people stood on the platform to welcome it, a man and a woman.

Annie had mixed feelings about coming home to the Collingwood area. She felt like a new and different person. Her sojourn in Cobourg had been a life saver. Annie knew she would have never survived if she had stayed here in the state that she was in or, had she, would have dwindled to some half-life existence.

She had learned so much, about herself, about Life. The young woman was grateful to her mother for sending her away from the farm in Nottawa. She had plans now. She would stay for a month or two here to set things straight about rumours. She wanted people to see she was sane and confident of herself. Much of this was for her parents' sake. If it wasn't for them, she would not have returned at all.

There was a new life waiting back in Cobourg. That bustling, advanced town had welcomed her and she had made many new friends. The doctor's nephew who himself had just become a full-fledged medical man had asked for her hand in marriage. It would be a good and happy life for her. Security and peace of mind would be hers and he was a good man.

As Annie McClory stepped down from the train, she looked very different. Her hair was swept up in little coils on top of her head, and it was complimented by a wide-brimmed hat. She wore a bustled dress of the latest fashion and carried a silk parasol. On her hands were white gloves and she held a pretty handbag.

Annie saw a couple at the end of the platform but had trouble recognizing her parents. It looked like her mother but the man didn't seem to fit the memory she had of her father. She strained her eyes attempting to focus.

The two people who stood on the platform were silent with surprise as the lady of style descended the steps from the train. *Could that beautiful lady be my Annie?* thought Ruby, self-consciously glancing down at her own homemade dimity dress. But her face lit up with happiness at the transformation in the girl.

Far from the wild-eyed, forlorn creature he had expected to see, George Freenan couldn't take his eyes off the woman he had waited these months to see again. He was speechless and humbled by her serene beauty.

As they walked toward her, Ruby took the lead and grabbed the hand of the woman who looked incredulously past her mother to the man who stood quietly behind, hat in hand. Ruby was flustered because she hadn't rehearsed how to present the man to her daughter, so blurted out absurdly, "You remember George, my dear?" then looked pleadingly into her daughter's eyes.

Annie never did return to Cobourg. But Amanda left the vicinity to return to her beloved Toronto that summer. George signed a paper that gave his wife full rights to her father's inheritance. He waived his husbandly interest in her fortune. A new word was bandied around by the local townspeople. *Divorce.* It wasn't that it was a completely new thing, but it was most unusual and had never been heard of occurring in this small community. It was rumoured that the storekeeper was going to get one.

Annie moved into the large rustic log house that had been in George's family for three generations and eventually became his wife. In the three years before her death, Ida Freenan's wish was fulfilled. The house was again happy. Because Amanda and George had joint custody of the children, who were now in their teens, they spent much of their time with George and Annie.

As time went on, people became less concerned with the affairs of others and more concerned about the future as the twentieth century drew closer. There were more and more people now filtering into Collingwood. There were those who felt it would someday be a great metropolis. Those of the old ones who would repeat a tale and relish a scandal grew older and died along with the others. The story of George and Annie was forgotten by most of the populace or faded into obscurity as do all stories in time. They were able to live peacefully without social stigma and had many friends.

Annie never forgot the great debt she owed her parents for helping her in her time of need. The years brought George and Annie two more children of their own, a boy then a girl. Annie used to love to sit in the evenings and spin or write poetry. She loved this house and farm and never had any further desire to return to Cobourg.

After all, this was her home. She was brought up in this area, had suffered here, and her heart was here as it had always been. In one of her letters to her dear Aunt in Cobourg, she enclosed a poem to show her of her new-found happiness.

> Country house golden in the fields
> Of yesterday harvest
> Brown beam house, lofty sunset barn
> Glorious russet home
> Where fowl and cattle mingle
>
> Gently cooing, flutters dawn over this scene
> And two lie protecting and protected
> By wings of loved ones
> And all is bliss, enchantment reality
> In the heavy beamed house
> Huge and countrified
> In the ever-reaching barn grounds

Golden in the dawn
Amber at noonday
Topaz at eve-glory.

Winnie became the talk of Collingwood in another way. Her reputation as a socialite and hostess spread far and wide. To receive an invitation for a dinner party, salon, or ball at Trelawny was now the goal of every lady of polite society.

Rumours of Miss Winifred Conroy's dubious relationship with Gordon Welch and her lowly beginnings were ignored by most. Those of monied classes were not questioned in regard to their morality. They had a morality of their own, it seemed. Rather, she was considered avant-garde and very modern in her behaviour.

Men of high standing sought her favours in conversation for she was considered to have a charming wit and could discuss many subjects with knowledge and understanding. Before it was definitely known she was claimed by the owner of the house as his, a number of marriage proposals came her way from outstanding men in various occupations and from a number of surrounding communities. She was considered a jewel that would grace the household of any socially aspiring man. Her charm was discussed and much praised, and she was said to have a piquant beauty.

Eventually, the belle married her benefactor in a church ceremony, which was the envy of all eligible women of the county. The lavish reception at the house which followed was described in the society column and discussed for months after in the town. Disappointed suitors despaired at coming to know of their final rejection by the belle. A number of broken hearts ensued.

Caitlin and Mr. Delaine were wedded in Toronto and returned to Collingwood after six months, Delaine having brought his little family to Midland to stay for two months while he travelled to Manitoba on survey assignment.

Their return to Collingwood was met with revived memories of unfortunate past events and some open hostility. The townsfolk remembered the uncanny death of the cuckolded Bill Pratz, the flight of the wife beforehand, and the marriage a fait accompli to this much older man was all too much for many of them. They took it upon themselves to place blame and make conjecture. A couple of ugly episodes ensued. One night, the two were "shivareed" by a bunch of drunken rowdies who made a mess of their home and scared Caitlin half to death.

She shivered in the corner with little Willie while Lawrence tried to reason with them and failing that tried to singlehandedly throw them out of the house. He only ended up battered and unconscious after which they shamefacedly elected to leave the devastated family alone. Some kind and wise person, upon hearing of plans to shivaree the couple, had gone to the sheriff who met the culprits on their way out.

He hastily told them that if they didn't clean up the mess they'd made, he'd throw them all in the clink and fine them handsomely on top of it. This primitive shivaree ritual was pure annoyance to him and hopefully would become a thing of the past. He sent one of the blokes for the doctor on threat of a beating and a furious Doc Rostrum returned and mentally made a note of all involved for a future calling out.

Fortunately, Delaine was not seriously injured with only a mild concussion, scratches, and bruising. Their life was back in order before a month and after that, strangely, they had no more trouble with the townspeople. As a matter of fact, the latter made no small effort to be friendly. Caitlin put it down to the influence of the good doctor who was an extremely influential man in the town in his own way.

Winnie and Gordon Welch had a grand ball to celebrate one year of their marriage in 1882. Winnie looked about her and smiled with satisfaction. Everything was perfect in preparation for the night.

She looked down at the large opal ring on her hand, which stone was one of Australia's finest gems, next to the filagree wedding band. She felt the now familiar quickening in her tummy. She had known for some time she was to have a child but had waited for this night to tell her husband. She was not to know now that this was the first of eight children she would have to Gordon Welch.

The orchestra had been brought from Toronto especially for the evening like that first ball she had helped Eulalie to arrange. When the dancing began, she looked around the room with Gordon at her side. Her eyes fell on Eulalie and Sam Woodrow. When they saw her, they raised their glasses to her and smiled. She was glad that Sam forgave her and was gratified to see the couple's contentment. Who would have thought that the adventurous and smooth Sam and the beautiful, flighty Eulalie would settle down to sedate marital bliss?

"Darling, I have something I'd like to tell you." Winnie caught her husband's hand and looked into his face. He smiled and gave her a look that contained a fleetingly delightful mixture of happiness, intrigued puzzlement and amusement.

She had seen that look of indulgence before and loved him for it. As she was about to open her mouth to tell him of her surprise, he suddenly looked behind her and said, "Oh, do wait with your news for one moment, my Love. Here is someone I would like you to meet." He smilingly led her around to see a handsome couple who had just come in the door.

The lady was a singularly beautiful woman, not in the same way as Eulalie, but every bit as lovely with raven hair adorned by an attractive slash of white in the front. Her beauty was without artifice. Her neck and shoulders were blue white alabaster without benefit of talcum powder and she had hauntingly large grey eyes. The gentleman was considerably her senior but had kindly eyes and a quiet dignity that was quite remarkable.

"I should like you to meet an old and dear friend of mine, Winnie."

"I do wish you would leave the old part out, Gordon." The man looked lovingly at his young companion. "I have been trying to live that down for the longest time."

Gordon laughed and continued, "This is Lawrence Delaine and his wife, Caitlin." He turned to Winnie and said, "This is the first time I have had the honour of meeting Caitlin although I have heard a great deal about her over the years from Lawrence." To Caitlin now, he spoke, "I am so very happy to have you both in my home at last." He kissed her hand. "I have longed to introduce you to my wife, and I feel that you two will have much in common. I have a feeling that you will become great friends."

EPILOGUE

A book has more than one ending, just as a cat has more than one name. It is I, the Ghost speaking.

In the voice that a book begins, so must it end and so, therefore, I will say a few words reverently, forcefully.

Ghosts are fragments. The Huron Indians felt there were two parts to the soul. Part of me is still back there, in that time. I still remember Mimi's long hair. So long she could sit on it. To think all that beauty is dust now. And I remember the black hair of my sweet daughter whom I so greatly wronged.

Yes, I remember the dark hair of my sweet daughter and the long chestnut hair of my lover, the woman I loved. I was a stubborn old man. But I know that they loved me and so forgave the wrong I did them. And I take some comfort in that.

For although I am dead, part of me still haunts Collingwood. I walk along the old tracks of the railway that run out along the man-made peninsula, which is part of the old dry dock. They are deserted now and overgrown with weeds.

I stare into the wide stretches of bay water into Georgian Bay or Lake Manitoulin as it was once called. I do this over and over again and sometimes I see her there, an apparition like myself, but just the top half of her body as I remember it. And her long chestnut tresses blow toward shore like the wind in the waves. She looks at me beseechingly and stretches her bare, white arms out to me. But before I can reach her, she fades away.

This tells me that I am not ready for her yet. There is still something to be purged from me. The writing of this book is part of my cleansing. I know it must be for lately the vision of her has lasted longer, and when I reach my hand out to her, I feel I am getting closer to that time when we can be together again.

THE END

I moved from Toronto to Collingwood, Ontario in 1986 but have always been inspired to write about this area and wrote poetry about nearby Wasaga Beach years ago, captivated with its natural beauty and mystery.

This historic area of Canada with inland sea, escarpment, endless beaches, scenic farmlands and resourceful people served to stimulate my imagination, resulting in "The Belle of Collingwood".

I hope you enjoyed this story.

Best Wishes,

Marjorie Day

Printed in the United States
By Bookmasters